Rose Terry Cooke

Happy Dodd

Rose Terry Cooke

Happy Dodd

ISBN/EAN: 9783337407414

Printed in Europe, USA, Canada, Australia, Japan

Cover: Foto ©Andreas Hilbeck / pixelio.de

More available books at **www.hansebooks.com**

OR,

"SHE HATH DONE WHAT SHE COULD."

BY
ROSE TERRY COOKE.

I DEDICATE THIS BOOK

TO THE

MEMORY OF MY MOTHER,

Anne Wright Hurlbut Terry,

TO WHOSE PATIENT CARE I OWE THE POWER TO WRITE AT ALL;

AND WHO IN A LIFE STRAITENED BY CIRCUMSTANCE,

AND HARASSED BY DAILY TROUBLES, FAITH-

FULLY AND CONSCIENTIOUSLY DID WHAT

SHE COULD, AND HAS GONE

TO HER REST AND

REWARD.

ROSE TERRY COOKE.

HAPPY DODD;

OR,

"SHE HATH DONE WHAT SHE COULD."

———•———

CHAPTER I.

IT was the first Sunday in May, and there were
to be a few persons admitted to membership in Mr.
Payson's church, the first church of Canterbury.
As he called their names, they came out into the
aisle ; and the fourth, answering to the name of
Happilona Dodd, came from the side slips, and so
stood half facing the congregation.

She was a young girl with a dark, thin face,
slight and small of stature, very plainly dressed,
and as she walked up, she limped a little. Nothing
about her attracted the eye but the sensitive expression of her lips, and the innocent awe of her
large brown eyes as she lifted them to hear what
Mr. Payson was saying.

"My dear friends, having fulfilled the require-
ments of Him who said 'He that believeth and is bap-
tized shall be saved,' ' observe all things whatsoever
I have commanded you, and lo I am with you alway,
even unto the end of the world,' we understand from
your presence here that you desire to enter the visible church of Christ on earth: that you take God to
be your father and king, Christ to be your redeemer and friend, and the Divine Spirit to be your
teacher and helper. You also intend and hope to
be loving and faithful members of this household
of faith : to consider and treat its members as of
your Father's family, and to work with them in
Christian duty and fellowship ; to help those who
are not yet children of the kingdom, as well as
those who are. This is your desire and intention?"

Those who were standing bowed their heads, and
then the church arose, and Mr. Payson went on :

"We then welcome you to this little assemblage
of believers as brethren and fellow-heirs together
of the gospel of Christ, soldiers of our company
in the army of the Lord. Therefore, beloved, fight
the good fight of faith ; lay hold on eternal life ;
endure hardness as good soldiers of Christ Jesus ;
and may he deliver you from every evil work, and
preserve you to his heavenly kingdom ! "

As he closed, the church still standing, as if by
spontaneous consent, sang the good old hymn ;

"Let saints below in concert sing
With those to glory gone;
For all the children of our King
In heaven and earth are one."

After this came the benediction, and those who
were not to share in the Supper went out from
among them. The service was almost silently con-
ducted, only with Christ's words, a short prayer,
and a hymn. Happilona sat by her mother's side,
and felt like a tired child who has got home at last.
When the service was over Mr. Payson said:

"I have a few words to say to our new members.
My dear friends, you have now sealed your agree-
ment with God. Hear the words of the Lord: 'Ye
are my friends if ye do whatsoever I command you.'
The test of your life in Christ is not what you feel,
your deep sorrow for sin, or your lofty joy in holi-
ness; but what you *do*, as the result of a living
principle within. Joy and sorrow are the secrets
of your own hearts with Him who made you; but
your deeds are the flower and fruit of the new life,
which is also his work. For men do not gather
grapes of thorns; therefore strive to abide in the
Lord, and in his strength bear fruit abundantly;
and may he pronounce on every one of you the
commendation he bestowed on a penitent sinner
of old time: 'She hath done what she could.' "

"That was a good word, Happy," said the widow

Dodd, as the two went home together in the soft spring sunshine.

"Which one, mother? I thought they were all good."

"So they were; but I mean that last: 'She hath done what she could.' It always seemed to me such a comfort. We can't all do great things for our Master; but something we can all do. Poor Mary! she had nothing better than her box of precious ointment; knew no other way to show her love to her forgiving Saviour than to lavish the best and costliest thing in her possession upon his tired feet. It seemed wasteful to Judas; he did not understand her spirit; but the Lord answered for her, for he saw the love that lay back of the lavishness. 'She hath done what she could.' That is a thought for poor folks, Happy."

"It doesn't seem as if I could ever do anything, mother," the girl answered sadly. "If I were strong, or very smart, or knew how to do anything."

"If you could do what you can't, eh?"

Mrs. Dodd smiled as she said it.

"Don't be troubled to-day, Happy. There are plenty of little things; living is pretty much all little things. If you keep step with these, you will be ready for larger ones when the Lord sends them."

They were at home now; and as soon as the girl
laid off her outer dress, she spread the table for
their Sunday lunch. They were poor people, and
there was little but the necessary food within their
reach, but neatness and order made it more pala-
table than better fare served carelessly. As Mrs.
Dodd saw how neatly her daughter spread the
clean cloth and set on the bread, cheese, and cups
of cold tea, she thought that even here she was
doing what she could; but she did not say so, for
life had taught her that young plants grow best
with least observation; she had said more than was
her custom to-day; now she would leave this new
life in shade and silence to seek the sun after its
own fashion.

That night, after their early supper, Mr. Fox,
the Sunday-school superintendent, came in. He was
a brisk, pleasant, active sort of man, and had known
Happy and her mother many years, both as attend-
ants at the school and personally; for Mrs. Dodd,
who was a tailoress by trade, had worked much in
his family, and was still employed there, as his boys
had not all outgrown her services. He knew very
well how Happilona had been brought up; not with
much education at school, for she had always been
a delicate child, and at one time long confined to
the house with the trouble that had left her lame,
but with the utmost care of a good and sensible

mother, whose fund of Scriptural knowledge was
an astonishment to Mr. Fox himself.

Mrs. Dodd had none of the ordinary helps to
scriptural study but an old concordance, which had
been her father's; for she was the child of a poor
country minister, and being left an orphan at
eighteen had married a brilliant young lawyer, of
whose dissipated habits she was quite ignorant.
After several years of sorrow and struggle, this
man died, and left her penniless and helpless, with
three little children in the graveyard, and one
scarce a month old in her arms.

She was naturally a woman of energy and endurance, but there seemed nothing for her to do
unless she learned a trade; so she went into Canterbury, found work in a tailor's shop, and before
long made friends and an humble living for herself
and child. In all this period she had learned to
cling more and more to the only Friend who seemed
left to her at first; and she read and re-read her
Bible till it was as familiar to her as the breath she
breathed. Out of it little Happy — who wore her
grandmother's quaint title, shortened into this
pleasant diminutive — learned to read. Her childish sorrows were allayed by Bible stories, for her
mother could afford no baby-books or toys for her
beyond a rag-doll of her own making; and as the
child grew older she was accustomed to hear her

mother refer in every strait to the Bible for guidance or consolation. It was, truly, daily bread to
this poor woman. She had no maps, no voluminous
commentaries, no vindications of its divinity, to
help her understand it ; her Bible proved itself; and
a diviner Spirit than that of man opened its pages
for her, and taught her its heights and depths.
" The meek will he guide in judgment, and the
meek will he teach his way," was a promise abundantly fulfilled here.

Mr. Fox's errand to-night was to ask Happy to
take a class of little girls in the Sunday-school,
whose teacher had just married and left Canterbury.

" O Mr. Fox, I can't ! " the girl answered quickly,
coloring as she spoke.

" Well, well, Miss Happy, nobody can do what
they can't. I don't want to urge you unpleasantly ;
but there's reason in things, you know, and as a
good Yankee I have a right to ask questions. Why
can't you ? "

" I don't know, Mr. Fox.

" Don't you? that's bad. You know how to
read, perhaps ? "

Happy could not help laughing. " Oh, yes, I
know how to read. But I should be afraid of
them, Mr. Fox."

" Of the little girls? Why, they never bite !

they are quite small too — from nine to twelve, all
of them, I should say."

Mrs. Dodd looked on in silence ; she understood
Happy's objections, but she saw Mr. Fox did too,
and she preferred he should combat them in his
own way.

" O – h ! " said the girl, " you know what I mean,
sir. I am sure I could not teach them anything."

"At least you can try, Happy. If you find it is
impossible, I will relieve you ; but come next Sunday, early, and I'll take you to the class. There
are five of them. Adelaide Palmer is Squire
Palmer's daughter, — an only child, and perhaps a
spoiled child ; you might do a great deal for her.
Helen Sands is one of the doctor's family. You
know Dr. Sands ? "

" Yes, indeed we do ! " said Mrs. Dodd. " We
know him gratefully too ; he has been very good
to us."

" There, Happy ; you see there is another reason
for you. Julia Calhoun, I guess, is a good girl.
She is Mr. John Calhoun's daughter, the dry-goods
merchant on Main Street. Mary Gray I don't
know much about. Mrs. Gray is an odd woman,
and I think her father was a coarse, blunt man.
Poor child ! she'll need helping, if she takes after
her mother, and girls most always do."

" Oh, I wish they did, Mr. Fox ! " interrupted

Happy, eagerly, looking at her mother with such loving and admiring eyes that Mr. Fox's kindly laugh was a little tremulous.

"Well, perhaps we can't expect it always, my dear; but I hope you will follow the rule," he said, gently.

Mrs. Dodd's eyes were full of tears. Happy did not often express the deep feeling she had for her mother, and it was very dear to that mother when she did. She could not speak at once, and Mr. Fox went on:

"The last of the five is Ruth Holden. If looks tell true, she is the flower of your flock; but she is a very shy and lovely flower, to be handled gently. She has an invalid mother, and her father is a selfish, hard-headed man of business; she has to grow in a stone-wall. Happy, you must help her climb up and over it."

Mr. Fox certainly knew his business. Before he was through, Happy felt a personal interest in the children she had never spoken with, though one or two she knew by sight.

"I'll try!" she said, looking up with a sweet, shy smile at the superintendent.

"Angels can do no more, Miss Happy. I shall expect to see you at a quarter to nine, then, next Sunday morning. Good-night to you both."

When he had left the room, the girl turned to her mother with a wistful face.

"Mother, do you suppose I can?"

"You only promised to try, dearie! Nobody knows what they can do without a trial. There's a good Bible word for you, at any rate: 'If thy presence go not with us, carry us not up hence.' The Lord never gives us work to do that can't be done; that was Pharoah's way, not his. There's the bell for evening service, we can go there anyway, and that is to-day's duty: we haven't got to to-morrow's work yet, much less next Sunday's."

CHAPTER II.

THERE were plenty of daily duties in Happy's life; her place in this small household enabled her mother to support them both, for it set her free from home anxieties.

Happy did all the cooking, made and mended their clothes, and kept the house, or rather the tenement, neat and orderly. Three little rooms on the second floor of a house do not seem to involve much work, but Happy was not strong. And beside, she was lame: the evening always found her well tired, and glad to rest in the old chair that was once her grandmother's; and if there was no extra sewing to be done, her mother read to her. This week they studied the Sunday-school lesson together with more diligence than ever; for it was now to be the girl who should give, where hitherto she had only received. The lesson was in the first chapter of Matthew: and these were not the days of Union lessons, or Sunday-school papers, or helps. The Superintendent gave out a lesson, it is true,

from one of the old books ; but the classes were by
no means held to it, and Mrs. Dodd had advised
Happy to begin the New Testament with her class,
and go on, chapter after chapter.

Sunday morning dawned bright and clear, and
Happy, inwardly trembling, arrived punctually at
the chapel, and was put in her place by Mr. Fox,
who formally introduced her to the class when they
had all arrived. Adelaide Palmer was as fine as
silk and velvet and feathers could make a child ;
rather pretty, and full of insolent affectation. She
bent her head languidly to the new teacher, and
stared at her black alpaca dress, gray cloth sacque,
and felt hat with only a bow and band of black
velvet, as if she were inspecting some natural
curiosity. Helen Sands, who thought Addy Palmer was wonderful and lovely on account of her
fine clothes, saw the look and tittered softly.
Happy's cheek burned, but it was not with cow-
ardly dread ; she was indignant. Mary Gray
nodded to her in a careless way, but with no in-
spection ; Julia Calhoun, tall, sensible, and evidently
bright, with a pleasant expression, shook hands, and
turned a cold face on Addy and Helen.

"I shall like her," thought Happy, "but I shall
love this one "—as Ruth Holden, blushing like the
flower itself, held out to her a shell-pink tea-rose
in a geranium leaf.

"Would you like it?" the child said softly, in a voice so sweet the young girl wanted to kiss her on the spot.

Ruth was indeed lovely: the fair silken hair brushed closely back and falling in heavy masses over her shoulders, left unveiled a face whose regular features were absolutely illuminated by a complexion clear and splendid as sun-tinted snow; great gray eyes fringed with long lashes, — eyes as deep and clear as jewels, and full of feeling and purity,— looked with a sort of divine candor into her teacher's. If Happy had been unworthy of that gaze, she would have shrunk from its pure searching; but she herself was almost as innocent as Ruth, so she only smiled at her, and received an answering ray of light from the child's face, which was fairly radiant when she was pleased, though sad in repose. For Ruth was not altogether happy; her mother was always hovering on the brink of death, and could not brood this bird of Paradise as its delicate, sensitive nature needed. Perhaps it was better for her that even so early life should harden rather than enervate the tender plant; but she seemed so made to be cherished and guarded that Happy thought to herself many times afterward how much darker the ways of God were than those of man, but how much better!

This first lesson was not without its difficulties. Addy Palmer played with her rings, and jingled her chain and cross, while Happy tried to explain the lesson. Helen Sands' eyes roamed far and wide about the chapel, quick to note every new dress or fresh hat, and much more interested in the contemplation of the Granger family, three girls always heaped with finery, than she was in the lesson.

But Julia Calhoun listened with a certain critical expression ; Mary Gray looked at her Bible, if nothing more; and Ruth Holden's face was like a clouded sky in summer, when the winds chase the white fleeces across the blue heaven, and shade and sun give to earth the expression of living thought. Without knowing it, Happy had a graphic way of stating things as if she had seen them yesterday, and a simple earnestness of speech very pleasant to children. Ruth's sweet lips parted in breathless interest as, after reading the chapter half through, the teacher said, " Let's try to see it now. Think of those wise old men coming to Jerusalem, to look for the King of the Jews. I wonder how they knew what the star in the east meant ? Perhaps God told them in dreams, as he did Joseph. Then you see Herod was troubled. I suppose he felt very much as Queen Victoria would now if some people should go to London and begin looking for a new king of England. How do you think you should feel, Helen, in her place ? "

" Oh, dear ! I can't suppose, Miss Dodd."

"Can't you try?"

"No; I never could suppose anything," yawned Helen, staring with all her might at some visitor who had just entered in a new spring suit. Julia Calhoun came to the rescue.

"I think she'd be awfully scared, and I guess Herod was."

"Yes, indeed," Happy went on. "But he wasn't too scared to think: he knew a good deal, I suppose, about what to do in an emergency; he had been king long enough for that. The first thing to do was to find out all these wise men knew, and then he sent them off to find out more, and come back and tell him. How glad they must have been to see the star, when they got out of the city, going right before them to show the way."

"Do you suppose it was a real star?" asked Mary Gray, looking up suddenly.

Now Happy had been troubled in her own mind as to what she should do in case the scholars questioned her too deeply for her knowledge.

"What *shall* I do, mother?" she had said only the night before—"if the girls ask me something I don't know?"

"Tell them you don't know it, Happy. Truth is always better than guessing. There is a great deal in the Bible nobody understands; why should you expect to explain it all?"

So she simply answered Mary :

" I don't know.   Whatever it was, it showed them
the way.   I think Mary must have been surprised
to see these three old men come in to the door of
the stall and give her baby such beautiful things,
and fall down on their knees before him.   I wonder
what she thought ; her head must have been full of
ideas about the Holy Child."

" I thought it was shepherds came first to see
him," said Julia.

" Yes, that is in another Gospel — in Luke."

" Why aren't they all alike ? " said Mary Gray.

" Because they were written by four different
people : I don't think any two persons in the world
seeing anything happen could tell about it just the
same way, even if they saw it from the same
place."

" Why not ? " asked Addy Palmer, who happened
to have been sharply reproved, a day or two before,
by her school teacher, for misrepresenting something in school, and hoped to get a certain justifica-
tion out of Miss Dodd's opinion.

" Because they are not made alike : some people
don't notice or know half that goes on before their
eyes, and some see every little thing."

" Then you don't believe it's a lie always if a
person can't tell a thing just as it happened ? "

" Nothing is a lie that is not meant to deceive ; if

you mean people to understand what you tell them
to be true, when you know it is not true, that is a
lie, whoever says it."

Addy Palmer's eyes dropped, and she said no
more, and Happy went on.

" And now comes something that makes me think
these wise men must have been told about Jesus
Christ by God himself, and sent to see him, for the
twelfth verse says : ' And being warned of God in a
dream that they should not return to Herod, they
departed into their own country another way.' So
you see Herod did not find out as much as he meant
to. He did not know God was standing in his way ;
he did not think about God at all, probably. I think
we will not go any further to-day in the chapter,
but just stop here, and see what lessons there are to
learn from these verses.

" One is that it is a good plan to go to the Bible
for advice and teaching. Even Herod found this ;
for when he wanted to know about Christ he went
to the Jewish priests, and they told him what the
Bible said. If we always go to the Bible, we shall
find some help or leading in every time of trouble
or joy."

" About everything ? " said Ruth, with a little
trembling in her voice, and very wistful eyes.

" Yes, dear, about everything of real importance."

" I suppose even the Bible wouldn't tell about

dresses and bonnets!" said Julia, with a sort of
sarcasm in her voice, as Addy Palmer, next her in
the class, was gazing in an absorbed fashion at the
Grangers, who had previously occupied Helen's attention.

"Yes, it does, something," answered Happy,
smiling.

"Why, what?" exclaimed Helen and Addy in a
breath.

"Suppose you all look and see what you can find
in the Bible before next Sunday, about dress.   You
all have reference Bibles; take for the text first
Timothy, second chapter, ninth verse."

Addy looked out the text directly, and showed it
to Helen, who made a queer little face, thinking no
one saw her.   Miss Dodd did, but she went on.

"And another thing is to give all we can to God :
our greatest treasures ; the things we like best and
think most of.   The wise men brought gold and
costly perfumes and gave them to the Holy Child to
show their love and reverence ; and if we love him
we shall give him what we love best, and that is
generally our own selves.   These two teachings are
enough, perhaps, to remember to-day.   Now will
you all tell me what you would have liked best to
see, that we have read about?"

Happy did this with a half-conscious idea of making
it a test question ; and to some extent it served that

purpose: the girls hung back at first, and were shy; she had to press them a little.

"Suppose you speak in order: what would you have liked best?" looking at Adelaide Palmer.

"Oh! the treasures. I wonder what they were!"

"That's just what I was wishing," said Helen Sands.

Julia Calhoun thought a moment.

"I'd have liked to see how Mary acted when the wise men came in."

And Ruth went on, all her face flushing with emotion:

"O, Miss Dodd, I wish I could have seen the baby!"

Poor little Ruth! her tiny sisters both lay in the graveyard, but her loving heart kept them in sweet remembrance.

"I'd have chosen to see the wise men, and ask them about the star," said Mary Gray.

Just then the bell rang, for there had been much said not chronicled here, and they turned about to sing. The lesson was not after any very scientific or orderly fashion; it was the way Happy had been used to read the Bible and talk it over with her mother: simple enough, and akin to the "foolishness of preaching," but it had interested the children, and their criticisms on the new teacher were gentle,—except that Addy Palmer sniffed at her dress, and

Helen Sands said she hadn't any style; but as
neither of these possessions are great aids to teaching the Bible, Happy would not have been disturbed
by them.

"O, mother, how tired I am!" she said, as they
got home after the service. "But I like it ever so
much better than I thought I should, and I like
some of the children."

"That is good, dearie; then you have found one
thing you can do."

"One thing I like to do, mother."

Happy had not yet found out that the two are
almost identical.

CHAPTER III.

AFTER Happy got fairly to know her Sunday school class, she began to love them, and to enjoy teaching them. It is impossible to teach the gospel without a personal interest in those who learn it. The secret of all preaching lies also in this personal interest in the audience; not individual interest; for this is impossible, but the vivid, loving consciousness that men are indeed brethren, however they evade or ignore the kinship; kindred according to the flesh, whom the eager faith and anxiety of him who speaks are striving to heal and save through Christ, the Elder Brother.

It is to be owned that Happy had some trouble with Miss Palmer's indolent and insolent affectation, and Helen Sands's rattle-pated folly, and love for fashion and finery; but she had discovered, under Mary Gray's rough exterior, honesty and a kind heart, though veiled by the unconquerable shyness which made her so blunt. Julia Calhoun would have troubled her a little, her mind was so speculative, her questions so keen and logical, had not Happy learned to say frankly, "I do not know." These four little words were like a talisman to her, on which she rested herself from many a doubt and fear; for the reverse side of this inscription was always, "God knows."

As for Ruth Holden, there was no doubt in Happy's mind that the child was sweeter and better than ever any child had been before. Ruth's faults were slow of discovery, and more negative than her virtues. She was morbid, introverted, impatient of other people's failings, and very proud, with that subtle kind of pride which is not for daily use, and wears the mask of a virtue, even of humility, when it is visible. But all this Happy did not yet discover; she only loved her, with all her heart, and longed to do something to show it, as all love longs.

In her week-day life this poor girl was shielded from some things by her very poverty and weakness. She could not go out to work because she was needed to do the home duties; these might have been set aside somewhat, had her health allowed her to work in a shop, but she was too delicate for such confinement. Such light needlework as she could find to do occupied all her spare time, and helped a little; but it was her mother's object to keep up the girl's strength, and build up her constitution while she could; for Mrs. Dodd knew

very well that the time was coming when Happy
would have to take care of herself, and her best
weapons of war in the fight with poverty would be
health and strength.

It is not to be supposed that the girl's spiritual
life went on in perfect calmness; of "fightings
within" there were as yet none, but "fears without" had begun. As she sat alone one day, working at the straw plaiting which happened to be
to-day's task, she heard a slow step come up the
stairway, and the door opening let in old Miss
Lavinia Greene, the other tailoress in the little
town; an aged woman with whom Mrs. Dodd
herself had learned her trade, but who was now
unable to sew from an attack of paralysis some
years since, which had given her head and her
hands a constant tremulous motion that put a stop
to their usefulness in most ways. She had laid up
a little money, enough to live on with great care;
and her sole amusement was visiting her old acquaintance, and interesting herself in their affairs,
whether they liked it or not.

She had been out of town for a month or two
now; but her first thought on coming home was to
call at Mrs. Dodd's, and "visit with" Happy.

"Well, well!" said she, as she sat down in the
arm-chair, and recovered her breath with a little
effort. "How be ye both, Happy?"

" Pretty well, ma'am, thank you."

" And I've heard say you jined the church sence
I was to Northport."

" Yes'm," said Happy, in a low tone.

" Well, I'm glad on't.   I hope ye'll act up to it.
I s'pose you feel real overflowing' jest now; as
though you was ready to die any minnit, and rather
die than not.   Fust love; full assurance o' hope, 'nd
sech like.   Dear me! I've been through the hull on't."

Happy stared at her with wide eyes; this had
not been at all her experience, but rather " whereas
I was blind, now I see "; and she had not yet been
launched into that hopeless maze of self-analyzing
which some people consider a necessity of religion.
" Miss Lavinny " was opening that gate for her
now.   She went on :

" 'Twon't last, though; there's trials an' tribula-
tions a waitin' for ye ; trouble for everybody in this
world; 'fliction, back-slidin', loss of evidences,
death ; dear knows what.   All your trouble is to
come ; but ef you've got the root of the matter in
ye it's a help.   Yes ; it's really quite a help.   But
you needn't expect to feel uplifted as you do now,
not by no means."

" But I don't feel uplifted, Miss Lavinny," said
Happy, simply.

" You don't? don't feel sure o' heaven, and aint
shoutin' in your heart for joy every minnit ? "

" No, ma'am."

" For the land's sakes ! Ain't you sartain sure
you're a Christian, and you'd go to heaven right off
if you was to die suddin ? "

" Oh dear ! " and the tears were in Happy's eyes
as well as her voice. " I hadn't thought about it
much any way. I ain't sure of anything, Miss
Lavinny, except that the Lord Jesus died to save
sinners, and I do love him. I know I do."

The color rose to her pale dark cheek as she
spoke ; but Miss Lavinny shook her trembling head.

" Well ; mabbe you be converted ; but them aint
my experiences, nor they aint what used to be
folkses in my day. You'd better examine your
feelin's, Happilony ; see to your evidences bein'
straight, be sure you're born again before you set
out to be a professor ; I'm real afraid you're under a
mistake," — and here, having done her duty as she
fancied it, Miss Lavinia branched off into a stream
of gossip past and present, which fell on heedless
ears, for Happy was grieved inexpressibly, and
afraid in her humble soul that she had indeed been
too hasty in calling herself a Christian, and too self-
conceited in avowing it to others. By-and-by this
unpleasant visitor rose and went away, leaving
Happy with another pang of self-reproach to tor-
ment her, by insinuating, as she left, that she saw
she was not welcome as usual. " But them that

fetches reproof and rebuke is miser'ble comforters,
I know. I done it for your good, for all that,
Happilony ; and flatterin' lips won't never be laid to
my charge ! "

With which painfully true sentiment Miss Greene
shut the door behind her snappishly, and left the
girl to her own thoughts.

They were not pleasant ones ; there are few
people who can begin to criticise, examine, or look
for faults in their inward hearts, without discovering much to pain and perplex them. Happy had
youth and ignorance in her favor, but still the minutes crept slowly and bitterly away till it was time
for her mother to come. Mrs. Dodd noticed at
once the cloud on her child's face, and the brief,
constrained answers she gave her few ordinary questions, and she was not a woman to let any trouble
vex another soul if she could help it ; so she gently
and quietly drew from Happy the story of Miss
Greene's visit, and her own tears and troubles.
Mrs. Dodd did not offer any present counsel ; she
only said :

"Never mind, now, dear ; I have an errand to do
after supper, and I want you to go with me ; when
we come back we will talk all this over." So after
tea she said ; " I went to Mrs. Ives's to-day, you
know, and she says a woman down in Horn Lane is
sick, and almost without food for herself or her

children. Mrs. Ives cannot go, of course, she is
not able to walk yet, so she wants me to see about
it, and I thought you'd like to go too."

Happy was only too glad of a chance to walk
with her mother, and they soon found the way to
Horn Lane ; it was just at the edge of the village;
and close by the little river ; the soft summer air
was sweet with all the odors of woods and fields,
but the filthy tenement in which Ann Gladding
lived was shut tight against all outer air or odor.
Sick with typhoid fever, with a drunken husband,
and four little children, the old story of sin and
misery was repeated here in full. It was no new
tale to Mrs. Dodd ; but Happy had never come in
contact with such things and it struck to her heart.
She stood for a moment still and frightened, and
then, at her mother's suggestion, took the children
out of the stifling room on to the doorstep, and
amused them while Mrs. Dodd did what she could
to make the sick woman more comfortable, promising to fetch help for the night, and come herself in
the morning ; then she coaxed the children up to
their wretched attic, with Happy's help, washed
their faces, fed them with the slices of brown bread
and butter she had brought, and put them all to
bed. This was not much, but nothing more could
be done, except to stop in at a neighbor's, and get
Mrs. Foley to sit up all night with Ann Gladding,

as Mrs. Dodd could not conveniently do so till she
made some arrangements about her work for the
rest of the week.

Happy had forgotten all about her own troubles,
till her mother said, as she lit the lamp and sat
down beside it with her sewing; " Well, dear, what
about your own troubles ? "

" Why, mother! I declare, I forgot them, surely.
I was so troubled about poor Ann."

Mrs. Dodd smiled.

" That is a pretty good way, Happy; a better
still is 'looking unto Jesus.' Hear what he says,
and nobody else can trouble you. He never said
that we must be sure of heaven, or sure of conver-
sion, or very happy in our minds, or have a certain
round of feelings, to be saved; he said, 'Believe in
me:' 'If ye love me, keep my commandments,'
and the other side of that, 'He that hath my commandments and keepeth them, he it is that loveth
me.' Here is the commandment and the proof. If
you love God, you will show it in your life; words
and feelings are only leaves, fair and pleasant,
but not of any use; it is fruit the Lord of the
vineyard wants; and it is just as true now as it was
in Christ's early life, that grapes do not grow on
thorns, or figs on thistles."

" But mother; some good people don't act so."

" I don't think that is our business exactly,

Happy. The Master never said, 'Go toil to-day in' your neighbor's 'vineyard.' Other people are *other* people, and if they do not do just as we like or wish, all the more reason for us to do better. 'Every man shall bear his own burdens,' the Bible says; and I think this is what it means, — we are answerable only for our own, not for other people's."

"But, mother, don't it say too, 'bear ye one another's burdens' ?"

"Yes, dear, only put on the rest of the verse, 'and so fulfill the law of Christ.' We *shall* bear our own burdens to the judgment seat, whether we choose to or not; but we are told as Christians, to help one another, bearing other's burdens as Christ did, by trying to make them easier to carry, or by sharing them. He healed the sick and raised the dead; and we can help sick people, and tell the dying about him who will raise them from the grave. He fed the hungry with a miracle; we can feed one or two out of our own store. He made people happy at Cana by turning water into wine, because wine was a need and a custom at such places, and this poor man had not enough. Our Lord did not do this to countenance intemperance, as some people like to say, but to show that he wanted everybody to be happy as well as good; whenever you can make people happy, it is something to do for him who stooped even to help the

common wants of common and poor people, for
their pleasure. And this brings us round again to
you, Happy ; whenever Miss Lavinia's fears and
doubts trouble you again, dear, don't sit down and
think about them, go out and help or comfort somebody that needs either comfort or help."

"But what if I can't find anybody, mother?"

"Then take the Bible and read about Christ.
To look at him is to see our own redemption from
all evil, our surety, and our safety ; for 'your life is
hid with Christ in God.'"

"O mother, how good the Bible is!"

Mrs. Dodd's eye kindled and her lip trembled.
Happy would never know *how* good till she had
lived her life, and found in its pages the word
of the Lord, new every morning and fresh every
evening," the "daily bread," without which no
man's soul can live.

CHAPTER IV.

THE next week gave Happy plenty to do. Ann Gladding continued to be very ill, and though Mrs. Ives and other good women offered help in the way of money and food, Mrs. Dodd had to administer it, and more than once she sat all night by the poor woman, and took such care of her as nobody else could do.

"Why must you go, mother?" said Happy, one day, as she saw how pale and tired her mother looked, while she prepared to spend another night with Ann.

"There doesn't seem to be anybody else to go to-night, Happy. Mrs. Foley can't leave her baby again, and the other neighbors have had their turn."

"Haven't you had yours?" asked Happy, wistfully.

"Not if I can go, and no one else can, dear. Don't you remember that little verse in the paper last week? translated, it said, from an old hymn:

Thou wast weary seeking me,
Crucified to set me free!

I think of that so often since I saw it. How tired
Christ must have been, going about day after day,
teaching and preaching, homeless, hungry, poor.
Oh! Happy, we can't begin to do that for him!"

"Mother, I always wondered he came to be poor;
it seems as if rich people could do so much more,
and were thought of so much more in the world.
If Christ had been a great king now; it does seem
as if he could have done more good."

"That is what the Jews thought; but just see
how many more people are poor than rich. It was
the common people who heard him gladly; just such
folks as you and I, Happy. We can tell him now
just what troubles us, how we are tired and discouraged and poor, and know he can feel exactly
how we suffer, for so he suffered; but could you go
to Queen Victoria, and tell her how it made your
head ache to sit and sew, and how irritable you feel
when you are all worn out with fine stitching, or
how discontented when you are weak and can't
eat poor fare, and then ask her to help you to be
patient?"

Happy laughed. "Of course you couldn't; but
all these things we can take to the Lord, who lived
for us as well as died for us, and tell him about
them. 'For we have not a high-priest which cannot

be touched with the feeling of our infirmities, but was in all points tempted like as we are, yet without sin.'"

"Mother, are you really glad we are poor?" said Happy, looking wistfully up into her mother's face, for Mrs. Dodd had risen to put on her hat and go over to Horn Lane. The question was hard; the honest motherly heart reminded her how many times she had longed to be able to get advice from some skillful physician, change of air, good and pleasant food for her child, fruit and flowers to tempt her sickly appetite and refresh her beauty-loving eye. Happy did not know how her mother loved her. Do we any of us know till the grave holds the one patient heart that yearned over us, faulty and foolish as we might be, even unto the end? But even craving mother-love can find eternal rest in the heart of God, and Mrs. Dodd had found it. A smile that was born of pain long silenced lit her pale face as she answered:

"Shall not the Judge of all the earth do right, Happy? I have almost learned to be content with his allowance of this world. If ever I want more — and sometimes, to my shame, I do — I think that he knows best, and that I have nothing to say about it."

It had been a life-long lesson to her mother, and Happy had not yet attained to it; but she sat down

to read over her lesson for the next Sunday, and
kept on until a knock at the door roused her. It
was little Gay Packard, whose father and mother
lived on the lower floor ; whatever the child's name
was, she had always called herself "Gay," and the
name fitted her so well it clung to her. Her father
was a carpenter, a dreamy sort of man, whose trade
barely supported his small family, he spent so much
time in small inventions that never seemed to do
him or any one else any good ; his wife was a frivolous, improvident sort of woman, who delighted to
go to dances and shows of all kinds, and was sure
to send little Gay, her only child, up to Mrs. Dodd's
rooms to be cared for. At first she had taken the
child with her everywhere, and the little thing had
slept through many a firemen's ball or masonic
dance, on a heap of shawls in the corner, or sat up
in a state of unnatural excitement through circus
entertainments and minstrel shows as often as they
came about, until Mrs. Dodd had noticed it, and
invited the mother to send her baby upstairs, where
she could sleep on the lounge all night, and be fresh
and happy next day. To-night she came again, with
her tiny pleading question, "P'ease, Happy, tan I
stay wiz you? Mamma's dorn away!" Happy did
want to study her lesson, but she could not turn
little Gay back, so she closed the Bible with a sigh,
and took the small girl into her arms, thinking

silently, "I wonder if I ought to stop learning my
lesson, and play with her;" and even while she
petted Gay, whom she dearly loved, her thought
went wandering about among Bible words of which
she knew so many, thanks to her mother's teaching,
and she recalled the words of Jesus about little
children. Perhaps Gay had come to teach her a
lesson! At any rate she was here, and must be
cared for; the lesson could wait. And her own
lesson came instead; it was of doing the hour's duty
even when it seemed to interfere with a greater:
and, long after, she recalled it. Now she began to
tell Gay a Bible story, and watching her sweet wide
eyes and the eager interest she took in hearing about
little Joseph for the fortieth time at least. Happy
thought of the other children scattered about Lake
Street, where she lived, — children who did not go
to Sunday-school. Could she get them together
Sundays after church, and tell them stories, and sing
hymns to them ? Gay fell asleep in her arms while
she was thinking and planning about it ; and when
she had carefully put the little thing to bed on the
lounge, and resumed her Bible reading, she found
the new idea even more absorbing than the child,
and when her own bed-time came fell asleep with
the thought in her heart. But this week's work
began again with the morning. Mrs. Dodd brought
home two of Ann's children, the two youngest, for

Happy to take care of.   This was disagreeable
enough ; the girl and boy were rude, dirty, ungov-
erned — contrasts of the strongest to Gay Packard,
who was at least clean and gentle.   Hitherto Happy
had found it easy to do good, now it was to be hard.
In vain she tried to amuse them.   Her mother had
but a few moments to take her hurried breakfast
before she must go to her day's work at Mrs. Ives's ;
for though she had been all night at Ann Gladding's
she could not afford to lose a day.

   " Mrs. Ives is going to give me some old suits of
the children's for them," she said to Happy, as they
sat at breakfast, while the two children supped up
some brown bread and milk out of a bowl, with
noises and squabbling that forcibly recalled pigs at
a trough.   " Then we can wash them to-night and
put on clean things ; those rags are past mending.
But you will have to endure them to-day, dear,
there's no help for it.   Ann's life depends on quiet,
and " — Here, as if to illustrate the unuttered comment, Nan fell to pulling Jack's hair because he
took altogether too large a share of the breakfast,
and Jack retaliated with the iron spoon ; between
them the yellow bowl fell to the floor and broke in
two, and the milk flew far and wide over the rag
carpet.   Happy's face fell ; she ran to wipe up the
milk, but not before her mother saw the dismayed
look.   She pitied her heartily, but she knew very

well that pity is sometimes best unspoken: it is
rarely a tonic. She only said with a very bright
smile, which seemed to Happy a little too pleasant
for the occasion:

"I think you'll need a text to-day, Happy; here's
a good one: 'Thou therefore endure hardness, as a
good soldier of Christ Jesus.'"

As her mother closed the door it suddenly returned to Happy where she had last heard those
words, and the whole scene of her reception into the
church came back with them. She felt as if a
trumpet had sounded the recall to her post, almost
as if she had slept on guard and just awakened.
Honest and simple in her desire to serve her Master,
she stopped the train of disagreeable reflections that
threatened her comfort, and went vigorously to work
to conquer a peace with these rebellious little creatures. It was a hard day's work. Nan was the
least trouble; but to keep Jack, quite unused to
anything short of absolute freedom, a whole day in
the house, seemed impossible, but Happy knew if
once she let him out of her sight he would not stop
short of home, and he was quite too young to hear
to reason: all she could do was to amuse him, and
this was, as she said at night, harder work than
washing.

She tried Bible stories, and for a time they interested him, but soon he began to yawn and

fidget; then she sung to them. Nan did not like
singing, and made faces at Jack when he tried to
join in the chorus, as Happy showed him. Happily,
just after noon a violent thunder-storm came up,
and the rain lasted two or three hours, during which
the children got thoroughly frightened by the severity of the tempest, and were glad enough to curl up
on the floor at Happy's feet, and hear about Noah
and the Ark; but as soon as the rain ceased they
were more restless than ever, and when Mrs. Dodd
came home at night she found Happy tired enough,
the room in dire confusion, and Jack tied firmly to
the leg of the bedstead, the only possible way to
keep him at home, while Nan sulked and pouted
in the corner, and would have rebelled furiously
but for Jack's captivity. Mrs. Dodd was more used
to children than Happy; she did not scold them, as
they expected, but unpacked a basket of gingerbread and cheese, which Mrs. Ives had sent, and,
untying Jack, set them both down to supper,
adding a mug of weak tea as a treat. Then she
helped Happy set things to rights, and after they
were both refreshed by their own supper, they
washed the children, dressed them in some old
night-gowns of Robby Ives's, and Mrs. Dodd made
a bed for them out of her winter comfortables in
the little attic which served her for many things,
and now seemed a delightful chamber to these little

people, who were more weary from their unusual bath than from the long day's naughtiness.

"O, mother!" said Happy, "I never had such a time in my life. I never *did* see such children."

Mrs. Dodd looked both troubled and amused. "There are plenty far worse ones in the world, dear; and perhaps they will fall in your way to help."

"But, mother, they don't seem to care a bit; they don't like to be done good to."

Mrs. Dodd laughed outright. "Poor child! did you suppose they would? Do you think you would like the first lesson if anybody should teach you to swim? It's like teaching them the use of a new element to try to make them good."

"I didn't try to, much, mother; only enough to get along with them. I wanted to please them and make them happy, and they did not even seem to be thankful."

Her mother's face clouded. "If you go on that ground, Happy, it will be cut from under your feet at once. Our orders are plain on that point as on every other: 'Lend, hoping for nothing again.' You must learn that gratitude is a Christian virtue, and rare at that. Beside, your business is simply what you can do, and the doing of it; not how it is received. You will find men and women, elegant, refined, educated, even professing to lead Christian

lives, no more ready to acknowledge faithful and
kindly service than Nan and Jack. But that must
not stop your service; you are not answerable for
their short-comings, but you are for your own.
And, Happy, are you always grateful to God? If
he forsook us because we render him no return,
where should we be? But 'he is kind to the un-
thankful and the evil.' Is that enough of a sermon
to sleep on, dear?"

Happy kissed her mother in silence. "Oh! what
should I do without her?" she thought as she fell
asleep.

CHAPTER V.

HAPPY'S second day with Jack and Nan was not quite so bad as the first; their clean clothes seemed to impress them with a little self-respect; but still they were hard to get along with. Rough and rude by birth and breeding, Happy could not but contrast them with little Gay Packard's gentle, caressing ways.

"Say!" shouted Jack; "gimme a knife, can't ye? I want ter whittle a narrer out o' this pine stick,"— the pine stick being Mrs. Dodd's yard stick.

"Don't ye!" shouted back Nan. "Don't ye fetch him no knife, he'll cut up orful if ye do; he'll whittle everything! he ain't got no bow here neither to fit a narrer to, so there!"

"Hang your picter!" responded Jack.

"Oh Jack!" said Happy, horrified at the expletive.

"Well, what's up now?" the impudent little fellow demanded.

"You mustn't use such expressions here," said Happy, sternly.

Jack thrust his tongue out at her and winked furiously, while Nan tittered.

"Par and mar says cuss words," said she, stopping her laughter to extinguish Happy with a positive fact.

"*Nobody* can say them here," was the calm reply.

"Say, gimme a knife," Jack retorted, regardless of the episode ; and this style of speech went on all day. Happy was at her wit's end, and when her mother came home was delighted to hear that Ann Gladding was so much better they could go back the next morning.

"You could not bear them much longer — could you?" said Mrs. Dodd, with a smile, as she saw her girl's face light up.

"Oh mother! I have tried ; I've done all I knew how to do, and I'm so ashamed."

Her mother knew very well that this would not be the first of Happy's troubles in her attempts to do good ; but, strange to say, her counsel was not comfort, she only said : "Narrow is the way, and few there be that walk therein."

"But, mother, I am ashamed to think it isn't pleasant to me to do good. I thought I should like it, and I know I ought to, but I'm only sick and tired."

"Why, Happy! where did you ever learn that idea? Even Christ pleased not himself; he never promised that we should. All the promises speak of strife and weariness and trouble first; then peace and joy in God. If you could find the company of evil natures pleasant, would you think that a token of grace?"

Happy could not say anything, the tears choked her: like many another young girl, she had laid out for herself a lovely plan of doing good and being blessed in the way of duty. Her Sunday-school class was pleasant to her, almost without exception; for she began to perceive that she could sometimes interest even Helen Sands's flighty, shallow character, and stir the calm self-satisfaction of Addy Palmer's nature a little, and Happy was so honest and so earnest that a little token of good was of infinite promise to her. But these rough children were her first painful experience, and she had yet to learn, with many a sinking of heart, that to go down into the mud and slime of human nature, and try to cultivate its waste places, is a task of tiresome labor and slow return; that it is only God who can be forever patient, because he is perfect; and that humanity may labor for a long life, and yet scarce see the first green blade of harvest, but must learn to be content with sowing the seed, regardless of its springing. Her heart condemned her now

that she had not been more patient; she could not
know that these children considered her "orful
good," and that these two days of compulsory service and weary labor had really laid a foundation
for the Sunday afternoon class she had planned, far
more firmly than her own mere effort could have done.

Now a different task lay before her; Mr. Fox had
requested all the teachers in Sunday-school to visit
their scholars at their own homes, in order to know
their parents and establish a deeper relation between teachers and scholars than could be brought
about by the hour's association once a week. And
he also judged rightly enough that every teacher
could understand her scholars better if she knew
something of their home life and character; for
children, like older people, are very apt to put on
their best manners with their best clothes.

"O mother! I don't know how to do it," said
Happy, sitting on a little old-fashioned cricket at
her mother's knee after supper; that being the hour
they always had for counsel and conversation.

"Happy, you really ought to be called Miss
Much-Afraid," laughed Mrs. Dodd. She understood the girl's nature perfectly, but it would do no
good to sympathize with her. Happy was timid,
shy, very sensitive, with all her simplicity, to the
opinions of others; but she had a fund of moral
courage that when once roused enabled her to do

what she thought was right, even while she trembled and hung back for a time. This trait was her strength, and her Christian life was to build it up and heighten it; and it was to this her mother appealed.

"I guess you can do it, dear, even if you are afraid; do you remember going up to Dr. Sands's office one day, three or four years back, to have some teeth out? I never shall forget how you sat up in the chair, and kept saying, 'Oh, I can't Doctor! I certainly can't! Don't, please! I can't bear it!' and yet opened your mouth and sat quite still when he was ready, and had all those long roots pulled out without stirring hand or foot. How the Doctor laughed when it was over!"

"Yes, mother, and I never forgot what he said; 'Well, little girl, you're one of the kind that said "I will not," but afterward repented and went.' I did not know what he meant, exactly; but I think I do now."

"That's it. You will go this week, I know, because you ought to. I would go to Mrs. Sands first; she has known you this long time and then I should go next to Mr. Palmer's."

"O, mother!"

But this was all Happy said; the next day after her work was done, she put on her Sunday dress, and began the unpleasant round.

Nobody expects to see a martyr in a neat cambric dress, with a piqué sacque and little straw hat: but after all there was a spark of kindred spirit in Happy's dark eye as she set her lips firmly and limped along the sidewalk. Duty impelled them both; theirs to dying, hers to living; but fire is fire, whether it be the slight spark of a match or the roar of a burning city.

She rang the bell at Dr. Sands's house, and was shown into the sitting-room by Eddy Sands, who came to the door, and favored her with a stare and a nod. Mrs. Sands was a good-natured, easy, lazy sort of woman, naturally; a woman who tried to be a Christian, and really was one, but not energetically. Grace enabled Mrs. Sands to lead a benevolent and painstaking life, one of some self-denial, but it did not make her alert and active like Mrs. Dodd; for even grace does not give us new traits, but guides and governs the old, — a fact which would encourage many a desponding Christian if they would but lay it to heart. She was very pleasant and cordial to Happy; called Helen to come in and see her; sent Eddy for a glass of water; and with a good deal of effort rose from her chair and went into the garden to gather some flowers, which she sent to Mrs. Dodd. Helen went to get a string to tie them, and Mrs. Sands said to Happy:

"Nelly is getting very fond of you, my dear; she says Miss Happy is the best teacher she ever had; and that is a good deal for Miss Nell to admit."

Happy colored with pleasure, and gave Helen a heart-felt kiss as she took the flowers, and said "Thank you," and "Good-bye."

"That's a nice girl," said Mrs. Sands to herself.

And so the first call was over, happily. But two doors off Mrs. Palmer lived. Her husband was rich, and the house was a large wooden mansion set in the middle of a green yard. Happy knew Mr. Palmer both by sight and hearing; a "smart" man of business, intelligent, active, loving and making money; all things to all men, not for the apostle's blessed reason, — that he might "save some," — but that he might increase his own goods, and attract customers continually, to that end. Everybody liked him but poor or sensitive people. Mrs. Palmer was a woman with only two or three ideas, and one of them was "style." Happy was shown into the dark parlor by an Irish girl who answered the bell, and after sitting half an hour in the deep twilight of the blinded and curtained room, on a small and trembling chair evidently made only to look at, Mrs. Palmer sailed in, dressed in the very latest fashion; for she always went to New York with her husband twice a year, and consulted the windows in Sixth Avenue with eager eyes and retentive memory. She gave Happy some chill fingers to shake, and having discovered who she was, began to talk to her.

Now, Mrs. Palmer's grammar did not justify her dress, and the poor, plain girl who sat there by her, spoke far better English than she did. Happy was astonished to hear her begin.

"Well, Addy said she guessed you'd call after what Mister Fox said a Sunday. How's she getting along to the class? Addy's smart enough when she's a mind to; I didn't think 'twas real ne-*cess*-ary to have her go to Sunday-school, but the rest they went, and she done it before I knew ; that was to Miss Falkland's class — she that was married before you took the girls. Don't you want to see Addy ? "

" Yes, ma'am, I should like to," said Happy.

And Mrs. Palmer, opening the door, shrieked up stairs: " Addy-laide ! come down , come into the parlor ; there's somebody to see you."

But Addy bounced out of a side door almost into her mother's arms. " Don't holler so, ma, for goodness sake. What on earth's the matter ? "

" Come into the parlor ? "

"I won't ! I ain't fit to be seen now. My hair ain't crimped, and I've got my old dress on.

" Sh ! sh ! it's nobody but Happy Dodd ; you're dressed good enough to see her."

And being of the same opinion, Addy marched
into the parlor; greeted Happy with a nod and a
hand-thrust; sat down on the piano stool, and
began drumming on the piano cover.

"Don't do that, Addy; you'll scratch that rosewood; it cost too much to finger that way."

"Mercy, ma! I ain't hurting it."

"Yes, you be. Your pa give eight hundred dollars for that down to York last year; that's too
much to resk, ain't it, Happy?"

Addy did not wait for her teacher's answer.

"Oh, never mind the old piano! Say, Miss
Dodd, don't you want to see my new Bible?"

Of course Happy did. She was keen enough to
perceive that Adelaide — who had some of her
father's shrewdness — wanted to change the subject; and was all ready to admire the red morocco
Bible, with gilt clasps and ornaments, when Adelaide brought it. She made a short call here, for
other company came in; but she left feeling that
she had learned more about this scholar, and was
better able to teach her than ever before. In
neither of these calls had Happy spoken of religious matters; it was never her way to speak
much of what she felt most deeply, and she had
once heard Mr. Payson say at an evening meeting:

"Do not make religion a bore to those who do
not possess it by constantly throwing it in their

way, either by talking to or at them. Human
nature is perverse, and turns instinctively from
what is too much pressed upon it. Act out your
faith, live it ; ' let your light so shine.' The man or
woman who is just, true, pure, generous, kindly,
and a professed follower of Christ, is the best of all
preachers and teachers."

So Happy went home (for the afternoon was far
advanced, and her walk to the " court end " of the
village was long) neither encouraged much nor
discouraged at all; but on the whole glad that a
part of her duty was done, and that it had not been
too formidable. She found little Gay at the door to
meet her, for her mother had gone away on a pic-
nic, and would not be home till late. It rested
Happy to have the tender arms clasped about her
neck, and the soft small cheek laid against hers.

" I'se glad you tamed, Happy. I was 'fraid on
the stairs. I loves you."

" And I love you, darling," said the girl, as she
gave back warmly the child's fond kiss.

CHAPTER VI.

LONG before Happy began her class in Sunday-school she had begun teaching, though with but one unconscious scholar, — little Gay. To her she had preached the gospel with all the earnestness of youthful faith; and Christ was as real a personage to little Gay as Happy herself, only that she did not see him; and many a sudden thrill the child had sent to her father's heart by her constant allusions to the things of another world, — a world which seemed as familiar to her thought as that she lived in. With an instinct of reverence Happy had taught her, by much patient trial, to speak the name of the Lord distinctly and slowly: and when her father or her mother would say " Gay is a good girl to-day," she answered often:

" I's glad. Jesus Christ likes to have Gay dood."

" How do you know? " asked her mother, one day, half irritated by the child's frequent reference to him whom she herself would not acknowledge as Master.

"Bibel says so," answered Gay, with serene satisfaction; for this was Happy's answer to all her
own baby questioning.

A child may be taken to-day into the Lord's arms
and blessed, even as when he walked on earth; and
Happy could not but hope he had spoken to her
little darling, baby as she was, for she seemed daily
to grow more loving, more gentle, and more obedient. Her very delicate organization perhaps kept
her from the ordinary temptations of children ; poor
food, insufficient clothing, weak lungs, the result of
neglected colds and careless exposure, all helped
extinguish her animal spirits, and want of fresh air
made her languid and dull. Happy did not know
how delicate the child really was; and Mrs. Dodd
saw her so little that her more experienced eye did
not detect the rapid progress of this poor baby
toward a better home. This very night that Happy
found her waiting on the stairs, Gay was seized with
a sudden fever: she woke several times in the night
with sharp outcry, and Mrs. Dodd gave her some
simple remedy she had, but without avail. By day-
break she was decidedly ill, and as her mother had
not yet returned, having found her sister at the pic-
nic, who had persuaded her to stay all night at her
house, Mrs. Dodd woke the father and sent him for
the doctor.

Mr. Packard had been half drunk the night before,

as he often was; but though he woke trembling and irritable, the shock sobered him, for if he had loved anything on earth beside himself that thing was little Gay. In half an hour he had brought Dr. Sands to the child's bedside, and altogether unnerved, and unable to see her suffer, had driven over to Scranton to fetch her mother, in the doctor's gig. It was a case of diptheria, Dr. Sands said, — a disease that, like a coward, steals first and most fiercely upon the feeblest victims. Gay's trouble was short, for she offered no resistance. Happy nursed her like a mother: she could not give her little darling into Mrs. Dodd's hands. After some hours of evident suffering the child looked up into Happy's face and smiled.

"O Doctor! she is better," the girl cried out, with a look of vivid joy on her pale face. Tears stood in Mrs. Dodd's eyes, and the doctor's kind voice trembled a little as he said: "No, my dear; she is dying."

Happy recoiled as from some dreadful blow: then sudden courage possessed her, and she bent over little Gay, and said softly that baby-prayer, hallowed by so many childish lips for so many years, "Now I lay me down to sleep." She said it clearly and slowly, and the child evidently heard, for she tried to lift her little hands to fold them, but she could not; but when Happy had finished she looked at her with a solemn brightness in her eyes.

"Good-bye, little Gay," said Happy; and in a hoarse whisper the child said: "Dood-bye," and was gone out of time forever. Mrs. Dodd's voice broke the mortal silence, with "Suffer little children to come unto me, and forbid them not"—

She had no time to finish the text, for the door opened and Mrs. Packard rushed in. Weak, selfish, faulty, and a careless mother, yet she was a mother, and her child lay dead before her; and with the sudden passion of a weak, undisciplined nature in its first grief, she raved and wept and stormed, till Happy felt as if the heavenly calm of the dead baby was profaned. Her husband stood by the bedside, all unconscious except of that tiny sleeper. He could not control his wife at any time; he did not try now. The doctor went out at once; he was in great haste, and had only waited for his gig, to go to the other end of the town to a dying patient. Mrs. Dodd did not say anything: she did not know what to say, in fact; for with her quick capacity of sympathy she felt every throb of that mother's wretched heart, and lived over again the dying of her three lost children. But Happy could not bear it long; she stepped up to Mrs. Packard's side, and laid her hand tenderly on her hot forehead.

"Don't, dear!" she said softly; "Jesus Christ has taken Gay home: she is all safe. Don't cry, please!"

Mrs. Packard pushed her hand off and looked up in her face with red and streaming eyes: "Don't! Much you know about it, Happy Dodd! I don't care who's got her when it ain't me! You ain't her mother! She's my baby! O Gay, Gay!" and here a wild burst of hysterics swept over the poor feeble soul, and Mrs. Dodd drew Happy away into the living-room.

"Sit down, Happy," she said, "and drink this hot tea. Human nature won't stand everything, and you haven't eaten a bit since last night: it's four o'clock now."

It was well for Happy that she had been taught obedience so early that it had become an instinct, for she ate and drank mechanically, and then lay down and fell asleep from pure exhaustion. When she awoke Gay had been taken down stairs, and Mrs. Packard's stormy grief had subsided into sullen gloom: her husband was going about the house doing what he could to make it orderly and decent, while she sat in a rocking-chair, rocking, and uttering heavy sighs, but silent and resentful. It was almost dark when Happy opened her eyes to see her mother sitting by the window, but the fading glitter of day across her cheek showed that it was wet with tears. Happy was on her feet in an instant.

"Mother, dear!"

Mrs. Dodd looked at her with the tenderest, saddest look she had ever shown to Happy.

' I was thinking about my own three babies,
Happy, and that poor woman down stairs." It all
come back to the girl now ; in her sudden waking
she had seen and felt her mother's tears before she
remembered little Gay. She laid her head on her
mother's knee and cried bitterly. Mrs. Dodd did
not try to control that frank outflow of sorrow, for
this was Happy's first experience of death, and she
was only a girl ; tears were the natural and healthy
expression of feeling ; it is only the oft stricken who
can receive a blow and make no outcry.

Presently Happy looked up. " O mother ! why
did God take the dear little thing away ? "

" I do not know, dear ; God knows. I could tell
you what I think about it, but that would only be
my thoughts. Happy, if you live long enough, there
will be a great many things happen to you and yours,
that you cannot understand ; try to give up understanding them, and then you will have peace. God
is infinite, and we are only his limited feeble creatures: to measure his ways by our thoughts is to
try pouring the great sea into a tea-cup. ' Canst
thou by searching find out God ? canst thou find out
the Almighty unto perfection ? It is as high as
heaven: what canst thou do ? deeper than hell:
what canst thou know ? The measure thereof is

larger than the earth and broader than the sea. If
he cut off and shut up, or gather together, then
who can hinder him?'"

There was an unusual solemnity in Mrs. Dodd's
voice as she spoke, and her words fell deep into
Happy's soul: she never forgot them. Both were
silent for a while, and then her mother said: "Will
you go down stairs with me now, Happy?"

The girl knew what she meant; but in all her life
she had never seen the face of death, and she
naturally shrank back. But her mother did not
put the subject away: she had her own reasons for
wishing her girl to become acquainted with that
dread presence first in so lovely a manifestation as
that which lay below stairs; for while Happy slept,
Mrs. Dodd had dressed the fair shape in its last
attire, and laid it in the crib, where it seemed to
her only sleeping.

"There is nothing sad for you to see, Happy,"
she said. "We must all face death some day, and
why not now? Gay is asleep, only asleep forever,
till time shall be no more."

But it was not the look of sleep to Happy, when
she followed her mother into that shaded room, and
looked at that waxen shape on its fresh pillow; the
blue-veined lids were calm beyond any look of life,
even its deepest slumber; the wan, tiny hands
never wore that rigid clasp before; and the soft

curls were still and shining above the baby forehead; no breath stirred those silken rings, or parted
those pale lips; no pulse moved the folds of the
snowy night-dress, or throbbed in the small throat.
No! it was death, death itself! beautiful, but
dreadful in its beauty.   Happy could not look long,
it was not her Gay who lay there; she turned away
with a shiver, and heard her mother whisper softly,
" He is not here !   He is risen !" and the words
quickened her sinking heart, even as of old time
they comforted the Marys at the sepulchre.   Then
they went into the kitchen where Mrs. Packard
still sat, sullen and wretched, rocking to and fro.
Her husband stood by the window looking out into
the yard, grieved, awkward, unoccupied; longing to
have something to do or say, yet filled with a
certain sense of impropriety if he should do or say
anything.   He looked round in a relieved way when
Mrs. Dodd and Happy came in.   " Have a chair,"
he said, placing two out in the middle of the floor.
Mrs. Dodd sat down, but Happy did instinctively
the best thing, — she knelt down by the childless
woman, put her head in her lap, and burst into
tears.   Mrs. Packard could not bear it; hot and
slow her own tears gathered and fell.

"Don't! oh, don't!" she said, hoarsely.   "Don't
you cry! it's me that ought to cry forever; you've
been real good to — to her; you told her things she

oughter know, and I didn't. If she's reelly gone
where you say, you showed her how, 't wan't me.
My baby's gone, and I shan't never see her — oh
dear, oh dear!"

"Yes, you will!" whispered Happy; but she
said no more. The great grief beside her sealed
her lips. When Mrs. Packard stopped, the man
began, "That's so! Happilony, you've been dreadful good to Gay, we shan't never forget it of ye;
but she's dead all the same, you know; dead an'
gone," and with an air of bewildered pain he
walked into the bed-room and shut the door, to be
alone with his child. Mrs. Dodd beckoned Happy
to come away; there was nothing to be said here
and now. "They talk to the grief of those whom
Thou hast wounded," had been her own bitter
experience; she knew that nothing but love has a
right to speak to grief, and here was only neighborly
kindness, Christian desire to bear their burdens,
honest pity. Their turn would come by and by.
To-day it was best to leave that fair, pale shape,
and the divine Spirit that speaks even from dead
lips, to do their work of ministry. Two days after
there was a simple funeral; all the relatives living
out of town, and most of them far away, only Mrs.
Packard's sister came from Scranton, and a few
neighbors stepped in. Mr. Payson prayed, and read
the Bible verses appropriate to the hour, and at the

grave made another prayer, and then they left little Gay's earthly vesture in its earthly bed.

Happy was deeply moved. It seemed more utter loss than ever to leave the sweet little face, the clinging arms, the golden head, alone and cold in the lonely graveyard; and her mother read those natural thoughts with a mother's keenness. "Don't seek the living among the dead, Happy," she said, as they turned away. "Look up. This is one thing you have done for the Master; one thing you could and did. You have brought a little child to him, and he has taken her in his arms and blessed her."

The words sounded to Happy like a consecration. and she thanked God and took courage.

CHAPTER VII.

HAPPY went to the Sunday-school class, the next Sunday, solemnized and saddened both, and talked to them with the earnestness of one who for the first time looks into a grave. This is quite another feeling from that of later years; it is full of novelty, of awe, sometimes of terror. There is nothing more beautiful and more gentle than the way in which God prepares a long life for its end; the breaking of slight ties, the pause of pain and slow recognition; then another removal, and another pause; till at last we learn death by heart, as it were, and being drawn quietly over to the great company who have gone before us, by the strong cords of memory, of love, of longing and regret, we scarcely know if our life is here or there; and lie down in our turn, serenely and trustfully, at the Lord's word, knowing that to die is to go home at last.

The girls in Happy's class wondered at their teacher, there was such new depth of feeling in her eye and voice; such solemn, tender earnestness, such a fresh glow of faith in all she said. Gay's death had brought the teacher to be taught of God; and she felt as if nothing must be left undone or unsaid to bring these little ones also to the Master. Addy was restless and uneasy; she had a conscience that made her uncomfortable often, though home influences helped to dull its voice.

Helen Sands was more quiet than usual, but her eye still wandered about the room, and her attention was not fixed. Julia Calhoun listened with steadfast countenance; and Mary Gray gave no sign except that she looked at her book, even while Happy was talking most earnestly. Ruth nestled closer than ever to her teacher; tears gathered in her beautiful clear eyes, and the warm color rose in her cheeks; before Happy had finished telling them about little Gay, those tears fell softly and unconsciously, and Julia's eyes were also dim. The hour was too short for Happy; her lesson was not finished when the bell rang. After the concluding hymn and prayer were over, she went out with her class; an unusual thing, for she generally waited for her mother, who had a Bible class of older girls, which Happy had belonged to until her promotion to a teacher's place. But to-day she kept with her children, as if unwilling to let them go away from her; and to her amusement, even in her serious thoughts, she heard Addy say to Julia Calhoun: "O Jule! don't you think Miss Dodd called to our house last week! Did she go to see you?"

"No," answered Julia, "but I guess she will."

"She came to our house too!" put in Helen Sands in her usual careless way.

Mary said nothing; but just before they reached the church, Ruth, who was clinging to Happy's hand all the way, looked up and said softly, "Won't you come and see mamma and me, Miss Happy?"

Mary heard her, and said, curtly, "Me, too?"

"Of course I will. I am coming to see you all; last week little Gay's death stopped me; I meant to have seen you then."

Happy's face glowed as she saw the pleased expression on those three young faces, for Julia had lingered too, as if to speak; and her heart glowed also. This was pleasant; how much more pleasant than the rough, dirty manners and persons of Nan and Jack Gladding! But Mr. Payson's sermon put a different train of ideas into her head; it was a sermon on practical religion, and the text was,

"For the Son of Man is come to seek and to save that which is lost." The special message that struck Happy to-day was this:

"The lost! My dear friends, the lost are not generally an agreeable class of persons to seek or to save. There are many 'lost,' it is true, among

people of refinement and culture; but the mass,
those whom you are most likely to have opportunity
to help, are the poor and the ignorant. There is no
sentiment about this work; its objects are coarse,
dirty, rough, too often profane and drunken, repul-
sive to every sense of soul or body, yet over them
divine pity hovers and longs; can you do less? It
is pleasant and beautiful to do good in the way we
too often read of, visiting the neat and pious poor,
or reasoning with the polite and cultivated unbe-
liever; but it is not pleasant to follow in his steps
who went unto 'spirits in prison.' It is yours to
go to such spirits yet in the prison of ignorance,
filth, and sin; and you will find it hard work, disagreeable, tiresome, sometimes loathsome; but, my
dear friends, it is the Lord's work; can you afford
to be fastidious? Can you dare to despise or pass
by any soul he died for, whatever its surroundings
may be? Take with you this vial of odor, 'Lord,
I do this for thee'! and the waste places will
blossom as the rose. You will share the very joy
of him who descended into the depths to save you;
and you will show that the faith which is in you is
so instinct with life and love, so absolute a reality,
that you will preach the gospel of Christ without
being aware of it."

Happy took this into her soul. Her own delicate
nature and organization wrought in her a certain

indolence and shrinking from pain or trouble that
she was fully aware of, though without really knowing how much excuse the willing spirit had in the
weak flesh. She determined, as she sat there, to
begin her Sunday afternoon experiment with the
children of her neighbors at once; and longed to
get home and talk it over with her mother; but to
her intense disgust Miss Lavinia Greene joined
them, and Mrs. Dodd asked her to come in and
take supper. Happy's heart sank within her; but
Miss Greene was delighted; she was fluent as usual,
all the way, and having taken off her bonnet and
shawl, possessed herself of the cushioned rocker
and the biggest fan, and sat down by the open
window.

It was early in September now, and the day had
been as hot as some September days are; but
Happy would not let her mother get the tea,
although she felt unusually tired; she thought any
work was better than sitting down to entertain
Miss Lavinia. It did not enter into her head just
now that she had any duties except toward "the
lost," and Miss Lavinia was a church-member in
good and regular standing. But Happy was not to
escape; Miss Greene liked to garnish her food with
voluble conversation.

"Well, Happy," she began, "we had a real good
sermon to-day, didn't we? I call that a most an

excellent sermon; but 'twan't real perfect; of
course, there ain't nothin' human that is."

Mrs. Dodd smiled involuntarily, for this was the
key-note of Miss Lavinia's character,—that nothing
was just right, on earth, certainly. If her criticisms
aimed higher, she at least kept them to herself, but
now she went on.

"I do think there's some folks ' lost,' so to speak,
seemin'ly, as it might be, who don't come under
neither o' them heads of his'n, — folks that ain't
cultered, nor rich, nor stuck up, nor ain't dirty and
swearin', and ignorant nuther. Folks like Sam ·
Rice, now. You remember him, don't ye, Almiry?
He that was sister's son to Aunt Bliss down to
Haddam. Why, he was a dreadful clean man, an' I
dono as he ever swore; and he wan't ignorant
nuther; he could write a pretty good letter, and he
took the Weekly Courant reg'lar, and read every
speck on't, even to the _add_-vertisements, — so's to
get his money's wuth, I expect, for he had money ;
but, the land's sakes ! he might better ha' been
poor, he was so awful mean. Why, Miss Rice she
didn't never have more'n one caliker gown to her
name, an' an old alipacky for a go-to-meeting'. He
was too mean for anythin'. Why, he sold the man
to the store a barrel o' cider, and they 'greed on the
cost, an' when he come to bring it he charged two
cents for the bung, as sure's you're born; and he

fetched eggs to Miss Blisses fust cousin's folks, and
called eleven on 'em a dozen when one was double
yolked! Land sakes! I'd rather try for't with the
biggest heathen in forrin' parts, that is to say, as it
were, about convertin' on 'em, as to try to fetch
Sam Rice round. Them's the kind there can't
nobody but the Lord tech."

" The Lord has got to touch everybody, Miss
Lavinny," said Mrs. Dodd, smiling; for this Sam
Rice she knew to be a life-long aversion of her
guest's, and that, the more she tried to excuse him,
the higher Miss Greene's indignation over him
would rise. It is sometimes the truest effort of
peace-making and charity to be silent, but Miss
Lavinia was not to be put down so.

" Well, I know that, but I was speakin' of folkses
tryin' to do sech people good. I do suppose when
the Lord makes sech hard folks he can break 'em,
but other people can't. Why, he's a larfin-stock,
and a hissin', as Scripter says, to all the town. I
call to mind now what 'Bijah Greene, my fust
cousin, sed about him once; we was a joggin' along
to mill, for he was a goin' over to get fodder, an' I
took the chance to ride over to Mill Hollow, havin'
a spell of work over there, and we come by Powder Hill I see a crop of rye a growin'. on to the
edge o' that steep precipice like, where 't goes
down square to the brook. 'Mercy to me!' says I,

'look a there, Bijah! who on airth ever driv critturs
to plough in that pokerish place?' 'Hem!' sez
he; 'that's Sam Rice's lot; he'd plant rye on the
edge of nowhere ef he thought 'twould grow.' "

"Where is Abijah now?" broke in Mrs. Dodd,
and happily the subject changed, and the cousin's
family and prospects were discussed for the next
half-hour. Then Miss Lavinia suddenly charged
on Happy. "Well, Happilony, how do you get
along to Sunday-school? Seems to me as ef you
was kinder young to hev that are class; they're a
pretty set-up lot, I guess. Do you like 'em?"

"Yes, ma'am," said Happy, half angry, half
amused.

"Well, I never! There's that Palmer gal. Her
folks are stuck up, I guess. I know them Palmers
stock an' lock, as Bijah says; and the Doctor's girl,
she's a flippety thing. That Calhoun girl, I reckon
she's one o' them that's good stuff ef it ain't spiled
in the sewin' and shapin'. Miss Gray's girl, she's a
queer one; her ma's as odd as Dick's hat-band, and
she takes after her some, I expect; he was a dreadful rough cretur, but sound an' good when you
come to reelly know him. I used ter tell our folks
that Gray was jest like a chestnut burr, you got
your fingers full o' prickles tryin' to get the meat,
but 'twas good when you got it; mebbe she is;
don't ye lose heart over that one, she'll come out

right by-and-by, I feel to believe. That little
Holden cretur, she's a real leetle blossom, but she's
got queer streaks. I knowed her folks consid'ble
along back. They don't think no small beans o'
themselves; and they're so everlastin' elegunt, 'nd
eddicated, 'nd gener'ly high strung; they see other
folkses failin's real spry, and haint got a mortal
sight o' charity for 'em neither. But she's as
pretty behaved a girl as you want ter see, she is.
Well, I hope ye'll get along with 'em, Happy, and
won't make no great o' mistakes. It's an orful
responsibility now, I tell you. *I* couldn't never
undertake it, old as I be, but I'm glad if you can."

"There is help for us all, Miss Lavinny," Mrs.
Dodd said calmly; "'I have laid help upon one
who is mighty to save,' the Bible says, and if
Happy finds she cannot keep the class, she can give
it up. It's what we can do that is required, you
know, not what we can't."

"That's so!" was Miss Greene's answer; "and
if she don't never do nothin' outside, Happy's a
real help and comfort to you, Almiry. I wish't I
had one just like her." The keen gray eyes
softened as she spoke, and Happy looked up in
amazement.

"O mother!" she said, after Miss Lavinia was
gone, "I was so sorry she came, and now I'm sorry
for her."

"She is a poor, lonely old woman, Happy. I ask
her to come here because it is one of the few places
where she has a friend; and she is one of the
household, after all."

"I forgot that," said Happy, simply.

"You don't know her yet, Happy. Under all
this sharp talk, and strong like or dislike for people,
she has a warm, generous, true heart. If Sam Rice
were sick or in trouble to-morrow, Miss Lavinny
would go to help him in a minute. She has very
keen eyes to understand character, and is not back-
ward to speak of anybody, but she is good, and
sincerely Christian. What you do for her is done
for ' one of these '; and she is lonely enough to
make me pity her sincerely, all the more that I
have got you, my child, and she has got nobody."

Happy's arms were round her mother in a
moment.

"Oh, I'm so sorry I was vexed about her.
Mother dear, do ask her here every Sunday."

"Don't go over the other edge now, Happy.
No, indeed! I can't afford to give all my Sundays to
her; there are other places where she goes, and I
think you have a right to me more than half the
time, haven't you? Now get your bonnet, it is
time for evening meeting."

CHAPTER VIII.

THE next week Happy began again to call on her class. The first place she came to was Mrs. Gray's, who opened the door herself, being a woman whose way was always to do a thing herself rather than wait to have it done by another. Happy had no pleasant experience here: Mrs. Gray was not in a good humor, and she was one of those "well-meaning" people who never seem to get beyond "meaning." She took Happy into the room where she was sitting at work, which happened to be her bedroom: it was cluttered with patterns, shreds, half-made garments, which were partly stitched on the machine, and waited now for further basting.

"Sit down, sit down," she said, pushing a heap of cloth, scissors, spools and patterns off a chair. "Mary ain't at home; how's your ma?"

Happy answered; and Mrs. Gray went on: "I suppose Mary pesters you a good deal; she's dreadful queer; she takes after her pa. He *was* the queerest!

Well, you're pretty young to have a class anyway.
Are you gettin' tired?"

"Oh no!" said Happy, earnestly.

"And Mary don't put you out any?"

"Not at all, ma'am; Mary does not trouble me.
I only wish I could make it more interesting for her.
I'm afraid she finds the lesson dull sometimes."

"Like enough she does; 'tain't to be expected
anybody like you could make it real interesting."
Happy colored, but Mrs. Gray went on. "Law!
you needn't mind me: I'm real blunt, that's my
way. I don't say things softly. I'm blunt always;
but you no need to resent it."

It did not seem to Happy that it was a valid excuse
for such coarse incivility that it was Mrs. Gray's
"way;" but in her slight experience she had not
discovered that this lady was only one of many
people who excuse themselves for being rude in this
fashion; fondly deluding themselves — but nobody
else — with the idea that honesty covers a multitude
of their sins, and that to mean well is equivalent to
behaving well. Strange that even a lifetime spent
without the affection and confidence of others, even
the alienation of those allied to them by the strongest ties, does not, cannot, convince them that the
fruits of the Spirit are "love, joy, peace, long-suffer-
ing, gentleness, goodness." Yet Mrs. Gray called
and believed herself a Christian; unaware that her

own child had often thought in her heart, though
her lips as yet had never uttered it, "If mother is a
Christian, then I don't want to be one!" No doubt
Mrs. Gray would have been shocked and pained to
know this. But the Lord does not always break
such delusive fetters: he melts them away more
often, by ways which the wearers know not, till
they are free. Nor did Happy know how often
Mary Gray compared her gentle manner, and sweet,
quiet voice, with her mother's harsh, loud tones and
exasperating language; it was this contrast which
made Mary so devoted to her teacher as she really
was at heart, though the time had not come yet for
her to show it, or Happy to feel it. But this call
did good in one way, it awoke in Happy's mind
sincere pity for Mary, and made her unconsciously
show her so much care and tenderness that Mary's
ideal of a good woman wore, all her life long, the
semblance of this poor, pale, limping girl.

At Mrs. Calhoun's she found only Julia at home.
The bright, sensible face lit up as she saw her
teacher; she led her into a pleasant sunny parlor,
put her into a rocking-chair by the open window,
where scents of late mignonette and lingering pinks
came in on the soft air, and brought her a plate of
fresh peaches, sweet and splendid with long days of
sun. Happy was not accustomed to such petting:
it moved her strangely; and while Julia sat looking

on with glowing face and keen, bright eyes, enjoying
the fruit quite as much as Happy did, and enter-
taining her with a real girl's talk, gay and vivid, the
child did not know how near the tears were to her
teacher's lids, or how fully Happy understood and
loved the frank, generous, genial spirit that promised to bless the world about her some day, as
benignly as now she ministered to her teacher. In
the midst of their talk Mrs. Calhoun came in; a
handsome, cheery, lady-like woman, with whom the
tailoress's daughter felt as much at home as with
her own mother as far as being at ease in conversation, and having no sense of discomfort went. Happy
had yet to learn that some people are ladies and
gentlemen in every position in life, and some in none.
She only thought, as she left that hospitable house,
what a peaceful and pleasant lot in life had fallen to
Julia Calhoun, and was glad with all her heart that
the child had such goodly shelter; for next to Ruth
Holden her heart had gone out to this one of her
little flock.

When she entered the yard at Mr. Holden's, Ruth
saw her from the window, and ran out to meet her,
all her soft wealth of hair flying about her shoulders, and her beautiful face lit up like a blossom in
the sun. She gave Happy a warm kiss, without a
word, and, drawing her into the house, sat down on
a stool at her feet, and looked up at her with silent

happiness. Happy stroked the fair locks back from
the child's face, and began to talk to her quietly
about some small, indifferent things; for she was
almost startled at the vivid excitement that lit those
clear eyes and flushed the sensitive, speaking face.
Ruth was fond of very few people; but those whom
she loved she loved strongly, almost passionately,—
a temperament to be dreaded, as far as peace in this
world is concerned; that temperament for which,
above all others, there is no rest on earth, no abiding
happiness, but in the sure love of God. Presently,
after the indifferent matters of the weather and the
plants in the window, had been discussed, and Ruth
had shown her mocking-bird and her gray kitty to
Miss Happy, she turned quickly, and said, "Would
you like to see mamma?"

"Of course I should, dear, if she is well enough
to be visited."

Ruth ran off to see, and after a few minutes'
absence led Happy into a room where Mrs. Holden
lay on a broad sofa: a delicate-looking woman, no
longer handsome, for illness had robbed her face of
its once resplendent bloom, and lined it with pain
and trouble. But not even care and sickness could
obliterate the vivid smile, or destroy the soft, refined voice with which she welcomed Happy; yet
strange it seemed to the girl that this lovely, gentle,
intelligent, and apparently affectionate mother, was

the only one out of all the five whom she had seen
in her visits who did not profess to be a Christian
woman.   Happy could not understand it ; she knew
that Mrs. Holden belonged to no church before she
went to see her ; and she had expected to find her a
fretful, weary, irritated, and irritating invalid ; and
she found, instead, the aspect and manners of a saint.
She was not old or experienced enough to see that
nature had given this woman one of those enviable
natures which skim the surface of trouble and ignore
its depths ; a nature so apt to see only the bright
side of things that even illness, which in her case
was more weakness and languor than pain, could not
thoroughly discompose' her soft, nerveless temperament.   She had no wants such as rasp and discourage
poor people who cannot work ; every luxury that
money could purchase was showered upon her ;
poverty and distress never showed their bitter or
pitiful faces in her quiet chamber ; she was not
called upon for help or sympathy ; she had not the
keen craving intellect that might have made her
restless, or the love for her kind that would have
left her lonely.   Plenty of pleasant novels, warm
soft wraps, delicate food, flowers, — all these made
her life easy and lovely as a sweet dream, and so she
was gliding on toward its end.   Ruth loved her, it
was evident in every look of her face, in the careful
gentleness of step and movement, in the way she

arranged her mother's wraps, and shaded the intrusive sunshine that had crept round to an unguarded crack. But she was no real mother to the child; there was nothing in her of that self-forgetful, patient, all-enduring, all-forgiving gentleness that is the very type and shadow of divine love and care. "As one whom his mother comforteth!" Oh! what a wide, deep world of meaning lies in that tender simile to all who have known a real mother! Is there any love like unto this love, except His who has said "So will I comfort you?"

Mrs. Holden did not say much to Happy. She was gentle in phrase and subject: spoke of "my darling Ruth" in a shallow way that did not impress her honest little visitor as she meant to have it. She gave Happy a few roses from the conservatory, and said she was glad to have Ruth fond of her new teacher, as she had seemed rather to dislike the last one, and Sunday-schools made a pleasant change for the child, she was shut up at home so much with mamma and the governess.

Ruth colored a little, and Happy wondered privately how Mrs. Holden came to let her go at all, not knowing that Ruth had a good grandmother who had persuaded her father into this measure; for Grandma Holden fully understood her daughter-in-law, and though she did not live with her, yet the homestead was not far off, and was Ruth's city of

refuge, — a place where she had learned more than
in Sunday-school, before ever she was allowed to
join the class.

The call here was short.   Mrs. Holden showed
signs of fatigue to Ruth's practised eye, and she
asked her teacher to come out into the garden.   So
Happy said good-by, and Mrs. Holden relapsed into
her novel, while Ruth, delighted to have her dear
Miss Happy all to herself, gleaned the flower-beds
while she talked to her about her grandmother, her
pets, and the gardener's baby, and sent Happy home
with a sheaf of fragrant leaves and blossoms that
scented the tenement-house for days, so carefully
were they tended.

This duty over, Happy began on the less pleasant
task of organizing her class of poor children.   Her
mother advised her to begin with a few, and get
them to bring in others, as time went on, and they
learned to like it ; so she began with Nan and Jack,
who promised, reluctantly enough, to come over on
Sunday, after meeting, being bribed by promises of
an apple apiece, and a ginger-cake if they were very
good.   To these she added one little girl in the next
house, — a pale, weak, dark-eyed child, whose father
was a Canadian Frenchman, a charcoal-burner, and
a godless, reckless fellow, emphatically one "of the
baser sort." Polly's mother was an Irishwoman,
but was so given to drink that she knew little and

cared less what her child did on Sundays, as that
was her day of leisure, and what she called pleasure.
Mrs. Lagré went to mass early on that day and
dragged Polly with her : a ceremonial observance
she would on no account omit, as she had it to set
off against the late hours, when ceremonies or rites
counted for nothing, and Pauline could run wild.
With these three promised, Happy looked forward
somewhat fearfully to the opening of her experiment ; but with simple faith she carried her fears to
her Father, and tried to lay them down at his feet.
This is one of the latest lessons, however, that the
Christian life accepts ; we are so doubtful, our faith
is so small, our acceptance of heavenly truths so
partial and so unreal, that we are very slow to feel
how much God can and will do for the childlike,
trusting spirit. Happy prayed most earnestly ; and
the mere communing with Him who is invisible, that
is prayer, over and above petition, steadied and
strengthened her courage, and lifted her for the
time into a higher plane of life and thought. But
still she feared much when in the lingering course
of the week little practical difficulties beset her, and
she forgot the help that was promised. Sometimes
she wished she had not undertaken such a work,
and was almost ready to give it up on the spot ; but
unexpected aid came in. Mrs. Ives heard through
Mrs. Dodd of Happy's plan, and sent her in a parcel

of gay lithographs on Scripture subjects, her own
children were tired of; and several half worn pic-
ture-books with songs and stories, the relics of an
infant-school that once existed in Canterbury, and
which Mrs. Ives had taught. This was a wonderful
help to Happy, as it proved, and took a certain
weight off her mind now. She was very much
obliged to Mrs. Ives, and yet it never occurred to
her that such an obviously human and commonplace
assistance could be an answer to prayer for help and
guidance. She had forgotten about the sparrow
which falleth not to the ground unnoted of its
Maker.

CHAPTER IX.

SUNDAY afternoon came, and Happy's three scholars with it. Nan and Jack had remembered their former experience, and their faces showed a laudable effort at cleanliness, in streaks of different shading that were literal "water-marks"; but Pauline had not even attempted so much toilet; she was dirty and ragged, and smelt of bad tobacco, almost to the extinction of Happy's odorous bouquet. However, she was willing to have her face and hands washed, and then they all sat down on the wash-bench.

"Say! where's them apples?" was Jack's first outcry, and no attention could be secured from him till three red apples and as many ginger-cakes were arranged on the ends of the clock-shelf, in plain sight. Then he consented to hear a story about Adam and Eve in the garden, and was by no means reserved in his comments. Happy tried to make them feel how beautiful Paradise was; but her

images and descriptions were quite above their
heads ; at last, in despair, she said :

"Now you all think what sort of things you
would like to have grow in a splendid great garden
where you were going to live."

There was a moment's pause, and then Polly's
piping voice squealed out "Cabbidges!"

"Oh, I don't mean things just to eat!" said
Happy, smiling in spite of herself, "but things nice
to see ; things to make it pleasant."

"Cabbidges!" squealed persistent Polly.

"Sho!" said Nan, in contempt. "I'd rather
have pertaters an' plums."

"I go in for peanuts!" shouted Jack: "ready
roasted too ; them's the fellers."

Mrs. Dodd, in the next room, could not help
laughing at the tone of despair in Happy's answer.

"Perhaps they did have all those things, only not
roasted peanuts, Jack."

"No, sir-ree! I guess they didn't. Ef they'd ha'
had 'em there, she wouldn't a' ben such a everlastin' fool as to go in fur an apple."

Poor Happy! She thought it was wisdom to let
the descriptive part of the lesson alone, and go into
the moral.

"But you see now how bad it is not to mind
what God says. If Eve had let the apple alone,
she could have stayed always in that lovely place."

"I've picked lots of apples off other folkses trees," said Nan, with an air of profound experience; "but they didn't never do nothin' to me."

"Perhaps they didn't see you," said Happy. "If they had, you might have been punished too; but God saw you, Nan."

"Did he?" the child said carelessly; "well, I didn't see him, and nobody didn't do nothin' to me anyway."

Happy's heart sank: she had never come in contact with such ignorance before. She knew the charcoal-burners in and about Canterbury were a reckless race; but she thought the Gladdings, who were Yankees bred and born, were better instructed, or, rather less ignorant than the foreign part of their class. But the Gladdings belonged to a certain type of New England people little known to the world at large; poor, isolated on some lonely hill-farm, or bleak shanty by a solitary pond; supported by the intermittent labor of their indolent hands on the products of the acre or two they either rent or "take"; getting a little money by the sale of berries, fish, herbs and roots, or rough baskets; now and then joining a charcoal job; their luxuries being whiskey and maple sugar, and their food pork and potatoes with occasional "cabbidges." This class of people are more like the beasts of the field than many a savage tribe. Crimes of the most

revolting character are common among them; they
seem to know neither law nor gospel, but exist on
the extreme outskirts of many a New England
village uncared for, unconsidered : a deeper heathen
than the idolater of the South Seas, for they have
not even the pretence of a God. From such an
ancestry as this the Gladdings came. The parents
of these children had, indeed, lately moved into
Canterbury, because Mr. Payson, who knew that
"to seek" went before "to save," had hunted
them up over on Poverty Plains and Powder Hill,
and secured for these two at least, Gladding and
Lagré, work at the foundry, and a shelter in the
tenements in Horn Lane that might have been
decent if the woman had cared to keep them so.
The children had just begun to go to district school;
but they were as ignorant as the average African
heathen; and Happy found that the story of the
Fall, and its lesson, was far beyond them.

Jack interrupted her with his own comment:
"Well, ef she knowed she was goin' to be turned
out, she was a fool, an' no mistake; just fur an
apple, ho! "

"Jack! Jack! you must not use such words
where I am! "

Jack stared, and Nan and Polly giggled.

" Why, I didn't say nothin'! " he muttered.

" Yes, you did, Jack; I don't like to hear such

words. I want to have you be a good boy, and
please God, and go to live with him, when you die,
in a much nicer place than Paradise was."

"Die!" exclaimed Jack, with great scorn, "me
die! ho! that's a good un! why, I ain't old 'nough
to die; it's old folkses bizness, dyin' is. P-r-r!"
and with this indescribable sound of mockery and
contempt from his puckered lips he turned and
looked at Nan's rosy, dirty visage, and stuck his
finger into her cheek as if it had been an apple
dumpling. "S'pose you'll talk about this young un
dyin' next, won't ye?" and Nan giggled because
Jack did.

"Stop!" said Happy. "I want to tell you
something that happened right here in this next
room last week. A dear, pretty, good little girl,
not as old as you or Nan either, did die almost two
weeks ago, only a day or two after you were here;
right on my bed."

"Jingo!" said Jack; but the little girls looked
awed. Happy did not reprove Jack for his expletive, she had the sense not to weaken the point she
had evidently made.

"What'd she die for?" piped Polly.

"She was very sick indeed, sick only a little
while, too; and then God thought she had better
die and go to live with him."

"I'd jest as lieve's not!" said Jack, putting his

hands in his pockets, and setting up a defiant whistle. Happy was so moved with remembrance of her dear little Gay, that she went on, careless of Jack's interruption, and told the children all about her illness and death, and about her baby efforts to be good and "please Jesus Christ," till her voice trembled and choked with tender memories. Nan looked on with open mouth, Jack stared fixedly out of the window, and Polly played with her thumbs all the time.

After this she tried to teach them a hymn-tune. Polly seemed to catch it quickly, but Jack and Nan made horrid discord, and defied both tune and time. When they had taken their apples and cakes and gone home, promising to come next Sunday, Happy sat down by the window, which she had opened to freshen the close air, and leaned her head sadly against the casing. This was hard work, — work that she never dreamed of; how could she do it? Mr. Payson's sermon came back to her — or one sentence of it, — " Lord, I do this for thee!" But then it did not seem as if she had done or could do anything. Her mother found her in this mood, but she did nothing except stoop and kiss her gently. Happy caught her arm, and leaned her tired face against it.

" O mother! you heard them? Did you ever see children like that? "

"A great many times," said Mrs. Dodd, quietly.
"But what can I do?"

"I think I wouldn't give them stories altogether,
Happy; tell them one Bible story every time, show
them the pictures, but don't try to explain it; they
are too young. People try to make children understand everything they learn, but it can't be. Children's minds are not able to take in much at a time,
but they can remember words; and long after, these
words will come back to them understandingly. I
would teach them the Commandments, one by one,
if I were you; and if they ask questions, either
answer them simply or not at all. Then when they
have got the ground of the law by heart, go to the
gospel, and teach them texts about Christ and salvation. Don't be in a hurry for results, Happy;
they are God's harvest, not yours. You can plant
the seed, even among thorns, but you can do no
more." Happy would hardly have been quite as
discouraged could she have heard Polly quavering
to her baby-sister the old hymn-tune she had
learned that afternoon, and the words of the first
verse.

> "'Come!' said Jesus' sacred voice,
> 'Come, and make my paths your choice.
> I will guide you to your home;
> Weary wanderer, hither come.'"*

Polly had a good memory as well as a quick ear, and Happy had taught her to say the words plainly. As it was only one verse, the task was easy ; and while she sang it over and over with shrill repetition to François in the cradle, Andrew Lagré, smoking his pipe on the doorstep, heard the reiterated air and words again and again till they took possession of his idle faculties, and he sung them next day, going about his work, merely to get them out of his head, he said, when one of the workmen cursed him for psalm-singing — cursed him because those words brought back his own childhood, Sunday-school lessons, his dead mother, his lost life; and stirred the first tears in his eyes that had moistened them for years. Truly Happy had sown the seed of a running-vine in this instance, for it came up far out of her sight. Jack and Nan went home, pleased enough with their apples, but not particularly heedful of the good words they had heard ; only quite resolute to go again, the early red apples were so good.

This week Mrs. Packard came up stairs to see her neighbors ; she was composed enough now to thank them, and she did so more gently and earnestly than seemed possible in her. She brought Happy a little painted mug that had been Gay's chief treasure.

"I want you to have it, Happy," she said, half

crying. "Gay set everything by it; 'nd I can't
bear to see it round. You was dreadful good to
her; I can't never tell you how much we think
about it, Packard and me. And that makes me
think, Mis' Dodd, he's got a stool for you, a kind
of a cricket-like, so's to rest your foot on while
you're a sewin'. It's bigger'n that one you use,
and if you've got a bit of old carpet, or drugget, or
something, he'll cover it real slick."

"That's exactly what I do want very much," said
Mrs. Dodd, looking as pleased as she felt, for she
knew how to be a cheerful taker as well as a cheerful giver. "And I have got a piece of new carpet
that will be just the thing. Mrs. Ives gave it to
me for a soapstone bag, but I did hate to cut it up;
it's a remnant of her old parlor carpet, and it's real
pretty."

So Mrs. Packard went away, carrying the carpet
in her hand, her heart lightened of a part of its
burden, her sense of obligation, that bitter yoke to
the souls of so many people, eased mightily.

There was a new thing to be done before Sunday,
an event that the people of Mr. Payson's church
looked forward to with deep interest; the minister
had gone away on Monday to be married, and was
to bring his wife home on Saturday. Nothing less
would serve his people than to celebrate the occasion with a donation-party Saturday afternoon; so

some of the leading ladies of the society held
counsel with Delia Lamb, Mr. Payson's "hired
girl," and agreed that she should do nothing about
providing for their arrival, but leave it all to the
ladies, who announced at the Wednesday sewing-
society that the congregation were invited to be at
the parsonage at eleven o'clock Saturday morning,
in order to prepare for and receive their minister
when the one o'clock train should arrive. Mrs.
Dodd liked to do her share in all such things, however small that must be. She was not disturbed by
any false shame about sending little matters; but
to-day she could not find anything available among
her stores but a little jar of pickles. However,
just after the Thursday evening meeting, Delia
Lamb joined her; for Delia was from the same town
where Mrs. Dodd had lived through her marriage,
and had always kept up the old acquaintance.

"Stop a minute, Mis' Dodd; wait just a minute
till I fetch my breath. I want ter see ye about
somethin'. You've heered about this donation
party, haint ye?"

"Yes, I have; and I mean to go too, Delia."

"I knew you would, you're on hand mostly when
there's something to do. Lots of folks can talk,
but there ain't so many to do. Now, if it ain't
impudent to ask, what be you goin' to carry for
vittles?"

"I haven't got anything but a jar of little cucumber pickles, Delia. I don't put up preserves, as many do; we can a little, just for sickness, but everybody will carry cake and canned fruit."

"Mercy to me, I guess they will! there'll be cake enough for a weddin', and stacks of biscuit, besides a bushel of pears and peaches, that'll spile, like enough, afore they get eat up; what there won't nobody fetch is jest what we'll want the most, an' I'm under bonds, as you may say, not to lift a finger to do a thing, and that's why I come to-night. I want you to make a loaf o' rye bread for the minister; he sets by fresh rye bread a sight: and I know you make it first-rate."

"I will," said Mrs. Dodd; and having done her errand, Delia bid her a curt good-night, and turned off toward the parsonage.

"Mother!" said Happy, indignantly, "you won't send such a little thing to the minister's as a loaf of rye bread, will you?"—for Happy had her failings, like other people, and one of them was a certain 'pride of appearance; she might be willing to *be* poor, though that was doubtful, but to *seem* poor, even when it came to offerings given to the dear minister, this was hard. She could comprehend Mary's breaking her alabaster box of precious ointment over the feet of Christ, but never fully approved of the widow's mite; she would rather have given nothing. Mrs. Dodd thought it was wise to answer only the outside of her question.

" Why, certainly I shall, Happy. I am glad to know just what he likes." And neither of them said any more about the loaf, till the expected Saturday morning arrived, and with the light sweet sphere in their basket, beside the brown pickle-jar, Happy and her mother set out for the parsonage.

.

CHAPTER X.

IT was a splendid October day, the world outside was gay with color, and the brilliant trees, steeped in softened sunshine, only seemed to glow more deeply for the light veil of mist; the air was calm and sweet; not a breath of wind stirred the scarlet and yellow splendors of the maples and elms about the parsonage, but within all was noise and confusion when our friends arrived.

The house was old and simple; a coat of fresh paint made it look very white, and as to the blinds very green; but the furniture, the carpets, were inexpensive, and not new; for Mr. Payson had lived in Canterbury five years now, having come there with an invalid wife who had used her own taste as to furnishing, and, though she died within the year, had left her record in the cheerful rich coloring, the comfort, the real value and use of the articles she had chosen. The house lay fair to the south; both living-rooms and the kitchen had windows that way, and the minister's study and bedroom

were over the dining-room and parlor : a little room
down stairs did duty as library; it was small, but
held easily all the volumes not wanted up stairs.
There were gay chintz curtains all about the house:
nothing more costly, even in the parlor; and there
the warm red carpet, the open fireplace with its
shining brasses, and two or three fine engravings
simply framed and hung low on the pale buff walls,
made the room so attractive that all the splendors
of Mrs. Palmer's best parlor, or Mrs. Holden's
artistic, dim, tranquil drawing-room, could not give
the guest such a sense of cheer and welcome as the
homely brightness of this small square room.   The
dining-room was darker, and a wood-stove replaced
the fire; but that too was of a homely hearty aspect
always, and now, being dressed with boughs and
garlands of gorgeous leaves, and the table at its full
length, spread with all sorts of viands, it was hard
to say which was pleasantest.   All the house was
fragrant with the last lingering flowers : sheaves of
chrysanthemums shed their refined odor of bitter
sweetness on the shelf in either room ; baskets of
mignonette, with here and there a late rose, and
lavish branches of sweet verbena, seemed to welcome
the company ; and the crowd of people, laughing,
talking, arranging and rearranging, as gifts poured
in, were pleasant to behold, they seemed so happy.

Mrs. Dodd spoke to one and another, shook hands

with some, nodded to others, but held her way straight on to the kitchen, where Delia Lamb sat bolt upright in her chair, her Sunday gown and best collar indicating a holiday, but her hands folded in her lap in evidently unwilling idleness. She began to laugh as soon as she caught Mrs. Dodd's eye, and said, when she had come near enough to hear,

" Well, here I be! Of all things for me to be settin' down in my Sunday gown, doin' nothin', of a Saturday; but they wouldn't hear to my stirrin' a mite. You fetched that bread, didn't you, Mis' Dodd ? "

" Here it is, and the pickles too: what shall I do with them, Delia ? "

" Oh, jest slice up the bread and set it next hand to the minister's place, to the end of the table next the winder. They calc'late to make him and her set down, and the rest wait on 'em. My sakes! it's jest as I told ye! biscuit and cake to kill, and only one loaf o' bread beside yourn. Mis' Potter sent that, and it is the beateree for bread, but 'tain't rye. I'd set the pickles right into the pantry, if I was you; there's seven different kinds on the table now, 'nd I guess that'll do for sourin': but you'd oughter see the pies ! "

Language seemed to fail Delia here, she lifted up her hands and let them fall in despair; Mrs. Dodd knew why, when she saw two long shelves covered

with these dainties; some appetizing enough, with
flaky crusts and gold or crimson hearts, others sealed
and heavy-looking, suggestive of unlimited dyspep-
sia. What became of this squadron nobody ever
knew; but, weeks after, Delia was heard to say sur-
veying the vacant shelves with a satisfied nod, "I'm
thankful to goodness we keep a pig!"

Happy soon found something to do; for though
there were plenty, as Delia foretold, to talk, there
were few to begin the doing. Mrs. Dodd was at
once pressed into service in the pantry, and it fell
to Happy's lot to help arrange the table. As soon
as her taste and deftness were perceived, this was
left to her entirely; for the elder ladies were inspecting and rearranging up-stairs, and the younger
ones had their own affairs to whisper and laugh
over, the "men-folks" not being expected till Mr.
Payson should arrive. Happy enjoyed her work
mightily; she had a natural appreciation of beauty
and daintiness, and under her hands the long table
assumed order and grace. She put fringes of geranium leaves about the only basket of late peaches on
the table; and decked the plates of yellow pears
with dark garnet leaves from a shrub-oak in the
yard; while here and there among the green grape-
leaves that seemed to underlie a great heap of purple,
dull pink, and yellow-green bunches of grapes, she
set a fiery nasturtium blossom flecked with velvet

dashes; and on every loaf of whitely glittering cake laid a tiny cluster of two or three bright leaves in sharp contrast with the spotless icing. Everybody exclaimed, when at last the decoration was finished, it was so beautifully done, and Happy was more pleased than anybody else, it seemed to make up for the slight gifts her mother had brought; while Mrs. Dodd looked on smiling, and thought even here Happy had done what she could, and, as it came about, what nobody else there could do.

Everything was ready and more than ready before the minister got home. His heart was in his eyes and on his lips when he saw how his people had welcomed him and his wife; he shook hands with them all, and gave each a grateful and friendly word. Happy was among the last, for she had been absorbed in watching Mrs. Payson. The girl had no friends of her own age, for her health and her needful home-keeping had prevented her making acquaintance with the girls who would otherwise have been her comrades, and Mrs. Dodd did not like that class of companions for her daughter well enough to make any effort to bring them together. Like the average American girl in city or country, the young women in Canterbury who worked for their living were loud-voiced, giggling, frivolous creatures; lovers of cheap finery, promiscuous balls, beaux, low amusements, and anything that their hard-earned money would bring them in the way of pleasure.

With such as these Happy had nothing in common ; her aims and her tastes were not theirs ; yet often she was very lonely, and wished in her secret heart she had one friend, older and wiser and better than she, whom she could visit now and then in the long days when her mother was away ; and she had a half-conscious feeling that she might find such a friend in the minister's wife, if she were disposed to be friendly ; since in a New England parish the minister is expected to share his official duties with his wife to a certain extent, and the congregation feel a prescriptive right to her time, — which is not always agreeable, or even possible, to every woman. So now Happy watched for Mrs. Payson eagerly, and saw, hanging on the minister's arm, a tall, slender, young woman, not handsome, not blooming, with dark hair and serious, tender, dark eyes, a face both lovely and lovable, and, when a smile kindled on the firm, delicate lips, almost radiant. Happy made up her mind then and there, that here was the friend her girlish heart longed for ; and when the minister introduced her to his wife ; she colored and smiled so expressively that Mrs. Payson said to herself, " What a sweet look she has ! I must find out all about her."

Great was Happy's delight to hear the array

of the table admired warmly by the new-comers;
and she was hardly less pleased, when, having said
a few and fervent word of thanks to the Giver of
daily bread, and seating himself in his place, Mr.
Payson smiled and said, with a pleasant look :

" Somebody has ministered to my special taste.
Eleanor, taste this rye bread : it is perfect, I know,
before I have tasted it."

Happy discovered that the right gift is the best
gift, whatever it be ; and her mother hearing the
minister's comment, and seeing Happy's face, knew
she had learned that lesson without any of her help.
And the girl also had unconsciously won the recognition she most coveted ; for, inquiring of Delia who
ordered the table so beautifully, Mrs. Payson learned
it was the same young girl whom she had already
noted, and renewed her resolution to make acquaintance with her at once.

" Are you very tired, dear ? " said Mrs. Dodd,
when they reached home after the donation party ;
and Happy threw herself down in the easy-chair
with a sigh of relief, replying :

" Yes, I am, mother, but it's a good tired ; we have
had such a nice time ; and I think the minister's
wife is perfectly lovely."

Mrs. Dodd did not feel inclined to dispute the
matter, for her older and keener eyes had also passed
favorable judgment on Mrs. Payson ; so Happy went

on : " Isn't it queer how different people seem to other people ? "

" That's rather a blind saying, Happy.   What do you mean ? "

" Oh ! I was thinking what I heard Mrs. Palmer say to somebody, when she saw the minister's wife. ' Well,' said she, ' I've took a good look at her, and I don't believe but what the fire'll fly some, in the kitchen : them eyes don't look as though she could be browbeat, and Delia Lamb's a real masterful piece.'   But I didn't think that about Mrs. Payson. I thought her eyes were kind and sweet, mother, didn't you ? "

" Yes, I did, Happy ; but I thought they looked decided too.   I should say Mrs. Payson had natu- rally a warm, quick temper, but controlled it well. Temper is a good thing if it is kept under.   I re- member father was very fond of a saying, out of some old divine's writings : ' Anger is one of the sinews of the soul ; he that wants it, hath a maimed mind.'   You know the Bible says, ' Be ye angry and sin not.' "

" I never could understand that, mother."

" I suppose it means there are some things we ought to be angry about : a great injustice, or cruelty, inflicted on others, or open and shameless sin.   But I don't at all think Mrs. Payson and Delia will have trouble, though they both have naturally quick tempers. Delia has got the rein on hers too."

"Mother, didn't you know Delia before you came here to live, a good while?"

"I used to go to school with her in Dorset, Happy; she is only a little older than I am."

"I shouldn't think she would like to hire out," said Happy, thoughtfully.

"Why not?"

"Oh! it must be dreadful to be a servant; I should think she would have gone out sewing, or to a factory, or taught school, if she had to earn her living."

"She did very much better, Happy. Her father was a poor farmer, and a drunkard at that, and her mother bed-ridden. Delia only went to school a little while, she could not be spared at home. She never had education enough to teach; but she had to learn housework, for she had to do it. When her mother died she was twenty-five, and her father would have been a town pauper but for her help. Delia has a great deal of pride naturally, but she is an honest Christian woman; and she told me once how she sat down and 'figured out' as she said, her best course. If she went out to sew, her health would give way, for she was used to stirring about and having plenty of air; she had seen too many seamstresses break down not to dread that sort of

work, for if she lost her health she could not support her father or herself; then factory work would
be equally confining, and though wages were good
she would have her board to pay, whereas, if she
went out to service, she would have the work she
was used to, good food, some time to herself, and
wages that, with the rent of their old house, would
provide for her father ; so she went to live at Squire
Ellis's. She said, ' It went against the grain consider'ble at first, but I'd made up my mind deliberate,
and I wan't a goin' to back down with the first wind
that blew. I said to myself, sez I, " Delye Lamb,
ef you ain't respectable enough to be hired help,
you ain't respectable enough for anything !" an' I
stuck to that; it helped me mightily to call to mind
what the Lord said: "But I am among you as he
that serveth." ' She was quite right, Happy ; she
is a healthy, happy woman to-day. Her father died
in a year or two after she went to the Judge's, but
Delia had found her place, and kept it. Every right-
minded person who knows her respects her : the rest
she is not concerned about."

"But mother, does she have any friends ? "

"Plenty, Happy. There is many a house in this
town where Delia is always welcome. She is not
invited to parties, or asked out to tea, though sometimes Miss Lavinny or Widow Skinner do get hold
of her when the minister's away ; but her work does

not leave her time for much visiting, and Delia knows it is not her place to visit familiarly at houses where she has still kind and true friends. Happy, if I should die before you, I should ask nothing better for you than such a home in such a family as that where Delia is fixed."

Happy did not answer. She could not face either the possibility of her mother's death, or her own taking a menial position. But Mrs. Dodd's words did just what she intended — set Happy thinking, and prepared the way for a future that might, no doubt, be long delayed, yet also might arrive suddenly. She had sowed this seed in its place; and there she left it, with a silent prayer that God would give the increase in his time.

CHAPTER XI.

HAPPY's little Sunday-class gathered accessions very slowly; sometimes a new face would be seen one Sunday, and never again; those who did come were uncertain and unpunctual in attendance at first; but before the spring came there were six who could be counted on, three beside Nan and Jack and Pauline. It sometimes seemed to Happy that going from her well-dressed, intelligent class in the morning to these wild children in the afternoon, was like going from a flower garden to an unreclaimed swamp; yet for this first year she seemed to have made as little impression on her "good" class as in the last six months on her "bad" one, for in this way she distinguished them to herself. Indeed, if there were any signs of progress, it was among the younger set; for they began to wear clean faces, brushed shoes, ill-mended clothes; and the girls showed an instinct for ornament that Mrs. Dodd advised Happy to respect, as a symptom, however slight and poor, of awakening self-respect.

It is a late lesson, but Mrs. Dodd had learned it, that God does not give us any trait of character, bad or good, that has not or may not have its use, that was not, as he sent it, for his good purpose: that is not still capable of being washed from the soil and taint of sin, and enlisted into his service who maketh even the wrath of man to praise him. But as to improvement openly toward the love of God and his service, there was none visible. She could not see that any one of them liked anything of the Bible but its stories: by dint of constant repetition they had learned the commandments, the beatitudes, texts about Christ and his work, and the twenty-third Psalm, beside singing several hymns to such old tunes as Happy herself had been brought up to link inseparably to certain words. "Fountain," to Cowper's dear old verses — verses that shrivel into dry leaves before the touch of criticism and taste, but are full of odors, as the prayers of the saints, to thousands of weary and heavy-laden souls; "Coronation," quaint in joyful triumph; "Mear," celebrating in its plaintive, peaceful cadence,

> "Those to glory gone;"

"Windham," woful as its words about the broad road to death; "Cambridge," sweet and full of happy repeat as a love-song, yet consecrated beyond

mortal passion or pain; "Tallis," whose punctual
beat caught quickly the uneducated ear ; and even
forlorn old "China," which Polly privately confided
to Nan she hated, because "it sounds 'zactly like
our old Bose, when ma shut him up in the barn,
and he howled awful."

All this seed as yet showed no sign of germina-
tion, it lay "buried long in dust"; and equally
dead lay, or seemed to lie, the fair garden-spot that
Happy delighted in.   Addy was as conceited and as
vain as ever; Helen Sands as light-minded and
facile ; Julia as sensible, intelligent, and interested ;
and Ruth as charming.   If there was any change, it
was in Mary Gray.   She was as blunt as usual, but
not quite as rough.   Her words were few and un-
polished, but she was more careful that they should
not seem disrespectful or rude, and her interest in
the lessons certainly grew; yet she was not the
scholar to whom Happy looked with most interest,
or of whom, in fact, she expected anything.   As
the spring went on into summer, there seemed to
be no change in either of Happy's flocks, except
one which was external,— Adelaide Palmer's family
removed to Ohio ; and though the girl seemed a
little moved when she said good-bye to Happy, and
thanked her for the small Testament which she
gave her in parting, Happy felt deeply and bitterly
that Adelaide left her unimproved, unchanged.

Her heart sank, she was ready to cry when she went home that day.

"O mother!" she said, "haven't you a good word for me? I am so discouraged!"

"There are plenty in the Bible," gravely answered Mrs. Dodd. "Try for yourself, Happy." As she spoke, texts came one after another into the girl's mind.

"Is the Lord's hand shortened that he cannot save?" "God giveth the increase." "In due season ye shall reap, if ye faint not." And involuntarily she spoke them aloud.

Mrs. Dodd smiled. "You are learning fast, Happy; 'he that watereth shall be watered again.' I wish you could see how simple your duty is, my child, — *only* to plant and water; you cannot quicken the seed or hurry the harvest."

"Perhaps I shall be patient sometime, mother."

"Perhaps so; but it may be a long time first. Your life is all to come yet; you have been so shut up, so by yourself always, that it is beginning to live, to you, now."

That night, when the six children came to their school, they all wondered at Miss Happy's sad face, and tried in various ways to please her; quaint childish efforts, but sweet enough to the girl, who had almost despaired of their having hearts at all. The tears stood in her eyes as Pauline patted her

cheek with a rough brown hand. Robby Gunn
offered her a bit of his precious chewing-gum, and
his little sister Mandy nestled up against her arm,
and sung with her clear, shrill voice louder than
any of the rest, having heretofore refused stoutly to
sing at all, pretending to be very shy. Happy recognized the good intent in all of them, but was
most pleased when, just after sunset, Jack and Nan
came back with flushed triumphant faces, and a
great bunch of wild roses.

"She an' me went down to Moss's swamp for
'em!" said Jack. "I knowed you'd think a heap
of 'em, cos they smell so sweet. Don't you rek'lect
how you sot by them flowers somebody give ye last
fall, cos they was sweet?"

"Yes, indeed I do!" said Happy, coloring with
pleasure; "and I shall think just as much of these,
and more, Jack; thank you ever so much, and Nan,
too." She stooped and kissed them both; Nan
returning the caress heartily, and Jack submitting
in a shamefaced fashion, heartily glad it was dusk,
and no boys about.

"Your wilderness has blossomed like a rose,
hasn't it?" said Mrs. Dodd, as Happy arranged the
delicate, fragrant blossoms in an old pitcher, and
set it on the stand. "Take courage, Happy; there
is a little lookout for dawn, now, isn't there?"

Happy was glad to acknowledge it; but still her

heart ached over Addie Palmer, and she prayed for her that night with increased earnestness.

People who do not believe in prayer lose a wonderful rest and refuge. When time and space, the wants, the bitterness, or the duties of life, separate us from those we love so far that our help is useless to them, our voices silent, our eyes blind ; when we know that suffering, illness, danger, death, may lie in wait for them every hour, and no strength or longing of ours can avail to help them, where do they fly, what hope or comfort do they have, who cannot give their beloved into the safe-keeping of an omnipotent God ; who cannot pour out their tortured and anxious hearts to Him who heareth and answereth prayer ? The next Sunday came, and to Happy's great surprise Mary Gray lingered behind the rest of the class, and said, in a low tone :

" Miss Happy, can I speak to you ? "

The infant school-room, just across the vestibule, happened to be empty at the time, so Happy drew the child in there.

" What is it, dear ? " she said softly.

" Oh ! I can't talk here ; can I come to your house some time ? "

" Yes ; come to-morrow afternoon. I shall be all alone. Come right over after school."

" Don't tell anybody, will you, please ? " said Mary, abruptly.

"No;" and, much wondering, Happy took her hand, and without further words they walked over to church together.

It had been a terrible eff rt to the shy, blunt child to say this much, and Happy partly understood it, but she thought M ry had got into some trouble at school, perhaps, and needed her help; she was utterly surprised v'hen, the next afternoon, her visitor, having arrived punctually, and sat some minutes in dumb, awkward silence, suddenly threw herself down by Happy's knee, and, burying her head in her lap, sobbed out: "Oh, I do want to be good!"

Happy felt as if a blow had struck her. Mary Gray! a girl whom hitherto she had classed with the most hopeless of her children; and yet she was here, simply, honestly, asking the question of all questions, without any preamble. It was the old cry, "What shall I do to be saved?" in other words. Happy obeyed her first impulse, and, bending her head over the child's, said in a low voice, "Dear Lord, help this child of thine to be like thee; show her how to be good, and help her every day of her life."

Mary rose from the floor and laid her head on Happy's shoulder; the burden seemed lifted from both their hearts, and laid where it could be well borne — in the arms of the Saviour.

"And you must try, too, dear," said Happy, gently and firmly.

"I do try a little; but it seems as if I never, never, could be good!" the child answered; and as Happy led her on, she told in her own way how deeply she had felt many things that she had heard in the class; things Happy had thought uttered in vain, yet here, on dry ground, they had taken root. Poor child! it was among thorns. With the usual reaction of naturally shy people who once make up their minds to freedom of speech, Mary poured out her whole soul to Happy; how she had never wanted to be a Christian till lately, because some Christians were so cross and hateful. Happy could supply the original of this portrait; her humility did not suggest that she herself had been one reason of the avowed recent change in Mary's opinion — that she meant her teacher when she said she did want to be like some Christians who were good.

"You want to be like Christ?" she suggested to the earnest speaker.

"O, Miss Happy, I can't! I don't know. I want to be good, and I ain't a bit; you don't know how hateful I am at home, and everywhere. Nobody likes me; but I don't care so much for that, I don't like myself at all, and that's the worst of it."

Happy had so newly been over all this path she
could show the doubting, trembling feet its earliest
steps, and set the little pilgrim's face toward the
wicket gate.   They parted after an hour of quiet,
tender talk, with a very earnest kiss.   Happy's
heart full of anxious thankfulness, and Mary, with
a steady purpose that was to work out its ends in
its own fashion, and some time brighten into the
perfect day.

Mrs. Dodd listened to the story of it all with the
deepest pleasure; she longed to have her child receive some earnest of that faithfulness on which
she trusted her own soul; for she felt that the time
was fast coming when Happy must be left to feel
that faithful Saviour's help to the uttermost; when
she should have to leave her darling to walk the
world's ways without her.   She had long known
that her life was in danger from an insidious disease
that was ready now to do its worst, within, at most,
the next few months: and she had passed through
a conflict of feeling that it is neither possible nor
best to describe, as she foresaw her own suffering,
her certain death, and, worst of all, Happy's lonely
and unhappy condition when she should be left to
such a life as that of a poor, sickly, and comparatively friendless woman must be.   Now, after much
prayer and long pangs of both flesh and spirit, she
had attained a certain standpoint of endurance and

courage, if not of peace ; peaceful she could not be
while she had yet to tell Happy what lay before
them both. She had deferred it so long because
she thought the girl's physical feebleness could not
bear a protracted strain of anxiety and distress :
but within the last year Happy had been growing
stronger, and Doctor Sands had given Mrs. Dodd
some hope that her child would outgrow her con-
stitutional troubles. This hope strengthened Mrs.
Dodd's resolution ; she prayed hourly and earnestly
for help, for strength, to break the matter to
Happy. Her own personal share of the coming
sorrow she had long faced ; and now came the
bitterer pang. She made up her mind first to go
and see Miss Lavinia Greene, and lay the matter
before her : for not only was she the oldest and
best friend Mrs. Dodd had left, but with all her
oddities she had a kind heart and keen " common "
sense, as this least common of all traits is called ;
and she knew that in any event Happy would find
in her a kind and friendly counsellor. Then Mr.
Payson must know ; on him too she depended to
watch over Happy's spiritual life so far as one soul
can watch for another. After these she would tell
Happy.

CHAPTER XII.

IT was late in the week when Mrs. Dodd took a day to herself, and leaving Happy busy and smiling over her work, walked to Miss Greene's little house on the hill. A very small house indeed, standing on a slip of ground between two others of ordinary size; but as the spinster herself said: " All mine! the hull on't, from ridge-pole to sullar floor; and I tell ye that's consider'ble when you come to be sixty year old, with next to nothin' to live on. Furni-toor's good too, if it *was* my grandsir's — solid cherry, 'nd fust-rate hair-cloth, no gimcracks; but the best on't is bein' mine."

As Mrs. Dodd entered she found Miss Lavinia knitting, as usual; this was her afternoon and eve-ning work when no sewing was in hand. The house was exquisitely clean; two small rooms below, with a shed opening from the further one, and two above these, with a tiny attic, was all the room she had, but it was enough. The parlor, with due respect for New England traditions, was shut up, darkened, held sacred to rare visitors, an occasional tea-drinking, or quilting, and the front bed-room served for like emergences. One stove warmed both the sitting-room and the old lady's bed-room above, and in winter served to cook her meals ; in summer a little sheet-iron stove, in the shed, did this duty. Everything was simple, and rather grim ; "the beautiful" was a worship unknown to Miss Lavinia, her household gods were cleanliness and order.

She was very glad to see Mrs. Dodd, though she noticed and commented on her pale face and tired look, and was eager to give her some refreshment. But the widow wished to make her communication at once, for she had nerved herself to the task, and wanted it over with ; so, refusing Miss Greene's offer she sat down, and told her story in a few forcible words, then laid her head back against the cushion of the old-fashioned rocker she sat in, and gave way, with one or two bitter tears and sobs, to a natural agony, for the thing she knew and dreaded seemed more than ever dreadful, now it took shape in speech. Miss Lavinia lifted and dropped her hand with the unmistakable gesture of surprise and dismay ; her wrinkled face grew pale.

" You don't tell me ! " she said with dimming eyes and faltering voice. " You poor cretur ! and you've knowed this all along and kep' it to yourself ? The lands' sakes! Why didn't you let me know on't afore?"

"What good would it have done, Aunt Lavinny?" she answered. "I saw Dr. Sands more than a year ago, and he advised me to do nothing; he thought it might be years before I had any trouble, and to go to a surgeon and be operated on might be sure death; at any rate could only delay the end, and was dreadfully expensive. I thought it over, and prayed it over, and did what seemed best. I do not regret it now, for I did the best I knew how at the time."

"There can't nobody do no more than that any-how; but how come it about that you're troubled with it so quick?"

"Oh, when I watched with Ann Gladding last year, the poor thing was delirious; and, as I was trying to give her a powder, she threw her arms out and gave me such a blow, right there. I did not really know I was hurt at first, I felt so anxious about her; but I felt that I was bruised next day, and that was the beginning. It has been mercifully slow, and so far I have not needed any quieting medicine; but lately it grows worse every week, and now I've got to tell Happy."

Miss Lavinia got up from her chair and went and stared out of the window. Her self-possession was shaken, she wanted to recover it before she spoke;

so she made a few vigorous swallows, secretly dried her eyes on the edge of the chintz curtain, cleared her throat stoutly, as if a heavy cold possessed her and was to be resisted, and then went back to her chair.

"You're good grit, that's a fact!" she said in a tone that was almost cheery. "Now we know the wust on't; and let me tell ye there *is* wuss things 'n a cancer: you don't believe it, but what ef you was to be bit by a mad dog and hev hydrophoby? Or what ef you had spine complaint and couldn't never sit up nor move to the longest day you live?"

Mrs. Dodd shook her head with a faint smile; she knew well that to be bed-ridden, with Happy to tend her, would be sweeter than separation for all the rest of Happy's mortal life.

"Well, figger it as you're a mind to; mabbe you'll die of somethin' else, arter all. Try to look at the bright side on't, ef ye can."

"I have, Aunt Vinny, and the bright side for me is heaven."

Miss Lavinia swallowed again; there was something in her friend's sad calmness that moved her unusually. But she was not to be daunted by emotion; she returned to the subject.

"Well, is there anything under the canopy I can do for ye? Talk's talk and nothin' more; and feelin's ain't worth a red cent without they come to facts, no more'n flowers that ain't fruit-blows. Ef there's a mortal thing I can do to help ye, or chirk ye up, I want to do it, right off."

"I want you to do something for me by and by, Aunt Vinny. When I am gone, I want you to be a friend to Happilona."

"I'll begin right off; for I tell you, Almiry Dodd, you make a real mistake to think o' tellin' on her till you can't dodge it. Let the poor gal alone; time enough to take trouble when the Lord sends it; don't you go 'nd rile up her sperrits weeks an' weeks afore you need to: it ain't right nor best, now I tell ye."

"But there are so many things I must say to her! I want to advise her for the future: to tell her how to act when I am gone, to — "

"You can't do it!" interrupted Miss Greene, fiercely: "you're overreachin' into the Lord's kingdom. How do *you* know what a day 'll bring forth? You may go an' plan, an' advise, an'foresee, and when you're gone some pesky thing or 'nother 'll jump up jest where it hadn't oughter have, and your idees ain't anything but hampers to other folks. It's jist like them long-winded wills folks make sometimes, providin' for three generations. There's Jane Jinkins; didn't her grandsir leave her the old homestead for life, then to go to her nieces, and ain't it ruined her with taxes an' sich,

and fin'lly been sold up and left her poorer 'n dirt
when she might ha' sold it and had a good livin',
ef Grandsir Payne hadn't 'lotted on providin' for
them that wasn't born ? '

" But I must say some things to her," Mrs.
Dodd said, piteously.

" Well ; can't you write 'em down ? they won't
hurt half so bad on paper as they will coming out
in your kinder hurt, sorrowful voice, and they'll
stay by. Advice that's writ, sticks ; it's there : it
don't slip your mind. But ten to one if you was to
sit down now and give her an hour's real talkin',
what with feelin' bad, an' cryin', an' thinkin' a heap
more of losin' you than what you was a sayin',
she'll forget it straight off. You hear to me,
Almiry."

" Perhaps you are right, but I won't make any
rash resolution ; the thing can wait a week or two,
surely, and will bear thinking of. But Aunt
Vinny, I want to talk to you a little about what
is to come."

" Well, talk away. I'm old and tough, Almiry.
I've had my own troubles, an' mebbe I can give ye
the good word. Anyway, I'm fust rate to hearken
when I sit down to it."

" Well, I want to tell you what there is for
Happy. My life is insured for two thousand
dollars. I have made out to pay the premium

regularly, and it's paid up to August.   Then there's
five hundred in the Savings bank, that Aunt Susan
willed to me, and there's our little things at home.
Happy has got plenty of clothes, and she is well
enough to sew a little.   But what is to support her?
The interest money won't."

" Well, I guess not.   Land! money's a desirable
thing sometimes, ain't it?   I've heered say the Lord
shows what he thinks of it by them he gives it to,
and, gener'lly speakin', rich folks is a poor sort; but
they ain't all.   You wouldn't want her to go into a
factory, now?"

" No, indeed!   Happy could not endure that sort
of life or companionship : she is too pure and simple
to combine with the sort of girls who work in those
places."

" And she ain't eddoocated to teach."

" No : she has not had health or means to study,
and, if she had, school-teaching is the hardest work
and the poorest pay a woman can do ; nor is she
able to go out tailoring as I have, she never learned
the trade, and, besides it is dying out; there's a
ready-made shop here now, it was opened last week."

" Well, what in creation do ye think she oughter
do?   I wish't I had enough to take her an' keep
her; but I hev to pinch severe, and visit round a
heap to get along myself."

" I know that, Aunt Vinny ; and besides, if you

could help her, I'd rather Happy should be independent and help herself, it's better and safer for
her. My idea is for her to go and live out in some
family where she will be well treated and cared for.
She would make a good child's nurse, or she could
do second work."

"For mercy's sakes, Almiry Dodd! Your Happy
live out?"

"Why not, auntie?"

Miss Lavinia's mind was racked for an answer,
but it was as one that beateth the air, none came;
so she fell back on conventionalities.

"Why, why, 'tain't reely respectable."

"Don't you respect Delia Lamb?"

"Oh! Delye, why, I dono but I do: certain,
certain, Delye's a real good woman. But then her
folks was — well — why, Almiry, your pa was a settled minister!"

"But, Aunt Lavinia, what was Jesus Christ?
What did he say? 'But I am among you as he
that serveth.' After that, are any of us too good
to take the lowest place?"

"Well, I know, yes, but consider them times;
besides, Almiry, 'twould kinder shut her away from
folks."

"I know all that: but isn't she shut away now?
Who has she but me for company? She never has
been with other girls here; they weren't her sort;

and, Aunt Vinny, the matter narrows down very
much. Happy cannot get her living in any other
way that I see. In a respectable family she would
have good food, and some care at least, and tolerable
wages. Doing any other work she must be lonely
and uncomfortable. Promise me that you will stand
by her if she takes this course, and befriend her."

" Why, of course; did you think I wouldn't, Almiry? I'll do by Happy just the same as ef she was
mine, you'd better b'lieve. I hain't got much worldly goods, and I don't make no rash promises, for ye
can't never tell how things 'll turn out. But this I
will say, if I'm spared and have my faculties I'll
befriend Happy for certain, just as true as I can."

Mrs Dodd was reassured and comforted, and having at last consented to the cup of tea Miss Lavinia
insisted on brewing for her, she went on to Mr.
Payson's and laid her case before him.

If he did not receive the confidence just as Miss
Lavinia did, he was even more help and comfort to
Mrs. Dodd, for the very reason that he did not and
could not feel for her so deeply. But he approved
of her plans fully; for it had long been a hobby of
his that a better class of poor people should take up
domestic service as a means of support, Delia Lamb
having worked out the problem in his own household, where she was held dear and valuable. He,
too, promised to help Happy in any way he could,

and further her plans; and after a kind and honest talk with Mrs. Dodd about her own outlook for the future, in both worlds, he calmed and soothed her troubled soul with a very earnest and tender prayer; and she left him to go home, tired indeed, but unspeakably comforted; and so upheld by the good grace of God that even Happy's beaming welcome and loving attention did not move her calm, or destroy her serenity.

That night she sat up late writing a long letter; for it was not her way to put off a really important thing, and she wanted to be sure of a few last words with her darling, whatever happened. And it was well that she did so: for though she did not know it, the disease that outwardly threatened her had also worked its fatal will within, in painless, secret swiftness. The over-exertion, the excitement of the day before, perhaps lent its little aid; but early the next morning a violent hemorrhage told the story of the enemy within, and when Dr. Sands reached her bedside, she was almost beyond his cares.

"Thank God!" he said, fervently, as he saw how still, how peaceful, was that bloodless face. Happy looked at him as if she did not hear or know what he said: long afterward she discovered that she too ought to have thanked God for this merciful ending, for peace instead of agony, weakness unto death instead of mortal pangs. Poor child! the blow was

unfelt yet ; she was like a walking dreamer. Her
mother rallied a little under the doctor's treatment ;
only a little — just enough to say, " I have laid help
upon One who is mighty." Then she smiled at
Happy, sighed like a weary child just as it sleeps,
and was gone. Happy was motherless.

CHAPTER XIII.

IT is one of God's great mercies that a heavy blow stuns either mind or body. Happy could no more believe her mother was dead than she could credit the fictions of a bad dream; she knew it, but she did not feel it. A strange trance seemed to possess her. People came and went: the Packards below stairs remembered how she had cared for them when little Gay died, and did a thousand little things for her that no one else could do. Miss Greene came and stayed with her till the funeral, sleeping down stairs on Mrs. Packard's lounge, — for nothing could persuade Happy to leave the kitchen while her mother lay cold and stark in the room that had served them for bedroom and parlor. She did not forget her duties, dull as her apprehension seemed to be of other things; the blessed routine of work upheld her, as it does all who are chained in its wholesome fetters. Her mother's employers were all kind, with practical kindness. One sent in bread, another cake, a third

cold meat, after the friendly country custom in
time of trouble, that a stricken family may have
time to attend to the necessities of grief. Julia'
Calhoun, sensible as ever, brought her a black dress
and hat of her cousin's to wear to the funeral;
Ruth sent a basket of lovely flowers; but Mary
Gray came herself, and, putting her arms round
Happy, kissed her over and over, and brought the
first tears into her eyes. By-and-by the funeral
took place; still like a dream to the solitary
mourner. She saw that dear dead shape carried
out forever from her sight, and she followed with
firm steps to the little graveyard, and with calm
face heard both funeral prayer and psalm.

"She bears it wonderful," Mrs. Packard whispered to Miss Greene as they walked home together,
Happy just preceding them with Mr. Payson.

"Bears it!" answered Miss Lavinia, with a
sniff. "She don't know it yet, she's asleep. Bless
ye! the hull on t's to come. I'd ruther seen her
scream and cry and holler than be so dumb and
sot!" And she was right; the reaction, if it ever
came, promised to be severe, and Miss Lavinia set
herself to help the poor girl if she could. The day
after the funeral was Sunday, and Happy could not
rouse herself to go to church; she lay on the lounge
helpless as a child, and Miss Lavinia, who had come
over after service, went down to the well for some

water, and felt her gown pulled smartly, as she was
tilting the bucket.   Looking round, she saw a boy,
clean, and not ragged, but patched enough to tell
of poverty.

"What *air* you a pullin' me for?" she demanded
sharply.

Jack—for it was Jack—answered, "Say! where's
teacher?"

"Who be you? an' who's she?"

"Me? oh! I'm Jack Gladding.   Where's Miss
Happy? is she sick?"

"Why, no, she ain't sick; but she's about as bad
off.   Don't ye know her ma's dead?"

Jack nodded, and went on: "Jest you tell her
Fred Park's agoin' to hear us read to-day, cos we
thought she wouldn't want ter.   Ki! won't Fred
have good old times long o' us?   Mebbe we'll behave, though, seein' it's for once.   You tell her,
will ye?"

Miss Lavinia promised, and Jack went off, whis-
tling, his cap on one side and his hands in his
pockets, though his heart secretly ached to see
Happy, and he was as sorry for her as he knew how
to be!

"Boys are unaccountable things," was the spinster's verdict, as she took her dripping pitcher up
stairs, and delivered the message to Happy, who
seemed not to hear it at all.   A few days went on

in this listless, dull fashion, broken, every now and
then, by a keen flash of agony as the new and
dreadful " mother-want " made itself daily felt.
Unaccustomed to endure trouble, as yet undisciplined by life, Happy had fallen in her first battle,
and lay wounded almost to death. Mr. Payson
came to see her, talked to her, prayed with her, all
to no purpose. " They talk to the grief of those
whom Thou hast wounded," repeated itself over
and over in his mind as he went away, resolving to
send his wife the next day, — for he believed her
consolatory powers were unlimited ; but she could
do no more. One after another came in on the same
friendly errand ; but kind words, tender admoni-
tions, advice, pity, sympathy, all seemed only to
make her cringe and quiver the more. " Whom oil
and balsams wound, what salve can cure ? "

Miss Lavinia had waited her time ; it was now
two weeks since Mrs. Dodd died, and one day the
old lady took her knitting and went over, determined to rouse Happy from the selfish abandonment
of her grief, and show her a better way. She
plunged, as usual, into the middle of things.
" Happilony," she said, " I've come a puppus to
take ye to do. Do you think you're actin' as a
professin' Christian oughter, or as your mother
would ha' had ye ? "

Happy cried out like a struck child, and made an

imploring gesture; she could not bear to hear her
mother spoken of yet. "Oh, don't! don't!" she
said.

"Well, I must. I promised Almiry I'd be a
friend to you, and I mean to be. Happy, do you
think it's a doin' what the Lord would have you to
do to set here, day in an' day out, mournin' and
idlin' while there's your two Sunday classes want
seein' to, and you've got to look forrard to gettin'
your livin'?"

"I don't want to live," she answered hopelessly.

"That ain't nothin' to the puppus; you ain't the
fust nor you won't be the last in that fix; folks
can't die when they want to, no more'n they can
live when they want to."

"Oh, if mother could have said one word to
me!" sobbed Happy, stung into life by Miss Lavinia's trenchant words.

"Well, it might ha' ben worse, a heap. She did
look at ye, lovin' Happy, for I heered the doctor
say he never see sech a look as she giv' ye; what ef
she hadn't even giv' ye that, and hadn't seen ye at
all, nor knowed you loved her, an' died so without
the least knowledge of your bein' beside of her?"
Miss Lavinia's voice trembled. "You haint measured the depths yet, child! there's others ben
through them waters of affliction, and hed all the
waves and billows go clear over them. Now rouse

up and think what you'd oughter do, and then do
it. Do you think these folks down stairs 'll hev
much opinion of religion if they see you givin' up
as though there wan't no better world, and no help
in the Bible, and no help for you nor your mother
neither ? "

The loyal soul in Happy's breast responded to
this appeal; she felt that she had not done her
duty; that she was selfish, even in her grief, to
ignore and neglect her duties as she had done. She
lifted her tired head from the lounge, and looked at
Miss Lavinia with eyes that had already a little
light in their tear-dimmed outlook. " I will try,
Aunt Vinny ! " she said humbly but resolutely.
Miss Lavinia said nothing, but took down the Bible
and read aloud the ninety-first Psalm. Her voice
was cracked, her accent quaint; but her heart went
into the wonderful words, and they were like the
sound of a trumpet to her hearer. She recalled by
some subtle chain of association, her mother's
counsel to her after Gay died : and like David she
arose from the earth, and changed her apparel, and
came into the house of the Lord and worshipped,
for the very next Sunday found her as usual with
her class. They were all eager to see her; without
being really conscious of it, there had been a feeling of curiosity in all their minds as to how Happy
could or would bear such a loss. Mary knew how

she had seemed to love her mother, and though
she could not feel what the loss was, she loved
Happy too much not to pity her. Julia could best
of all understand this sorrow, for her own mother was
dear and beloved above all things to her. Helen
Sands never thought deeply about anything; but
her father and mother had spoken so pityingly and
tenderly of Happy since her trouble, and Mrs.
Sands, having made a great effort to go and see her,
had reported her so entirely prostrated with grief
that Helen was surprised into sudden interest. She
sidled up to Happy, and put her hand into hers, with
the first symptom of affection she had ever shown:

"O Miss Happy! I'm so glad you've come; ma
said she didn't believe you would be able."

A low, sad voice answered: "I could not have
come, Nellie, without help; do you remember the
text we talked about last time? 'Wait on the
Lord; be of good courage, and he shall strengthen
thy heart; wait, I say, on the Lord.' I have been
there for help, and found it. I want to tell all of
you to-day that it is true. God will help us to bear
the most dreadful trouble if we ask him, for he has
helped me."

The tears filled Happy's eyes as she bore this
testimony to the suffering grace of God, and the
children looked as if some new revelation had been
made to them. Helen for once was effectually

sobered : and, in all her after life, she never forgot
this witness to the reality of spiritual things.   Julia,
too, felt it deeply, and Mary Gray's heart throbbed
with a new sympathy for her teacher.   If God
could so help Happy to bear a great and dreadful
sorrow, was there anything he could not do, even to
helping her to a new and better life ?   Ruth Holden
was the only one who did not enter into the spirit
of the hour.   It seemed dreadful to her that Happy
should so openly speak of her suffering and her
comfort.   There was not much talk about the lesson, for Happy's soul was full of her mother, and
she was as one whose lips are filled with a necessity
to preach the gospel.   Never before had heaven
seemed so actual to her, death such a certainty, sin
and separation from God so dreadful.   The time
was too short for all she had to say ; but she said
enough to convince her class that, whatever they
might think or feel about religion, it was a deep and
daily reality to her.   After church was over she
went up into Horn Lane to find her smaller scholars, and tell them to come as usual ; and when the
hour came they were all there, and one more with
them, — not a child but a young man with a pleasant face, who said at once : " I only come a minute
to say I'd tried to read to the children these two
Sundays back, for I guessed you wouldn't like to
have 'em scatter."

"Thank you very much," said Happy. And he
went away hearing Jack burst out, before he was
well through the door, with, —

"That feller's Fred Park. Ain't he good ?"

"What made him think about reading to you ?"
said Happy.

"Oh, I d'n know! guess he hadn't got nothin'
else to do Sundays."

"He comed becos pa singed my hymn at him, 'nd
he wanted to have me sing a lot more," squeaked
Polly, with a little· perk of her head sideways, as if
she were personally flattered on her singing.

Happy could not help smiling.

Nan added: "He works to the foundry, with
Poll's pa."

But for all this information Happy did not know
till long afterward that this young man was brought
to Lagré's house by Polly's hymn, which her father
had caught and sung at his work, and which had
aroused in Fred Park's mind all the childhood he
had passed under the loving care of a Christian
mother, all his lessons at Sunday-school in the far-
off Vermont village, the quiet happy days so long
gone, and made him long for some better life than
the rough, dissipated one he was living ; for even
this slight seed had taken root, though among
thorns.

When the children were quiet, Happy read to

them about Christ's raising Lazarus ; she had not thought of the chapter before, but suddenly it seemed the right thing to read.

As it came to Jack's turn to read out the verse "Jesus wept," he looked up abruptly. "What made him do that for ? "

The question was one that for a moment Happy knew not how to answer; hitherto she had taken the ordinary view of those divine tears, — that Christ wept with the weeping sisters ; but then she thought why should he weep who was about to restore the dead to life and end the sorrow of the mourners ? and another answer to Jack's question threw a ray of light into her mind as if from on high.

"I think he was sorry to bring back Lazarus to this world, Jack."

"Sorry ! I guess not ! Folk's don't want to be dead, *I* don't b'lieve ! not much ! "

"But you see, Jack, the Lord knew all about this world and all about heaven, and he knew how good it was to be safe with God, never to be sick, or sad, or hungry, or tired any more : and he was sorry to bring him back to such a life as this life is."

"Say ! " put in Jack, just at this period, evidently desirous of confuting Happy's idea by a practical application, "say, would you cry if your ma could be fetched back agin ? "

Happy turned pale; strive as she would, this test was too hard; her eyes wandered involuntarily back to the Bible page. "Then said the Jews, Behold how he loved him!" Yes, indeed; not in their narrow human sense, but as God loves, — for the good of the beloved. Happy found her answer here.

"I am not good like Jesus Christ, Jack. He did not think about himself at all, he thought of what was good for Lazarus. I hope he will help me in time to be glad that my mother is safe and happy: so glad that I shall not want to have her back. I do now, sometimes; but that is because I am not good enough."

Jack was silenced; he said no more through the lesson, but listened with unusual gravity. After the rest had gone he still lingered, and coming up to Happy said, very gruffly: "*I* think you're good 'nuf, I don't want ye no better, there!" and then took to his heels.

Happy's tears came thick and fast; partly because Jack's speech touched her sore heart tenderly; partly to think of the sharp comfort that had newly come to her out of the story of Bethany. As she moved about her room setting things to rights, some long-forgotten lines sung themselves over to her, half-remembered:

Have we so loved her well and long,
That we would call her from her song,
The lifted voices of that throng
    Who see the face of God:
And fetter her to sense and sin,
Fightings without and fears within,—
The crown of victory yet to win,
The valley to be trod ?

O Lord, thou lovest, thou art love,
Thy glory doth our grief reprove;
Thy heart enfolds her far above
    This loving that we boast.

This was all she could remember, but it was enough
to sing her to sleep that night, and many another.

CHAPTER XIV.

THIS Sunday once over Happy felt that she had again laid hold upon life; and praying long and earnestly for courage and guidance, she resolved on Monday to look things in the face, and set her life in order. If she had been rich, with nothing to do but nurse her sorrow, or try by change of scene and companionship to forget what had happened, she would have had a far more hopeless outlook. Work — or rather the necessity of work — is a true blessing, though it wears a dark disguise; the curse of Eden was only a curse to Paradise, but, like God's will always, was both good and fit for man's new world of sin and sorrow. Nothing is so good for the aching of a lonely heart as labor that must be done: nothing so sure a preventive of sin as work that leaves no time for temptation to coax or caress us; when we cannot die, when we must live, and grudge the necessity of living bereft of those most dear, then to have had earnest work a necessity to

support that life, is the very gift of God, the real
angel of consolation.

Happy had got to earn her own living ; she knew
it, she dreaded it ; and though it was set before her
as the duty of the day, she did not know how to go
about it. But she did the wisest thing she could
do ; went for Miss Greene to come and stay with
her through the day, again, and give her some
advice.

" And now, Aunt Vinny, what must I do first ! "
she said, with so much faith in both the will and
power of the old lady to help her, that Miss Lavinia's
sharp eyes grew a little dim.

" The first thing's to know what you've got to do
with, Happy ; take stock o' your tools, so to speak,
seemin'ly. I had a talk with Almiry that day she
come up to my house. I know she had her life
insured."

" Yes, she had, for two thousand dollars."

" Well, so fur so good.   You'd as good as not take
them papers to the minister, and he'll fix it for you ;
but you won't lay hands on the money for a month
or two, mabbe ; and then you'll have to look about
how to put it out, safe, to int'rest. She had some in
the Savin's Bank too, didn't she ? "

Happy went to find the book ; there was a credit
of three hundred and fifty dollars there.

" Some o' that, Happilony, you'll have to pay for

buryin' of her; I expect it will be about fifty dollars. It's an awful shame to waste so much money on buryin' folks."

"O, Aunt Lavinny!" sobbed Happy. "It was the last thing I could do for her. I did not care. I wanted everything to be nice."

"I ain't scoldin' of ye, Happilony, not a bit; you acted accordin' to your light, an' if that was darkness you wan't no way to blame. I know how you felt; natur is natur, but it doos crop out amazin' queer by times. But now we're on't, I want to say, don't you never waste no finery on my poor perishin' body. I'd as lives return to airth in a pine box as a rosewood one, and the airth had jest as lives have me. I don't want no trimmin's and gimcracks inside nor outside; put an old gownd onto the remains, and a pine coffin to hold 'em, and ef anybody talks, let 'em. Talk don't make nor mend folks, partiklarly dead folks. I'd ruther, forty times over, be buried as poor as poverty, and save my dollars for the livin' that needs 'em, than to put 'em underground for the sake of an hour's show; and so'd your ma say ef she'd ha' know'd it; her sense was amazin'. Well, you done your best, child. Law! if everybody done their best the millennium would set right in, but I expect it won't, not this year. Now we've settled that bisness, we'll lay it by, long

with the fifty to pay for 't; thet leaves ye three
hundred in cash.   Rent paid, ain't it ? "

"It was paid, two weeks ago, up to the first of
next month.   Mother said she had the money then,
and so she'd pay it up to then, and have it off her
mind."

" Then you've got a week to consider on't ; but
to-day's here and the week ain't. Hev you got
stores in the house ? "

" Wood enough, we were going to get some next
week ; and there is some tea and sugar, and some
pork, and a few potatoes."

" Well, you can buy what other vittles you want
as you go along ; and a week 'll give you time enough
to pack up these things."

" O Aunt Lavinia ! shall I have to go away from
here ? "

" I don't see but what you will, Happy , you can't
live alone allus, and you dono yet what you be a
goin' to do ; but I want to tell ye somethin'.   After
Almiry died, I went round fixin' and slickin' up
things for the funeral, — for you wan't able to do
nothin', naterally enough ; it's sprouts a heavy blow
breaks down, not tough old boughs like me — that's
had their growth an' their blowth and got used to
winds.   However, as I was sayin' I was puttin' up
a mite, an' I come acrost this letter in Almiry's big
Bible.   I mistrust she writ it the night afore she

died, for she said so much to me that day that I
reckoned she didn't mean to wait no great before
tellin' you. I took liberty to lay up the letter,
knowin' you were, so to speak, as it might be, on-
qualified for readin' on't just then ; so I kep' it, an'
here 'tis. I'm a goin' home now, for I left my wash-
in' in the suds to come along o' you, but you jest set
down and read that letter, and read it over agin, —
I expect it'll help you a sight — and I'll come in to-
morrer, after my chores is done up, and we'll talk
things over."

So, taking up her bonnet, Miss Greene went away,
with a true and delicate consideration for Happy
that many a better educated person might have failed
in, and left the poor girl to read the last words of a
mother whose heart and hand had never ceased to
comfort and support her child, and even in dying
had made an effort to smile for Happy's sake.

It is hard to read a letter with streaming eyes and
sobbing breath. Happy laid it down many times
before she could gain composure enough to reach
the end ; and then she read and re-read it over and
over. It was a long letter, and written in full view
of her coming death and Happy's loneliness ; but
though the tender yearning mother's heart over-
flowed in those pages, the Christian's triumphant
faith shone there also. And it was practical as
well ; Mrs. Dodd advised Happy to put her money

in some safe investment under Mr. Payson's advice, and, as it was not enough to support her, to let the interest accumulate for a time of need, when she should be old or unfit for work; so far all was pleasant, but when Happy came to the advice as to her work, and found that her mother had wished her to go out to service, she laid down the letter, choked with emotions she would have found it hard to analyze. Happy was not perfect by any means : what she would have called " proper pride " was a strong trait in her character. Theoretically, she considered herself a great sinner and an humble follower of Christ; but when these faiths came to a practical test, they were threads only. She could not bear the idea of being a servant. With a flushed face and hurried pulse she took up the letter ; all the arguments which her mother had used in conversation with Miss Vinny she had recapitulated here, but they did not prove convincing to Happy; it was a very hard trial to her temper and her humility, and for a time seemed impossible to bear. She walked up and down the room wringing her hands, and trying to devise some other means of support. She knew very well that she could not do factory work, neither could she sit and sew all day ; the unwelcome conviction that her mother knew best kept forcing itself upon her as fast as pride and pain set it aside. At last she recollected herself, and on her knees asked

for light and help as she had done before, but with
far deeper sense of need, more definite dependence.
Prayer in its very utterance gives peace ; whatever
storms rend or drench us for the moment, the soul
breathes a calmer and diviner air, rises into the light
which is above the clouds, and sees the earth as it
looks from beyond our troubled atmosphere, a scene
of grief and trial that is but for a time, that will
vanish in the glow and glory of eternity.

It is in this way that prayer is answered sometimes
while yet we are speaking ; with the tranquility of a
nobler position toward both God and man comes
purer judgment, a juster appreciation of all things,
and godliness becomes profitable to this life as well
as the next. Happy lifted her head from her hands
with a look of humble patience that showed where
she had found rest. She was tired, for the struggle
was long and hard ; so while the kettle was heating
to make her tea she sat down by the window and
opened the Bible ; a few verses helped the calm that
possessed her. She had opened to the eighth chapter
of Romans ; and, as she read on and on, feeling as
the wonderful ascending of the argument brought
her nearer and nearer to its splendid burst of triumph
at the end, that she too could enter into that chain
of reasoning as one who knew its propositions and
inferences by heart, one who was a child of God —
"and if children then heirs, heirs of God, and joint-

heirs with Christ; if so be that we suffer with him, that we may also be glorified together." Joint-heir with Christ! What did this mean? Happy asked herself what were his possessions in this world? Poverty, contempt, ridicule, no place to lay his head; hunger and thirst; only here and there one gleam of love, or pity, or appreciation; only now and then an hour of rest. His friends and followers were the humblest of earth,—laboring men who left even that labor to follow him; and he " was among them as him that serveth," ministering to disease, filth, sin, with his own hands; crucified between two thieves; dying in shame, agony, and darkness! And for what?

> " Oh, love divine, what hast thou done?
> The Lord of glory died for me,"

Were the words that sprung into Happy's mind for answer; and following them came another text: " The disciple is not above his master, nor the servant above his lord. It is enough for the disciple that he be as his master, and the servant as his lord."

The words seemed almost spoken in her ear, they so fitted her present need; and as she came to the glorious climax of the chapter, beginning, " And we know that all things work together for good to them that love God," and went on to the exulting shout which ends it, she entered in with all her heart to the

abounding joy and faith of the apostle, and repeated
aloud, to and for herself, "For I am persuaded that
neither death, nor life, nor angels, nor principalities,
nor powers, nor things present, nor things to come,
nor height, nor depth, nor any other creature, shall
be able to separate us from the love of God which is
in Christ Jesus our Lord."

Things looked differently to Happy now: and it
is "now" that we live.   Life seemed easy to her
laid beside that of her Master, even though it should
be a life of humiliation and service, and she went to
sleep comforted and strengthened.

In the morning Miss Greene came.   "Well,
I see you read that letter, Happy, and I guess
you know more'n you did about Almiry's idees,
don't ye?"

"Yes, I do, Aunt Vinny.   Did she tell you what
she wanted me to do?"

"Certin, certin: she an' me talked it all over.
I'm free to say I didn't altogether and tee-totally
agree with her at the fust: but she was a most a
master hand for sense, Happy.   I come round and
giv' in as soon as I chewed on it a spell, and I was a
makin' up my mind to come over an' tell her she
was in the right on't when I heered she was gone.
Well: heaven's the better for her, a sight, and earth
the wuss."

Happy could not speak for a moment; and Miss

Lavinia wiped her full eyes. " But, Aunt Vinny, what had I better do to find a place ? "

" Ask the minister ; or — no. I'd ruther ask Mis' Payson. Wherever you be, you'll hev to do with the women-folks of the house ; and men don't know no more about what women be to home, in their fam'lies, than they know about what grows in the moon. Mercy to me ! I've knowed more'n one man that wan't no more aware o' what his wife was like, and how she acted in her own house, than nothin'. Men are queer creturs : take 'em in a business kind o' view, as it were, so to speak, and they're sharper'n whittled lightin' to see what's a goin' on ; but come to get a woman under their eyes and they're blind as old bats. We'll see Mis' Payson right off. As for your things, Happilony, I should git red of the biggest part ; send 'em up to the auction store, and sell 'em. What you want to keep, you can set up in my garret. I may as well tell ye now, I've ben and gone and got my will drawed out to leave ye that little house o' mine, when I've got through with't. You'll allers hev a ruff over your head any way ; and there's a leetle money too. There ain't none very near to me left, you see, and I'd as lives you'd hev it as the next one. Don't say nothin', child ; don't thank me aforehand : it's waste words. Mabbe you'll die fust : who knows ? But there's one more thing — don't you set your mind

on all plain sailin' an' clear sky ahead ; there's trials
in everybody's life, and there's agoin' to be in yourn ;
but jest you hark to me a bit, and I'll give ye a mite
o' advice. Don't overdo ; don't whew into everything as though there wan't no more days in the
week : you won't half do your work, and you'll quite
kill yourself, if you do. Folks has got some duties
to their own bodies. And don't you be put upon
more'n is fair ; some folks think hired help ain't
human creeturs, but the help don't agree· with 'em.
I ain't afraid you'll talk too much, or do anything
that ain't all square ; but I be afraid you'll do too
much, and them you live with won't think no more
of ye than if you do jest what you'd ought to, an'
no more. Well, that's enough. I'll come round
agin this afternoon, and we'll go over to Mis' Payson's, if you want to. It's jest as good to have it
over with right away, as to wait." And Happy
thought it was.

CHAPTER XV.

THE next morning Happy went to Mrs. Payson
alone; Miss Lavinia had a headache, and could not
be with her, but it was not a very formidable matter
to see Mrs. Payson. Happy felt already that she
was a friend, for she had been there once or twice
since Mrs. Dodd's death, though it happened that
the girl was either sleeping, or " had gone to the
grave to weep there," like the women of all the
ages, — before and since Scripture recorded it of
the Marys, — every time the minister or his wife
tried to see her. There was something so kindly
and reassuring in Mrs. Payson's voice, her smile,
her simple, cordial manner, that Happy felt her
heart lightened at once. Mrs. Payson was a woman
whom almost everybody liked ; and those who did
not, were to be pitied, her husband said, for they
lost a great deal. She brought Happy into her
pleasant parlor, which was in daily use, and, giving
her an easy-chair, took up her sewing, which she

had laid down to go to the door, in order to make the interview as little formal as possible.

Happilona was naturally a simple, direct little person ; her way was to go at once to the point, and she did this now by asking Mrs. Payson to read her mother's letter. When that lady finished, and put the paper down, her expressive face showed deep feeling.

" My dear," she said, " your mother was an extraordinary woman."

" Yes, ma'am," was all Happy could answer.

" I think she was right in her advice to you, entirely right ; though it is not what I should have expected, or you either probably." She saw from Happy's face that she had judged right in regard to this. " I do not see what else you could do, not being strong. I don't think you'll find it pleasant at first, Happy ; you have never been obliged to act under the orders of a stranger, and it will be irksome ; your pride will be wounded many a time, and your feelings hurt ; but, my dear, have the sense to say to yourself, ' This is the duty God gives me ; I must do it for him.' Your course is very plain ; you must earn your living, and this is the only way you can earn it ; but you can make that way evil or good, as you choose. I have seen a servant loved and respected as much as any woman I ever knew ; and you can be."

Happy looked up and smiled; the words might
have seemed harsh and hard had they not been
uttered in the gentlest voice, with the tenderest
manner. Aunt Lavinia had given much the same
advice to her, but it rasped on her nature, though
she felt its goodness. Mrs. Payson was like her
mother, she thought, and she looked up with a
beaming face.

"I will try," she said.

Mrs. Payson smiled back. "And I will try to
help you, Happy. Have you heard of any place?"

"No, ma'am. I thought perhaps you might
know of one."

"I will look about the parish and see. Meantime
there is no reason — is there? — why you cannot
stay with me to-day. I should like to have you."

So Happy stayed; and the rest from work, and
absence from the place where she missed her mother
every hour, did her good. By-and-by Mr. Payson
came in; he was glad to see her. "You have been
talking with my wife," he said. "I am sure that
did you good, Happy."

"Yes, sir, it did; she talks like mother."

The minister's eyes beamed. "That is a real
compliment, my dear, one that is honest and earnest
both."

Mrs. Payson had left the room a moment as her
husband came in, and now she said, as she entered:

"Mr. Payson, the first thing you do, please, is to read this letter, and give Happy your advice; she has had mine, but I want her to have yours."

Happy looked at him while he sat reading, and thought how nice it would be to live with two such people; they had quite won her lonely heart, not only by their real kindness, but by the charm of their pleasant, cordial manners. How much does life owe to a kindly manner! Here were two persons whom everybody liked; not because they were any better, any wealthier, any more intellectual, than a thousand others about them, but simply because they were agreeable; took pains to be neatly and properly dressed, and to be friendly with all men. If Mr. Payson had gone about the parish with his head held down, his coat soiled, and his shoes unblacked, long, rough locks brushing his coat collar, and a face of gloom and ill-humor, now and then expanding into a sour, reluctant smile, which it was his duty to wrench to the surface for an acquaintance; or if Mrs. Payson had been a selfish, sloppy, whining woman, — all the power for good which drew people towards them would have been changed into a power of repelling the very souls they were set to lure into the fold. When Paul said he was made " all things to all men, that I might by all means save some "; and again, " Even as I please all men in all things, not seeking my own profit, but the profit of many, that they might be saved," — did he not mean something like this constant effort to win others to love the gospel, that in and to themselves was so sweet and lovely ?

While Happy waited, the thought went through her mind that it was a good thing to be so lovable, so agreeable ; and she resolved to try and be pleasant herself, even in trouble, for the sake of other people.

When Mr. Payson had read the letter, he gave her almost exactly the same advice his wife had ; and, much helped and strengthened, Happy went home to her lonely rooms ; oh, how lonely now ! worse and worse each day ; so full of her mother's presence and atmosphere that to enter them was a fresh pang every time. It was one good thing in going to service, she thought, that those rooms would be left behind her entirely. She was not strong enough to bear such a haunted solitude ; an entire change would be welcome.

The week passed ; a little work was sent in to her that she could do, and it was promptly paid for ; she did not have to take any more money from the bank, and kind Mrs. Ives, herself confined these two months to the house, sent her over some little delicacies that tempted her to eat, and so gave her more strength. Happy lived through the days as we all overlive such days, in a dumb endurance,

a dull pain, a "constant anguish of patience," till
Sunday came once more.

As she sat with her class about her, waiting for
Mr. Fox to open school, it suddenly struck her that
perhaps, if she went out to service, she would have
to give them up, or rather they would give her up.
With this thought in her mind, she looked at the
fresh young faces about her. Helen Sands, she felt
sure, would leave her; perhaps Julia; Mary, she
thought, would stay ; but as to Ruth ! — here was a
doubt. Happy's eyes filled at the possibility , she
loved that child so dearly, and was so anxious to do
her good, that an idea of separation pained her.
But the verse for the day recalled her, — " Casting
all your care upon Him, for he careth for you." As
the children repeated it in unison, the last words
rested and reigned in Happy's soul. " He careth
for you ! " Then what could harm her? What
if she could not do Ruth any more good? was not
God able to take her into his own care ? So she
laid her anxiety aside, and went on with the lesson.
After it was over, Mrs. Payson stopped her a moment, and said :

" Can you come over to see me in the morning,
Happy ? "

" Yes, ma'am,"—but her heart beat as she said it.

After church came a little visit from Miss Vinny,
and then her younger class.

" What shall you do with 'em when you move out ? " said Aunt Vinny, as she tied on her bonnet to go home.

" I'm sure I don't know, auntie. I have got that to arrange ; for, wherever I go, I must have this hour to myself, and perhaps in the morning."

" Well, don't worry about that now : ef you conclude to keep 'em, you can take my kitchen for a Sunday or two till you get a better place."

Happy knew this was a great deal for Miss Lavinia to offer, and she determined to trouble her as little as possible ; she could have got a room in the attic of the tenement house where the children lived, but there were many objections to that.

They were very good to-day, — as good as untamed children in high spirits could be ; they sung with all energy, and really tried to please her ; and when the hour was over, Happy kissed them all round, with a sort of feeling that they were her own, — a feeling intensified by her own loneliness.

" I shall come and see you all, this week," she said, after the last hymn was sung.

" Oh, goody ! goody ! " screamed the little girls ; the boys only looked pleased, but that was enough for Happy. After they went away, Mrs. Packard came up stairs and asked her to come down and eat her supper with them. Happy was glad to go, for Sunday evening was a hard time for her. She was

warmly welcomed by both, and urged to eat as
much as would have sufficed her for all day ; but it
was their measure of hospitality, and she knew and
was grateful for it.

Mrs. Packard was a woman inquisitive by nature,
and never taught to repress that unpleasant trait;
she plunged at once into a series of questions, and
was surprised to hear of Happy's plans.

" Well, I declare ! " she said ; " I should think
you'd a sight rather go into a shop, or a store, or
take in sewin'. I don't mean to cast ye down, but
livin' out does seem a mean business for you,
Happy."

Here was the other side confronting her. Happy
did not feel strong to argue ; she could not convinc-
ingly put herself down when that self sided with
Mrs. Packard.

" I am not a bit healthy and strong, you know,
Mrs. Packard. I must do what I can."

" That's so ! " said Mr. Packard, who had hitherto
been very silent. " You've got to use the boards
you've got, if you ha'n't got them you'd oughter
hev. I've done j'iner work enough for that; and
folks has got to make the best o' what they be
a'ready. I wish you good luck, Happy ; and I want
you should remember that as long as she and me are
round, you can allers come here and stay here jest
as long as you're a mind to." He did not wait to

hear Happy's thanks, but pushed his chair aside and
went quickly out of the door. Little Gay's fair
face rose up distinctly before him and choked his
speech ; he had never forgotten her.

"Well! he means it," put in his wife, "an' so do
I, Happilony. Luman's a heap changed since Gay
died; and I know I'd ought to be a better woman.
I must try for't, that's a fact. He don't drink a
mite now ; and goes to Methodist meetin' reg'lar."

"Oh, I'm so glad!" exclaimed Happy.

"Well, I b'lieve you be. I b'lieve in your ma's
kind of religion and your'n too. If I can get that
kind, I'm bound to have it."

"There isn't but one kind," said Happy, smiling.
"Mother's was the only right kind, Mrs. Packard.
I mean to try to be like her, too ; for she tried to be
like Christ."

"I expect she did, Happy. She's been the best
friend me and Luman ever had. If she hadn't ha'
lent him that hundred an' fifty dollars last spring, I
dono where we'd hev ben now."

"What?" said Happy, surprised.

"Why, we owed that to Squire Jakeway over to
the store, and we owed it more'n three year; and he
got real obstopolous one day, and your ma heered
him talkin' smart to Luman, for he'd come here to
take him to do about that bill; so she stepped in
when he was gone, and offered to help us, and let

us have the money right off. But she wouldn't take no note nor nothin', but she ses: 'I know you will pay me when you get ready, Mr. Packard, I can trust you: the money will be Happy's before long, and we don't want int'rest, we're both intrested enough in you a'ready,' and then she kinder laughed, and Luman he choked right up, but he kinder sputtered out an' said he'd pay if he lived, every cent on't, int'rest and all. And so he will, Happy; he's got twenty dollars a'ready in the Savin's bank, in your name, so'st he can't never draw it out himself. Mercy on me! don't you cry like that, child!" for Happy's tears fell fast. "I thought you knowed all about it. And, moreover, I was goin' to say, if you want to keep up with that little Sunday class o' yourn, why you can have 'em in our kitchen every time. It'll do us a heap o' good to have ye; and maybe you'll stop to tea now and then, and see how we're gettin' along."

Happy thanked her with all her heart, and went off early to church in order to stop and tell Miss Lavinia she should not need to trouble her with the children, and also about her mother's goodness to the Packards.

"Jest like her!" exclaimed Aunt Vinny. "She was the scripturalest woman I ever see; she didn't let her right hand — that's you, Happy — know what her left hand was a doin' never. And that

tells what puzzled me a lot; Almiry told me she'd
got five hundred dollars in the Savin's bank, and
there wa'nt but three hundred an' fifty, you know,
when we found the book. I expect she forgot,
when she was a talking to me, how she'd lent that
to Packard. She never did think nothin' o' what
she done herself, but everything o' what other folks
done for her. Well! it takes poor folks to help
poor folks, arter all!"

CHAPTER XVI.

MONDAY morning, after her work was done, Happy went round to Mrs. Payson's, and was welcomed warmly. " I think I have got just the right place for you, Happy," said Mrs. Payson ; "right, that is, as to work and wages : whether it will be altogether pleasant, time must prove. Mrs. Holden wants a young girl to wait on her, and do some light sewing ; mend Ruth's clothes, and make some of them ; and do any little thing she may want done. Rather desultory sort of work, but not likely to prove hard, and she offers twelve dollars a month."

Happy stood silent ; was it pleasure or pain that stayed her speech at the thought of living under the same roof with Ruth Holden in a servant's capacity ? She could not tell herself. Would Ruth like to have her there in such a position ? Could she stoop from her dainty, delicate pride to care for Happy ? These thoughts flashed across the poor girl's mind with a sudden thrill. Ruth had been the idol of her imagination, and to be lowered in her eyes seemed bitter; but Mrs. Payson's voice recalled her. "What is it, Happy? what troubles you?" Happy blushed, but could not explain; she only said, "I think it seems to be a good place, as you say, Mrs. Payson, for work and wages. One thing I should like to know, shall I have time to teach my classes on Sunday?"

"I should think so certainly: there cannot be much need of you there on Sunday: old Mrs. Holden always spends the day at her son's house, and is a good deal with his wife; one or the other stays at home with her; you must stipulate for this leave of absence to begin with. It is best to begin right: then there will be less trouble or complaint afterward. One thing, however, Happy, you will have to consider: perhaps your class in Sunday-school will not all attend it as they have done before."

Happy colored up to her hair.

"My dear, you will have to encounter prejudice, of course; you will find people look down on you now, who did not before; your pride will suffer, but I hope and think you have faith and courage enough to do what clearly seems your duty, in spite of other people's opinions and your own shrinking."

Happy did not feel sure: she smiled a little sadly. Mrs. Payson's words were kind, and gently uttered, but their sense was hard and bitter: she said for answer, "I can try." It was all she dared say, for

Happy was only a poor, timid, lonely young girl, bereaved of her only relative, cast on the world to fight for her life, with her faith yet new and chiefly untried. But her intention was honest and her heart sincere: she did love God, and meant to serve him. Life looked pitiless enough to her just now, but her resolution was firm to do the best she could. In this spirit, accordingly, she went over to see Mrs. Holden in the afternoon.

Mrs. Payson had been before her, so that the way was prepared, and she was taken at once to Mrs. Holden's room. That lady was as languid, as elegant, as delicate looking as when Happy last saw her, a year before, but there was an indescribable change and chill in her manner; you felt the hand of steel under the silken glove, the exacting, loveless, selfish nature betrayed itself. None of Mrs. Holden's servants loved her. They served her well, even punctiliously, for she made it necessary; but she never regarded them from any stand-point but her own. They were there to do her work, not to have joys or sorrows or interests of their own; and if that work was neglected or ill done, her words could be as fluent and sharp as the words of any vulgar virago, — for she was not a lady at heart, though it would have been to her an unendurable insult to be thought otherwise.

Happy suited her in one respect; the girl had no

family to call her away, or to be perpetually coming
to see her.   She made some demur about the Sunday
observances, though she did not object to one week-
day evening ; but finding Happy was firm about this
matter, and being really desirous to get the girl into
her family, she at last agreed that after nine o'clock
on Sunday morning she should have the day to
herself; a matter very easy in reality, since Happy's
duties had nothing to do with the house except as
she took care of Mrs. Holden's room and Ruth's on
Mondays, while the second girl helped the cook.

"But you can't expect your class in the church
school will stay with you now," said Mrs. Holden,
pointedly.

Happy's face flushed, but she quietly answered,
"Perhaps not, ma'am ; but if they do not, I shall
want to join Mrs. Payson's Bible class."

The lady said no more ; it was nothing to her
what this girl did, yet it had chafed her a little to
have Happy make any stipulations, and she had said
what she did in order to "put her down," as she
phrased it to herself.   It did not have just this
effect ; but it did serve to show Happy that Ruth
at least would not come under her instruction
again.   She said as much to Mrs. Payson, when she
went back to tell her that she had engaged to go to
Mrs. Holden's the next week.

"You are mistaken about that, Happy," said

Mrs. Payson. "You will have ten times more chance to teach Ruth now than you ever had before; not by positive lessons but by example, which is the strongest teaching. I see you are very fond of Ruth, and now God has put you just where your affection for her will be another inducement to live a christian life. I often think our spiritual lives are like the growth of a vine ; the great Gardener of the vineyard gives us one help after another ; but, Happy, remember *all these are to help us climb!* We go up, or fall. If you live as you ought to daily and hourly, live as you can, with Christ's help, you will be of far more service in bringing Ruth to your Master than you can be in the Sunday class.

Happy's face brightened at the thought, and then sobered again ; for if the idea was glad it was also solemn. Mrs. Payson saw the thought in the transparent countenance, and said gently, "Who is sufficient for these things ? My grace is sufficient for thee, for my strength is made perfect in weakness." That was the right word for Happy ; she went home more resolute and more humble too, and began to make her few preparations for leaving the rooms where so much of her dear dead past had been spent. Not much could be done to-night ; she was tired, and knew that she must not waste her strength, but the next morning her painful task began.

To fold and lay aside her mother's clothing was like re-opening her grave to Happy; hot tears fell thick and fast over the familiar garments that brought back the face she should see no more, the voice she could never hear again ; but it had to be done, and she laid them all reverently away in her mother's trunk before she did anything else, in order to have the worst over at once. Her own possessions were to wait till the last, for they should go directly to Mrs. Holden's house ; the rest were to be stored in Miss Greene's little attic, and how to get them there was the next question. But while Happy was eating her dinner, she bethought herself that she must let her little class know that they were to meet hereafter in Mrs. Packard's kitchen, and perhaps Jack could tell her of some one she could get to take her furniture and boxes over to Miss Greene's house. If Mr. Packard had been at home he could have helped her ; but he was out of town at work, and only came home Saturday at night to spend Sunday. Jack looked rather amazed at Miss Happy's appeal, but was not wanting to himself at such a responsible moment ; he thrust one hand in a ragged pocket, and searched under his cap for an idea with the other, after the manner of boys, then slapped his knee as if struck with a sudden ray of intelligence.

"Well, there's Fred Park ! he's out of a job. I'll

bet a cookey he'll scare up a team somewhere so's to
fetch them things for ye."

"I'll pay him what is right, you know," said
Happy. "I don't want to hire a big truck-wagon,
and pay a dollar; one horse in a lumber wagon will
do for me, Jack."

"Yes, sir-ree. All right. I'll fix that job to-
morrer mornin', sure. When air you agoin' to
move?"

"Friday, as early as I can. You'll let me know
to-morrow?"

"You see," was the brief answer, and bristling
with importance, Jack sauntered off, having promised to come to Mrs. Packard's house on Sunday.
He was a happy boy! If inward and outward
growth were simultaneous, Jack would have been
an inch taller within the next hour; fortunately for
his already too brief garments, he did not leave
them any farther behind in reality, however he felt.

On Friday, the horse, wagon, and driver came
punctually to the door.

Fred Park in rough and worn clothes, but scrupulously clean and neat, was so alert, so smiling, so
careful of Happy's goods and chattels, and so considerate of her slight strength, that Mrs. Packard
began to look about her, and wonder if Happy
noted this unusual attention, but she did not; nothing was farther from her thoughts than the man

who carried her furniture carefully, and was so civil
to her. She had heart and hands both full, for she
was leaving her home ; humble and poor enough,
and lately haunted with the saddest of earth's memories, but, after all, as she felt on leaving it, her
home. There are people who do not know what
that little word means ; who compass sea and land
for pleasure or forgetfulness, and never care to find
the peace and content that lie about their hearths
who " dwell among their own,"—people who leave
the most pleasant dwellings and the dearest friends
to try and feed the restless unease that consumes
them with fresh sights and alien faces : but Happy
was not of this kind, and she felt a bitter pang as
the last of her possessions went out from the door,
and her home was desolate. She said good-bye to
Mrs. Packard, and preceded the wagon to Miss
Greene's, where Fred Park again made himself useful ; and soon the dark little attic was heaped with
boxes, chairs, bed and bedding, — for Happy had
not tried to sell anything, hoping some time or other
to need the dear old things again.

"What shall I pay you?" she asked Fred Park,
when the moving was finished.

"Well: the team ain't mine, you see, Sam Smith
he let me have it : he'll want fifty cents for't. Ef
'twas my team—but it's his'n, you see."

"And how much for you?" again asked Happy.

"Oh!—well,—why, I don't want nothin'. I
come to help ye."

Happy colored with embarrassment.

" But I meant to pay you, and I want to."

"I know it. I know ye did; but really I don't
want anythin'; it can go tow'rds your helpin' them
youngsters. I expect you don't get paid for that,
do ye?"

Happy laughed. She saw the young man would
not take money for his services; she thought he
was grateful for her teaching the children: perhaps
he was a relative of some among them. With instinctive tact she dropped the matter, and gave him
the half dollar, saying, " Thank you for helping
me; I am much obliged."

" You're as welcome as you are obliged," responded Fred, giving her a good look out of his dark eyes
as he drove away, as if she were pleasant to look at.

" He's everlastin' spry, ain't he?" began Miss
Lavinia. " I never saw a handier feller in all my
days: where did you get him, Happy?"

Happy told her, and though Miss Lavinia, like
Mrs. Packard, had her own feminine speculations
about Fred Park, she too kept them to herself. It
was early days to put such notions into Happy's
head, she thought; so she said nothing, but turned
her attention toward putting dinner on the table,
which had been delayed for Happy's sake.

" And hain't you had no misgivin's yet, Happy ? "
she asked, between the bits of pie which her knife
conveyed slowly and meditatively to her mouth, as
they were finishing dinner.

"I've had a plenty, Aunt Vinny ! "

" Well, 'twouldn't be nateral if you didn't. I
expect folks that never mistrust trouble's comin' on,
ain't never ready for it. But I do think, Happilony, the wust on't 's the fust on't. There ain't no
sitooation in life but what'll hev trouble along with
it ; only make up your mind to 't, and it won't
trouble you no great. She ain't your sort of a
woman noway : and the girl's real pretty, but she
ain't perfect, no more'n you an' I be. Land ! if you
want to know folks, just hire out to 'em ! They
take their wigs off afore the help, so to speak,
seemin'ly. They're awful pleasant spoken an' gen-
teel outside, amongst folks, but the kitchen fetches
'em, I tell ye. A real lady's a lady to hired gals jest
as much as she is to the minister's wife, but that
kind is skerce. There's fine clothes, and fine manners a plenty ; but first-rate innardly fine folks is
skerce for certain'. Old Mis' Holden's one of the
saints of th' airth, but she don't live there. My ! I
don't b'lieve she ever giv' one thought to what was
best for herself in twenty year back ! she jest lives
in other folks. I ain't free to say I think there's a
heap o' comfort for them that does *live* so. Bible

says Love your neighbor as yourself, and ef you
hain't got any self, where's your measure, eh? and
I don't b'lieve she has got any. She's good enough
to die any day. I know you'll think a heap of her.
But don't ye get disheartened, Happy. Look to
the Lord as your ma did; and when you want
cretur help come right around here, and I'll do
what I can for ye always. I promised Almiry I'd
be a friend to her girl for all time, Providence per-
mittin', and I ain't no promise-breaker."

Happy got up and put her arms around Miss
Vinny, and kissed her. It was all the answer she
could make, but it was enough.

CHAPTER XVII.

SUNDAY morning Happy got ready for Sunday-school with a beating heart; she knew that by this time all her class must know she was about to be a servant, and her pride rose up like an armed man to daunt her. Only after a very earnest prayer for help and strength did her courage return; and when she arrived at the chapel, and found nobody in her seat, a wave of heart-sickness came over her, till she looked about and saw that very few people were there anywhere; she had come half an hour too soon.

By-and-by Mary Gray came in, smiling at Happy, with a tender and quiet look, such as she scarcely ever wore. It did Happy more good than the child knew; and as Mary nestled down beside her, and gave her hand a loving pressure, she could hardly resist the impulse to turn and kiss her. Then came Julia, bright and fluent as usual; and last of all, Helen Sands, reluctant and pouting — for, truth to tell, she had rebelled at the thought of being taught

by a "hired girl," as she expressed herself, and
might have been allowed by her easy mother to
stay at home, for the sake of peace, had not the
doctor opportunely come in to breakfast, as doctors
will, after everybody else was through, and heard
Nellie arguing the matter with her mother in the
bedroom.

"Helen, come here," he said peremptorily.
"What is this fuss about?"

Helen hung her head. "Oh, nothing much, pa!
only I don't want to go to Sunday-school."

"Why not?"

"Well, you see, Happy Dodd she's going to live
at Mr. Holden's, going to live out there, and — "

Here Eddy bounced in, and took up the hesitating story. "And Nell can't go to Sunday-school to
a hired girl! Just like girls! mean as dirt! I'd
like to know — "

"And I'd like you to be quiet, Ned," sternly in-
terpolated the doctor.

"Helen, are you really so silly as this? Why
isn't Happy Dodd as good a teacher for you to-day
as she was a week ago?"

There was no answer.

"If you object to her being a 'hired girl,' as you
say, your objection extends to me. I am a 'hired
man,' and hired to a few hundred people instead
of one. This is utter nonsense. Happy Dodd is a

good, brave girl. I respect her more than I ever
did, and I only hope you may live to be half as
good as she is. Put on your bonnet, and go as
usual."

When Dr. Sands said as much as this in his
family, it was final ; he did not often have time or
opportunity to govern his children, unhappily for
them ; but he never admitted any disobedience to
orders. So Helen, in a rebellious and petulant
humor enough, went off to the chapel.

But she was the last ; Ruth did not appear. She
did not wish to go, nor did her mother wish to have
her. The idea of Happy coming to the house as a
servant both pleased and displeased her. She really
loved her teacher, and would miss the class ; but to
put herself under the instruction of a servant was
something altogether out of the question. It was
impossible to change their relations one day out
of seven ; she must stay at home, of course. So
she put on her hat and idled about the garden till it
should be church time, as she always went in the
morning with her father. Grandma Holden found
her there when she came over, after her usual
custom, to sit with her daughter-in-law during the
first service.

" Why, Ruth, dear ! " she said, " are you ill
to-day ? "

" No, ma'am," Ruth answered.

"I thought you must be, not to be at Sunday-school," the old lady went on, fixing her mild gray eyes on Ruth's face, where the swift color was rising.

"Grandma! don't you know Happy Dodd is coming here to be mamma's seamstress? Of course I can't go to Sunday-school to her!"

"O — h!" said grandma; but the tone was so significant that it stung Ruth far more than any words to which she could have given answer; and she turned away saying to herself: "Oh, dear! I wish grandma *would* let me alone. I can't help it."

And while this little scene went on, Happy also was telling herself that, after all, it was best so. Ruth was right to stay away; it saved much awkwardness, many false positions; but Ruth could not quite satisfy herself, and Grandma Holden, actuated as much by contempt for her daughter-in-law's airs as by a desire to set Ruth right and do justice to Happy, could only complicate matters by farther speech, and, being pretty clear-sighted, did not mention the subject again, but left it to arrange itself.

Happy set herself to her teaching more earnestly than ever, and when the lesson was over said simply, "I am very glad you came to-day." Helen fidgetted about and did not look at her, but Julia and Mary both answered with such a smile that

Happy could have thanked them over again. In the afternoon her little class gathered in Mrs. Packard's kitchen, and behaved better than usual. Perhaps the change of place had something to do with it; perhaps the fact that just as they were scrambling after their hats and bonnets Fred Park appeared at the door, with a basket of wild plums.

"There!" shouted Jack. "There he is, Poll! Nan, look a'here! Say, Fred Park, we've been awful good; good as pie, hain't we?" appealing to Happy, who gave unqualified assent. Then he went on confidentially : "He told us he'd fetch around suthin' if we was extry good to-day. Oh, my eye! ain't them nice?"

The young man laughed at the eager faces, and, sitting down on the shed step proceeded to divide the plums; first offering Happy a splendid sheaf of cardinal-flowers tangled in a misty garland of wild clematis, through whose faint delicate whiteness the scarlet spikes glowed like fire through smoke. Happy was delighted : her love of flowers amounted to a passion, and the woods and fields were an unknown volume to her life as yet. She was pleased, too, at the kindness; for she had few friends, and whatever little thing was done for her assumed disproportionate value in her eyes.

Fred Park waited and walked home to Miss Lavinia's with her, after she had gathered up her books and said good-bye to the children. Happy did not ask him in, and Miss Vinny was getting tea in the kitchen, so she did not see him. If she had, Happy's eyes might have been opened. then and there; but as it was, she went on her way, careless of any intention on anybody's part to meddle with her life; intent only on doing what she could for God and her fellow-men.

She went to Mrs. Holden early in the morning, her trunk having gone there the week before, and was shown to a little room in the attic, close under the roof, with part of a window in it, the other part belonging to the next and larger room, where the cook and chambermaid slept. But at any rate this was her room, to be shared with no one; and she made it look as homelike as she could, putting a few little things of her own about it, and her mother's Bible and hymn-book on the stand. Then she went down stairs and learned what she could of her new duties before Mrs. Holden was ready to see her. She met Ruth in the lower hall, and was about to pass her with a gentle, grave bow, but the child's real feeling prevailed; she held out her hand to Happy, and said, coloring, "I'm glad you've come."

Happy was glad too, now: but she did not presume on this welcome; she went her way quietly, and tried to do her duty.

No doubt this duty was hard and irksome. There were many days when she found it impossible to please Mrs. Holden, and almost equally impossible to keep her temper under the provocation it received.

Happy had been carefully shielded from the roughness of life, and now every little thing irritated her morbid sensitiveness. Her mother had been exquisitely gentle even to her faults, and to be called stupid, a fool, a perfect blunderer, and other disagreeable epithets, hurt her cruelly ; and it hurt her more to find that the temper she thought she had under such control was only asleep for want of exercise.

Many and many a time her tongue burned and her lips opened to answer some unjust reproof or unkind speech ; but a look at Ruth's fair troubled face, if she were present, a thought of her mother's counsels, lifted up her heart to Him who alone could give her self-control, and who did give it. She found, after much effort at keeping her temper, that the surest way was to say to herself a text of Scripture .or utter a brief prayer before she answered any exasperating question, or made any remark that was necessary ; in any case she kept silence as far as she could. It helped her much to know that Ruth's eyes were always watching her. Poor human nature ! Its weakness is so great that

to live as in God's sight is the hardest thing for us
to do.   Faith is so faint that the heavenly vision is
dulled in the best of us; and even our gracious
Lord made provision for this failing of the flesh
when he transferred his personality practically to
his disciples, saying, "Inasmuch as ye have done it
unto one of the least of these, ye have done it unto
me."

"Happy," said Ruth, one day, sitting down by
her in the sewing-room, for Mrs. Holden was asleep
and needed no particular attention, "Happy, why
do you always shut your lips and keep quite still a
minute when mamma scolds you?"

Happy looked into the child's clear eyes, half in
doubt if she should answer; then she said, "I say a
text or a little prayer before I speak, Ruth; lest I
should speak too quickly."

Ruth did not say anything more, she went quietly
away to think it over; here was somebody who
really did try to be good every day, whose religion
was an hourly help to her.   She knew very well
that her own speech was not so guided or guarded,
even toward her mother; and the lesson went home
to her heart, all the more that it was involuntary.
Happy had her own troubles, too, with the other
servants; they were Irish, and, like many of their
class, resented the fact that a "Yankee" should be
set among them, and in a rather higher position;

and it was equally unpleasant to her to be obliged to
have a certain sort of companionship with them, in
her regular round of daily duties.

Her naturally delicate appetite was not enticed by
the careless, sloppy fashion in which the kitchen
table was spread, and the half-cold meals did not
tempt her; she ate so little that she actually grew
weak at first for want of food, and was so glad of
her Sunday supper at Miss Lavinia's that the good
old woman suspected the state of things, and kept
her supplied with private stores of gingerbread and
biscuit that were very welcome. But by quietly
doing her duty, and showing whatever small kindness
came in her way to Ann and Katy, by helping with
a heavy ironing now and then out of her own working hours, — for she did not sew in the evenings, —
or by showing Ann some new way of preserving
fruit or coaxing savory dishes out of little remnants
when the butcher failed to appear, — things she had
learned from her mother, — and by a thousand name-
less tokens of good-will, a pleasant word here and
there, or even a kindly smile, she found the way to
their warm Irish hearts: and Ann, noticing her
want of appetite, began to keep the food warm, the
tea hot, the toast crisp, for " the poor cratur;" and
Katy laid the dishes in better order, noticing that
Happy would silently rearrange them sometimes,
and put on a clean cloth more than once a week,

since she had so much help about her extra ironing.
Little things all of them, but so are the leaves that
make up a tree's verdure and beauty; so are the
petals that clustering together shape the perfect
rose; and so are the sparrows that crowd and chirp
in thousands about us, yet no one of these falls to
the ground unheeded, and — "Are ye not better
than many sparrows?" shall not "all these things
be added unto you"?

CHAPTER XVIII.

In the course of a few weeks Happy came to know Grandma Holden. She was sent to "the other house," as the old homestead was called, on various errands, and soon learned to admire and to love this lovely old lady, whose life was a constant practice and teaching of the gospel. Almost all Madam Holden's children were dead ; she had watched every one of them down to the river's brink with unfaltering courage and cheer, and unsparing devotion. Her only daughter, a widow too, was traveling in Europe ; one son was at the South, the other was Ruth's father : out of eight, these three alone remained. Her husband died after an illness of years that bore heavily on mind and body ; and though she could never speak of him without tears springing to her tender eyes, there was always a smile to follow, fresh and faithful as a rainbow, to attest her cheerful submission to God's better will.

Old as she was, her soft hair had not one silver thread in its thick bands, and her spare figure

moved with a gentle alacrity that denied her years.
As Miss Lavinia had said, she was a woman with no
self, a woman who lived in and for her own people.
It is true, the circle in which she so moved was
small, and time was still narrowing it; but she gave
to it all she had to give, the whole of a full cup,—
a rich and devoted nature. The duty lying nearest
her was always done, fully. Perhaps China and the
isles of the sea were left out of that circumference;
but her family, her friends, her neighbors, were in
no case neglected. She "stood in her lot" to the
end of her days. If we all did as much, would the
days of millennial peace tarry so long?

From her, Happy had a great lesson to learn : the
lesson of loving. Not after the elective fashion of
this world's love, which goes where it is attracted
only, and as often goes to destroy as to protect and
honor, but as God loves, — with pity, pardon, and
insight. Grandma Holden found something lovely
in every soul with which she came in contact: some
spark of the life that once came from the breath of
God, and which is so rarely all extinguished so long
as living lasts. Happy had been loved: loved as
few mothers even love their children. And her own
heart had gone out to her class-children, especially
to Ruth ; but she held herself aloof from most
people, because she did not like them. That this
was not right had never crossed her mind ; she did

not enjoy it in other people's manner towards her,
but it seemed inevitable in herself.   It was a study
and a revelation to her to watch Grandma Holden's
friendly manner to everybody.   To see how she
found something in each to love, to admire, or to
respect; yet not for want of discrimination into
character.   Her eyes were keen to observe and dis-
cern; but she had that charity which "hopeth all
things and endureth all things," "suffereth long and
is kind," "thinketh no evil," and "seeketh not its
own."   This last type of heavenly love was especially
Madam Holden's own; having no self-consciousness
to be jarred or wounded by the neglect or unkind-
ness of the world about her, she never perceived
that it was unkind or neglectful; and having the
largest hope and charity for everybody else, she was
so deeply humble, so sensible of her own shortcom-
ings, that Mr. Payson had said of her: "Madam
Holden sees everybody's goodness but her own, and
loves everybody but herself."

It is true that she loved Ruth more now than any
other creature; but in tenderest feeling for our
human nature it is recorded of one disciple that he
was him "whom Jesus loved;" and after that shall
the peculiar tenderness of one heart for another be
blamed as sin?   In this matter she soon found quick
sympathy with Happy, and unconsciously they
worked together for the child's good.   Mr. Holden

did not cross the path of any of his servants often.
He was a cold, stern man in manner: if he had
a heart, it was kept for one or two. So the winter
went on less miserably than Happy had feared; she
learned what her work was in the house, and did it
faithfully; but she had one embarrassment. Fred
Park had found out where she lived, and had called
to see her. Happy had no place to receive him,
and no wish to have visitors there, she knew it
would not please Mrs. Holden, nor did she want to
take the two or three friends she had into the kitch-
en, where Ann and Katy abided. It was unpleasant
to have to tell the young man that she could not see
company, but it had to be done; and it seemed a new
and painful element in her present position that she
must give up her friends' society entirely, except
as she saw Miss Lavinia every Sunday. But Fred
Park found this out very soon; he joined her always after her little class was over, and walked with
her down to Aunt Vinny's; and that sharp-eyed
spinster began to look at him over her spectacles,
and resolved to find out all about him before she
would ask him in to tea.

Happy was young, innocent, almost friendless; it
is not strange that she soon found a shy pleasure in
this first attention she had ever received; that she
learned to expect him with more pleasure than she
was conscious of, or that it made her restless and

troubled to think she had no place in which to show
him in return some friendliness and hospitality.

Her afternoon class had increased during the
winter; there were eight of them now, and Jack
and Nan, by right of first-comers, felt a certain responsibility for their own behavior as examples, that
did them a deal of good: they grew so quiet, so
helpful, so affectionate, that Happy " thanked God
and took courage " in regard to them daily.   Of her
other class less was to be said: Mary Gray, being in
deep earnest, had gone on in the Christian life so
far that she was anxious now to become a member
of the visible church ; her mother was móved to her
very soul by the child's experience, which she well
knew was not the result of her own teaching or
example.   It was not to her that Mary had come for
help or sympathy, but to that poor lame servant-girl
who was teacher of her class.

With all her faults, Mrs. Gray was an honest
woman.   She had never lived as she should have
lived since the first year she had professed religion;
her faith had become feeble and her works few.
Mr. Payson's simple and direct preaching had made
her uneasy often ; gradually the frost was coming
out of this fallow field, and the sod being broken to
admit the sun's rays.   Mary observed an unusual
softness and gentleness in her mother's manner ; and
when she told her of her purpose to join the church,

she was astonished, and even agitated, to have her
mother kiss her, and feel the warm tears on her face.
Mrs. Gray would have liked to go forward with Mary
and renew her own vows; she did renew them in her
heart; and when she saw Happy's sweet moved face
bent on Mary as she approached the altar, Mrs. Gray
felt for the first time how much she had done for
her child which should have been her own work,
and resolved to be a better mother. Happy had
done more than she knew. Julia and Helen looked
on also. Whatever their thoughts were, they did
not at once show; that they were not the same
thoughts was certain from the difference in the two
characters. Ruth, too, did not see without emotion
this companion come forward to profess her faith:
she did not say much about it to Happy; but her
wistful face on which the color came and went, as
she looked on, said a great deal.

It was spring now, and Mrs. Holden was always
better in spring, and therefore less petulant and exacting; so that, in one respect, life became easier
than usual to Happy, though she had more real
work to do in the needful preparations for summer,
which involved much sewing, altering, and repairing. But this she did not mind; her heart and
head were filled with a delight daily growing dearer,
she was fast becoming deeply attached to Fred
Park. He had been so kind to her, so careful of

her all winter. But for him she would have fallen
often on the icy streets, — for, lame as she was, she
missed her mother's helpful arm in the evening ;
and when Fred found out she went punctually to
evening meeting on Thursday, he always waited for
her at Mrs. Holden's gate, and came home with her
after service. Now that spring was here, many
bunches of wild flowers found their way to her,
and were carefully treasured, in a mug that had
been hers since she could remember, on her window-
sill ; and one beautiful day in June she really went
to drive outside of the village, for the first time in
her life. She had asked leave of absence for the
afternoon, as Mrs. Holden was to go away for the
day and night with Ruth, and Fred Park was
waiting for her at the garden gate. In all her life
Happy never forgot that day ; the beauty of the
hillsides fresh with the exquisite young verdure of
the season, the wayside flowers, the birds, the
fragrant air, made the hours seem like paradise, as
sweet and as brief ; and to be with a companion
who watched her kindling face with undisguised
pleasure, tried to anticipate her wishes, shared or
seemed to share in her enjoyment, and cared for
her comfort in every way he knew, added very
much to the pleasure of the drive. Many a tired
and sated woman taking her daily drive in ease
might have envied this poor lame servant-girl,

jogging along after one miserable horse in an old wagon. Elusive happiness! it is like the wind that bloweth where it listeth; it dances for some rejoicing hearts in even a purple spire of grass, lives in a child's laugh, smiles in a tranquil pool of water, sparkles in the stars, or laughs in a dandelion; fairy sprite, escaping the eager touch that woos it, alighting where it is scarcely known by name, falling on just and unjust, never snared by human devices, never fettered to time or circumstance; gone while scarce tasted; and oftenest like a rainbow glittering on falling tears! How much better is peace! calm, divine, immortal, looking unto God as the Rock that shadows in a weary land, making no haste and unafraid of terrors. This indeed passeth understanding; it is the atmosphere of heaven, the light of His face; but happiness is mortal sunshine, and endureth but a moment. That night while Happy was sitting in the moonlight in her room, wrapped in a sort of delightful, intangible dream, that glorified all things, and made the life she had so dreaded seem full of hope and promise, Ann and Katy came up to their room. They too had been out, Ann in the afternoon, Katy in the evening. They evidently thought Happy was asleep, for they lowered their voices; but she could not help hearing, and, the first thing, Ann arrested her attention.

"Sure, it's that Park feller. I know'd him in a minnit."

"Well, an' ain't it a pity?" responded kindly Katy. "The gurrl ain't knowin' to him no more'n she is to the Imperor of Rooshy."

"An' why should she? Did iver you see a more innosinter piece in the wurld than she is? The mother kep' her up like a cosset lamb."

"Surely! an' how would she know the firrst thing about a feller like him. I'm thinkin', I'll tell her somethin' maybee, Ann."

"An' it's the fool av the wurlld you'll be, Katy Doyle, av you do that; sure, why would you be interferin' betwixt two like that? Let 'em alone! She'll get insinsed some way: there's lot's knows him besides you an' me. You'd get a turn of her tongue av you said a word, for all she's so dacent."

They said no more, but Happy sat there stunned. What were they talking about? Fred Park? She was indignant. What could these Irish girls know about him? He was good, too good for them to understand. Who else had ever been so kind to her? She reasoned herself into quiet,—if it could be called reasoning where all the arguments were on one side, and the conclusion foregone.

It did not occur to her till the next morning that she had forgotten to read her Bible or say her prayers, and this for the first time for years. Poor

Happy! She was absorbed in a dream that only visits such as her. Youth, innocence, inexperience, all cherished and fostered the vision, and the will was bribed to let her sleep. She went about her daily duties in an abstracted way, so different from the quiet but thorough attention she had hitherto given them, that both Mrs. Holden and Ruth noticed it; one sharply, the other shyly, — but to remonstrance or question she gave no answer except a timid excuse; the blush that flooded her pale dark face spoke for her.

"What are you about, Happy?" said Mrs. Holden angrily, one day. "Those chairs are all set crooked, and you did not put away my shawls last night, or bring up the collars this morning. You are getting too careless to endure. Have you been falling in love, or what is the matter with you?"

Happy looked at her aghast. She felt insulted; hot tears filled her eyes, and her face grew scarlet. Just in time she remembered herself, and mentally asked help to be quiet and respectful; but Mrs. Holden had turned away to speak from the window to her husband, and Happy escaped with the shawls she was folding to put in a camphor chest up stairs. She felt as if a gulf had opened before her. Her unconsciousness was gone. She could not go on dreaming now; for in her hitherto secluded life her

ideas of love had been pure and shy, and now,—
could it be true? — she had let her heart go away
from her without the asking. She was ashamed,
but yet thrilled with new happiness; and no friend
to help or sympathize with her, no mother to
comfort her; she bent her head on her hands and
in a few hurried words asked God to help her and .
bless her — and him. An honest prayer, both
heard and answered; but not as she would have
had it did the answer come, but in His way and
time.

Ruth looked at her shyly and tenderly often. At
last she said, " Are you ill, Happy ? " " No," was
all the answer, except a smile that was both sad and
sweet, and Ruth asked no more questions; a native
perception and delicacy withheld her, but she could
not refrain from many a wistful look at Happy's
changing face.

It was reserved for Aunt Lavinia, with her keen
tongue and unsparing solicitude for Happy's good,
to open the girl's eyes, and show her in what a path
she was treading. For Miss Vinny had a deal of
the Areopagite spirit, and spent much of her time
" either to tell or to hear some new thing ; " and
what she succinctly termed Happy's " proceedings "
had come to her ears in the exchange of gossip
about the little town, and grieved her much; for

she was old and astute, and knew all about Fred
Park and his habits, and had no faith at all in his
temporary reformation. In fact, this world-wise
spinster found nothing so hard to believe in as any
reform: it was a page in her record both worn and
blotted.

CHAPTER XIX.

THE next Sunday, when Happy came to her little class she found a great bunch of wild honeysuckles waiting for her.

"Say!" shouted Jack. "Fred Park said I must fetch them to ye, Miss Happy; them's pinxter bloomies."

"They are very, very pretty," said Happy, stepping into the next room to lay aside her bonnet and speak to Mrs. Packard. Jack waylaid her as she came out, his queer freckled face and sparkling eyes alight with sly mischief.

"Say,—ain't he gettin' sweet on you, ain't Fred? I bet he is."

"Jack!" said Happy, coloring violently, "don't talk in that way; it is not right or proper. I cannot have it."

"Fac'! for all that," rejoined the irrepressible boy.

Happy wisely said no more, but began the lesson at once. She was disturbed very much lately by the discovery that other people knew and talked about her intimacy with Fred Park. It had been a pleasure of her own, so dear, so unacknowledged, that she did not once think it was seen and commented on ; and she felt uneasy that the tone of these comments was not altogether respectful to him, but rather pitiful of her. When school was over, she gathered up her flowers to go, saying quietly to Jack : " Tell Mr. Park I am much obliged to him."

" Well, he was a comin' to fetch 'em hisself," answered the unabashed Jack, " but he had a reg'lar high a Sat'day night ; I see him when he come up stairs ; can't fool me sayin' he's sick abed to-day. Sho ! I guess I know ! seen dad too many times ! "

Happy did not say anything. She turned away sick at heart, and slowly went over to Miss Vinny's.

" Well, if you haint got a bow-pot now ! " exclaimed the old lady, as her guest came in with the sheaf of glowing roseate blooms in her hand. "Don't lay 'em down, Happy, they're dreadful sticky ; wait till I fetch a jar for 'em," — and she brought out of the cupboard an old blue china vase, in which the soft, deep pink blossoms shone resplendent.

" Han'some, ain't they ! "

Miss Lavinia's one passion now was for flowers. Her little yard was gay with them all the year ; not merely the commonest, but beds of brilliant tulips,

clumps of June lilies, scarlet amaryllis, the great
flaming cup of the perennial poppy, deep pansies,
spicy carnations, rare roses, rank geraniums ; all the
result of her skill and care, — for the least slip
budded, bloomed, and grew to greatness under her
deft handling. She surveyed these wild flowers
with the sidelong look of a bird, her head on one
side and her face beaming. But suddenly she
looked round at Happy.

"Why! what on earth ails ye, child ?" she exclaimed. "You're whiter than chalk. Ain't you
a doin' too much this weather, Happy ?"

"Oh no, Aunt Vinny ; the weather is good, I'm
sure. I don't feel very well," — and Happy burst
into tears.

"Well, I am beat now! Come along into the
parlor, child, and lay down on the sofy; you're
overdone, and you'll feel better when you've rested
a spell. I guess we won't go to meetin' to-night;
you can lay here on the sofy, an' I'll set in the
winder and smell the flowers. That honeysuckle's
bu'stin' full of blows, and the dew fetches the smell
out." So Happy lay still till tea was ready, her
sore heart aching beyond the power of sweet odors
or the tranquil summer twilight to soothe. But
after tea, when Miss Vinny was safely established
in the high-backed chair, she overthrew Happy's
brief equanimity directly.

"You hain't told me yet where you got them wild blows?"

"Somebody sent them to me," Happy managed to say.

"H'm! somebody's nobody! Well, I ain't given to ondoo cur'osity, but I guess you've gin' me an openin' to say somethin', Happy, thet I've ben hankerin' to say quite a while. I expect I know who giv'.ye them flowers; and I don't suppose you know a thing about the feller, no more'n a baby."

"I do, Aunt Vinny," sobbed the girl. "I heard something to-day by accident."

"Well, I'm glad you hev. I hated awfully to break it to you, so to speak, seemin'ly; I reckon he's ben courtin' on ye quite a spell."

"Oh, no, auntie! he never said a word; he's only been so kind."

"Kind! oh land! dredful kind, them sort is! kind to themselves. He ain't nobody for you to go with, Happy. I've heered consider'ble talk about it lately, an' I made up my mind to open your eyes pretty quick. Why, he's got turned up where he was a workin' more'n ten times, 'cause he got drunk as a fool!"

Expressive phrase, "drunk as a fool!" Did any one ever know of a wise man who got drunk? it is fools only who deliberately degrade themselves. They may be intellectual, kind-hearted, affectionate, but over all is folly of the worst and weakest kind.

Happy shuddered at the idea. She did not know before how she loved this man, how deeply his kindness had entered her heart. Miss Greene laid down her spectacles, and looked at her pitifully, solemnly.

" Happy, I'd rather, a sight, see you lie on that sofa stone-dead, than to see you a drunkard's wife ; and if your mother could speak out of her grave she'd tell you so herself. You ain't no way strong nor healthy anyway : and I should hate to have you marry the best man that ever was, and git broke down with care and trouble ; it's bad enough to be sick by yourself without havin' a husband and children to look after, and like enough, more'n probable, a sickly set o' them, too ; but there ain't nothin' like marryin' a drunkard. I haint never told ye, Happy, but seems as though I'd ought to, now or never ; your father drinkt himself to death, after starvin' his wife and babies clean to death, some of 'em ; Almiry didn't but jest live, and there's three little graves in Bassett beside his that tell the story."

" Your father was a real smart man, Happy, a likely man, well appearing, and as tonguey! I've heered folks say Lawyer Dodd could make a jury b'lieve black was white ef he set out to; but he hadn't sense enough to quit drinkin'. Folks won-

dered Almiry darst to marry him, but, mercy to
me! she wan't but eighteen, and she never knowed
but what he was clear perfection till after they was
married. I tell ye, men folks is awful cute about
that; when they're courtin', the words of their
mouth is smoother'n butter, as the Bible says, but
in their heart is war ; quick as ever they've got their
way, the butter melts, I tell ye! Well, you didn't
never know your father ; thanks be to praise, he
died when you was four weeks old. ' Ta'n't jest
nateral or scripteral to be thankful when a man's
dead, because you might think he'd live to repent,
mebbe ; but I guess the Lord spares 'em jest as long
as there's any hope o' that, and he knows best
anyway."

"Did you ever see my father, Aunt Vinny?"
asked Happy.

"Yes, I see him once, jest before he and Almiry
was married ; he come to Canterbury, and Delye
Lamb, she come in, too, in the stage that day ; she
and me was mates to school, so I was expectin' her,
and when the stage come in, I see this spry young
fellow a settin' up with the driver, and he nodded
to Delye, and sez I, ' Who is he?' and sez she,
' That's Lawyer Dodd, that's a goin' to marry our
minister's daughter.' He was real good lookin'.
But there 'tis, you see, Happy ; he'd begun it then ;
fust thing he run into the tavern and called for

brandy ; we was waitin' in the parlor for Delye's
cousin, who got belated somehow.   His looks, nor
his learnin', nor his gifts didn't save him, and he
dragged her down to the edge with him afore he
had to let go.   Why, Happilony, she'd rise out o'
the grave, if she could, to save you from marryin' a
drinkin' man."

Happy felt the weight of a dreadful conviction
settling round her heart; she was crushed every
way , one way involved a life-long sorrow, the other
an equally enduring trouble that might be shared
by her friends, if no more ; she shrank from facing
either alternative.

"O, Aunt Vinny !" she said after a moment's
silence, "don't you think there is any hope for
such people ? can't they be cured ? "

"I don't calculate to limit the Lord's mercy,
Happy.   Saul was an awful cretur when he was
struck down by grace.   But I don't want *you* to be
tryin' your hand at reformin' a young fellow like
that.   You'd die a doin' of it, ef you made out ;
and there ain't any man thinks a heap of a woman
who'll marry him to convert him.   'Tain't but a
chance, and you resk your life on it, ef nothing
more.   You hain't no right to gamble with yourself
that way.   I s'pose the Lord can turn a drunkard
from his cups, but I don't think a girl can.   If it's
cuttin' off the right hand or puttin' out the right

eye, Happy, hear to me, and do it! If it's gone so
fur as that with you, it'll come dredful hard. I've
ben there myself, now, to own it; and I know it's
the heaviest kind of a cross, and it seems as if you
couldn't never carry it; but the Lord'll help, bless
the Lord! I'm a livin' woman this day, beholden
to nobody; nobody blamin' of me for bringin' 'em
into a world of sin and pain and shame; nobody to
molest me nor make me afraid; a clear conscience
and a home o' my own, — and he died in the poor-
house years back, — died of the tremens. I tell
you it was hard in the time on't, cruel as the grave,
Happy; but I sought for strength, and got it, and
there's plenty to-day where that come from."

Miss Vinny's eyes shone through tears. Her
poor old head shook harder than ever; her wrinkled
cheek glowed with a spot of wintry red; and her
voice had no uncertain sound, but rang like a call
to battle in Happy's ears. Would she too conquer?
Her heart sank; but Miss Vinny went on.

" Mind ye, I ain't sayin' a word against marriage:
it's ordained of the Lord, when things are all right;
but them that goes against their light ain't ordained
I expect. I know there's married-folks a heap happier than I be; but then I dono for certain that the
main end of living is to be happy. The catechism
don't put it so, nor the Bible neither. Happiness
comes in jest as the blossoms do,—sort of consolin',

you know ; but the reel thing is doin' your duty,
and when that's done, why, there's solid comfort;
and this world don't end it."

Happy was much moved by this confidence of
Miss Lavinia's ; it is a great encouragement to know
that others have tried the depths of pain and loss
before us, and come up out of them alive and whole.
It is in this that the power of Christ's life lies; that
he did not come as king and conqueror, but as one
who endured all the trials of our own existence, —
for the poor he tasted poverty , for the tempted,
trial ; for the forsaken, desertion in his sore need, the
desertion of his dearest friends ; for the dying, the
very bitterest bitterness of death ! There is no
pang of ours he has not known, from the sorrows
of childhood to the last agonies of violent death ;
no grief he cannot feel with us ; no anguish he does
not understand and pity. His sympathy is the
sympathy of experience, the experience of humanity ; but his love and help are all divine, all power-
ful. Wonderful union of heart and hand ! mighty
provision of God for man ; truly Immanuel, God
with us ; and who can be against us ?

But who is sufficient for these things ! If they
were our daily thought and hope, life would lose its
terrors and death smile. As it is, let us all pray, —
" Lord, increase our faith." Happy had need to
use this petition now, for her heart failed her. She

could only give Miss Vinny mute tokens of her
gratitude ; and when the time came she went home
without a word, and left the honeysuckles behind
her. Miss Lavinia did not remind her of them.

There were a few things to do after she reached
home; Mrs. Holden's pitcher of ice-water and plate
of biscuits to prepare, and her room to arrange for
the night: and Ruth's hair to be brushed and
braided. She went through this mechanically;
though Ruth, seeing how heavy her eyes were, and
how listless her motions, asked if she were ill.
Happy said yes, because she had no explanation to
offer, and she did indeed feel sick unto death ; but
it was heart-sickness.

There was little sleep for her that night. She
pined as never before for her mother's face, her
voice, her tender arm. Many times she fell on her
knees by the bedside, and with burning tears
prayed for help to do right. Prayed, as she
thought, for strength to make her own life miserable forever; to break her own heart, — and that
heart itself rebelled against the prayer. It was
daylight before she fell into troubled sleep.

CHAPTER XX.

HAPPY had plenty of work to do the next day, and it proved a blessing, as work always does to the troubled; but still a heavy cloud hung over her. She did not doubt her duty, it was plain before her face; the way in which she should walk was hard, steep, toilsome, lonely, but it was unmistakable, and though flesh and heart failed, she knew she must pursue that path. She had tried in her weakness and distress to see how she might evade it, but her upright conscience baffled every such attempt; she had prayed then for strength, and God had given her that certainty of duty which is in itself strength. The temptation that conquers us is that which blinds us first, which assails our reason with potent but specious arguments, to which we listen because we do not see the face of the tempter, and have no will to refute his reasoning; but Miss Lavinia had done Happy good service, her eyes were opened. Now she only longed to have it over. It is so hard for women to wait, either for good or evil, and

Happy was a timid woman. She did not know when she should see Fred Park again: she both dreaded and desired to see him, and she could not expect to do so till Thursday ; on that day he generally waited for her after the evening lecture ; she thought he went too, but now this little delusion vanished. The week seemed very long, and she was sad and quiet as never before ; but her dream was over. She attended to her duties with punctual alacrity, forgot nothing, neglected nothing. Mrs. Holden had no fault to find, for as long as she was served well, it mattered little to her whether her servants were ill or well; she liked a placid, pleasant face about her, but, if everything else was right, she did not care much about Happy's sad eyes and pale cheeks ; and she could not help herself here ; no order of hers would restore the sparkle and color to that pallid, quiet countenance. Ruth noticed it, and was kind in a thousand little ways, every one of which went to Happy's grateful heart, for she was grateful ; that rarest of human traits was both native and educated within her. Whoever did anything for Happy never was forgotten ; a kind word, a gentle look even, won a place at once in her memory, and no bright flower, 'beautiful sunset, or unusual pleasure failed to lift up her heart thankfully to God who " giveth us all things richly to enjoy." Rare virtue ! it is not of this world! Here we may spend strength, time, health, life itself, in the service of those we love, and be dismissed and forgotten like a lame horse or a worn-out garment at the first caprice ; the promises and vows of affection and interest all swept away, the ties of years snapped, the services that wasted our souls and bodies are all set aside, and we sent out with quivering, aching, bleeding hearts to find our way in the wilderness alone. But thank God ! this is not the fashion of his children. Gratitude is a Christian grace alone ; the ties of blood, the assurances of friendship, the vows of love, may — do — all fail us, but the brotherhood of God's family is true, unfailing, eternal. Madam Holden, too, perceived that something was very wrong with Happy, and in her gentle way tried to help her ; but she was too well-bred to intrude herself even upon a servant's confidence. Instinctively she felt that the girl was in some strait that she must pass alone ; but in her daily prayers Happy was earnestly remembered ; and the gentle tenderness, unusual in its open demonstration, of every look and tone, showed such sympathy and consideration that it descended like the dew on that feverish, throbbing sorrow.

But Happy was not to escape without further distress. Mrs. Payson sent for her, when the dreaded Thursday evening came, to stop there on

her way to the chapel. She had heard these rumors
about Fred Park and his attentions at sewing-society
the afternoon before ; for this town, like all others,
had such an institution attached to each of its
churches, and the strife of tongues was equal to the
toil of fingers whenever they met. This occasion
served as substitute for a local paper, for here the
events of the day were not only recorded, but commented on, and marginal notes added both to record
and commentary, till the tiniest fact rustled and
strutted in such elaborate garments as scarce to be
recognized. Mrs. Payson had heard there, to her
great trouble and amazement, that Happy was going
to marry a man who was a hopeless drunkard of
the lowest description, — not only poor, but always
on the brink of delirium tremens, and whose only
recommendation seemed to be that he could not
live long in such a reckless course of dissipation.
She trembled for Happy, and, feeling in some sort
responsible for her, sent at once for her to come to
the parsonage. Mr. Payson was out of town, or
she would have devolved this unpleasant office on
him ; and in doing so would have discovered the
true state of the case. Fred Park was, in fact, an
able workman, and could always command a good
place and fair wages as long as he was sober ; but
he inherited a taste for alcohol. His father was a
drunkard before him, and the dreadful heritage

of appetite had at times full possession of the son.
He had more than once lost his place for this reason,
and when he came to himself his repentance was
deep and bitter; but he had never learned that his
own strength was weakness, or found out the only
help that avails in such a trouble. When Happy
came in, she saw Mrs. Payson was disturbed; but
she was not prepared for the question that followed
her welcome, — an abrupt question enough, for
Mrs. Payson was not a person to evade or delay a
disagreeable necessity.

"Happy, are you going to be married?" she said.

"No, ma'am!" was her indignant rejoinder.

"Oh, I am so glad!" replied Mrs. Payson, as her
face brightened. "I heard you were engaged to
such a bad man, my dear, and I wanted to ask you
to consider the matter — to look at it thoroughly
before it was too late."

Happy said nothing; her face was crimson, and
the tears stood in her eyes. Mrs. Payson was not
quite satisfied.

"Do you know a young man by the name of
Park?" she went on.

"Yes, ma'am."

"And is he attentive to you, Happy?"

"He is very kind to me, Mrs. Payson."

The minister's wife sighed; what could she do?
There was a quiet dignity about the girl that

seemed to enforce silence, yet she could not let her
go unwarned.

" Happy," she said gently, " I think you know I
want to be your friend, and I must warn you, however unpleasant it is to do it, that this young man
is not a fit associate for you ; not a proper man for
you to marry. Dear Happy, I hear he is a drunkard;
do beware ! "

Happy's momentary anger had passed away ; she
recognized the voice of real interest and affection.

" I do not mean to marry him, Mrs. Payson ; he
has never asked me ; I hope he never will. And I
know about him too."

The tears ran over now, and Mrs. Payson was so
moved she put her arms about Happy as her mother
might have done, kissed her, and stroked her shining hair. Happy never forgot that comforting
caress ; she had liked Mrs. Payson before, she loved
her now.

" Faithful are the wounds of a friend," were the
words that came into her heart ; though she did not
speak them. She only said, very shyly :

" I expect to see him to-night; I shall try to say
something to him. I must tell him what I know ;
but I don't know how to say it."

She gave a look to Mrs. Payson that said far more
than her words ; it told of an unspoken dread and
anguish that made her friend's heart ache. " Take

no thought how or what ye shall speak, for it shall
be given you in that hour what ye shall speak,"
rose involuntarily to Mrs. Payson's lips, and Happy
went away with the words ringing in her ears.

"I don't know," said Mrs. Payson afterward to
her husband, "whether I had any right to use so
solemn a text for such a purpose, but it seemed to
come to me."

"Why not, Eleanor? If the Bible is not good
for every day, it is good for nothing. Look at the
context; is it likely Happy will ever be called to
bear harder 'testimony' to her faith than this,
though it is not before 'rulers and governors?' I
believe we wrong the intention of our Father when
we do not use the living bread for daily bread.
The Bible was not made for the Sabbath any more
than man, but equally made for him. I believe
there is provision in it for our commonest needs, for
our hourly perplexities; that what are called 'common sense' and 'worldly wisdom' are to be drawn
from that treasury in as large a measure as the
spiritual teaching and divine promises it offers;
that the book of God is as profitable for the life
that now is as godliness. When your father and
mother wrote to you at school, were their letters
only about your studies and your future occupa-
tions? Did they not give you counsel about your
health and your manners, your dress, your com-

panions, your enjoyments? 'If ye, then, being
evil, know how to give good gifts unto your children, how much more shall your Father in
heaven?'"

Mrs. Payson sighed. "Oh, if one could only
remember it always, how much easier life would
be!"

"And how much better! We do not use our
very blessings. I am glad poor Happy was armed
with that promise, it must and will help her."

And it did. She met Fred Park as usual at the
gate, but to-night she did not take his arm; a little
omission, but in her a noticeable one, for her lameness always rendered help agreeable.

"Do let me help you!" he said, as she stumbled
now and then on the uneven walk.

"I would rather help you, Mr. Park," she answered in a low, firm voice, but so low that he did
not catch the meaning of the words and went on.

"Miss Happy! I wish you would let me help you
and take care of you always; you are the most like
my mother of any woman I ever saw. I think a lot
of my mother, but I like you better than anybody.
Will you be my wife?"

The moonlight shone full on Happy's face as she
turned it towards him, but it could scarce have
been paler in full day.

"No," she said, "please don't ask me. I wanted

to tell you to-night that I could not walk with you
any more. I did not know till Sunday that —
that — " Her voice faltered and broke here.

" That I wasn't good enough for you! O, Happy, I knew that long ago! But I want you all the
more to make me better. I love you because you
are so good, and I want help if ever a fellow did.
I want you to help me."

" I can't," said Happy, choking.

" You won't! you don't love me! why don't you
tell the truth ? " fiercely ejaculated the man. " If
you loved me, you would be glad to help and save
me."

" *I* cannot save you," said Happy.

" You can! you can! If I had a home and a
good sweet wife, do you think I'd ever touch a
drop again? A poor shiftless fellow like me must
go to the devil, of course. There's no help."

" Oh, don't! " said Happy, trembling. " Don't
talk like that. Don't you believe in God ? "

" I believe in you, anyway; you could make me
right over, Happy Dodd, and you'd try if you loved
me."

Happy turned round and looked into his face
with clear, sad eyes ; her voice did not falter, nor
her cheek flush ; truly it was given her in that hour
what she should say. " I do love you. I love you
more than anybody in the world, and it is dreadful

to think I ought to give you up, but I must do it.
I cannot do what is wrong to-day because it may be
good some time hereafter. I have only to-day to
be sure of. I must do right now if it breaks my
heart. I cannot marry you."

The steady, sorrowful voice, her great sad eyes,
the pure truth and principle of her words, that
came slowly, as if the chill lips were reluctant to
utter them, but obeyed a higher will than her own,
awed her hearer while they bitterly pained him.
They had just reached Mrs. Holden's garden gate,
for this talk had followed on a long silence after
they had left the chapel yard, and Happy refused
his arm. They both paused a moment. The fragrance of summer was around them, the silence of
night, and the flooding glory of a full moon. Fred
Park looked at the pale little girl who had dealt
him the hardest blow of his life; the unmistakable
agony written on her face assured him that she too
suffered, — suffered voluntarily and deeply, rather
than do wrong. He was young enough, and honest
enough to believe and respect her the more for her
own faith and honesty; he stooped down and kissed
her gently, — the first and last kiss of such love
that Happy ever felt upon her lips.

"Good-bye!" he said. "I believe you are good,
Happy, good as an angel, but you've been the end
of me."

It was an idle word, but it smote Happy to the heart. Had she done right? the terrible doubt flashed across her; she turned sick and faint; had she sold her life's happiness only to destroy this man? Again the word of God came to her rescue: "Let us do evil that good may come; whose damnation is just." The text roused her like a heavenly voice.

"No!" she said firmly. "It is not in my power to do that. God can help and save you, not a weak woman. If you want to be a good man, he is ready to make you one. Good-bye." And, entering in, she shut the gate between them, and shut him out, in more senses than one.

He went back to the place he lived in so disturbed and dismayed, that he fled at once to the old solace of the bottle; and while Happy was on her knees praying for him and for herself with streaming tears, he was drinking deeper and deeper the cup of shame and madness. She had cast her bread indeed on deep and stormy waters; would she ever find it again?

CHAPTER XXI.

A sort of sad peace now settled over Happy's life ;
it was the reward of painful duty fairly done.
There were many heavy hours to endure. She
knew the ordinary outlook of a girl's life was closed
for her, finally. She was one of those women who
can have but one love, though they may have many
and warm affections, and she instinctively felt that
she should never marry any one else. Not altogether
out of girlish romance did this idea take hold of
her : a few words Miss Vinny dropped had rankled
in her mind. She knew she had no right, as well as
no wish, to be a burden on any man's hands, and to
hand down her sad inheritance of delicacy and disease to another generation. It made it easy for her
to take this view of the subject because she could
not marry Fred Park. Had she been strong and
healthy, the idea would not have dwelt with her that
her life was ended here in one sense ; for many a
woman has married on no higher plane than sincere
affection and respect, and gone through life happily

enough, transferring to her children the devotion
that should have been her husband's, — and many
another woman has been shipwrecked by the same
experiment! But Happy had no temptation to try
it. She faced her duty in this case once for all, and,
having seen its force, turned to her work, resolved
to live from day to day by God's help, leaving to-
morrow in his hands who alone knoweth what a day
may bring forth. She never saw Fred Park again.
By the carouse of that Sunday night and its conse-
quent effects he lost his place at the foundry, and
went back to his home at Wilford. This was another
help to her. It would have been hard to meet him,
now and then, after what had passed. She heard
of his leaving through Jack, who seemed to feel
aggrieved at his own loss, and with his preternatural
sharpness laid it to Happy's account, and even hinted
at his conviction more than once.

But soon a new interest came into her life. Mrs.
Packard had a little girl born about the end of July,
and wishing Happy to name it, she called it Almira,
after her mother, — and her lonely heart warmed to
the little helpless creature from that moment. She
petted it at every odd time she could get away from
her work. She sewed for it, getting up by daylight
for that purpose. She watched its childish ailments
with motherly anxiety, and she prayed for it daily
with tender longing and hopeful faith. The soft

small fingers that grasped her own, the flickering
baby smile, the utter dependence, — all appealed to
her heart, and taught her many a lesson of her own
weakness and need of trust. "Except ye become
as little children" is a word that cannot be fully
understood but by those who have loved and cared
for a little child, and seen its change from feeble
silence into the full delight and utter faith of baby-
hood; who have watched its growth, beguiled its
sorrows, soothed its fears, clothed, fed, tended it,
hovered over its sick-bed, wept over its faults, and
loved it with an everlasting love, that neither time,
nor change, nor separation can weaken, — a love
that lives for and in the hope of a future life together,
and can bear all things in that prospect. This is the
love that interprets God the Father to our human
apprehension, that expounds his patient, gentle,
tender, and unfailing affection, and makes us cry
mightily for that new birth which shall create us
into his little children, and give us a right to such
overwhelming affection, such almighty care. Happy
had not the fear for her pet's future that had troubled
her for little Gay; for both Mr. and Mrs. Packard
had become church members, and were trying honestly to live the new life they had entered on. She
did not know how much her own example had done
for her friends. She had done what she could in
her own small sphere of usefulness, and the results

were widening beyond her own comprehension. Here already were two people whose first attention to religion she had aroused by her teachings to their child, and fixed by her words at that child's death-bed, and her faithful devotion to Christian duty, ever since, in her little school. It is one of the typical lessons God give us in our school-book of nature, — this increase of unconscious influence beyond thought or hope. For, look at the smallest pebble, a weary insect, a frosted leaf even, dropped on the pond's smooth surface, — how the rings, be they faint or strong, go circling outward, one on another, larger and larger, till they reach the very shore, and with tiny plash and recoil feed the thirsty roots of grass and blossoms in a wide circumference! Or, drop but one small drop of perfume in a room, how the particles separate almost infinitely, and go floating on their fragrant errand through the air, from door to door, until the house is "filled with the odor of the ointment." And we find a new and wonderful significance in the "golden vials full of odors, that are the prayers of saints."

But Happy's conscious work also had its increase. Her little class recruited its ranks again and again, till the place was too strait for them, and the labor too great to be thoroughly done. Aunt Lavinia had watched her through her great trial with deep and loving interest, though she had forborne speech on

the subject, — a self-denial most grateful to the girl,
who hardly comprehended what an effort it was to
her kind old friend. There were very few people
for whom she would have restrained her curiosity
and her comments so far. But she loved Happy
now better than any one else; for she too was almost
alone in the world, her few relatives so distant and
so far separated from her that Happy seemed nearer
and dearer than any of them. She saw now that
Happy's hands were over-full, and advised her to
look for a larger room, and find some one to help
her teach.

"Why don't you take one or two of them girls
out of your other class to help ye, child? It'll do
'em heaps of good, folks never half learn a thing
till they've taught it to somebody else."

Happy had not thought of this.

"I will, Aunt Vinny," she said; "there's Mary
will be glad to help me, and Julia. I shall not need
Helen."

"Nor they won't need her, neither; she's flightier
'n a lightnin' bug. I never see sech a little sperrit;
lace 'nd ribbins inside of her head where there 'd
ought to be brains; a clear skittermalink."

The last word was too much for Happy, she
laughed outright.

"What is that, Aunt Vinny? I never heard that
word before."

"Well, it's one o' my words. I dono but I've got
as good a right to make words as them that gets up
dictionaries. I know they couldn't find all them
words anywhere; they fill up out o' their heads.
Gracious! think of them big lexingtons, as he calls
'em, in the minister's book-case."

Happy laughed again.

"It's a good word anyhow, if it makes you laugh,"
went on Miss Vinny, looking over her spectacles.
"You don't laugh half enough, Happy. Don't you
know what Solomon says, — 'a merry heart doeth
good like a medicine?' I want to see ye spunk up
and be spry again. I guess the cold weather 'll
kinder brace you up, so to speak, as it were."

"I will ask the girls, Aunt Vinny; but what can
I do about a bigger room?"

"Jest you ask old Mis' Holden; I shouldn't wonder if she know'd some place you could hev. She's
lived here all her days, and knows 'most everybody;
they'd hear to her, certin; if there was a place to be
had, why, she'd have it a mile afore any other woman
in the town."

It was a piece of strategy on Miss Lavinia's part
to send Happy to Madam Holden; for she knew
very well that this lady had both the will and the
money to help forward in any good work, and would
be more than likely to hire a good room for this
growing mission-school, and pay the rent. She did

not know that Madam Holden was entirely unaware
of Happy's enterprise, or that the founding of a
school of this sort had long been a scheme in the old
lady's mind, only waiting for younger hands to be
able and willing to carry it out. She was at once
surprised and delighted to find this poor girl, out of
her own desire to work for her Master, with little
or no exterior help, had begun and carried on for
two or three years the work she had been planning
and waiting for so long. She readily promised to
find a room for them, and pledged herself to pay the
rent as long as the school should exist. It now remained to find the teachers. To Happy's surprise
Julia was eager to help her; but Mary hung back,
and was doubtful. She had thought it would be
the other way; but the truth was that Mary was so
conscientious and so distrustful of herself that she
feared her own power of teaching others was not
enough to warrant the attempt; while Julia, capable
and confident, had not learned humility as yet, or
the weakness of her own strength, and did not shrink
from an enterprise that looked so easy.

Mrs. Holden during the next week found a large,
light room in one of the tenements on Lake Street,
which she had cleaned, whitewashed, papered with
a cheerful paper, a few Scripture prints hung up
about it, some short benches brought in, and as it
was nearing winter, a little wood-stove put up, and

a large closet in the entry filled with wood. The keys to this closet and the room were both put into Jack's hands, and he was given charge of the apartment. This post of trust did him a great deal of good, his self-respect was aroused, and he determined to deserve so much confidence; there was always now a clean bright room ready for the classes, a sparkling fire in winter, a bunch of fresh wild flowers, and a pail of cool water, in summer. Jack had grown to be neat, handy, helpful, and affectionate under Happy's persistent teaching, and Nan also had much improved; the rest progressed more slowly, with the exception of Pauline Lagré. Her quick French nature made her swift to see and adopt whatever she liked: she too had learned to be neat and clean personally; but an inborn love of finery ruled her little bosom, and her attempts at dress were pitifully ludicrous at times. Mary's class was selected out of the girls, Julia took charge of the boys, while Happy kept the larger share of the older boys and girls both, and the school went on and prospered. Their own training in Sunday-school proved of much advantage to both Mary and Julia; they could follow Happy's simple, direct method of teaching with ease, and it became a habit with them to look over the afternoon lesson in their own class in the morning, and talk about all the points that were likely to come up with the children. This at last interested

Helen Sands; she begged to have "ever so little a class," too; and having given her charge of four children just learning to read, Happy was surprised to see with what tact and skill she managed the restless youngsters, and how patiently and pleasantly she taught them. She did not know that Helen was really at heart more attached to her than to any one out of her own family; what her father said was law and gospel to Nellie, and she added to her love for her teacher a respect that was borrowed from Dr. Sands' estimate of Happy. She never had forgotten what he said to her on that day when she hesitated about going to the class again because Happy was a servant: "I only hope you may live to be half as good as she is." This fired Helen's ambition: under all her levity and folly she had a good deal of affection and some sense, and all that was good in her, her teacher had gradually drawn out, as heat colors those sympathetic inks that were before invisible, and fills a blank space with valuable inscriptions. Her father noticed the change at home; he saw that his little girl was becoming more thoughtful, more loving, more unselfish, by slow degrees; and in his heart he thanked Happy; but never with his lips! Why do we not oftener say pleasant things to each other? We do not hesitate to find fault, to fret, to scold even, to let the law of *un*kindness rule our lips but how often we shut them on the tender

word, the well-earned praise, the hearty commendation, the real gratitude we feel! It is not so with
Him who should be our example. " Well done,
good and faithful servant! " is his language ; and
this reward is set before us in his word. " If
there be any virtue, if there be any praise, — think
on these things." " Whatsoever is lovely, and of
good report."

I remember well the saying of a little child whose
unconscious wisdom taught me much while I was
with her. Her father found fault with her once,
as was his custom, — for he was one of those who
are more apt to criticise than to commend.

" Papa! " said the little thing, looking up at him
with soulful eyes. " Why does you always find
fault wiz me, and nebber, nebber says I am a dood
dirl, even when I is dood ? "

It was a hard question to answer, and it betrayed
a hard experience for a child. Why do we not all
sweeten the lives of those about us with kindly
words, since by words we shall be justified or
condemned ?

But Happy had learned this lesson out of her
own need ; her unselfish spirit ministered to others
that for which she had pined herself, and Helen fed
like an air-plant on her earnest commendation and
her approving smiles. The winter Happy had so
dreaded passed peacefully and pleasantly, to her

surprise and gratitude ; her darkness was lightened
by the light of heaven, and she said in her heart,
looking back, the words of her favorite hymn :

> "Ye fearful saints, fresh courage take,
> The clouds ye so much dread
> Are big with mercy, and shall break
> In blessings on your head."

CHAPTER XXII.

As the winter went on, Mrs. Holden seemed not quite as well. She was less exacting, but more helpless, and Happy was never so necessary to her as now ; she would gladly have taken her from her Sunday work, but for the fear that she would leave her. Her dependence roused all Happy's generous and kindly feeling ; she turned from her own trouble to help another's need, and so helped herself. It is to the selfish soul grief becomes a hopeless burden, not to those who aid and sympathize with their fellow-sufferers and so forget themselves. Toward spring the feebleness rather increased, for the weather was unusually damp and cold, and though the leaves came in their season they seemed to appear reluctantly and sparsely, and the few flowers shivered in the bitter east winds that prevailed. Mrs. Holden suffered from rheumatism now, the result of debility and the damper weather, and the doctor ordered her removal to a room up-stairs that might be drier. Happy's lameness made it hard for

her to go up and down, and, for fear she should be
useless to her, Mrs. Holden had every convenience
for her service brought to the second floor that was
possible. Beside she began to feel a certain affection for her faithful, patient attendant, that it was
difficult to withhold; for the coldest nature will at
last warm to constant, tender service, and Happy
pitied Mrs. Holden from her very heart. As summer came on, still damp, though warmer, the invalid evidently continued to sink; an insidious
disease had fastened on her that the best medical
care and the most intelligent nursing could only
alleviate and delay; there was much lifting to do at
times, and at length a professional nurse was called
in to help. Mrs. Holden did not like this, she preferred to have Happy, and only yielded in the fear
of losing her altogether, for she was growing tired
and pale. Now Dr. Sands ordered her out of doors
daily, and she did the errands, or walked in the
garden an hour every morning. At these times she
saw more of Ruth, who was not allowed to be
much in her mother's room, and who began to feel
from the coming of the nurse, that this illness was
more serious than the long invalidism which she
was used to, and which had never alarmed her.
She went to Happy for comfort and hope; comfort
she found, but hope was not in the honest answers
that met her questioning, and her heart began to

ache in the daily darkening of the prospect before
her, — a prospect which seemed to have no bright
vista beyond the clouds, for Ruth knew well that
her mother had not even professed to be religious.
Her father was a member of the visible church,
what Miss Lavinia called a " Sunday Christian ; "
and though Ruth loved him dearly, his influence
on her was not toward better things. He wore the
name of Christ in vain as far as his life or words
went ; selfish, hard, arrogant, and dogmatic, he was
a man whom no one out of his own household
loved, and few in it. Whatever softness of heart
he had was kept for Ruth and his wife ; the world
at large shrank from contact with him, and in the
church he was a cipher, except for punctual attendance. Madam Holden and Happy were the
only two actual Christians with whom Ruth had
come in contact, and they preached her a continual
sermon ; but even they could not comfort her now.

" O Happy ! " she said, " I cannot, cannot bear to
have mamma die! What shall I do ? Oh! what
shall I do ? "

" Dear Ruth, you cannot do anything to help her
now," said Happy, very tenderly. " All you can
do for yourself is to ask God to help you bear the
great trouble."

Ruth turned sadly away ; her usual reserve and
pride had for a moment given way under the heavy

pressure of impending loss; but Happy's words sealed her lips. She did not like to be talked to — "preached at," as she phrased it; she would shut her grief in her own heart, and endure it. Mrs. Holden could not, by the end of June, be left at night without watchers; weak, pained, weary, she needed many things in the hot, sleepless hours, and Happy's patience was unfailing. From her heart she pitied this delicate, suffering woman, who was going down to her grave hopeless and careless of what lay beyond it; and she sent up many a fervent prayer for the soul that was gradually losing its temporal habitation, but had made no provision for that which is eternal. Mrs. Holden watched her more closely than she knew; she liked to look at the pale, calm face, bent over the Bible that was her close companion, — a sad face enough at times, but sure to brighten as she read, though often the reading paused while she bent her head on her hand; tired, as her observer thought, of reading; in fact, giving thanks for the " unspeakable gift," or asking earnestly that it might be given to her who was only a looker-on. Toward the end of the summer Happy received a heavy blow; she learned through Miss Vinny, that Fred Park had been intoxicated deeply on the night she last saw him, and that for this reason he lost his place in the foundry. She felt, in the first bitterness of this news, that this

was the result of her refusing him, that he had
indeed been right when he said she had finished his
life, and she could not bear the thought. All this
sacrifice had been in vain then ; the offering was not
accepted, the mighty effort was useless, she had
only shipwrecked him, and spoiled her own future.
A sort of hopeless darkness fell over her, and she
was ready almost to despair. Aunt Vinny saw the
effect her tale produced in Happy's death-white
cheek, and the speechless agony in her eyes ; and,
with her own quick intuition sharpened by experience of a like grief, she divined at once how things
stood, though Happy had never told her anything
about her walk from chapel, or their final parting.

"Now don't you think I told ye right, Happy ? "
she said, knowing very well that condolence was
not the right thing now ; " he wasn't no feller for
you to marry. A man that'll take comfort in drink
is a poor cretur any way, and it didn't show no
great hold of yourn on him that he'd go and hev a
spree right off, afore you took him to do about his
ways an' customs."

" O Aunt Vinny ! who told you ? " exclaimed the
astonished girl.

" Nobody told me, but I can see through a mill-
stone, old as I be, specially ef there's a hole in the
middle on't, as there gener'ly is. It don't take no
great powers o' mind to put two an' two together,

Happy. I know'd your trouble, poor child, and I felt for ye ; but there ain't no use talkin' about them sort of things. Let sleepin' dogs lie, I say ; if you rouse 'em up they bark and bite worse'n Dr. Wattses in the hymn-book."

" Auntie ! sometimes I think I was all wrong and selfish about — that person ; perhaps I might have helped him to be a better man."

" Now don't you believe no such nonsense ; a man that can't restrain himself before he's married, ain't a goin' to do it afterward. I tell ye, they'll do more'n forty times as much for a girl as they will for their wife, any day. I know 'em ! Men folks are curus ; the Bible says their hearts is deceitful and desper'tely wicked, and Scripter don't lie. You hear to me, Happy ; if you'd married that Park feller, you'd have been a drunkard's wife to the end of the chapter, and a short chapter too ! "

Nevertheless, though her mind accepted Miss Lavinia's opinion, Happy's heart was heavy still, with pain and anxiety for the man she loved so much ; her face was very sad that night as Mrs. Holden watched it, but she also saw it brighten under the unfailing sunshine of her Bible. As Happy came to the bedside to give Mrs. Holden some water, the invalid said in her weak voice, " What are you reading, Happy ? "

" The Bible, ma'am."

"Do you like to read that, really?"

"I love it!" the girl answered with hearty emphasis.

"Read a little to me: I've almost forgotten how it sounds; and I am so tired of lying awake aching."

Happy's voice thrilled with emotion as she repeated, rather than read, the chapter of consolation that is the very voice of heaven to suffering and fear.

"Let not your heart be troubled: ye believe in God, believe also in me." She read on very slowly and distinctly to the fifteenth verse; there she paused. Mrs. Holden did not ask her to go on; and Happy, thinking she was asleep, went back softly to the lamp, where she bowed her head on her precious Bible, and prayed as never before for that dying soul.

But Mrs. Holden did not sleep. The words she had heard were going over and over in her mind, especially that wonderful tender reproach: "Have I been so long with thee, Philip, and yet hast thou not known me?" The question seemed pointed at her. So long! so long! so many years since, as a little child, her mother had read to her from the Bible, and taught her the prayers all forgotten now. The early orphanage, her life afterwards with gay, careless people; her marriage to a man who cared for none of these things except to pro-

fess them, — all these had overlain the teachings
of her dear mother : but the quickening word recalled those teachings to life. Her mind was weak
with the exhaustion and pain of her body, and she
received ideas as a child does, simply and without
question.

Night after night now she asked Happy to read
to her ; she could bear only a little at a time, but on
that little she fed and rested as the starving on a
morsel of food. She said nothing to any one of a
new interest or an awakened hope ; but she clung
to those nightly readings, and when it was not
Happy's turn to watch with her, she always wanted
her "verses" before the nurse came in for the
night ; and more than once in her half-sleep, broken
by pain and fever, Happy heard whispered words
of childlike prayer, Bible words of comfort and
hope, the language of penitence and trembling faith
in Christ, drop in feeble whispers from the pale
lips. And when at last they gathered all about her
death-bed, though she scarce seemed to know the
kindred faces, or to feel a pang of parting grief,
they all heard the whisper, almost with her dying
breath: "I am the way." . . . "Be merciful to me
a sinner." . . . "Who died for us." . . . "Lord,
remember me ! "

This last prayer left a smile on her cold lips
that dwelt there after He had indeed remembered

her, and taken the weary spirit into his kingdom.

"God bless you, Happy!" said Madam Holden,
the next day, as the two stood together beside the
pallid shape, now resting in hope. "I knew some
one must have helped her. I had not courage.
You have done the good work, and done it faithfully."

"Oh no, Mrs. Holden! I only read to her. I too
did not dare to speak. It is the Lord's doing."

"And marvellous in our eyes, Happy. But you
did all you could, and the result is precious. I hope
the living will live to know and thank you as I do."

Happy looked at the peaceful dead with awe and
gratitude. A few late flowers had been laid on her
bosom by Ruth, but they were no quieter or
sweeter in their loveliness than the beautiful calm
face above them, in its expression of entire rest and
peace. She was glad that Ruth's last look at her
mother's face should take from it such a sweet
recollection, more glad that she had heard those
late, last words. And as she bent above the dead
she prayed with warm tears in her eyes for the
living; for she knew now, even better than ever,
that God is truly the hearer and answerer of
prayer.

After Mrs. Holden's death the household prepared to break up. Mr. Holden had long intended

to go abroad for a time, his health demanding both
rest and change; but he had been unwilling to
leave his wife in her delicate health, and she could
not attempt the voyage. Now he would take Ruth,
and join his sister in England, and then the three
would travel for at least a year; the servants were
to be dismissed, the house closed or let, and Happy
would be again without a home. But before she
had time to feel troubled about this prospect, Mrs.
Payson sent for her to come to the parsonage. She
found there a new inmate who had arrived during
Mrs. Holden's latter illness and death, and was
unknown to her till she was ushered into Mrs. Payson's bedroom and introduced to her two weeks'
old daughter.

Happy was delighted in the mother's happiness,
for she loved Mrs. Payson dearly, and knew how
deeply she had felt the loss of her first child, which
was only born to die; but when she found that she
herself was wanted to be baby's nurse, and help in
the household sewing, she was even more pleased.
This indeed would be home to her. Delia Lamb
would be a very different companion from Ann and
Katy, and to be an inmate of the minister's house
seemed to her like dwelling in the courts of the
sanctuary; she had not yet learned that even Paul
and Barnabas were "men of like passions with you,"
and Elias also, "subject to like passions as we are."

Her idea was that a minister was as uplifted in character as in office, and had put on the whole armor of righteousness for daily wear. She did not think that she could do him any good any more than the little captive maid knew what service she did Naaman, but rather looked to find her Christian life easier far in such surroundings and with such examples. She parted from Ruth with deep grief; and the child clung to her speechless and tearless, but with a grasp so close that it seemed hard to loose it, even when her father called her. She knew something now of Happy's worth, and reproached herself with the slight heed she had given to her teaching and her affection. Happy put into her hand a little book of texts, prayers, and promises for each day, and begged her to use it. She only answered with a kiss ; but, though no one knew it, a day never passed again that the tiny volume did not utter its message to Ruth's heart, received or not.

Mr. Holden unbent from his usual cold pride when he paid Happy her due. He thanked her simply but warmly for her kindness to his wife, and gave her a small ivory porte-monnaie with silver clasps that had been Mrs. Holden's, " for remembrance," he said. It was a useless toy, but when Happy opened it ten shining half-eagles fell out in her lap. Ruth, too, left with her grandmother a little trunk for Happy, "with my dear love"; and in it she found a good store of unworn clothing, a nice black silk dress, and a warm shawl that she had many a time folded and laid away in the dead mother's drawers. All this touched her, for she knew it was a kind recognition of faithful service. Here again she had done what she could, and even her humble ministry had been accepted of God and man.

CHAPTER XXIII.

THERE were two weeks yet for Mrs. Payson's nurse to stay with her, so Happy would have a little time to rest at Miss Lavinia's, which she was very glad to have, for Mrs. Holden's tedious illness had worn upon her more than she knew till it was over. The old lady was glad to have a visit from her, for in all this time Happy had grown dearer and dearer to her, till she was almost like a daughter to the lonely soul; and Happy took a daughter's place to her in many respects, — did her fine mending, trimmed her caps a little more like modern styles than the curious constructions she fashioned of herself, advised her about her dresses, begged slips for her from Mr. Holden's gardener, and sweetened that lonely life in a thousand ways, almost too trivial to mention, yet chronicled by a poet in the sweetest lyric of praise that ever a woman won:

"She doeth little kindnesses
That most leave undone, or despise:
For naught that sets one heart at ease,
And giveth happiness or peace,
Is low esteemed in her eyes."

Now too she had more time to see little Mira, who
was a year old, and to Happy's thought grew
sweeter and lovelier every day; she knew her now,
and would crow and stretch out her hands to go
to "Aunt Happy," from whose still, sad face, and
weary heart she coaxed and kissed away all grief
and bitterness for the time, with the wonderful
power of little children. Happy loved her with all
her strength; the pure, innocent, careless sweetness
of this baby, who had no thought for the morrow, and
no past to regret, was like healing dew to the girl who
had tasted life's bitterness, and still shrank from the
remembrance, and felt its acrid flavor on her lips.

"Don't ye get too fond of her!" exhorted Miss
Lavinia, with the unconscious paganism that lingers
with so many of us in this Christian dispensation;
"ef you think too much of her she'll up an' die,
jest as t'other one did. I don't believe in lovin'
folks too much; besides, it spiles children."

"Does it?" said Happy. "I shouldn't think it
would; I don't suppose anybody could love a child
more than mother did me; but she was very strict,
Aunt Vinny."

"Well, Almiry wa'n' folks; she was Almiry. It

don't work so with everybody; ta'n't one in forty
can govern a child right; mostly they let 'em have
every mortal thing they want, becos they think
they love 'em so much.   Love 'em! it's themselves
they love; they hain't no heart to do what's right
by a child, and fetch 'em up in the way they should
go, becos it hurts their feelin's to hear 'em holler!
Talk about moral suasion too! the land's sake!   A
good, smart little rod is the best kind o' 'suasion'
for th' everidge young ones."

"Mother never whipped me," said Happy.

"Well, I guess she did.   She giv' ye the awful-
lest spankin' when you wa'n't but six months old!
Why, 'twas the last year your grandpa lived, — old
Parson Robbins.   I was out to Bassett visitin'
round, and I chanced in.   You was a screamin',
and he was exhortin', and Almiry she sot there-
white as a sheet.   The parson he thought there was
no need on't, you was too little to take it in.   But
Almiry knowed.   She'd been a trying to change
your frock, and you didn't want to be ondressed a
mite.   You'd stiffen out like a stake, and your eyes
would shine!   But fin'lly she got the better of ye,
and you held still and was limpsy as a rag.   Then
she cried; I tell ye it hurt her!   She'd rather have
took a real flogging herself; but I've heered her
say time and ag'in that she never had no trouble
about your minding after that."

"I don't remember ever thinking I could disobey her, Aunt Vinny. I didn't want to mind always, and I used to try to beg off, but it never came to my mind that I could possibly do what she told me not to. That was one thing about her, she never could be teased out of her word; she knew what she meant, and meant it for sure."

"That's a fact; and children are a heap happier when they know jest exactly what they can and what they can't do, now I say for't! As for this persuadin' children to behave, it don't amount to the wuth of a pin. It comes to be nag, nag, nag, from mornin' till night, generally; or right down scoldin', sharp, hateful words, that cut worse'n rods, and stay by a sight longer. You make a child's flesh ache and sting when it's naughty, and it won't be naughty no great of times. Besides, that's the Lord's way, and I reckon his way's the best of all; when we don't behave we get hurt, — soul or body aches and cries out; and some of us learns and some don't, like other children. I don't believe but what sufferin' in the flesh is good for us; if it ain't, why did the Lord Jesus die on the cross? Scripter says: He 'sent his son in the likeness of sinful flesh,' and 'Christ hath suffered for us in the flesh'; and if them texts don't mean that the flesh of sinners is to suffer, why, then, I don't

know it, that's all. And if the Lord believes in
punishin' the flesh, we oughter."

It was a new idea to Happy that her mother had
ever punished her. As a child she remembered
strict training and constant oversight, but not
penalty. The truth was, she had been taught the
right way so early that habit had taken the strength
of nature, and being brought up literally in the
"nurture and admonition of the Lord," trained by
both the word and spirit of the Bible, she had
grown into the Christian life as naturally as the
fair young tree shoots upward toward the sky.
She knew little Mira would not be so faithfully and
carefully brought up. Already she had learned to
scream for what she wanted, and get it; for Mrs.
Packard, naturally a weak woman, and only very
lately a Christian, recalled with deep remorse her
neglect of little Gay, and could not bear to see the
child who had replaced her suffer for anything.
Happy could only pity and pray for her darling, —
but prayer and pity are mighty helps. In this
short vacation from her work she helped Mrs.
Packard get the baby ready for winter, and from
her own old clothes cut out and patched up sundry
garments for the youngest and poorest of her mission-school flock. She went often to see Madam
Holden, who always welcomed her, and invited her
warmly to come there as often as she could, not

only to see her, but to hear of Ruth, for whose fair
face and shy, sweet speech her grandmother and
Happy longed alike. She was out of their reach
now; far, far beyond care or help from either of
them. The worst evils of life might befall her, and
they were powerless to aid. But, happily for them,
they both knew and felt that she was in care of an
almighty love and power, and to Him they carried
their anxieties and were comforted.

When Happy began her life in the minister's
house, she thought her way would be all peace and
pleasantness. She was young and inexperienced,
and had not yet learned the lesson of all life: "this
is not your rest." Delia Lamb was kindly, but she
was also "smart"; and it "put her about" as she
expressed it, to have another inmate in the kitchen
where she had lived and ruled so long in solitary
state, and, like many another petty autocrat, she
liked to show her power. Happy was disappointed
and troubled here; she had hoped Delia would help
her learn the ways of a new place, but, instead, she
rather hindered her; for really she was herself in a
new place, the baby was an innovation. Mrs. Payson's nurse another and worse novelty to bear with,
and after having put up with the nurse's airs for
Mrs. Payson's sake a whole month, Delia's temper
was not tranquil, to say the least. Happy could
not complain or remonstrate; all she could do was

to endure silently and hope for better things. Mrs.
Payson, too, was not the cheery, bright, busy woman
she had known before. The unusual care which
she did not know how to meet wore on her strength
and spirits. She had everything to learn about the
management of a baby, as well as Happy. Its cries
frightened and pained her; it seemed so frail, so
helpless, so tiny, she was in hourly terror lest she
should do or leave undone something, and her
clouded, weary face was not inspiriting. She
leaned on Happy far more than Happy on her, so
that the girl was again becoming a support instead
of receiving strength and help.

Mr. Payson was in a sort of transition state also.
He missed the companionship of his wife more than
she knew, for her absorption in the baby was intense at present. His sleep was broken by its cries,
for hitherto the parsonage had been a very cave of
silence by night, standing alone in its large garden;
but walls nor doors prevented these little wailing
utterances from rousing him at all hours: even his
study was invaded by the sounds, and, like most
clergymen, he had never been trained or trained
himself to write under any but the most helpful
circumstances.

Would it not be well to have a professor of ab-
straction in our divinity schools, to teach the stu-
dents to write their sermons, as a woman does her

literary work, in the midst of noise, and subject to all kinds of interruption? No such professor had the handling of Mr. Payson; used to stillness, solitude, all quiet and undisturbed surroundings, he was driven to despair—and his old sermons! He grew irritated, nervous, (profanely spelled c-r-o-s-s!) prayed with no fervor, preached with no unction, and actually snapped at his wife before Happy. Mrs. Payson's eyes filled with tears, but before they fell she controlled them, moved to such effort by the sight of Happy's astonished face. The girl was one of those people who speak with their faces, unconscious entirely of the betrayal. She would have done anything rather than be disrespectful or reproachful to the minister; but her great, wide eyes full of pained astonishment he could not help interpreting, and he was humiliated and struck by this wordless reproof. He turned away, and went into his study; but the childlike look of that honest face followed him, and made him ashamed. When he preached, some weeks after, a sermon from the text, "And the Lord turned and looked upon Peter," his congregation thought it the best of all his always good discourses; but Happy never suspected that she had given occasion for all that eloquence. She only saw that things fretted the minister, and, after the first astonished recoil from the discovery that even a man of God is not perfect,

she set herself to make life easier for everybody
there, careless at what expense to herself. She
kept the baby soothed and quiet with that subtle
touch and charm some women have : she saw that
the doors were always closed ; she persuaded Mrs.
Payson to lie down every day, and let her take
baby on to the piazza when it was pleasant, or out
into the woodshed chamber when it rained, so that
peace returned once more to the study and the
nursery. Mrs. Payson grew stronger, and baby
more composed ; even Delia began to settle back
into the calm of old times, and though she never
openly repented of her disposition toward Happy
for the first few months of their life together, she
yet brought forth deeds worthy for repentance, and
made the kitchen a much more comfortable place
than it had been lately.

Often and often Happy remembered her mother's
words to her about trying to make people about her
happy as a religious duty, and the recollection stim-
ulated her to constant effort, not only to do what
was her understood duty, but also to make the path
smooth for those who walked beside her. The
baby knew her voice very soon, and would go to
sleep in her lap sooner than anywhere else, and
while the sweet autumn weather lasted she took it
out daily. By the time winter set in, the parsonage

was really homelike to her. She was Happy again, really as well as nominally.

The mission-school also flourished. The very fact of being in a room formally set apart for the purpose, not somebody's kitchen full of homely everyday surroundings, seemed to do the children good, to make them more respectful of the occasion.

Helen Sands was learning as much from her class as she taught them, though in another way; and Mary Gray, in spite of her self-distrust, was developing into a thorough and patient teacher. Julia had a good deal of trouble; self-confident and naturally dominant, she roused a spirit of opposition in her class that was hard to quell. Happy did not understand it; she never had any trouble with the children; but she could not tell Julia that the fault lay in herself, for she was not sure of it, and she hated to discourage the girl so early. So they worried on together, the children not loving their teacher at all, but roused and interested by her quick intellect and lively power of description; and the teacher intent on clipping these infant minds to the measure of her own ideas, or stretching them out to meet that measure, after the style of Procrustes, yet all the time exasperated to find that she could not remodel those natures according to her own standard, but must wait for time and God's help working in them before she could hope for their improvement. She had much to learn before she would be fit to teach, and it was hard for her to give up her will and her way, in the most stringent circumstances. But she was in the high road to knowledge, and Happy's calm, sweet manner and simple character were her best human example; she did not as yet recognize or strive after a divine pattern.

Before winter fairly came, Mrs. Holden heard from Ruth, who was happy among all the sights of Europe, with her father devoted to her, and her aunt as tender and careful of her as a mother could be — as her own mother never had been. She wrote a long letter to her grandmother, full of all she had seen, and did not forget an affectionate message to Happy at the end, which gave more pleasure far than the child could appreciate, for Happy's heart still clung to her with love and longing, and never a night passed that Ruth's name was not foremost in her prayers. A long quiet winter apparently lay before her now, a winter of work indeed, for the care of a little child is work for both brain and muscles, when it is thoroughly done: but a season of peace as far as she could forsee it so she set herself down to do her duty, thinking it promised no severity, but only life's daily bread to be broken in thankfulness — to take, eat and live.

CHAPTER XXIV.

As the winter went on, Happy grew more and more attached to Mrs. Payson's baby, as well as to the grown inmates of the house. There is nothing more bewitching to a real child-lover than to watch a baby's growth and daily development. Mrs. Payson was judicious; she knew that warmth and sleep and food enough were the simple conditions of her child's healthy life at first; and little Eunice never was disturbed to be exhibited to company, or made the victim of unrelaxing and stringent system. The nursery was always flooded with all the sunshine that was anywhere, and always had a breath of out-door air circulating through its warm precincts. The baby slept when it was sleepy, ate when it was hungry, basked in the sun, and grew so round, so rosy, so dimpled, as to be an example of what wonderful beauty lies in mere flesh and blood. As it grew older, and the vague baby smile grew into the benign look of infancy, Happy wondered, many a time, if truth lay in the dogmas she had so

long heard from the pulpit. Her head grew perplexed with questioning, her heart ached with the
tremendous possibilities of life for this fair, sweet
creature, who looked like a new white rose just
shyly parting its infolding leaves at the call of
June.

"Well, Happilony," said Miss Lavinia, one Sunday night, "I hear that baby is most amazin'
pritty."

"O Aunt Vinny! it is just the dearest, sweetest
little thing you ever saw in your life!"

"Han'some as a picter, I suppose."

"Yes, it is. I never saw such a child before.
Her skin is like snow, only warm-looking, and her
cheeks and lips real red : and her eyes so big and
blue they make you think of sand-violets, and her
hair is soft and yellow and curly ; and she is the
best child !"

Happy's expressive face darkened as she said
this; one of her doubts and fears came glooming
into the horizon.

"Aunt Vinny," she said, in a hesitating sort of
way, "does it seem natural — I mean does it seem
possible that dear, good baby can be totally de-
praved ?"

Aunt Lavinia looked at her over her spectacles
with the peculiar and forbidding emphasis that
mode of vision bestows.

" Well, of all things! if you ha'n't got aground
on doctrines. Happilony, you hear to me. You've
got common sense; and does it stand to reason that
the Lord that made you ha'n't got any? Now don't
you meddle with none of them deep things. He'll
do right whether or no; and them doctrines ain't
any of your business. There's enough to do in this
world, every minnit of time, without spendin' your
brains over them things. Don't ye know what happened when Samson wanted to feel the 'pillars
whereon the house standeth'? Why, fumblin'
around to ketch holt of 'em, and gettin' hold, he
pulled the house down atop of him! You go right
along and keep the command, and the Lord'll take
care of the house. Ain't he the maker and builder
on't?"

These were timely words, and Happy speculated
no longer about the baby's theological status; but
as she clasped the warm and tiny shape to her
bosom, and sung her to sleep with all the dear old
hymns that have echoed in the church of Christ so
many years, and inspired the army of the Lord in
their toilsome march and harassing warfare, she
lifted up her heart in fervent prayer for the child,
and found peace. In her love for little Eunice she
neither forgot nor neglected Mira, who learned to
look on Sunday for " Aunt Happy " with loving ex-
pectance, and to cling around her with such demon-

strations of love that the lonely girl clung to her in return with deep affection. It seemed to Happy, sometimes, as if these two babies were really sent to her for consolation, as if their innocent caresses were gradually restoring to her sore heart its patience and serenity. She did not know that such ministry would have been far less effectual to a different character from her own. She had to a remarkable degree the simplicity of a child herself. With but one aim in her quiet life, to do the will of her Master faithfully, she was as near the position of an obedient child as humanity in its older growth can attain, and was a daily realization of the picture Fenelon draws in his letter on simplicity: "This true simplicity . . . has the charm of truth and candor, and sheds around it, I know not what of pure and innocent, of cheerful and peaceful; a loveliness that wins us when we see it intimately and with pure eyes."

Unconsciously to herself she was becoming a power of good in the parsonage, where she had thought only of receiving help and instruction. Her single aim, her unselfish endeavor to lift the burdens of those around her, her tireless devotion to her duty, even the pleasant look on her thin, dark face, all inspirited and cheered the whole family. That the "life was the light of men" is no less true of the Lord's followers than of him; and

far deeper results than from teaching or preaching
may flow from these living epistles, that are known
and read of all men. Mr. Payson owned to himself
that Happy's presence had been a perpetual admonition to self-control and disciplined speech in his
own instance; Mrs. Payson leaned on her more and
more, daily; and Delia admitted her into full fellowship in the kitchen, sure that Happy would respect
her usages, and never contest her supremacy.
Quite unaware, she was becoming an important
member of the household, and winning affection
and respect that was deep and genuine. Being a
servant of God first, she found it neither hard nor
grievous to be a servant of men, and, looking back-
ward on her life, acknowledged her mother's wisdom in choosing this path for her, and the good
hand of God that had guided and blessed her so
far.

But another stroke awaited Happy, though it was
not a severe one; her way seemed to lie among the
dying, she thought, as she was sent for, one bitter
morning in March, to see Mrs. Packard, danger-
ously ill with sudden congestion of the lungs. She
was unable to speak when Happy got there; she
could only give her one grateful, loving look, and
then close her eyes forever. She was not a person
calculated to inspire any one with very deep affection. A slight and shallow nature had not been

improved by any training or education ; but she
was dear to Happy for the sake of old times, for
association with the mother whose memory hallowed
everything that had been near her to her danghter's
still longing heart; and dear, too, for little Gay's
sake, for Mira's, and for the recent but sincere Christian fellowship that existed between them. Both
man and wife had felt toward Happy that peculiar
respect and gratitude which fills us all toward the
human hand that has led or pointed us toward God.
It was to her they had both looked as a friend at
all times ; and often after the little class had left the
kitchen, while they still met there, Happy had been
used to go in for a quiet hour of reading and conversation with them, that they enjoyed and profited
by as much as the children did by her other teachings.   Mr. Packard turned to her now, in his overwhelming grief, as the one friend who could understand it; and little Mira, conscious only of some
trouble that frightened her, with puckered lip and
troubled face hid her head on Aunt Happy's shoulder as an unfailing refuge and comfort.   Mrs. Payson was very considerate ; she spared Happy as long
and as often as she could, till the funeral was over,
and some arrangement made for the care of the
child.   A sister of Mr. Packard's, a young girl
whose appearance and manner displeased Happy
more than she liked to acknowledge, came to live

with him. She was too young to understand the
duties required of her, and too silly and flighty to
devote herself to them. But for Happy's help and
advice, little Mira would have been ill provided for;
and the dirty, disorderly house overrun with Maria's
friends of both sexes, the wasteful housekeeping,
the careless ways of speech and action that she
brought with her from her factory life, all filled
Happy with dismay for Mira's future. She could
not help telling her fears to Aunt Lavinia, who had
grown into Happy's confidence as fully as her
mother could have wished. With all her quaint
speech and sharp tongue, the old lady was so genuine, so sensible, so kindly at heart, and now so fond
of Happy, that she filled a mother's place to her
more than either of them were aware. She comforted Happy now with her usual mixture of sense,
shrewdness, and real heartfelt trust.

"Don't cry over spilt milk, Happy, he done the
best he could; 'twas natural to want his sister there,
and if she ain't jest the right one she's in the right
place, and that's half the battle. Mebbe 'twill
sober her consid'ble in the end, and do her good,
but that ain't here nor there; we ain't no right to
vex ourselves about to-morrow; to-day's all we can
handle; the manna sp'iled when it was kep' over. I
know folks of your make do feel dreadful anxious
sometimes over what can't be known nor provided

for by anybody but the Lord. But he'll do it, as
sure as you're born, and it ain't your business to
make nor meddle with it. You can be kinder long-
sufferin' with her, and try to put her up gradual to
better ways, and that's all you can do. I've told ye
more'n four times, we ain't responsible to nobody
for what we can't do."

Happy felt the truth of Aunt Vinny's words,
particularly as they related to her own character.
She was naturally timid and despondent, and the
circumstances of her life had often led her into
temptation on these points. It is the latest of the
lessons that we learn, to preserve an unfaltering and
practical trust in the power and providence of God;
and she found it hard of attainment, as we all do.
But she followed Miss Vinny's advice, and whenever she could get a chance went to Mr. Packard's,
and before long established an influence over Maria
that was for good. She persuaded her to take a
class of very young children in her afternoon
school; and as she had a clear, sweet voice, and
good ear, Happy found her soon a valuable assistant. Mr. Packard felt his home to be so comfortless, during the first few months after his wife's
death, that it needed all the strength of his new-
found principles to keep him from relapsing into
old habits.

Like many another man, he had once found a

cheerful saloon warmed by a bright fire, a ready
welcome, a fragrant steam from the hot drink prof-
ferred him, and the society of other men, a very
pleasant exchange for a dull kitchen and tired-out
wife. Now, duty to God, like encircling arms,
possessed and protected him. It needs divine
strength to conquer the habits of years, whatever
it may be ; but divine strength is always ready, and
in its almighty power lies the only hope of the
slave to appetite. When Mr. Packard and his wife
both began to believe in Christ, their first aim was
for better things in daily living, led by Happy's example ; and now this aim bore fruit. She had died
in peace and trust ; he took up the dull burden of
life and made manful endeavor to endure to the
end. He had, to be sure, some help from his work,
which was now constant and paid well, and kept
him from home except at his meal-times ; but his
heart often sank within him at the dirt and confusion, he could not escape there, and when Maria
began to try to do better he recognized the effort at
once, and met it with eager praise and thanks, as
encouraging to her to receive as it was pleasant to
him to bestow.

Spring was close at hand in reality, midway over
in name, when Julia Calhoun told her class, one
Sunday, that she should be away the next two
meetings, and therefore Miss Dodd would take them

under her charge till she came back. This was received in silence; none of the children expressed
regret by word or look, and Julia was deeply
wounded. With all her fine traits, she was yet
self-conceited and over-confident, and she felt acute
mortification to think the class cared so little for
her absence. But a sharper lesson awaited her.

After school was over, and she went from the
door, she missed her handkerchief, and came back
for it. As she walked up-stairs, she heard talking
in the school-room. Polly Lagré and Nan were
waiting for Jack to shut the fires up securely, and
set the room in order before he left. Polly was in
Julia's class, and pausing on the upper stair her
teacher heard her say :

" Ain't I orful glad she's goin'! "

" Why, Poll, what's the matter of you? " asked
Jack.

" I don't like her not one single bit, and I love
Miss Happy."

" I guess everybody does," said Nan, quietly.

" Well, everybody don't love *her*, so there now! "
retorted Polly.

" She's jest as stuck up as she can live 'n breathe 'n
stick. She scolds orful! Miss Happy don't never.
She jest looks at you so kinder good and's if she
wanted to cry ; but Jooliar — "

" Shut up! " said Jack, harshly. " Don't you

know Miss Happy said you shouldn't talk bad
about folks.

" H'm ! I've heered her say plenty 'nough times
folks hadn't ought to be hateful. If Jooliar wa'n't
bad, I couldn't talk bad, could I ? heh ? "

" Stop it ! " said Jack again, imperatively. " I'm
boss here now, Poll ; you shan't sass the teachers
here. Miss Happy said we was fust-chop scholars,
and she 'pended on us to behave ; and if you can't
behave, you clear, Poll Lagré."

Julia waited to hear no more. She turned to go
home in a miserable humor. Was it true that she
could not make the children love her ? Was it *not*
true that she had always talked to and taught them
from a conscious height above their plane ? She
remembered hearing her mother laugh at the story
of a young girl who began to teach a class in a mission-school by saying, " We rich, come to you
poor." But had she not acted out the same spirit?
A Bible verse suddenly seized hold of her :

" Though he was rich, yet for your sakes he became poor, that ye through his poverty might be
rich."

It was an arrow that pierced through the joints
of the harness. Julia was sensible, clear-headed,
and candid ; she could not avoid the conclusions her
mind drew from her own conduct set beside the life
of Christ ; and in her three weeks' absence she

found that there was neither hope nor help for the harm she had done to herself and others except in a total change of heart and life.

Naturally proud and reticent, her struggle was long and severe, but at last the confident heart laid itself humbly and utterly at the feet of her Lord, and was at peace. Another of Happy's little flock had found the kingdom.

CHAPTER XXV.

It was with deep joy and gratitude that Happy received a letter from Julia recounting her new experience and avowing her change of feeling. "Dear Miss Happy," the closing sentence ran, " I don't believe I ever should have been a Christian if you had not been our teacher. You don't know how I thank you for all you have said to me, and for being so good yourself it made me want to be good too." The tears came to Happy's eyes as she read this; she felt, indeed, that Julia overrated her; but with this first impulse of humility came also the quick giving of thanks that she had been helped to bear witness to the power of God in the life of his humblest servant. It gave her strength to go on, and courage to endure, to know that two of her dear girls were at last gathered into her Master's service, and she prayed more and more earnestly for the rest.

This summer her little school increased greatly. Maria Packard drew in some of her girl-friends to

help her sing, and Happy managed to persuade
them to stay to a Bible-class which Madam Holden
consented to teach. Many of these brought in
their brothers and sisters for the sake of a place to
keep them quiet an hour or two, and Happy appealed to Mr. Fox to find her more teachers. He
laid the case before the Sunday-school one morning,
and soon had volunteers enough. The idea seemed
to take root thoroughly ; a mission-school had long
been wanted in Canterbury, and the cotton-mills
lately established there added to the need. Before
this summer was over, the room Madam Holden
had hired for them became too crowded ; and they
moved into the upper floor of the Adirondac Mill,
whose owner, Mr. Hart, was a member of Mr. Payson's church, and offered them this accommodation
till they could get a better. The contributions of
the church Sunday-school were now turned into
this channel, so that proper furniture was obtained,
with hymn-books and a small library ; and Mr.
Hart's son, a young man studying for the ministry,
was put in as superintendent.

To a person less humble and simple than Happy,
there would have been some pain in seeing the
whole thing, which she had begun and cherished so
long, taken so entirely out of her hands ; for though
she had still a large class, that was but an item.
But she only rejoiced to see the work grow so fast

and so strongly; for like many a little seed that
barely germinates at first, and pushes two small
leaflets feebly from the earth, struggling for life in
the chill storms of spring, but presently taking root
under ground, and gathering strength from the
earth that feeds it, springs up and branches mightily ; so this good foundation had begun suddenly to
branch and grow far beyond her thought. She did
not appreciate this as yet, or notice how often she
was consulted as to the management and organization of the school, for Happy was as unselfish as a
child of God should be, and had but one idea in
this matter, — that the very best work she could do
was the right work for the place. She had never
forgotten Mr. Payson's sermon about seeking and
saving the lost ; it had been at once a stimulus and
a help to her ever since. Now, as her class increased, she visited them at their homes as she
found time ; and many a poor woman blessed the
gentle face and kindly word that lit up their
wretched tenements now and then, though a few
repulsed and sneered at her. But these visits re-
vealed to Happy a new phase of life. Her innocent
eyes were opened to depths of sin and misery she
had never dreamed of ; she met with girls of her
own age old and hardened in vice, and shrunk with
horror from the spectacle ; but still the voice of her
Master sounded in her heart " to seek and save

that which was lost." This was his work ; it must, therefore, be hers, however she dreaded it or however she failed ; and she found very soon that no work is more discouraging than the conflict with poverty and sin together, no life more difficult to set right than one that is cankered with jealousy and hardened by want ; for she found in this class so much hatred and suspicion of those who were better off than themselves, so much bitterness of feeling toward their superiors, such distrust of kindness, such scorn of pity, such angry disdain of help, contradictorily mingled with such greed in accepting it, that over and over her heart sunk within her, and but for a higher help than nature afforded she would soon have despaired and left the field. As it was, after long hearing the words of such hopeless and faithless suffering and sin she encountered here, her own faith began sometimes to shake. She went in to Miss Lavinia one afternoon, after a tour among the homes of her scholars, looking so pale and tired that the old lady was disturbed about her.

" Set right down in the rocker, Happy, and take a drink o' tea ; you come jest in time. I was kinder tired myself ; I'd lopped down onto the sofy, when I happened to think I'd hev tea early, and now I'm glad on't. What hev you been a doin', child ? "

" Oh ! only visiting some of the folks in Horn Lane and Waterville, Aunt Vinny."

"Only! Well! I guess that's enough. 'Tain't an over clever place to go to anyway, and I guess you be tired."

"'Tisn't all tire, aunty; I'm so puzzled. I can't see into it."

"See into what?"

"Why, people's being so poor and bad."

"I dono as anybody asked of ye to see into it," dryly replied Aunt Lavinia.

"No, I suppose not, — but I can't help wondering. If being poor made them any better, why, that would be another thing; but it only seems to make them more and more hateful and mean and disagreeable every way."

"Well?"

"And — aunty — somehow I don't see how or why the Lord does put folks into such places where it seems as if they couldn't help being bad if they tried."

Miss Lavinia leaned back in her chair and looked sharply at Happy.

"If you've got so't you can't understand the Lord's ways, Happilony, mebbe you'd better stop. Folks that try dippin' up the sea into a pint cup, don't usually make it out. Why, child, what be you a doin'? Stop an' think a minnit. Didn't the Lord make 'em? and don't you expect he's goin' to care for 'em? If you can't see why, that don't

make no difference with him. Wa'n't Jesus Christ
so poor he hadn't even a tenement house to cover
him ? and what do these creturs want to complain
of ? Don't you try to find out the Lord by search-
in', Happy. Job did that for quite a spell, and it
wa'n't no use to him. You preach the gospel to
'em, and let him that fetched the gospel turn their
hearts to take it in. But you mind what I say,
Happilony. Of all the onprofitable, presumptoous,
foolish things a human cretur can do, there ain't
none like tryin' to measure God's ways by yourn.
The Bible don't give you no encouragement to do
it, nor common sense neither ; and you may say,
and it's real reliable, that if one does it, t'other
will. You jest do what you find to do, an' do it
with your might, and the Lord'll do his part, no
mistake."

Homely as the words were, they restored the
balance to Happy's troubled mind. She kept there-
after to her own province, and told the story of
Christ·the poor man, in such a heartfelt way that
more than one hungry soul laid hold of the manna
and fed thereon.

It was here that Happy found her place in life a
great help to her. To know that she was working
for her daily bread, and that in a position many of
those she visited, with the false and fatal pride so
common to poverty, and so degrading, would have

scorned to take, was so much in her favor with them ; and being poor herself gave a weight to her influence with them, and enabled her to set forth the work of Him who for our sakes became poor, with a convincing power that belongs only to sympathy and experience. She partly understood this, and in her heart thanked her dear, dead mother for the judicious choice of labor that had been so good for her and others. But she was to have one more and greater proof that the choice was blessed.

One of her girls, a cousin of Pauline Lagré, came to school one afternoon with red eyes, evidently from crying. Happy kept her after the class was over, and gently persuaded her to say what troubled her. The girl burst into a passion of sobbing, as she said :

" My sister's a dyin' ; she come home from York real sick last week ; doctor says she can't never get well." And here tears and sobs choked her.

" Would you like to have me come and see her, Katy ? " said Happy.

The girl's face brightened. " I wish you would ; she's orful bad ; she don't say much, but she coughs all night, most times."

So before the week was over, finding Mrs. Payson was going out to spend the day, taking baby with her, Happy asked leave to take the afternoon for her school visiting, and went first to Katy Parker's home in Horn Lane. It was a tenement on the second floor of a small house. Happy had been there before, but now she found a new inmate in the sitting-room, curled up in a little cot-bed ; a girl with a wan, childish face, haggard as from age, short dark hair, wild restless eyes, and a burning spot on either sallow cheek ; a wretched life, a polluted soul, beyond Happy's knowledge, but from its outward signs touching her quick sympathy. The girl hid her face, as Happy looked at her, with a quick giggle, as if ashamed of her shame, but she neither looked up nor spoke ; her mother, a fat, whining woman, rocked to and fro in her chair and wiped her eyes on a red handkerchief, but said little about Mary's illness, being voluble enough as to their wants and resources. Happy could do nothing ; her heart sank then, and failed her again and again in the after visits she made, to find how hopeless a task lay before her. The girl seemed to have no soul — no heart — to touch ; she was as indifferent to fear, or pity, or desire for good, as a doll might have been ; she liked the delicacies Mrs. Holden and Mrs. Payson sent her, was greedy for flowers and pictures, begged for candy and sweetmeats with pitiful eagerness, but seemed to have no thought beyond the hour. Earnestly, tearfully, Happy talked to her, but soul and body had been so long degraded and defiled that the immortal spark seemed deadened with the dying body. Happy could not understand it; but she learned one lesson over again when at last she picked out by degrees poor Mary's story. She had been put into a factory at thirteen years old. The work was hard, her food insufficient, her mother a selfish woman, with no sense of duty and no great affection for the sickly, cross girl, whose wages scantily fed and clothed her. Temptation had come in the child's way at a time when the mill shut down for a few weeks, and her place was filled, when it resumed operations, by an older and better hand; unwelcome at home, hungry as only a growing girl can be, knowing nothing good to teach or restrain her, she went into a saloon as waiter-girl, where her bright eyes and saucy tongue, and quick handiness made her acceptable. It is not needful to detail her career; she went from bad to worse, from deep to depth, and lay here at twenty-two an awful homily on the wickedness and neglect of those around her, and her own weakness. When at last she died, expressing no hope for the future, leaving no hope with those who had hoped and prayed for her, beyond what they might gather from her resolve if ever she got well again to be "a better girl, and not go out nights," Happy thanked God on her knees for her mother. But for her, she too might have been driven to the straits that had ruined

Mary, and perhaps been ruined too. She shuddered as she recalled the story of that old divine,
who, seeing a man pass to the gallows, cried out :
" There I go — but for the grace of God," and she
resolved to work more and pray with greater fervor
and frequency for the poor, whose needs she now
had measured more truly than ever. Mary Parker
had taught her both pity and charity ; and Horn
Lane owed more to the outcast in her death than
ever they had given to her life, though, with the
kindliness the poor so often show to each other in
emergency, the neighbors had done their best to
help and comfort Katy and her mother.

Mary is no ideal. Under another name she long
since lived and died, and her memory has been a
lesson of pain and profit both to the mission school
teacher who watched her go down to death as
darkly ignorant and careless as the beasts that
perish, to all human appearance.

Katy seemed sobered and impressed by her sister's death, but no definite result followed. She
gave Happy no trouble in the class, and was always
glad to see her at other times. The seed was sown
in tears and pain ; but it gave no sign of germina-
tion as yet, and Happy had learned to wait. She
could count Julia and Mary now as members of the
household of faith. She perceived that Helen was
growing more serious and unselfish to a marked

degree : and Adelaide Palmer and Ruth Holden she could pray for, and did, daily.

Out of her little class had sprung, as out of the mustard-seed, a branching tree. Jack Gladding and Nan were grown into helpful, trustworthy members of the school. Jack now removed to Mr. Hart's own class, and exerting a good influence, the result of Happy's training, on all the other boys ; and Nan, still with her, matured into a clean, loving, obedient little girl, an aid and comfort to her teacher, who looked back often with amused recollection to the first day she had seen the two children, — the day when her mother came home from nursing Ann to find them tied to the bed-post, while Happy was almost crying in despair and disgust at their very bad behavior. She wished her mother could see them now. Futile wish! but how many of us in our longings for the dear eyes and tender speech of the dead would not forget that they are happier and better far not to know even the best joys of this world? Why should we, how can we desire to disturb, for our own blessing, that peace of God which passeth understanding — the peace of death?

CHAPTER XXVI.

A YEAR went by now as placidly as some years do go, even in this changeful world. Little Eunice was a lovely, lisping child instead of a baby; and Happy loved her better day by day; she seemed to have grown into her very heart. Mira, who was older, showed the need of a mother's care, not in her dress, for Maria was proud of the pretty child, and decked her in all the cheap finery she could get, much as her mother would have done. She had plenty of food, too, and Maria looked after her in a certain sort of way, but there was no training attempted, no obedience asked or enforced; nothing done for her future welfare, to-day alone was considered: and Happy felt with pain that she was growing into a useless being, and must be one in the future, if not attended to now. Still, she had no remedy to offer. Mr. Packard often came of an evening to see her, bringing Mira with him, and though Happy knew these late hours were bad for the child, she could not feel quite willing to say so,

for she knew Maria was no companion for her
brother, and she hoped to do something even in
those few hours to gain an influence over Mira.
She drew fresh contrasts daily between the fresh,
childlike, obedient sweetness of little Una's character, and Mira's pert, forward, undisciplined disposition, and longed to help the motherless child to be
better; she did not know herself how her own influence had seconded Mrs. Payson's in the nursery,
and made it comparatively easy to train Eunice. It
is so much in the power of a nurse to undo a
mother's teachings, to indulge, and flatter, and
coax, and tyrannize, and make a child wretched
with injustice, or equally wretched with misplaced
kindness, that the wonder is mothers will ever trust
their children, at the early age when the habits of
character are forming, to the hands of ignorant and
careless girls, needing education themselves in its
simplest elements. Mrs. Payson fully recognized
the treasure she held in Happy, and began to
tremble now lest she should lose her, for her eyes
saw what Happy's as yet did not suspect, that Mr.
Packard's visits were not all on Mira's account; and
that they grew more frequent and longer as the
summer days came on. Mrs. Payson resolved at
last to say something to the girl about the matter,
both to relieve her own mind and prepare Happy
for the result of such attention.

"Happy," said she one day, sitting down in the nursery where Una was asleep, "don't you think Mr. Packard comes here very often ? "

"Yes, ma'am, I do," said Happy, frankly, "and I do wish he wouldn't. I don't know how to spare time to visit with him ; but I can't say anything on account of Mira. I am glad to have a chance to try to teach her something."

An amused smile touched Mrs. Payson's lips as she answered :

"But, Happy, did you never think he came here for some other reason than merely to bring Mira ? "

Happy said as unconsciously and openly as Una herself could have done, "Oh, yes'm. I know it isn't a bit pleasant for him at home. Maria is a good deal better than she used to be about the work, and keeping things clean and fixed up, but she has so many mates that come in nights to see her — and I suppose he doesn't care so much for young company."

Mrs. Payson laughed outright.

"I think he does care for some young company," she said. "Happy! did you never think that he came here to see you on an errand of his own ? "

Happy looked up, startled.

"It is time you understood it," Mrs. Payson went on, gravely, "for you will have to say yes or no before long."

" Oh, Mrs. Payson ! he don't — he can't — why, how can you think so ? "

" I have got eyes, Happy, and so has Delia, and I think she does not look kindly on Mr. Packard of late. We all love you Happy, and don't want to lose you."

Happy colored high.

" Do you think I want to go, ma'am ? " she asked reproachfully.

" I don't think you have considered the question yet, my dear. I want you to know it is coming and think seriously about it. There is a good work to do there if you have the heart to do it."

Mrs. Payson said this with great effort, for she thought it was her duty ; and when she had said it she got up and went away, leaving Happy's brain in a dull whirl of surprise, perplexity, distaste, and general trouble. Nor was Mrs. Payson tranquil herself ; she had spoken because she ought to, but the idea of losing Happy pained her deeply. In the few years of faithful service and trust she had passed at the parsonage, Happy had made herself almost a necessity ; she had fairly earned the love, respect, and confidence of the family, and was looked upon as one of their own number in the best sense. She gave not only help but counsel about matters in the nursery ; she knew, better than the mother, whose other cares often absorbed

all her attention, what Eunice needed, what little
evils threatened her, and what baby wants must be
gratified; she watched the child with tender vigi-
lance day and night, and reported any change in
her health at once to head-quarters ; there were no
neglected colds to ripen into croup ; no feverish
symptoms left to run riot ; no improper food allowed to pass the baby lips that desired to test all
things in that fashion ; that Una had grown so far
without any of the illness and suffering of ordinary
childish experience was owing to this watchful
care and devotion, and both Mr. and Mrs. Payson recognized the fact, and were abundantly
grateful, for Una was the very heart of the household. No wonder that they dreaded the thought
of Happy's leaving them ; no wonder that she had
made herself a place in their home as certain as
birth could have given her ; she had done everything her hand found to do under the sense of
God's right and her own duty to Him ; and such
service, however or whenever it be offered, is noble
and worthy.

> "A servant with this clause
> Makes drudgery divine."

Happy had long outlived the pangs of wounded
pride and the sense of degradation which troubled
her at first in Mrs. Holden's employment ; she felt

that she filled her place, that she was necessary, and to a woman of her stamp there is no sweeter feeling. Once convince such a woman that you cannot live without her, and there is no sacrifice she will not make, no labor she cannot endure in the light of that gratifying consciousness.

If Mr. Packard had known this trait of Happy's, his way would have been easier to begin with, and more successful in the end; but he was a timid man, and deeply conscious of his own inferiority to her; so he had made no sign in all his frequent visits of any peculiar interest in Happy, and she honestly thought he came chiefly for Mira's good, partly because home was not pleasant to him. She did not know one thing that impelled him; Maria had recently, to use her own phrase, "set up a beau," and Mr. Packard could see that before long he would be left alone again, for though Maria planned to retain her position in her brother's house if she married, her brother by no means intended that she should, as he disliked her lover more, every time he saw him, and avoided seeing him as often as was possible.

After Mrs. Payson left the nursery Happy became more and more perplexed; she felt at first that there must be some mistake, but recalling many things Mr. Packard had said and done lately, she began at last to suspect Mrs. Payson might be

in the right, and her idea was confirmed the next
day beyond doubt. It was Sunday; and as school
was coming together in the hall, Maria Packard,
leading little Mira, happened to reach the top of
the stairs at the same time with Happy. Maria was
chattering with another girl and did not see that
Mira's hat had fallen off her head, till she was
pulled back by the child who stopped for Happy
to pick it up and put it on.

Maria turned about to see what delayed her, and
nodded to Happy, who said pleasantly,

" This elastic is all worn out, Maria ; she couldn't
help losing her hat."

" Well, I shouldn't wonder," giggled Maria. "I
don't have no time to fuss over all them things! I
expect you'll do 'em up brown, Miss Dodd, when
you have her to look after; but 'twon't be all fun,
now, I tell you. The young one's got a will of her
own ; she wants tunin'."

Happy felt an angry color burn on her face, Maria's speech was so far from delicate or proper; it
would have been bad enough anywhere, but here a
dozen people heard it, three or four of them Maria's
friends, who giggled in chorus as she swept off into
the hall with Mira. One girl lingered behind, a
plain odd creature who recommended herself to
Maria's set of acquaintance by a keen tongue and
ready wit, but under it her heart was kind to those

who touched it kindly, and she had met Happy
often at Mary Parker's bedside, and helped her too;
she had never forgotten that faithful and tender
ministry.

"Don't mind her," she said now, very gently.
"She and her feller has had a fallen out, and she's
kind of riled: I know her! They'll make up to-
night, and she'll be as pleasant as a basket o' chips
— Land! I wonder what they'll do when they're
married, if they fight so like sixty now!"

Happy thanked her with a smile, but she could
not say a word; here was confirmation enough of
Mrs. Payson's correctness; Maria not only took it
for granted that her brother would marry Happy,
but she herself was to be married too, and leave
him alone; his need indeed was serious. But she
put these thoughts out of her head for a time, and
gave her whole attention to her pupils.

Jack had been promoted to the office of librarian,
of which he was very proud, and both he and Nan
now worked in the mill, and were able to be more
neatly dressed. Julia and Mary had persevered in
teaching, and around each of them gathered a large
and interesting class. Helen Sands was at the head
of the infant class, which had so greatly increased
as to really need a separate apartment. The school
was full to overflowing, and a new place of meeting
would soon be needed. Polly Lagré was in Julia's

care still, but had become very fond of her teacher,
for with the energy and decision natural to her,
Julia had gone on in her Christian life rapidly and
successfully, and was now as lovely as she was
useful. Mary Gray still had much to contend with,
both at home and in her own character, but she
worked courageously at her duties everywhere, and
bid fair to make a good and valuable woman. Her
heart opened to Happy in all its wants and troubles,
and they grew dearer and dearer to each other constantly,—though only these three were left. Helen
seemed gradually accepting a Christian life and
hope, though she did not acknowledge it yet, even
to herself; she was not a girl to undergo any deep
uprooting of old things, but rather one to grow
into a new life gradually, and to become a child
of God without any marked experience. Happy
longed sometimes to ask her why she took such
interest in Sunday school, worked so hard to
please and teach the little ones, and denied herself
as much as she did in order to visit them and win
them to love her, but she recalled what her mother
had often said to her that " sown seed should be let
alone," not dug up to see if it is growing ; so she
contented herself with observation and prayer.
To-day, after the school was over, and she had
made this little mental review of her older scholars
with satisfaction and hope, the subject that had

troubled her when she came in, suddenly sprang
upon her again as from an ambush, but the effort
she had made to put it aside and give all her
thoughts to the duty of the hour, had calmed and
strengthened her ; she could look contingencies in
the face now. Yet she was still perplexed, and on
her way to Miss Lavinia's house, where she as usual
took tea on Sundays, she thought over the matter
very seriously. There was Mira without a mother;
she loved the little creature dearly, and was grieved
to see her growing up without proper care ; and
there was Mr. Packard, in a sense, to be left homeless ; he was a good man, and had been a good friend
of hers and her mother's. Perhaps if he were left
alone he might fall back into bad habits and be lost.

These were all the arguments Happy thought of,
for the new plan of life that seemed to lie before
her to choose. To herself she did not give a
thought, consciously ; the prospect of a home of
her own which tempts so many women, and might
in other circumstances have tempted her, did not
occur to her ; she was at home in Mr. Payson's
house, and she had learned to trust her future with
God ; it might never come, she knew ; for beside
her own delicate organization, which so far had
only threatened trouble, but yet demanded constant
care over her daily physical life, she held a deep
and secret dread of her mother's malady, a disease

so sure to be hereditary that its probable occurrence
in her own case was never absent from her mind.
She felt that her life was not to be a long one, and
she was sure that her Master would care for its
peaceful ending; so no question of a home enticed
or disturbed her now. Against the idea of marry-
ing Mr. Packard, much arranged itself. She was
unwilling to leave Mrs. Payson; she loved her and
Una as if they had been her own kindred, and she
had a reverent affection for the minister that he
knew he did not really deserve, but whose very
honesty and purity led him unconsciously to a
higher plane of living that he might justify it.
She loved Delia too; in fact, Happy's nature, like
a flower whose bud, long delayed by storm and
frost, opens widely to the later sunshine, had ex-
panded into a breadth of sweetness and affection
under these home influences and the light of that
heaven into fitness for which she was striving to
enter, till she had become not only loving but
lovely, too.

No wonder Mr. Packard wanted her to bless his
home and make Mira into an image of herself, but
she did not feel any corresponding wish to do so.
The danger now was that she should in her ignorance and inexperience marry him from a sense of
duty, and make the greatest mistake a woman can
ever make under the influence of a good motive.

But Happy had not committed her way to the Lord in vain ; she prayed earnestly to be guided to right action, and her prayer was heard. She reached Miss Vinny's doorstep still undecided and anxious, unaware that her prayer was answered as well as heard, and equally unaware that Miss Vinny was to do her another of her many good services.

CHAPTER XXVII.

"WELL, I declare for 't! it seems an age o' Sun-days sence you was here, Happy," was the old lady's greeting.

"I meant to come Thursday night, Aunt Vinny," the girl replied, "but Delia wanted to go to lecture, and Mrs. Payson had company to tea, so I did the dishes after Una was asleep, and finally Mrs. Payson went to church too."

"Well! you're here now. I won't growl no more; but seems as though I wanted you more'n usual this week. I've been kinder left to myself, so to speak, seemin'ly. I didn't feel real cherk this week, so't I didn't go to sewin' s'ciety, and seems as if I didn't reelly know a thing."

Happy recognized the old lady's want; she knew how she really pined to hear about her friends, and how she depended on sewing society to supply that information. There is a good side to gossip as to many another reviled thing; its very derivation, "God-sib," tells of a common brotherhood under our Father, a family link that ought to and does make us eager to hear and tell about those who are nearest to us in this relation.

That innocent kindly tidings of our neighbors, friendly discussion of their positions and lives, news heard and told in a spirit of charity, does and will degenerate into scandal and slander, is the fault of our own evil, not of the abused intercourse, which ought to be pure and pleasant.

Reticent people are apt to cultivate their special trait as a virtue, and be proud of it, but extreme reticence is only the expression of dominant pride and masterful selfishness; it is a trait which virtually says, " I am holier than thou," in withdrawing from the common weal and woe its individual joys and sorrows; and demonstrates its origin by becoming always unlovely and repellant. Happy hardly knew how to open her heart to-day to Miss Lavinia, yet she needed her counsel, but the keen old eyes soon saw that something troubled her child's peace.

" What's the matter with you, Happy? " she asked anxiously; " there's an extra crease in your forrard, an' your eyes look tired; what is it? "

" Oh, Aunt Vinny! I'm real perplexed. I don't know how to tell you, for it isn't really anything to tell, but yet it is something to me, after all."

" Kinder curus, that is."

"Well, you see, Aunt Vinny, Mrs. Payson says, — and I don't know, maybe 'tis so, somebody wants — well — thinks about it perhaps — He hasn't said a word, not one word, Aunt Vinny! but I am so troubled. If I can't — why, I ought to let him know before he does ask me ; and if I can — but — oh dear ! "

" Clear as mud," emphatically declared the amused old lady. " Ef I hadn't had two idees in my head, I shouldn't never find out nothin' by you, Happilony ! but I've heered quite a consider'ble lot about you lately. Delye she's come here a spell back, mighty as Julius Cæsar, ragin' about some feller or 'nother that comes to see ye. I was beat when I found out 'twas Luman Packard ! of all things ! I might have knowed it ; there's a sight o' difference betwixt men folks and women ; you don't hear of one widder in a hundred gittin' married ag'in, but law ! a widower's got to be took care of ; I never knowed it to fail."

" But Aunt Vinny, don't think — well, *I* didn't think, but Mrs. Payson — "

" I dare to say ! I dare to say ! she spoke in meetin' afore the bell rung didn't she ? Well ! some folks will, and it's jest as good as not ; saves heaps of trouble. Mis' Payson's got good eyes I hain't no doubt : besides Delye a'n't blind, and ef his ears ha'n't burned some along back it ha'n't been for

want of reason. Now let's have it out, Happy;
nothin' like daylight to walk by. Be you goin' to
marry him? — that is ef he asks ye?"

"Aunt Vinny, I don't know."

"Hm —" growled the old lady. "Well, 'tis
time ye did. You a'n't set downright on mittenin'
of him then?"

"I ain't set on anything, aunty — I am so sorry
for Mira; she isn't half brought up, and now
Maria's going to be married, and he don't like the
man, and won't hear to their living there, and I
don't know what they will do."

"The amount on't is you think you'd oughter
step in and carry the hull thing on your own shoulders; kinder seems a duty like, does it?"

Happy's cheeks burned as she acknowledged this
had been her view of the case. Aunt Vinny looked
at her over those formidable glasses with an aspect
of critical investigation — "Happilony! Do you
reelly, truly, want to marry that man, whether or
no?"

Happy turned uneasily toward the window. She
could not answer at once; at last she said gently, —
"I don't know, Aunt Vinny."

"Folks gener'lly does know when they come to
that pi'nt," dryly remarked Aunt Vinny. "I know
ye consider'ble well, Happy Dodd; and I know
you're jest the cretur to go and do somethin' you

hadn't oughter do no more'n the man in the moon,
because folks want to have ye do it, and therefor
and thereby you think it's your bounden dooty.
Now I tell ye there's some things even in this here
contrairy state o' bein' that you'd ought to like to
do or you'd oughter let 'em alone. Same as 'tis
with vittles ; what don't taste good to ye don't set
well with ye never. Now this marryin' a'n't no
play ; one or t'other has got to draw the hull load
mostly, and it takes good heart to do that ; there is
some yokes that pull even fust go off, but there's
more don't, and if there's an off ox in the pair —
why t'other one catches it I tell ye. Ef you don't
feel as though you couldn't noways content yourself without goin' an' marryin' Luman Packard,
Amen ! but if you're goin' to because you think it's
right 'n proper to help him, why, don't ye never do
it. (Marryin' a man ain't like settin' along of him
nights and hearin' him talk pretty ; that's the fust
prayer ; there's lots an' lots o' meetin' after that.
And the worst on't is you can't git rid of 'em like a
pinchin' shoe, they're allers round, winter 'n summer, allers under foot so to speak as it were ; and it
wants an everlastin' sight of likin' to put up with
anybody that way. Besides, they're onreliable, the
best on 'em : they set on the sweetenin' fust,
always ; pork and potatoes is kep' in the pot till it
comes to be every-day, and when you can't help it

then you have to eat them things; and it takes real
fustrate everlastin' love to put up with things that
a'n't what they looked to be, when you find 'em
out fin'lly."

Happy had to smile, troubled as she was, but still
the idea of Mira stayed with her.

"It's mostly about Mira that I care, aunty; I
can't bear to see her spoiled."

"Wuss 'nd more so! Happy Dodd, you are re-
dikilous! 'Tain't Mira you'll hev to marry; and
'tain't your chore to bring her up; the Lord give
her to her pa and ma, not to you, noways. But it
'does seem as ef you couldn't sense what I mean.
Look here! do you like Luman Packard the way
you did that Park feller?"

Happy shrank as if from a blow. Miss Lavinia
had made her understand at last. She felt in the
sudden and mighty throb of her heart, in the recoil
of her whole nature, that the love she had thought
dead within her was only sleeping, and had risen
from its feigned grave to warn her against any
counterfeit of its power and permanence; for Happy was one of those women who can love but
once: a nature that only blooms a single time, and
then contents itself with a flowerless existence forever, though it grow and thrive otherwise.

"I know now, Aunt Vinny," she said, when
breath and color came back.

" Well, I hated to hurt ye, Happy, but it had to
be. You'd have repented, and you couldn't have
went, if I'd let ye go on the way you was a goin'.
I know you're sot on doin' what ye can for peace
and righteousness, more partikilar righteousness,
but you can't do this for neither. Say! ha'n't you
clean forgot besides what I more'n hinted to ye
once, that you wouldn't have no health to take
care o' a family, supposin' even you had oughter
take the chances of havin' 'em sickly little creturs
to be responsible for ? '

Happy's face paled ; in her anxiety to do what
was best for Mira, she had forgotten all- other con-
siderations.   She kissed Aunt Vinny without a
word, grateful to have been showed the abyss
before her, and have her mind set at rest ; and
went home quite resolved to let Mr. Packard
know, as well as she could, that his pursuit was
vain.

By having stringent engagements in the nursery
when he called, or slipping out of a side door when
she saw him coming up the path to the kitchen, so
that Delia could not find her, and could conscientiously tell him she was out, (which she was very
willing to do,) he at last began to understand that
Happy did not want to see him.   Then he quite
broke down, and was so openly and simply disappointed and miserable, that even Delia, dragon as

she had proved in Happy's behalf, begun to pity him. It is sweet to be pitied; there was a peculiar consolation in it coming from hard-headed, practical Delia; her sympathy seemed to endorse his suffering as genuine; his visits did not cease, but they were no longer for Happy; he poured his sorrows into Delia's ear, and drew strength from her counsel, till he began to think he could not live without her, and one night fairly went down on his knees to her in the wash-room, whither he had followed her busy steps for fear of interruption in the kitchen, and implored her to be his wife.

Delia was astounded. She had not once thought of this. She was flattered and touched both; her vanity — for in what woman has not this "stump of Dagon remained," even to hoary hairs? — her vanity was fed, and her heart softened toward a man who had not only suffered so much but had found such consolation in her. True, she was old enough to be his mother, but that is not considered in New England a fatal obstacle by any means, and Delia's feeling for Mr. Packard was rather the tenderness of a mother for a hurt child than the absorbing passion we denominate love. It was a good feeling to trust and to wear however: and she did not stop to analyze it in her astonishment at the offer and her equally surprising pleasure in it. How she accepted, Delia never quite knew, but she contrived to make her acceptance plain, and Mr. Packard went home that night a happy man.

But Delia felt obliged to tell Happy at once, and with ample apology.

" It does beat all how I come to do it," she said, frankly.

" I hadn't no more thought on't than the baby up stairs ; but he took on so dreadful bad when you giv' him the mittin Happy, that it kinder set me feelin' for him. I expect that was about it. And I want to say now, before things gits too fur, that ef you think different from what you did along back why I don't want to stand in your way none : and I reckon he'd whip round real spry if you jest looked his way, now."

" Oh, Delia," said Happy, " he wouldn't do any such a thing ! Besides, I haven't changed my mind, and I shan't. But you ought to give him more credit than that. I'm sure he could never think of anybody but you, now."

" I ain't so dredful sure o' that ; he ha'n't got no great o' backbone ; but then I've got enough for two."

" You're a great deal better for him than I could be, Dely. I am so glad about it : just as glad as I can be ; and you can't think how relieved I am about Mira. I did hate to have her grow up spoiled ; " and Happy seconded her words with a hearty kiss on Delia's cheek, which brought a suspicious dimness into the cool gray eyes.

"You're as clever as a robin, Happy. I guess you've done me more good than the minister an' meetin' together, since you've lived here, and I've strove to tell ye on't, frequent, but somehow I couldn't fetch round to. I guess I'll go now and tell Mis' Payson, for he's real onreasonable about waitin'; seems Maria's a goin' to git married next week, and he'd jest as lieves I'd come there right off. But I ain't a goin' to, now I tell ye. I shan't leave Mis' Payson in the suds not for no man that ever was born yet. I've got a fust cousin's widder over to Bassett, who's jest buried her only child, and she's got to fly round for a livin' like the rest on us; she's kep' boarders a spell, but it's wearin' work, and now Viohly's dead I guess she might like to come here; she's a most an excellent hand to cook vittles, and a capable piece. I've wish't I had her faculty, frequent."

So Delia went her way to astonish Mrs. Payson, and Happy sat down to her sewing, smiling to think of the turn things had taken, and thankful to be relieved of her anxiety about Mira.

Mrs. Payson was surprised enough, but accepted the position as well as she could. Aunt Lavinia was indignant and amazed both, but her sharp remonstrance did not move Delia a particle.

" Talk now, do talk : talk away, Lavinny Green ;
you don't make nor break me any! I'm real sick
o' housework, an' I want a change," for Delia
stoutly refused to confess to any sentiment in the
matter.

" Great change, I should think," retorted Aunt
Vinny ; " you won't do nothin' to Luman Packard's
I expect. Jest set with your hands in your lap.".

" Well, 'tain't jest the same thing doin' your own
work to what 'tis toilin' an' workin' for other folks.
I'm old enough to hanker after a home o' my own,
and belongin's, now I tell ye."

" You're old enough to know better'n to marry a
feller like him, Delye Lamb, twenty years younger'n
you be."

" Well! where's the harm on't if we're both on
us suited ? It's our own funeral I guess ; and one
thing is certin ; I shan't never have to take care of
an old man, that's the best on't."

" I'd as lieves take care o' two on 'em as that
skip-jack of a girl o' his'n."

" My! don't you let Happy hear that talk, Lavinny Greene ! She sets by Miry as though she
was bewitched ! "

" Happy ain't no rule. She ain't like folks.
She's one o' the Lord's own sort if ever there was
one ; she likes folks because they're poor, and sick
and wicked, not because they're likely."

"Well! I vum I don't!" frankly returned Delia. "Happy's most too good for common; she's one o' them that rejoices over repentin' sinners, and catches hold of 'em and helps pull 'em out of the horrible pit Scripter tells about. Now I'm free to confess I don't like 'em till they've got a goin'; but she's a real saint upon earth. Not but what she has her failin's, and I'm glad on't, and I hope she'll keep 'em a spell, for I don't want her to go to heaven yet awhile!"

Miss Lavinia was mollified by this simple admiration of her darling, so that the friends parted peaceably, and in due time the wedding took place in the minister's kitchen; and Mr. Packard soon became conscious he had fallen into good hands; a little stringent and persistent perhaps, but all the better both for him and Mira.

CHAPTER XXVIII.

It was in the course of the following winter that Happy went into the study, called by Mr. Payson, and received from him a letter; a fact which puzzled her a good deal till she opened it, as she had no correspondents at all. But it ran thus:

WILFORD, JAN. 1st, 18 —.

DEER MISS HAPPY:

I take my pen in hand to inform you that I am well and hope you injoy the same blessing but more to say I Remember Well them words you spoke the last time I see you; well I have experienced Relligion since I come to wilford and I've took the pledge and kep it so fur which is quite a spell — "

Happy's heart stood still with a sort of joyful terror. Was there a greater temptation lying in wait for her than she had ever yet known? — and yet an angel could not have felt a purer throb of joy and gratitude than she sent up to heaven before she dried the quick tears that would not· let her read the rest, and went on :

" And I see what you sed was correct; we are feeble cretures and can't do nothing without divine Help and I hope I shall keep on which I ask your prayers for to help me and I have a Helpmeet in my Wife Sarah Ann which I was married to a year come Febooary, and we have a little Boy. Wishing you all good and the lord's blessing besides for the good you done me I am yours to Command

FRED'K PARK."

She laid the letter down stunned. In that hour a hope died forever that she did not know before had existed ; a hope so much a part of her inner life that it had grown and strengthened without recognition, and she felt to blame for the very agony that accompanied its destruction.

It was well for her that the new baby who had recently arrived at the Parsonage was an exacting little creature, and that Una demanded even more care than usual since her mother could give her none.

The world would have seemed very empty to Happy but for those little clinging arms, and that baby helplessness. She could not stop to feel her grief fully till night came, and then she faced it; and in that full gaze saw that its indulgence was

wrong and must cease. To know that she ought
to do a thing was enough for Happy; on her knees
she sought for help, and shamed herself for losing
sight of the great blessing that had answered her
prayers in her own pain. Prayer does not always
bring us peace in its answer; but it brings always a
blessing, though it be in disguise; and this she
knew, though as yet she did not feel it; but went
about her work for days with a curious consciousness that her life was ended in all human interest;
— as if any life ever lost that, which had also found
an interest in the life to come! It was Sunday
before she had a chance to show Miss Lavinia the
letter; the old lady read it over twice.

"Just like a man!" was her sole comment, as
she dropped it into the fire. Happy did not answer
her; she longed to rescue the quickly shrivelled
paper, but she could not say so. Miss Vinny had
purposely put the last touch to her lingering weakness, as a surgeon probes a wound for its quicker
healing.

The coming spring was to bring Ruth Holden
back to Canterbury; her father had died abroad,
and she was coming with her aunt to live at Madam
Holden's. This was good news to Happy, who in
all this change and separation had never ceased to
love Ruth with a passion of affection, and to pray
for her as such love prays, "without ceasing." She

had seen Julia grow up, in all these years, into a
tall blooming girl, and Helen ripen into a little
woman; she looked up now instead of down into
Mary Gray's honest brown eyes, but she thought
of Ruth still as a child; when she stood by her at
last and found her a noble and beautiful young
girl, with the added poise and grace of education
and travel, her heart sank within her, and for once
Happy· thought of herself, and feared this elegant
and lovely creature could not look on her with any
tenderness, or scarce recollect her. But she was
mistaken; taught by a real grief and loss, — for she
had loved her father with all her heart — Ruth had
discovered that a real friend is the next best of
God's gifts to a parent, however humble that friend
may be; with all her pride and shy fastidiousness
she was a keen appreciator of character, and
Madam Holden's letters had kept her apprised of
Happy's work, and of her manifest interest in and
love for her old Sunday school darling, and Ruth
stooped to kiss Happy's little brown face with as
much warmth as Happy could have asked. It was
a pure delight to her to watch this fresh young
beauty; to see thought and feeling sweep over her
expressive face like cloud and sun, to hear her
gently modulated voice ask and answer all the questions that were heaped on her, and all she had to
put herself. Her graceful dress, a just interpreta-

tion of her taste and refinement, her soft abundant
hair, her clear keen eyes, and lovely lips and skin.
Happy studied as an artist might, but with a keener
passion. Ruth seemed to her altogether,

> "Too bright and good
> For human nature's daily food;"

but when she said shyly, as they were left alone for
a moment, " Happy, I have your little book still; it
has been a great comfort," Happy could not speak;
she turned away her head and closed her eyes to
thank God. Ruth understood it, but she too could
say no more. Happy's tears and troubles were all
forgotten now; at last even this one, above all
beloved, had come into the fold of safety! and she
was grateful and joyful as never before in all her
life.

It is true no doubt that Ruth's soul and salvation
were no more valuable than any other of her
scholars' in the abstract; but we do not live by
abstractions. God has so made us that we have
individual preferences and affections, and has given
us the divinest of all precedents in the dear disciple
"whom Jesus loved." Not that he did not love
the others, did not even yearn over Judas, but John
was especially dear to his human heart; and this is
recorded for our sakes, with that exquisite tenderness and compassion for human frailty that per-

vades the gospel, and is the very fragrance of the
Saviour's human life. For it is by these individual-
ities that we are educated for the life to come, it is
through them that we find our own level and position, and gravitate toward those who attract us
even as we ascend upward toward God when he
becomes to our souls "the chiefest among ten
thousand and altogether lovely," and beholding
Him we are changed into his likeness by mere sympathy and longing. There was but one now of
Happy's first class for whom she could not hope
and believe the best things. Addy Palmer she
heard nothing from. She must leave her in God's
hands, while still she prayed. There had been a
rumor in Canterbury that Addy had married a wild
young man without the consent and against the re-
monstrances of her friends, but this was only a
rumor. Mrs. Palmer had never alluded to it in any
of her infrequent letters to her one friend in the
town, so that Happy would not believe it could be
true. Time might give her some tidings of Adelaide, but whatever had happened her heart rested
on the presence and power of God in the girl's behalf; this could not fail her; this is "the shadow
of a great rock in a weary land," and under it the
saddest and the most anxious heart can rest, if only
it has found out that refuge and trusted in it.

Madam Holden began to see as the summer went

on that Happy was not well or strong; her face
paled, her eye drooped; she put her hand too often
to her side, and her lameness was more apparent
than ever.   The truth was that the big baby in the
household was too much for her strength; Mrs.
Payson was too feeble to carry him at all, and the
dead weight a heavy baby can be during his early
existence is a painful fact to those who have them
in charge.

Madam Holden devised a plan to rescue Happy
from this small tyrant at least for a time; she was
going to the sea-side with Ruth for a few months,
and she wanted Happy to go with them as their
maid; the service would be light, and the change
useful; and it was so evident the girl's health was
failing that she felt Mrs. Payson could not refuse to
find a temporary substitute and let her go.   The
idea was a glimpse of Paradise to Happy; to be
with Ruth and Madam Holden, and to see the
ocean; nothing so bright had ever lain in her way
before.   She did not like to leave Mrs. Payson and
Eunice and the baby; but she felt her own weakness in the languor that made her work so hard, at
times so impossible, and she hoped to come back
restored to strength and brightened in spirit.

Madam Holden undertook to arrange the matter
with Mrs. Payson, when on the morning of the
very day she was to see her about it, Delia walked

hastily into the nursery door, her face flushed, and
her bonnet awry.

"Happy!" said she, "git down your bonnet
quicker'n winkin', and hand them children over to
Betsey Ann. Miss Lavinny's been took with the
shockanum palsy and you've got to come right off."

Happy was pale and frightened enough, but
ready-witted as ever; she went to Mrs. Payson and
told her, then into the kitchen for Mrs. Lamb,
while Delia sat in the rocking-chair fanning herself
with her handkerchief, and puffing with the heat
and hurry. In ten minutes Happy was ready to go
with her, and when Mrs. Holden arrived at the
Parsonage in the afternoon and heard what had
happened, she resolved to say nothing about her
own plans, for she foresaw that Happy's would
perhaps be seriously and materially altered by this
event. They found poor Miss Vinny lying white and
speechless on her sofa in the parlor; a passing
neighbor had seen her lying by the doorstep insensi-
ble, and brought help; sending for the doctor and
Delia — Mrs. Packard — as soon as the old lady
could be taken into the house. Doctor Sands was
there when Happy went in; he did not say much
about the case, but desired to have a bed brought
into the parlor, and his patient made comfortable
there, as soon as possible. Happy attended to all
this; she knew where to find everything in the

house, and with Delia's help Miss Vinny's own bedstead was fetched down stairs and put up, a drugget from the garret spread over the carpet, and the
helpless woman undressed and laid on the pillows;
a look of relief passed over her rigid face, and
Delia sat down beside her and fanned her, while
Happy followed the doctor into the kitchen to ask
his opinion.

"It was some sudden shock," he said; "something that she was too old and weak to bear,
Happy. They found her dressed for a walk; she
had been somewhere; perhaps she had a painful
letter. Did you find anything of the sort about
her?"

"I didn't look, doctor; but here is her dress; I'll
see if there is anything in the pocket."

There was something; a something that ex-
plained the shock that had fallen upon Miss Vinny;
a letter hastily crumpled and thrust into the pocket
one might see, as if she wanted it out of her sight,
in the sudden dismay and pain it brought.

By hard labor and painful frugality Miss Lavinia
had laid by three thousand dollars; one thousand
was safe in the Canterbury Saving's Bank, the
other two she had been persuaded to invest in a
small farm, which her second cousin, that Abijah
Greene before mentioned, rented of her. He had
contrived either by a studied neglect of her interest

or an equally studied devotion to his own, to let
the land be sold for default of the taxes, which he
had promised to pay himself in consideration of an
abated rent. But being a shrewd Yankee he had
fallen back on a record of failing crops and " poor
luck," and allowed the land to be sold simply for
the value of his indebtedness. His mother-in-law,
being possessed of a little ready money, bought the
farm in for a tenth of its value, and kept Abijah on
as tenant for his wife's sake. Of course the farm
would be his in the end, as his wife was the only
child, and he had carefully contrived this neat little
piece of legal swindling to secure to himself a bit of
property which he had long coveted.

But to Miss Lavinia the loss had been a deadly
blow. If she had been proud of anything in the
world it was her independence ; for this she had
worked and endured and suffered ; and petty as her
resources were, needing to be eked out in every
conceivable way, still they were enough to keep
her without help from any one, and promised her a
life of peace and rest for the few years that life was
likely to last.

The shock of loss had been too much for a
frame already weakened by old age, and a mind
whose decent pride had become a habit as well as
a trait. She had hoped to hide her head in her
own house which yet remained to her, and endure

silently privation and even destitution, but nature
avenged itself on the worn body; she fell at the
very threshold of refuge, and circumstance, " that
most unspiritual God," laid open at least to her
friends, the secret she had hoped to keep to herself
while life lasted.

She was unable to speak, to move, to help herself
at all; just now she was unconscious of all around
her, but Doctor Sands said her mind would return
before long, and then it was important that familiar
surroundings should await her. In his heart he
knew that as far as man could see the best thing
for Miss Lavinia would be the sanctuary of death ;
peaceful altar, where all this world's dread blows
are averted, and the stricken soul escapes from
doubt and fear forever ! 'But death is a cure that
only the Great Healer can administer; man dare
not meddle with it ; it is not his to give ; he must
do his best to recall the unwilling soul from its temporary refuge, restore it again for the battle, disturb
the sleeper and arm him for the conflict, however
unwilling he be to do so.

There seemed to be no one but Happy for this
emergency. Delia could not leave little Mira who
was just getting up from scarlet fever, any longer;
she promised to let Mrs. Payson know directly, and
find somebody to fill Happy's place, for to-night at
least, and then left her to her watch and ward be-

side the lifeless old face whose set lineaments had yet a voice and language for Happy, saying to her eyes in the very words of scripture, " Thine own friend and thy father's friend forsake not."

CHAPTER XXIX.

IT was a hard night's watch for Happy; there was no active nursing to do, nothing more than to wet the dry lips, and wait for the change that might come; it was moonlight, and the rich odors of the flower-garden floated in at the open window with a crowd of remembrances on their sweet wings; that honeysuckle's breath brought back much to Happy's mind that she did not wish to recall, but night, in the silence of a sick-room, is not conducive to forgetfulness; to avoid those thoughts of the past which were as painful as profitless she began to consider the situation.

If Miss Vinny should ultimately recover, what prospect lay before her? Even if she recovered health entirely, which Doctor Sands admitted was doubtful at her age, she would yet be so poor and helpless that life would be a burden to her. She had no nearer relative than this cousin who had shown himself so unkindly a kinsman; there was nobody to help her literally. Happy knew that this

very money that had been lost, had been left to
her in Miss Vinny's will; she did not know that
Abijah Greene had found this out, and made it an
excuse to himself for his legal theft; saying to his
conscience, which sometimes pricked him a very
little, that Lavinny had no right to leave her money
to people who were not relatives, — that he only
took what should have been his own! Sophistry,
to be sure, but just such reasoning as stands many
a man in stead of the honor and honesty he pro-
fesses, but does not practice.

As she sat in the dim and fragrant silence thinking over these things, Happy at last and unwillingly
enough began to question whether it were not her
duty to leave Mrs. Payson's employment and come
to take her abode with Aunt Vinny as long as she
should live. The idea was not pleasant to her; the
Parsonage had come to be as much her home as any
place could be without her mother; her heart was
twined so closely about the children, Mrs. Payson,
and the minister too, that to leave them would be
a real exile to her. Then there was the present
prospect of a journey and a long time of association
with Ruth and Madam Holden, an outlook that but
a few hours before had been to her like cold water
to a thirsty soul; how could she give this up and
take up her dwelling with a helpless and no doubt
querulous old woman? Her heart rose rebelliously

against the thought, but like a flash certain curt and
apparently inconsequent passages of Scripture came
into her head. "Who died for us—" "Ye have
not yet resisted unto blood"—"thou therefore endure hardness"—"who pleased not himself"—
"him they compelled to bear the cross;" and on
this last word hung a fragment of a hymn she had
once been fond of repeating:—

> "Be mine the humble, helpless prayer,
> Compel me Lord to bear thy cross?

Had he not done that here? She hid her face in
her hands and prayed for help. Then the other
side of the question—Miss Lavinia's side—rose
up before her; if she lay there herself, stricken and
poor, what would she need and wish to have done
for her? there was no escaping the direct answer.
She was young; well, except for some over-fatigue;
she had more money of her own now than Miss
Greene had before her loss, for the interest of what
her mother left her had never been touched, and
her wants were so few and simple she had laid by
most of her wages, except what she contributed to
certain charities, chiefly the needs of her mission-
school pupils and their families; Miss Vinny had
the house and a thousand dollars left, with the interest on this money, and no rent to pay; with
whatever slight sewing Happy could find time to

do, they could live, simply but surely. She could rest there as well as at the sea-side, and the house-work would be a change for her. Before the birds began to sing the sun's coming, Happy was re-solved, not with any proud feeling of sacrifice or self-denial, but rather with a pitiful consciousness of short-coming and humiliation in that she had delayed such a decision at all, or considered it for a moment as possible to be avoided.

With daylight some awakening seemed to come to poor Miss Vinny, and before many hours she be-came conscious though still speechless, and her eyes followed Happy about with a look of wistful dumb devotion we see sometimes in the lesser creation, who look up to man in a silent worship, by no means justified always.

Delia came in about noon and offered to sit by her while Happy ran over to the Parsonage, to get some needful articles for her own use ; perhaps, she thought, to tell Mrs. Payson of her projected ar-rangement. To her great surprise she found Mary Gray installed in the nursery with the big baby in her lap, and little Una on a stool at her feet, listening with all her soul to a wonderful story. Happy was astonished and touched both ; it seemed Mary had called to see her just after she went out, and finding Mrs. Payson in such trouble volun-teered to help her, which she could the more readily do as her mother had left town and she was staying with Helen Sands for a few days. Her kind honest face charmed the children, instinctive judges of character as they are, and Mary was only too glad to do something at once for Happy and Mrs. Payson, whom she loved next to her teacher.

She was to be with them to-day, and then Helen Sands was coming to-morrow, and Julia the day after; they had arranged, she said, to take Happy's place with the children as long as was needful; and here was another reason for at once opening the matter of her permanent stay with Miss Vinny; so with a trembling heart she repaired to the sitting-room and stated her case to Mrs. Payson. It was an unpleasant surprise enough; but after the first shock and instinctive dismay were over, and she had calmly considered it, she too came to the unwilling conclusion that Happy's duty was plain however disagreeable it might be either for herself or other people, and Mrs. Payson was too earnest and honest a Christian to stand in the way of any one's known duty. She parted from Happy with tears and smiles both, promised her all the sewing she could afford to put out of the house, and was soon, by Mrs. Lamb's help, provided with a young girl who was said to be well-meaning, but proved herself nevertheless so dull, so awkward, and so unable to carry out any good intention she might have had, that Mrs. Payson sighed for Happy's quick intelligence and deft fingers almost hourly.

It is a tolerably good test of a person's real value to find how much they are missed in absence; there are many people who are ornamental, and agreeable, and pleasant, whom we can easily live without when they leave us, but there are a few who are the "salt unto humanity," whose loss takes the savor from our daily lives, and the sweetness from our enjoyment; who leave even in their temporary departure a gap no others can fill; whose death makes a void eternity alone can supply; and what makes the difference? Character! says a competent philosopher; but what makes that character? What, if not common sense and the grace of God combined? and both of these good gifts were Happy's. Mrs. Holden and Ruth were seriously disappointed, but they could not remonstrate, and many a time as Ruth thought in those bright summer days how Happy's eyes would have brightened at the sights and sounds of the sea, and how its fresh breezes would have colored the poor pale cheeks, and blown away the languidness of her tired soul and body, her heart went out with love and reverence both to the humble yet brave spirit that had so taken up its heavy burdens of duty and denial, and borne them day by day in the strength of the heavenly life.

But Happy found some compensations, as we all can if only we have the glad habit of looking for and welcoming them, rather than dwelling alone on loss and pain. As Miss Vinny grew slowly back into life she hung more and more on her dear inmate for cheer and solace; it was pitiful to see how broken she was for a few weeks, how wistfully she fixed her eyes on Happy as she went about the house at work, and with what faint remonstrance she took all her services. Then there was a certain freedom about the new life that was not unpleasing to Happy; she could go and come as she liked, and her classes could come and see her as was impossible before. Julia and Helen and Mary all improved the new position, and brightened the long weeks with their visits. Jack and Nan, and Pauline Lagré, who had never forgotten the times when Happy gathered them in her little kitchen, also found her out in her new home. And Jack proved of the greatest service; every morning before work he came to do whatever errands Happy had; he brought her wild flowers as in the dear old time, and luckily the pink honeysuckles were out of bloom now: Nan, too, came to sit by Miss Lavinia, frequently, and let Happy take a little walk; but as the summer passed by the old lady recovered the use of her tongue and her hands, though she

was still unable to walk, and she insisted on being
left to herself, at such times.

"I can holler, Happy, if anybody tries to pester
me, and I'd a heap rather set by myself than have
that little cretur a watchin' me the hull time as ef
I was a wax figger. You lock the front door when
you go up street 'nd there won't nobody come in
then. I'm trouble enough, anyhow, but I must do
what I can."

"I don't call you a trouble Aunt Vinny," Happy
answered very gently.

"Well, I don't suppose you do; but I've got my
senses agin, and I know I be. What on airth took
me to act so like all possessed jest because that
feller stole my money I dono. I never calc'lated to
tell you nothin' about it, and here fust I knew I
didn't know nothin', and next time here I was,
dumb as a horned critter, on the bed. Well, well,
well! the ways of Providence do beat all!"

"I should most think this was the way of improvidence, aunty," said Happy, smiling.

Miss Lavinia's face fired.

"Improvidence! not much! It's fust class
swindlin'. He did it a puppus. He know'd I'd
ha' paid them taxes ef he'd let me know how 'twas.
Don't talk to me about his "poor luck," as he tells
of; folks ha'n't no business to have any sort of
luck; besides, he's fore-handed and managin'

enough to make somethin' or nuther out of mullein
stalks, ef he wanted to. It's jest a game o' his'n.
And you hark to me, Happy; don't you never
trust no money of your'n to a man; there ain't
one on 'em but what'll take th' advantage of a
woman, specially if she's poor, every time. They
don't think women-folks has any right to money
anyhow, mabbe a man might look after his wife's
means for his own sake; I don't say but what they
would, but that ain't to do with the case; what's
her'n is his'n and he knows it everlastin well, but
come to anybody's else's wife, or any other woman
single or married, an' they a'n't nowhere; left out
in the cold every time."

"But dear Aunt Vinny," said Happy, troubled
by this bitter spirit in the old lady, "do you really
in your heart believe Mr. Greene meant to cheat
you? Perhaps we do him injustice. Maybe he
couldn't pay the taxes, and put off telling you
because he expected to, finally. Isn't he a Christian man?"

"He's a professor, ef that's what you mean; but
he ain't a practiser, an' there's the hull world betwixt them two sorts. Don't talk to me, Happy;
ef he hadn't knowed that land would come to her
eventooally, he'd ha' paid them taxes mighty quick,
if he'd had to borrer the money. I told him what
I hadn't ought to have told him, last time he come

here,— that I'd willed that place to you. There
was some talk about sellin' on't and buyin' stock
in the new railroad, and sez I, " Bijah," sez I,
" railroads is onreliable things; they're allus gitten
into trouble and bustin', so to speak, as it were, and
there a'n't nothin to fall back on; them old rails
won't sell; but land's right there till the eend of
the world, and I've willed that farm to Happy
Dodd, so't I won't run any resks." I see he looked
consider'ble riled, an' now I wish I'd held my
tongue. Ef the land was to be his'n he'd have
paid those taxes as sure as you're born. He a
Christian? don't you take the Lord's name in vain
like that, Happilony! I don't care a half a straw
what a man calls himself, I know a real Christian
man ain't onjust, and mean, and selfish, an' graspin',
and cross; that a'n't religion; not according to my
Bible. Folks don't pick figs off'n thistles to-day no
more'n they did in the Lord's time; you can tell
them by their fruits jest as well as you could then.
Didn't I jest catch that feller that come round
sellin' apple trees when that stick he told was a
Hu'lbut Stripe bore the fust time? That little
sour yaller thing wan't no more a Hu'lbut Stripe 'n
I'm a turkey! He didn't sell no more trees round
here, after that! Jest so with Abijah, his works
foller him, and they'll keep a doin' on't till he up
an' dies, ef he don't repent pretty quick. If there's

any kind o' talk makes me dead sick, it's to hear folks say when anybody does a mean thing, 'Oh! that's your Christianity!' when it's nothin' but the want on't. They've got sense to see a man's callin' himself a Frenchman don't make him one, but they hain't sense — or else they don't want to own it — to see a man ain't a Christian onless he acts real different from their ways."

Happy could not deny Aunt Vinny's logic; she knew very well what harm a mere profession does to the church and cause of Christ; how much contempt and scorn the hypocrite earns for that religion for which martyrs have died and saints lived. With her, faith and practice were as inseparable as life and breath; and she could not, even with the widest exercise of charity accept one as genuine without the other. This was the faith she had been taught by her mother's example, and the word of God; and this it was she strove to impress upon her scholars. Is there any other faith worth having? Is there any truth, or hope, or use in religion, by whatever name or sect it calls itself, if it does not purify our hearts and regulate our actions? If we are not more gentle, more patient, more kindly, true, generous, unselfish, and self-controlled. If we hate our neighbor, and grind the wages of the poor down to their lowest limit; if we are unjust, unlovely, of mean spirit and evil temper, then of what avail is any name, any profession, any rites and ceremonies that have passed over us ?

Where shall we find ourselves in that day when the stones of the causeway shall cry out against us, and the rocks refuse to cover us, and the Lord himself out of the heaven of heavens shall say as once before — " Where is thy brother ? "

CHAPTER XXX.

By winter Miss Vinny was able to be about the house, and apparently as well as ever; and her old spirit of independence awoke.

"Happilony," she said one day, "you've staid here quite a spell, and it's time you began to look out for yourself a mite now. I'm jest as good as I used to be for't I know, and I hadn't oughter be a takin' up your time no more."

Happy laughed gently.

"Oh, Aunt Vinny, I didn't think you would want to get rid of me just as soon as you got well."

"That's talk. I know ye consider'ble well by this time, child. I know you've been a spendin' money for me too. I can't help that, it's hard, — hard enough — to come onto your hands for all that time, but I ain't goin' to be nobody's burden. I expect I'm smart enough yet to cook, an' I'll get a couple of mill hands to board; that'll get my vittles, and that feller can't touch the thousand dollars I've got left; th' int'rest of that'll buy my

clothes, what few I want, an' mebbe pay my doctor's bill, little by little. I kin live, and I shan't
never forget what you done for me, but it's meaner
'n pusley to keep you here, and be a livin' on your
int'rest money when you ought to be arnin' more,
and I won't do it, so there now ! "

It took Happy a long time to combat successfully
Miss Vinny's resolution, but after a while she prevailed with her, having on her side a strong if secret wish of the poor old lady to keep such a friend
and companion with her in her last years, a wish
she yet tried to overcome and conceal with an unselfishness that touched Happy deeply. But at
length she yielded, and it became settled that
Happy should live with her as a companion, the
old lady doing the housework, and Happy taking in
sewing, and contributing her share to their mutual
expenses; Miss Vinny providing house, garden, and
fuel ; Happy food and light. It was a good thing
for them both, and the little home grew bright with
the cheerfulness of Happy's presence. She persuaded Miss Vinny to use the hitherto shut-up parlor daily, and to let in the sunshine at its two south
windows, usually kept closed after New England
fashion. Luckily the previous carpet had been
spotted, during Miss Vinny's occupancy of it as a
bedroom, in spite of Happy's precautions; so that
did not stand in the way ; and Dr. Sands had told

Miss Greene she must have sunlight and fresh air abundantly if ever she hoped to be strong again. Perhaps this motive alone would not have been sufficient, but he said at the same time that sun and air were equally necessary for Happy! Now no. room could be more pleasant; an old drugget that had been Mrs. Dodd's was fresh bound with some bits of scarlet flannel from the piece-bag; one or two cushions of dingy chintz recovered with gay patch-work, and a small afghan Mary Gray had knit for Happy the year before, as bright in its tints — being knit from the odds and ends of her own worsted work as well as Helen's and Julia's — as the gayest of autumnal foliage, was thrown over the back of Miss Vinny's chair. Ruth had brought from abroad one or two pictures for Happy; a fine chromolith of Alpine scenery, and a French litho-graph, beautifully colored, from a picture of Rosa Bonheur's. These were hung on the yellow-washed wall, and illuminated the room when sunshine failed. Being an old-fashioned house there was an open fire-place, from which Happy pulled away the board, and turned back the carpet which covered the hearth, then she rubbed up the brass andirons so long tucked away in the shed loft, with the shovel and tongs; and when such cold days came that the kitchen fire of coal would not suffice to warm both rooms through the open door, a fire was

built in the parlor, and brought such sparkling
cheer and freshness as only an open fire can give.
Polly Lagré's father provided them with cheap
wood, the refuse of his trade of charcoal burning,
and Jack cut and piled it at odd hours, so the expense was slight; and as Miss Vinny sat before the
blaze with her knitting, and looked at Happy by
the window sewing, with a face as peaceful as a
child's, she felt as if life was sweeter than ever
before.   Frost and tempest had assailed its thorny
aspect, and at length brought it from the bough,
but their rough ministry had also opened the burr,
and now the sweet and shining kernel showed
itself.

"I expect my last days is goin' to be my best
days," she said to Delia Packard, who was a frequent visitor. "I'm as comfortable as an old cat,
a purrin' away here afore the fire. I promised
Almiry I'd be as good to Happy as though she was
my own; but land! it's t'other eend fust. I tell ye!
She couldn't be no better to me ef I was her mother.
It beats all what a cretur she is!" and the old lady
paused to wipe her glasses.

"Well! she is a likely gal, I don't deny it," said
Delia with hearty emphasis, "and folks has found
it out. Look at old Mis' Holden, she sets the aw-
fullest store by Happy that ever was; and so does
Mis' Payson; and as for them that has been in her

class so long they fairly worship her; and there ain't nothin' them youngsters to the mission school won't do for her. It does beat all. Why, our Miry she thinks the sun rises an' sets in Happy's face, and so does the minister's Eunice. I tell you there's somethin' to folks when children like 'em like that."

"That's so," assented Miss Lavinia, as Happy came in with Mira clinging to her hand.

The winter was short and pleasant to Happy this year; personal troubles seemed to have left her stranded above their bitter tide now; but she had the troubles of others to bear still, discovering that the chorus of life is forever singing "this is not your rest." The winter brought a great depression in business all over the country; there was much suffering in Canterbury, the mills stopped running, and with want came disease, its terrible twin. Happy's heart and hands, as spring drew near, began to be overfilled with sympathy and work. At last she quite gave up sewing and devoted herself to the sick and suffering. Madam Holden and many other ladies in the town availed themselves of Happy's acquaintance with the needs of the people to put their alms into her hands, sure that they would be judiciously used, and with a strength whose continuance surprised herself she went about among the friends and relatives of the Sunday

school children, carrying relief for their wants, and
a kindly face and tender voice with them. Many a
worn cheek flushed with pleasure, and many a dull
eye brightened as Happy went in at the door; and
always after she had dispensed the food or clothing,
or delicacy for the very feeble, which she brought,
she had a word of hope or promise from the Bible
to drop into the grateful heart, or a hymn to hush
the fretful child, or a short simple prayer to utter,
almost always well received. This course was the
result of Miss Vinny's advice when Happy first
took up this shape of work for the Master.

"Look-a-here, Happy!" she said, "I want to
tell ye somethin'; you're sot on savin' souls as well
as bodies down there in the mill deestrick; now I
tell ye ef you've got any help for the bodies fetch
that along fust. 'Tain't no use to sow seed right
atop o' hard ground: you've got to dig it up an'
kinder meller it fust. I tell you poor folks feel a
heap more like listenin' to what you say after
they've had a meal o' vittles, than they do before.
It's natur, and you've got to take natur into account when you want to fetch in grace. Besides,
when anybody is faint-like and miser'ble for want
o' something in their stomachs, they don't care no
great about their souls. Look how the Lord done;
he didn't think hard o' them folks he preached to
for bein' hungry after they'd walked consider'ble

fur to hear him, and sot in the open air a spell. He knowed the word would stay by 'em better ef 'twas clinched so to speak, seemin'ly, with them loaves and fishes. I wish folks would call to mind more frequent than they do that verse that says, — 'He knoweth our frame; he remembereth that we are dust.' If we all thought on't it's my belief we should think more of the Lord above, and folks down here too."

As summer drew on, and the distress abated a little, the mission school began to increase more than ever, greatly owing to Happy's winter's work. Many sent their children for her sake who had laughed or scoffed at the idea.

The mill-hall grew full to overflowing; more teachers were needed and found; the lesser children were detailed into another room in a different building, and Helen had to have an assistant. Mrs. Holden began to consider seriously whether the time had not come to put into execution a project she had long had in mind. She had wealth enough for herself and her daughter, Ruth inherited a large property from her father, and beside this, would need nothing: Madam Holden yearly laid aside a part of her income for charity, and had added to it within a few years a legacy of several thousand dollars from a relative; there were ample funds here to build a large and convenient mission

chapel and school-rooms, and this seemed to be the
time. She was not a woman to delay or stay her
hand at any good work which she undertook; her
sympathy was in a certain sense limited; she did
the duty that lay nearest to her first, always; ad-
monished by the text that exhorts a man to attend
to his own household or be held faithless and infidel.
Here, right at her door, was a company of heathen;
the pressing question was to provide for these
neighbors, and to them she devoted all her care and
means. In a very short time a place was selected,
a plan approved, and workmen, carefully selected
from those who most needed work, busily engaged
in laying foundations and building walls. By autumn there would be room enough for all the children. But changes came both to the school and
Happy. Julia Calhoun, now one of the loveliest
young girls in Canterbury, married a clergyman
from a distant part of the State, and went away to
her new home. She parted from Happy with deep
feeling.

"If I am good at all, Frank, I owe it greatly to
that little woman," she said, as they turned away
from Happy's door.

"God bless her!" was the heartfelt answer; how
good he thought his wife Mr. Ireton did not try to
tell, but his face spoke for him.

Mary Gray left home too, but it was to teach.

To the great surprise of every one, Mrs. Gray had
recently married a rich farmer in the neighborhood
of Canterbury ; an old man, whose money had come
so hardly that he held it with a tight grip ; he had
two daughters, both indignant to have a mother
like Mrs. Gray set over them, and Mary's home was
destroyed too ; she was thrown upon her own exer-
tions for support, and preferred to find work as far
away from Canterbury as possible : so she took a
place in a large private school near Philadelphia.
She however, was still near to Happy, for they kept
up a steady correspondence, which was of great use
and comfort to both ; Happy's outlook into the
world and its need growing broader, and Mary's
anchorage strengthened and her heart refreshed by
Happy's works and words.

Of course the class in the church Sunday-school
was now broken up, as Helen alone was left of all
its members since Ruth had never returned to it ;
and now Happy thought it best to give all her time
to the other work, and took the hour and a half
before service to spend in Bible reading to three or
four old people in whom she had become interested
during her experience among the sick.   This was a
pleasant service to Happy, she loved the Bible so ;
and her earnest reading of its precious words gave
them an emphasis and power that were like rivets
to the heart of her hearers.

Miss Vinny almost grudged her loss on Sundays; she seemed to cling more closely day by day to the daughter she had found in her old age.

"I don't doubt them folks set a sight by you, Happy; but I declare for't I most begrutch you to 'em, I miss you so when you're gone. Mebbe it's made up to me in bein' so delightsome to hev you get back."

"Couldn't you go with me sometimes, Aunt Vinny? It isn't far down to the end of Horn Lane, and I know Granny Jakeway would be real glad to see you."

The idea pleased Miss Greene mightily; she took heart the very next Sunday, and spent an hour with the cheery little old woman, who was the nearest of Happy's audience. It did her a great deal of good. Granny Jakeway's poor and narrow attic, though its hard bed and scanty pine furniture were scrupulously neat, and the small sheet iron stove polished to its utmost capacity, contrasted strongly with Miss Lavinia's cosy little home. Sometimes she was disposed to fret over her loss and her poverty, to wish the Lord had done a little better by her in this world, to use her own phrase, but here was a woman to whom her surroundings would have been luxury, a woman, old, alone, miserably poor, and seriously infirm from rheumatism, who was yet so cheerful, so content, and as chirpy as a cricket; and had her tongue full of the Lord's mercy to her.

"Well!" said Miss Vinny, as she laid aside her bonnet and shawl after morning service, "I ain't too old to be lessoned yet, that's a fact, Happy. Mis' Jakeway has preached me one discourse to-day and somehow Parson Payson's sermon kinder followed it up. 'Godliness with contentment is great gain.' He handled it reasonable well, but 'twas a great betterment to keep a thinkin' of her all through it. Thinks me, whenever he'd up an' tell how it worked, that's Granny Jakeway to the life; seemed as though he'd set there along o' us two old creturs and heered her talk an hour before. 'Twas as good as a hull vollum of Barnes's Notes, now I tell ye. I've wrastled some after godliness along back, but I'm free to confess I hain't gin no great thought to the contentment part on't, but I ain't none too old to learn. Mebbe it's the last lesson. I wa'n't one o' them that got sent out o' school at four o'clock, and it's took me quite a spell to learn what I'd oughter, always."

Certainly the dear old lady took this lesson to heart as if it were the last; with the force of character that had always been great and did not seem to weaken with age, she set herself to practice contentment; she shut her lips over a certain habitual fault-finding that had marred the grace of her

Christian profession, and tried to see or to discover some good in everything, even in the pain and weakness of age, and the deprivations of comparative poverty; a poverty felt most keenly when she longed to relieve that of others.

"She's a ripenin' for heaven," was Delia Packard's comment. "As true as you live, Happy, she's a puttin' on the weddin' garment. She was allers good, but folks didn't mistrust it; she kep' her candle under a bushel, an' a bushel of chestnut burrs at that, but it's burnt 'em up now, and she'll be a shinin' light the rest of her days, but I tell ye they won't be many; that's as sure as cipherin' ! "

CHAPTER XXXI.

WITH autumn's approach the chapel drew near to completion. Happy had not been yet to see it, for it did not lie just in her way, and she was very busy. Ruth Holden had become engaged during the summer to a young man from Philadelphia, the son of an old friend of her father's, a Mr. Thorne ; and all her sewing that Happy could do was given to her. No sewing could ever be done with more dainty diligence, none ever had more prayers and more affection set in every tiny stitch; she dreaded the idea of parting with Ruth for what would probably be a life-time, but she rejoiced in her prospect for happiness, which seemed to be very great.

Mr. Thorne was a young man of education and character, in good business, having succeeded to his father's private banking-house; professedly a zealous Christian, with unexceptionable manners, the tastes and habits of a thorough gentleman, and he was of a family standing deservedly high for honor and honesty. Happy had seen him once, and her first impression of his face was not quite favorable; there was something weak about the mobile mouth, and restless about the light hazel eye that displeased her instinctive judgment; but she blamed herself on the spot for having even one disparaging thought about a man so dear to Ruth, and so evidently absorbed in and devoted to her own darling; they were to be married at Christmas, and Happy's fingers had to fly busily to complete Ruth's outfit, so that she had never been near the chapel all summer, and it was to be opened and dedicated on Thanksgiving Day, and all the school given a supper in the evening.

She had looked over the plans with Madam Holden, and given a modest opinion as to their merits, but further had nothing to do with it at all, being so fully occupied at home.

When Thanksgiving Day arrived Miss Vinny was determined to go to the dedication services, which took the place of the usual church services on that day; so dressed in her Sunday's best, and leaning heavily on Happy, she left early, in order to have quite enough time to reach there punctually. The way seemed very long to her, for of late she had lost strength; but when they came to the street where it stood, the sight of the neat brick building brought back the keen spark to her old eyes.

" Stop a minute, Happy; let's take a look at it

a ways off, so's to catch the sense of it; ain't it pretty? There's heaps o' room too, room and to spare. But what's them words on the marble slab above the second set o' windows? I can't see rightly, bein' it's all white."

Happy looked up at the inscription, but for a moment she thought her eyes, too, had failed her; yet another look proved their faithfulness.

"Oh!" she said, half aloud, as if something, neither pain nor pleasure nor astonishment, but moulded of all three, held her breath.

"What is it?" repeated Miss Lavinia, who did not hear the ejaculation distinctly.

"Why, Aunt Vinny! It doesn't seem as if it could be; but it's there; it certainly is. I a'n't asleep."

"For goodness sake, child! what be you up to? What's there? Can't you read?"

"I believe so," answered Happy, with a tremulous sort of laugh. "And yet it does seem to me, Aunt Vinny, that it says on that slab,

$$\mathfrak{D}\mathfrak{O}\mathfrak{D}\mathfrak{D} \ \ \mathfrak{C}\mathfrak{H}\mathfrak{A}\mathfrak{P}\mathfrak{E}\mathfrak{L}, \ 18\text{---}.$$

and under it,

"SHE HATH DONE WHAT SHE COULD."

"I'm glad on't!" exclaimed the old lady, eagerly. "I've set an' set an' wondered to see you, Happy,

workin' like a tiger all these years with them dirty
little creturs, and never thinkin' nothin' about it,
nor ef 'twas hard or easy, and now I'm glad other
folks feel to tell what you've did. I know jest
what you'd say if I'd let ye, and I've kinder comforted myself by thinkin' the Lord knew. And
He's the most consequence to be sure, but after
all, it is pleasant to human natur to have other
folks pleased with us, and human natur is common
property to all on us. 'If there be any virtoo, if
there be any praise, think on these things.' I expect Mis' Holden's got that tex' by heart."

"But Aunt Vinny, there's so many other people
have done just as much and more than I about this
school."

"Who begun it though? Who was't got them
three youngsters together in your ma's back-room,
and kep' it up in Mis' Packard's kitchen such a
spell? Somebody's got to put a mustard seed into
the ground to begin with, or 'twon't never be a
tree, big enough to hold all the fowls o' the air in
its branches. It's your child, Happy, if its growed
out of knowledge, and it had oughter be called
after your name; an' it's just like Mis' Holden to do
it; she ain't goin' to take nobody else's doo jest
becos she's got money; that ain't her; she's as
honest a woman as the Lord above ever made, and
I never see an honester thing done than puttin'

your name up there when she had a good 'nough
right, as things go, to set her own there.   She's
one o' the best."

"That she is!" Happy said warmly; and through
the whole service her beaming, blushing face was a
study to Madam Holden, who read in it all she tried
to say but could not find words enough to express.

Mr. Payson's sermon was from the text engraved
on the marble slab.   Aware of Happy's sincere
modesty, and respecting it, he only alluded to the
name of the chapel by explaining simply and without comment that it was given because the beginning of the school was from a small class, gathered,
and taught for some time, by Miss Happy Dodd ;
and then he went on to exhort his hearers on
the daily duties of life.   First, in as few words
and as clearly as possible, he laid before them all
the way of eternal life.   "'Come unto Me,' the
Saviour says, 'I am the way.'   But you ask, 'how
shall we come?   Christ is not here to hear us.'
My dear friends, there is your mistake.   He is.
Whoever, here and now, will say in his heart,
'Lord Jesus save me, and help me to live a new
life!' has come to him, and will in no wise be cast
out.   Repeat that prayer daily, and it will keep
leading you up to Him who died for you, died to
pay for your sins ; died because He loved you with
a love you cannot measure, or as yet believe.   And

when you have taken up life on the side of Christ,
and in His name, then you will do His work. But
you say again, 'How am I to do it? I have got to
earn my living; there is the house to take care of,
the children to clothe and feed, the daily bread to
be almost fought for, and by night I am so tired I
can't think or work.'"

A sort of sympathetic rustle passed through the
audience as he said this; they all felt the truth of
it for they were almost all poor and hard-working
people.

"Well, Christ knows all about that. He was
poor as you can be, poorer than any of you are, for
he had not a roof to cover his head, or a place to
lie down in, often and often; and felt both hunger
and thirst, and cold, as bitterly as ever you did,
just that he might show you that he could feel for
all your troubles, and enter into all your temptations; and when he tells you to do something for
,him, to show that you love him, he means it; but
he does not ask you to do what you cannot; only
what you can; and there is not in Canterbury, a
man or woman or child so poor, or so hard-worked,
or so tired or so ill, that they cannot show that they
love God and try to serve him. You can any one
of you learn to control your temper; to moderate
your tongue, using gentle and kind words to your
neighbors; to keep peace and order in your houses;

to be honest, temperate, helpful ; all this is just as
much work for our Master as preaching, teaching in
Sunday-school, or being a missionary, and will
please God as much, and help you grow fit to live
with him and for him just as surely as any work in
the world.

" ' She hath done what she could,' the Lord said ;
and yet all Mary did was to give to Christ the best
she had ; and that is all he wants of you.   And the
best any of us have is our heart, our love; give that
to God and the good life will grow out of it as
surely as the stalk of corn grows out of the little
kernel."

He made a very short sermon, knowing well that
a few words, simple, earnest, and distinct, are far
more impressive and useful than a long explanatory
and meandering discourse. Mr. Payson did not
think of himself, or the effect his sermon would
produce as a piece of thought, or learning, or ora-
tory; his business was to preach the gospel, and he
took example from the Lord's own sermons, which
were brief and pointed. An hour is more than the
feeble flesh of most congregations can endure phys-
ically, and one of our old divines was wont to say
that he could preach in twenty minutes more than
his people could practice in a week ; which is true.
It is not the gospel which demands a long sermon,

but the desire of the preacher to produce a sensation, or develop himself rather than his Master.

When Mr. Payson stopped to-day, his audience could have wished him to go on ; yet his words had deeply impressed and much enlightened most of them. After the benediction the children crowded round Happy with such glad faces and eager voices that Madam Holden could scarce make herself heard or seen. But Happy saw her, and putting away the little crowd with gentle hands, went up to her and Ruth who stood together, smiling to see how the little people loved her.

"Oh Mrs. Holden ! " was all she could say. The old lady laughed with a kindly sweetness that relieved Happy's embarassment.

"Well, Happy, that is enough," said Ruth ; " that oh ! expressed a great deal ; don't spoil it."

" My dear Happy," interposed the old lady, " I put your name up there because the school belongs to you, and will be your care always. It means more responsibility than praise to call it by your name."

Happy's face grew grave.

" ' I will watch for their souls as one that giveth account,' " came involuntarily to her lips.

" That is what it implies," said Madam Holden ; and then they turned to go up stairs and examine the school-rooms, while Ruth followed, admiring in her heart the simplicity, delicacy, and honesty of both these women, who, though their stations in life, and their earthly possessions differed so widely, yet showed the same pure and lofty aim, the same entire devotion to their Lord. "All ye are brethren," was the word that touched this unity of life in diversity of living, and brought back to her the dear old hymn that was Mr. Payson's favorite on communion Sundays —

> "Let saints below in concert sing
> With those to glory gone;
> For all the children of our King,
> In earth and heaven are one."

Ruth had but just entered into this family, and felt deeply that she had much to learn. Her lessons all lay before her; both outwardly and vitally differing from those which had touched and taught Happy; but for all gold there is a crucible, and if some needs a longer and a fiercer fire to refine it, and must first be crushed out of the ore rather than washed from the sand, it is all gold at last, and He who sits above the flaming furnace will not leave it till his own face smiles back from the pure and radiant surface.

The school-rooms Happy admired with all her heart. They were large, light, cheerful, and very convenient. Ruth's share in their furnishing had been to supply the maps and pictures, which were

very good of their kind; and in a light closet well
fitted with shelves, she showed Happy a pile of
pasteboard slips with loops attached, on each of
which was printed some text of Scripture in large
letters, so that every Sunday a new word might
attract attention, and be impressed on the children's
memory. The infant school-room was next to the
other, separated only by a small room fitted up for
the library, with a window opening into each school,
at which books were delivered.

This was a great change for the better; and
Happy ate her Thanksgiving dinner, to which Mr.
and Mrs. Packard and Mira had been asked, with a
heart full of most sincere thankfulness. At about
six o'clock they all went back, except Miss Vinny,
to the chapel, and found the large school-room set
with three long.tables, and spread with substantial
food as well as abundant dainties. The appetite of
mission-school children at a Thanksgiving or Christmas feast is a thing incredible to those who have
never watched it. The bright young girls of Mr.
Payson's congregation who waited on the children
could not make feet and hands fly fast enough to
serve the constant demands. Happy and Delia
both volunteered to help, and even Ruth Holden
laid aside her gloves and wrappings and filled cups
of coffee and mugs of milk with the expedition of
a trained waitress.

"For mercy's sakes," exclaimed Delia, in a momentary pause of the clatter, " be them youngsters
holler clear through, or hain't they eat nothing for
a week so's to hold the more now! As sure as I
live an' breathe I've give one boy, about ten or
eleven years old, two big helpin's of turkey, a thick
slice o' beef, four quarters o' pie, three doughnuts,
a big slice o' loaf-cake and two cookies ; he's got it
down by the aid of two mugs of milk and a great
dish o' coffee, and I make no doubt he'll want a
peck to the very least, of nuts and apples ! "

"Never mind, Mrs. Packard! " laughed Ruth.
"It is only for once, and I suppose they are chron-
ically hungry. Do you think any one of them ever
had enough of such food before ? "

"No, I don't suppose they did. I don't blame
'em none as I know of, but it's musical to see 'em
do it. I should think some of them little fellers
would bu'st, certain."

But no such catastrophe justified Delia's wisdom ;
after all was disposed of that the children could eat,
they had what remained divided among them to
carry home. And so abundant was the provision
that every one had something to take away as evi-
dence of the quality of the feast ; and there was no
reason to think, from their hearty enjoyment of
the games and the singing afterward, that any one
of the guests had been over-laden with the goods

provided for them. Aunt Vinny was still up,
though dozing in her chair when Happy got home,
and listened gladly to the story of the evening,
making characteristic comment.

" Well! it'll fill up the school mightily, that kind
o' thing. Some folks would say 'twan't good to
hire 'em to come, they'd oughter come from better
motives; but supposin' they haven't got the motives? 'Sow beside all waters,' Scripter says, and
furthermore ' thou knowest not which shall prosper,
this or that.' Yes; St. Paul wanted to save somebody, by any means, and you've got to bait your
hook accordin' to your fish. When they're saved
they'll know better; but savin' on 'em is our business, secondary to the Lord I mean. Now I guess
I'll go to bed, Happilony; I'm beat out with tired-
ness, but it's the best Thanksgivin' I ever see."

CHAPTER XXXII.

At Christmas Ruth was married. Her sewing had been sent home long before, done with such delicacy and neatness that Ruth and her grand-mother were both delighted; and with the piles of linen came a little silk and leather needle-book, so exquisitely made, and so daintily devised, that it excited everybody's wonder. Happy had sewed a piece of her heart into it, for the pale lavender lining was a bit of her mother's wedding bonnet which she had preserved safely to this day, as a relic of that mother's youth and transient happiness. And the tiny red strawberry that hung at one end and did duty as an emery-bag, had been her mother's work, and her own childish admiration; nothing was too good for Ruth that she had; and she had worked on the little toy till every stitch was set with distinct precision, and the soft flannel leaves were embroidered with as much elab-orate care as ever a young mother put on her first

baby's blanket.   It lived always after among Ruth's
treasures.

Happy, too, decorated the house for the wedding;
a profusion of trailing pine had been stored away
in the barn cellar, before frost came, for this purpose ; and with this, and graceful branches of hem-
lock, glittering clusters of Kalmia leaves, and
feathery bits of odorous pine, she adorned all the
rooms, grouping the hot-house flowers that were
sent from the city against soft backgrounds and in
little frames of dark rich green, more beautiful
than any succession of pictures ; for who can paint
the translucence of petals, the evanescent tints, the
airy grace of flowers in their delicate life ? or what
scent of manufacture reproduce the floating fragrance that makes a halo about them ?

At the appointed hour she waited for Ruth's
coming into the long parlor, half hidden behind a
great orange-tree in a tub.   She had gladly promised to witness the ceremony, and having first done
all she could in the dressing-room, and given the
last grace of arrangement to the supper table, she
had come in by a side-door, and stolen into shelter.
Very few people saw her, and nobody noticed her,
but she neither knew or cared ; her whole attention
was fixed on the beautiful figure draped in satin so
rich and white it looked like folds of solid moonlight, while a veil of the simplest and lightest sort

clung to it like a mist. Ruth wore no ornament
but a white rose Happy had nursed and coaxed all
winter that it might bloom now, but no other ornament was needed for the bright veiled head, the
tender shining eyes, the peach-bloom that came and
went on her face like flying clouds of dawn, and
the scarlet lips parted with the breathlessness of
her emotion.

She was the loveliest of brides, and for the moment Mr. Thorne's illuminated face swept away the
habitual look that had troubled Happy. Madam
Holden was serene and splendid as never before ;
she meant to do all honor to the occasion, and act
as if the wedding were a sunrise instead of a sunset to her, deeply as she felt the coming vacancy in
her household. Tears stood unbidden in Happy's
eyes as she listened to the ceremony ; it meant a
great deal to her that Ruth was passing out of her
orbit forever, as she thought ; she did not know yet
how small the world is, or how our lives touch at
points that seem impossible, and which we cannot
at all foresee.

But when all was over, and matters came back
to the quiet level that follows excitement and
change, Happy was diverted from thoughts of
Ruth by Miss Lavinia's increasing feebleness. The
old lady felt it herself, being too sensible and too
experienced not to know that her symptoms indi-

cated the end. She did not say much to Happy; she was not a woman who liked to express emotion, and she felt a great deal; death is at the least a solemn thing to encounter, even when it is deprived of its sting, and parting is sad, sad always, sadder than ever when we know of no definite time of re-union. Miss Lavinia had great natural courage, which added one element of strength; and her faith had been tried and proved strong by many vicissitudes; she could trust the Lord now, looking back on all the way by which he had led her, but she did shrink a little from the new and strange change which lay so close before her.

"I hate to leave you, Happy," she said one day. "Not but what I know you'll be took care of; the Lord'll see to that, an' I've did somethin' towards it, but it seems as though I shouldn't never know what to do without ye."

"But dear Aunt Vinny, you'll have the Lord to take care of you and comfort you there."

"Yes; I s'pose I shall. I know I shall; but somehow I don't feel to realize it. Seems as if I couldn't know nor feel nothing so much as your face, an' softly little hands, and your talk, Happy. I'm real feeble, and you're dreadful handy an' pleasant."

Happy smiled, very like a rainbow, for there were tears behind the smile.

"Oh, Aunt Vinny! Christ is altogether lovely, and almighty to help; you will find him a great deal nearer and better than you think."

"Then there's somethin' else," the old lady went on, taking no notice of Happy's tender words. "I allers did hate changes, and seems as if I couldn't stan' it to up and die right off, and not have any flesh and blood to me, so to speak, seemin'ly, but go off like a puff o' dandelion down. I b'lieve I am reelly afraid of the newness."

"Perhaps it won't seem new, Aunt Vinny; didn't you ever go to sleep in a strange place, and when you woke up wonder where you were for just a minute, and then it all came to you and seemed real natural?"

"Well, I dono but I have."

"I always thought dying must be like that. Anyway, I am sure it will not hurt us to go to God; and you won't feel this way always, either; don't you remember what Mr. Payson says so often, that God never gives us dying grace to live by? it is kept for time of need."

"Well, I guess that's so;" and the old lady lay back to rest, and ponder these things in her heart; but after that conversation Happy was careful to seek out and read to her all the consolatory and re-assuring passages of Scripture, all the sweet old hymns of triumph and faith, and the troubled ex-

pression gradually passed away from the worn face
and gave place to the calm of peace. Mr. Payson
came often to see her; so did Madam Holden; and
Delia Packard was there every day. Once she took
occasion in Delia's presence to say all she did say
about Happy's future.

"Now, Delye, I'm real glad you're here, for I
want to say somethin' to Happy that you'll call to
mind maybe, when I'm gone, if you ever see her
like to forget it. Happilony, I've willed this house
an' lot, and the thousand dollars that scamp Bijah
left me, to you. And here I want to say that I
forgive that cretur. I do forgive him now, truly,
but I think he's a real scamp all the same! As I
was sayin', what I've got I've willed to you, and I
want you to promise me you won't never sell the
house whilst you live, not onless it's greatly necessary. There a'n't nothin' for a woman like havin' a
house over her head that nobody can't get away
from her. I ha'n't said nothin' in the will about
it, for I didn't want to hamper ye none, and I
didn't want to take the chore of fixin' the futur
into my own hands. I've seen too many wills spile
folkses comfort that they meant to do the best for.
I don't want ye to be bound furthermore than by a
promise that you'll hold on to't if things is con-
formable."

"I will, Aunt Vinny."

"And moreover, ag'in, I want you to be sure not
to trust no man, not ef he's chief justice or presi-
dent of a bank, with your money, onless you have
a big hold on him. David said in his haste all men
was liars, and I guess he was as near about right as
though he had considered the matter. Anyway it's
safer not to trust the hull on 'em than 'tis to try
one an' lose all you've got. Use your common
sense, Happy; you've got enough on't. Don't be
a lettin' out your money without fust-class securi-
ties on't, as I did to 'Bijah. Look sharp at folkses
faces, and stick to your first ideas about 'em. The
Lord has fixed 'em so that what's inside will show
through, no matter how they kinder smear it over
with forever grinnin' or layin' on dignity; and He's
giv' some women-folks a kind o' defense as it were,
so to speak, in givin' of 'em eyes to see through
such pretenses. I tell ye, when I see a man always
smilin' an' smirkin' and bein' sweeter'n honey and
the honeycomb to all sorts o' folks, I don't take
none o' his sugar; it's sanded somewhere; similar
when I see one so pompous an' pious he can't be
touched with a ten-foot pole, and when I know he's
a hero to prayer-meetin', and snaps at his wife to
home, he ain't the man for my money; nor he ain't
one of them that'll ascend into the hill of the
Lord. Well, that's as much as'll do. Somebody
says, 'An honest man's the noblest work of God,'

and that's a fact: but He didn't make but a few o'
them works, not enough to go round; just you remember that, Happy."

These were the last words of human wisdom that
Miss Lavinia said; the effort to speak so much exhausted her.

"I guess I'll go to sleep a spell," she said, after
a little tea had refreshed her; so Happy replenished
the fire, and drew one curtain over the window before the bed, and then she and Delia sat down by
the blaze. Miss Lavinia slept very quietly, with
her hand under her cheek, like a tired child; the
fire flickered, crackled, purred, and sent out a low
sound of pleasant talk, but the watchers were silent; an indescribable feeling of hushed rest stole
over them. A silence of strange force seemed to
hold them speechless; there was no stir, no sound,
save of the gently burning fire; at last Delia looked
across at Happy, who answered the look only with
her eyes, but they both rose and went to the bedside; there the silence and the hush were con-
centred. Miss Vinny slept with her hand still
under her cheek, but she had awakened elsewhere,
this was the shell alone, the soul had gone home so
gently and so easily neither of those beside her had
been conscious of its exit; had she herself?

Happy only thought of her as awakening in a
strange place, and finding friends about her in a

moment; and she thanked God through her grief
that her dear friend had found His grace sufficient
for her in time of need, and taught her by experience that neither " life nor death " can " separate
us from the love of God which is in Christ Jesus
our Lord."

After the funeral was over, Happy came home to
her little house in a very lonely state of mind;
Delia, however, was close behind her.

" Well, Happy, I thought I'd come in a minute."

" Oh, Delia! I am so glad. It seems as if the
house was empty of everything, now Aunt Vinny
is gone."

" I expect it does, and I come to say to you that
Packard's got a job down to Chapinville, and if
you'd like to have Almiry and me come over and
stay nights, why we will; and I'll find one day anyway to spare, so'st I can help set things to rights,
and clean up a bit."

" That's just what I want, Delia. I did dread
being here alone just at first, I don't know why. I
was glad to stay where mother died."

" Well, you wan't all tired out nursin' her, and
you be now. It makes a heap o' difference with
folkses feelin's how their bodies be; jest the same I
expect as we all feel cherker and powerfuller in
new clean clothes than in old dirty ones. When
you've rested you won't be nowhere near lonesome."

"I couldn't help thinking, too, as I walked along back, how almost all the people I loved best have died ; isn't it strange, when I ain't any older ? "

"I dono as 'tis ; Gay died for want of lookin' after, I know by what I've heered your ma tell. Folks call it a mysterious providence when pretty little creturs like that is took away, but most times it's a mysterious improvidence I think ; ef you can't look after a child and take proper care on't, it'll die, same as a plant will, that's all. Then there was your ma, why she had cancer in her blood ; her grandmother had it, 'nd her aunt 'twas one of them things that can't be helped noway, because they're born in folks, like 'riginal sin and consumption. Luman's first wife she was keerless about herself an' ketched cold ; 'twan't anything strange she should die on't ; people do, quite frequent : and as for Lavinny, she'd got along beyond Scripter limits, well into the ' labor an' sorrow ' part on't. 'Twas queerer she should live so long than that she should up an' die I'm sure."

"Well, I guess you're right, Delia : but I felt so lonesome I couldn't help thinking about all those people."

" I guess you'd better think some about the livin', it would rest you more. Ha'n't you heard tell that she that was Julye Calhoun's a comin' home with her husband next week? I b'lieve he's goin' to exchange with Parson Payson one Sunday."

"Oh, I'm so glad!" exclaimed Happy, brightening at once. "I want to see Julia ever so much. I want to find out how she gets along and if she is happy."

"Don't ye ask her then ; married folks likes to appear dreadful pleased whether they be or not; you can't tell by what they say nor how they look, a mite. It's kinder like them freemasons, they keep the lodge tiled as they call it."

"Well, I'm not going to ask her," laughed Happy, "but I think her face will tell something.. Do come back to tea, Delia. I shall feel a great deal better if I have you and Mira at the table."

"Well, I guess I will. I know how 'tis with ye. But as soon as you get to work again you'll feel better, consider'ble. I used to tell old Doctor Griffin, over to Basset, that if he'd give folks work instead of pills he'd cure a sight more. I never shall forget as long as I'm spared the look he gin me when I said that; he kinder winked one eye at me real slow, and he says, says he, — ' 'Tain't good for them nor good for me to have 'em get well too fast, Delye.' My! how I laughed! I couldn't no more help it! but I knowed he was right, work's better'n paregoric any day."

"But I haven't any work to do, Delia."

"Well, you won't be long without it; folks of your make never be. It'll come."

Delia's prophesy was very soon fulfilled; a week was not over before she came in one day very hurriedly.

"There! I told ye so. Helen Sands she's took sick with fever, and the doctor thinks she's dangerous, and wants to have you come right over and take care of her; he says he see you with them folks to Horn Lane last year, and he'd ruther trust you with Nelly than a hospital nurse; but she's awful sick, you'd better believe: you git ready as fast as ever you can an' I'll fix up an' shut up for ye."

CHAPTER XXXIII.

HELEN SANDS was very ill indeed, as Happy saw at a glance, but this only roused her to quicker perception of need. There is one peculiar trait in women who are born with the rare faculty of nursing the sick, and that is readiness for an emergency. In five minutes Happy was ready, with every sense on the alert, and a cool head and deft fingers to do all that could be done for the sick girl.

In soundless slippers, her hair knotted and pinned away so closely it could not fall, however long she might be obliged to go without rest or refreshing; her dress a soft dark calico, relieved by plain white linen at the throat and wrists that could neither rustle nor be in the way, she sat down by the bedside and examined Helen's condition with the eye of an expert; her experience in Horn Lane had been good training; the doctor saw she understood the case, and with a sigh of relief betook himself to the patients outside his own house who anxiously awaited him. Happy more than justified Doctor

Sands's confidence; she watched every breath of
her patient, the slightest change of pulse she noted,
and recorded for the doctor; her hands were slight
and soft, but they had a wonderful magnetic power
in rubbing, the cool and yet vital touch seemed to
restore action to the feverish skin; and she knew
how to bathe the hot limbs without leaving damp-
ness all about the bedding, and the patient more
uncomfortable than ever. For many nights she
watched all night, though with help at hand if
she needed any. She dared not trust Helen to
any other care than her own, or take any less ob-
servant person's report of her condition. An hour
or two every day she slept, after taking a tepid
bath, and then ate her breakfast, and took an hour
more in the fresh air; this kept her ready for her
duty, and refreshed her, but for all that the strain
was very great. Helen continued delirious, not
fiercely, but with an odd uncertain fashion of lucid
and yet feverish intervals, and then the possession
of some fancy so peculiar that Happy was often
puzzled by the curious kinks of her mind. Once
she insisted on being served from a peculiar sort
of china, and refused to take food or drink from
any other, then again she would have no water
except from a neighbor's well, and she knew by
some preternatural instinct whenever for convenience's sake any one deceived her about these

things. Happy always told her the truth, it was best, she thought, and time proved it, for Helen at last refused to take either food or medicine from any other hand, and announced with her eyes glittering, and her face burning, more than ever,—

"She never tells lies. I can't trust the rest of you!"

After eleven nights of watching on Happy's part, Helen seemed to feel that she was doing too much, and she might lose her, and insisted she should lie down beside her every night instead of sitting up. This was harder still; the season was unusually warm for May, and the easier position made it almost impossible for Happy to keep awake, but Helen did not sleep at all; she wanted to be talked to, to have her long hair combed, and fine and soft as it was, this was like disentangling floss silk; then there were a thousand wild caprices to satisfy, and Happy attempted to fill all demands for the sake of quieting her.

Three weeks of this exhausting work were almost over when at last the fever began to abate, and the deathlike weakness to follow which is the natural result of such consuming fires. Now a new danger came in, danger of sinking and slipping out of life from pure exhaustion; but Happy could have help to combat this. Mary Gray came home to her mother's funeral, who had died suddenly,

and hearing Helen was so ill, came and offered her
services; Julia Ireton, too, had let her husband go
home without her, and she came to watch. Happy
trusted either of them to follow directions implic-
itly, and rouse her if any change occurred, and
therefore could get a good deal of the rest she so
much needed, but her anxiety was still very great,
for there was danger that in any one of the sinking
turns which every day and night seemed to lie in
wait for Helen, she might go out entirely like a
trembling spark.

"She is very low to-day," Doctor Sands said
sadly one morning as he came out of Helen's room
into the next one, where Happy lay on the sofa.
Mrs. Sands was utterly unable to help or even to
see the invalid; rheumatism in her feet and ankles
for some years had made her practically a cripple;
she could go about the lower part of the house in
a rolling chair, but stairs were an impossibility
to her.

"Yes, she is *very* low," the doctor went on.

"I think she is," said Happy.

"I hope she does not imagine how ill she is,
Happy. It might be the last touch; the least agi-
tation would put the candle out, entirely."

"I don't know," was all Happy could say; she
had her own idea about it; she had observed that
Helen had that sharpened hearing so peculiar to

some forms of illness, and she was by no means
sure that her father's comments had not reached
her ear before this. The doctor went softly back
to the bedside, and Happy followed him; Mary
Gray had just given the stimulant and tonic at the
prescribed hour, and Nelly seemed to have gained
a grain of strength from them, for she fixed her
great eyes on her father, opened her parched lips
slightly, and said in a hoarse whisper,

" I am not afraid ! " turned her eyes on Happy,
smiled, looked upward, and then closed them, for
even this had tired her.

The doctor broke down utterly, but left the
room at once; Happy slid to her knees by the pillow and bent her head in thankful prayer, and
Mary Gray's eyes filled; she knew very well what
thoughts were in Happy's heart, and to whom she
was telling them !

But after all Helen did not die; she stole back
to life very slowly and feebly. It was long before
Happy dared to leave her, but she herself broke
down from the severe exertion she had made, and
then Julia Ireton insisted on taking her home to
her own house in a wild delightful corner of the
State, where among hills, and brooks, and forests,
the village of Mr. Ireton's charge nestled like a
bird in its cradle hid in fresh foliage and rocked by
keen breezes. It would be vain to try to describe

the gratitude of Dr. Sands and his family for Happy's care of Helen.

The doctor knew very well that such nursing alone could have saved his child from death, for it was a case where mere medicine could do very little indeed; and he knew too that Happy's previous teachings had been the cause of Helen's calm and quiet acceptance of the fate she believed to be impending. But it was in vain that Happy was offered anything but gratitude.

" I can't, Doctor; don't ask me," she said, looking up at him with her heart in her sad dark eyes, when he wanted her to take just compensation. " Helen is one of my girls. I would and should do the same thing for any of them. When she pays your bill for medical attendance, I will send in mine for nursing."

The doctor said no more, but in all her after life she could never get any bill from Doctor Sands, or induce him to be paid for his own services; his answer invariably was, —

" We're not even yet, Happy."

Her stay in Hillside was delightful to Happy; she was more worn and tired than she knew, and the pure air among the hills, the fresh and living water of the mountain springs, the world about her, vivid with beauty and bloom, seemed more beautiful than her sense could grasp. She had no anxieties about her mission-class, for Mrs. Reynolds, Madam Holden's daughter, who had been visiting her only brother at the South since her return from Europe, but had come back to Ruth's wedding, and to live hereafter with her mother, was to teach it for her. Mrs. Reynolds was a slight, delicate, active woman, in heart and manner a thorough lady, and a conscientious Christian. She had suffered much in her life, and was glad to come home at last, her health being quite restored by a long stay abroad. Happy had scarcely made her acquaintance on account of Miss Lavinia's illness and death, and Helen's sickness, but Mrs. Reynolds knew her well from her mother and Ruth's report, and was glad to help her in any way she could.

Happy was more than glad to find that Julia's home life was as full and as happy as she wished it might be; as a minister's wife her position afforded room for the exercise of all her bright energy and activity. She had entered into Hillside like a bit of sunshine, stirred up everybody to faith and good works by her own cheerful and untiring example; her clear voice led the singing at evening meetings, and in Sunday-school; she taught a large Bible class with considerate dignity, and made it interesting to every member, and the sewing society took on fresh courage under her auspices. The young people of the church all loved her and gath-

ered round her for sympathy and counsel, and the
old people felt that her smiling face and cheery
words gave spice and impulse to their failing lives.
Her husband, a gentle, shy, studious man, seemed
to worship her as something wonderful that conde-
scended to bless him : Happy watched them with
wonder and pleasure, they were so essentially different, yet so fitted to supply each other's need ;
and the "like in difference" seemed to be so strong
a union between them. The danger was that Julia
might get too fully her own way in all things, and
the dominant faults of her character be fed by the
very use of them : but Happy had learned that she
must leave results with God ; she could only pray
for those she loved ; their life and their characters
were beyond her moulding ; she was unaware how,
even in this visit, her gentle considerate manner, her
humility and self-distrust, her quiet way of doing
some kindness, some unselfish act for every one
with whom she came in contact, her willingness to
yield, to wait, to bear the burdens of others, had
impressed Julia and taught her. It was Happy's
best usefulness that her example and her influence
enforced her words; before she left Hillside she
had made more than one friend, and Mr. Ireton
said, as he put her into the stage to return,

"How I wish you could stay with us always,
Miss Happy."

Mary Gray had kept house for her in her absence, and was at the door to meet her with a smile and a kiss; her home-coming was not sad, when such a welcome was ready, and she was glad to take up the old life again.

The Sunday school, too, welcomed her joyfully. Jack brought a dripping bunch of ivory pond-lilies to her door early that first Sunday morning. He had heard she was coming, and spent his Saturday in pursuit of these treasures which were somewhat rare about Canterbury. Jack had shot up into a tall lank boy; he was promoted in the mill and went to evening school, so that some sort of education was in his power, and he improved constantly. Happy might well be proud of him when she looked back on the days of their first acquaintance; and Nan, too, did her much credit. Pauline Lagré was still a little flighty and vain, dress was her chief delight: her wages were spent in finery, and there was not a ball or a dance among her sort in the village that she did not appear at, and demonstrate her nationality by her light feet and vivid enjoyment; but beyond this she was a good girl; she helped her mother with the younger children faithfully, and was always pleasant at home, and constant at the chapel both at school and church. Robby and Amanda, of whom we have made but brief mention before, had grown into a big boy and

girl, and were of that sturdy hard-headed type
sometimes found in New England; they were
orphans, and now lived in the same tenement house
with Granny Jakeway, who had taken them under
her kindly wing, and made her attic a home for
them; they both worked in the mill, earning a
scanty living, but it was better than to be supported
by the town, and Happy helped them as she could;
doing 'Manda's sewing, and from her small garden
adding many a savory mess of vegetables or fruit to
their slender fare.

Miss Lavinia, with characteristic forethought, had
set out in the tiny domain she owned, two apple
trees, both behind the house, in the little yard that
did not face the street, and in front she had put two
pear trees, a summer and a winter pear: a cherry
tree stood by the street, but like other trees of its
kind it bore more insects than fruit, and had to be
cut down. But the other fruit trees bore abundantly and added much to their owner's comfort.

After Happy came back from Hillside, quite as
well and strong as ever, there seemed to be a pause
in her work. Mary's vacation was over; she had
to go back to her teaching, and, after she left, the
house seemed lonely enough. Delia and Mira came
in often, and so did Mrs. Payson's children, and
Happy's love for Almira and Eunice had grown
with their growth; Una was very lovely; her clear

dark eyes and fresh color were beautiful, and her
sweet clinging ways made her friends everywhere.
Sam, who had been the baby, was a resolute and
aggressive young gentleman of his years, and ready
to wage war on all Happy's most cherished things
if she would have allowed him, but her rule in her
own house was absolute, and Sam found his de-
structiveness must go ungratified in that quarter.
Mira, under Delia's strict guidance, had become a
pleasant, obedient, useful little girl; she had no
beauty to make her interesting, but her neat dress
and smiling, rosy face went far toward that end,
and a more helpful little maiden never went about
a house.

"I've calc'lated to make her kinder independent
o' folks," said Delia. "There's no tellin' what may
come to her; what if I up'd and died? He'd
marry somebody real quick, men folks will; they're
helpless critters, an' I don't blame 'em, but I don't
want to have Almiry a burden on nobody's hands;
them that helps themselves and helps other folks is
always welcome come what will; but 'taint natur
that a great lazy sozzlin' girl is one a woman will
fellowship if she ain't noway related, nor if she is,
neither, for that matter! Ef she's got to have
another mother why I want to make it easy for
both of 'em, an' I guess 'twill be."

"You are very forehanded, Delia," said Happy, smiling.

"Well, it's better to be forehanded than after-handed anyhow; and 'tain't no harm to be pre—"

Here Jack burst in breathless.

"Say, Miss Happy! here's Rob to the door, I see him a tryin' to turn the handle, 'n he couldn't, it sticks, ye know. Well; he says there's a woman a dyin' or somethin', over to Granny Jakeway's, an' she wants you."

CHAPTER XXXIV.

HAPPY put on her bonnet and shawl and followed
Jack to the door where Robby was waiting in confusion to explain his errand, but it seemed to be no
more than Jack had previously told; neither of
them knew anything about the woman except that
she had a little girl with her.

Delia and Mira went their own way homeward,
and Happy locked the door and went down to
Horn Lane, wondering much what this would prove
to be. Granny Jakeway received her with a beaming smile, but a whispered welcome.

"Set down, deary, set down; she's fell asleep,
I'm thankful; she come in last night a lookin' for a
place to lodge. I expect she come in the Har'ford
stage, for she spoke about bein' on the river all
night; she's clean tired out; she didn't sleep
none for cryin' an' sobbin', I don't believe, and
the little cretur she cried too. I couldn't help
hearin' of 'em, for Mis' Smith she'd put 'em in the
back attic, that's her'n ye know, and there wan't

another crack in the house for 'em ; so I hobbled in,
and I see she was dreadful fevery, and I fixed her
some tea. I had kindlin's, thanks be to praise, so
I could warm it up real spry, and I gin the girl
some o' them cookies you sent over, she was hungry,
poor thing ! but the woman she couldn't eat none ;
she feels real bad, I tell ye ; bimeby, to'rds mornin',
she fell asleep, and I heard her callin' your name in
her sleep. I expect she knowed you sometime or
'nother, but ain't it a real providence that they
come here ? "

Happy thought it was ; but she also thought that
few poor and disabled old women like Granny
Jakeway would have welcomed a providence that
destroyed a night's rest and drew deeply on her
scanty stores, as evidently as Granny Jakeway did,
for she had brought both woman and child into
her own room and put them on her bed, where they
now slept soundly, the back attic being, as Happy
well knew, comfortless enough. And now the old
lady sat there beaming and nodding with satisfaction, quite ignoring the fact that her own rest was
gone, and her room invaded.

" ' I was a stranger and ye took me in,' " Happy
said softly. Granny's worn face lighted up.

" Bless the Lord ! " she ejaculated, for she was a
devout Methodist, and the response came naturally.
Then Happy stepped up to the bedside, and looked

at the sleepers; at first both seemed strange to her; the child was a pretty little girl, with long fair hair and delicate features; the woman's outlines were handsome, but her skin was sallow, her eyes sunken, her clothing like the child's, poor and dirty, but in its best estate had been only cheap finery, and her curling brown hair was twisted and tangled into the latest device of fashion.   As Happy looked, the face seemed to grow familiar, and the sleeper, stirring with the instinct that warns even in sleep of another human presence, at last turned over and opened her eyes.   As those prominent green-gray spheres fixed themselves upon Happy, they brought recognition.

"Addy Palmer!" she exclaimed.

Adelaide roused entirely now; her face grew dark and sad, and her eyes filled with tears.

"Oh, Miss Happy!" she said brokenly.   "Is it really you? and you haven't forgotten me?" then she sunk back on her pillow and sobbed bitterly.

Happy did her best to soothe and comfort her, for a long time in vain; at last she left her for a few moments and ran home, returning with material for a breakfast which she saw was the first thing needed.   Luckily Granny Jakeway's stock of fuel had just been replenished, and soon the fragrance of the steaming coffee and broiling steak seemed to rouse the child as well as the mother.   Happy left

her cooking for Granny to oversee; it was dinner
time for the old woman, and she too enjoyed the
prospect of a good meal, and was ready enough to
help prepare it, while Happy took the child up, and
washed its soiled face, braided the tangled hair, and
restored what order she could to the poor clothing.

"What is your name, dear?" she asked the little
thing, who was looking at her with innocent wide
blue eyes.

"Happy Dodd Hubbell," she answered, slowly
and distinctly. Happy felt the warm blood rush
into her face as she turned toward Adelaide who
was languidly watching them from her pillow.

"Yes, 'tis," she said, answering the look. "I
wanted something or other good to our house, so I
gave her your name. He didn't like it; said it was
outlandish, but that wasn't worth a cent to me. I
was bound to have one decent thing in the world
if I could, and I thought your name would help her
on, somehow."

Happy stooped and kissed her namesake with a
swelling heart; she did not once think of the high
appreciation Addy must have had for her character,
to cling so closely even to her peculiar and unusual
name; only two lines of an old hymn rung in her
ears, —

"Though seed lie buried long in dust,
It shan't deceive the hope," —

and she thanked God in her heart for this faint indication of a desire for better things. After Adelaide was refreshed by breakfast, and the little girl's hunger satisfied, Happy took them over to her own house, and sending little Happy out to play with the kitten in the kitchen, Addy lay down on the sofa and told her story. It was long and sad; one of the common tales of hurried, thoughtless marriage, deceit on either side, positive or tacit; a mutual discovery of mutual poverty, and then reproaches, recriminations, struggles for bread, ending in a sort of weak despair on her husband's part that drove him to intemperance, the specious consolation and fatal tempter of the poor and hungry.

Then the child was born, and, left without proper food, or care, or medical attention, Adelaide came to the very gates of death. The prospect sobered her, and as she crept back into life she resolved to do better, to be more unselfish, but the task was too hard. Her father and mother refused to help her, for she had married clandestinely and against their will; and she had never been taught to help herself; for the sake of dear life she took whatever work she could get; washing, ironing, sewing, — anything rather than her child should starve, and received her pay in food lest her husband should rob her of the money if she had it. With him things went on from bad to worse; he left her to

take care of herself, and outraged every duty he
owed her, and at last she obtained a divorce from
him, and set out with her child to return to Canterbury, hoping to find one friend there.

"I didn't know if you was dead or alive," she
said, as her story neared its end, "but I knew
you'd help me if you was alive, and they say
drowning folks catch at a straw. I'd kept my
watch and chain hid away always, so baby should
have it when she was grown; he thought I'd lost it,
and I let him think so, but you ought to have heard
him swear about it. He wanted it himself, and I
laughed behind his back to think it lay all safe
under a board in the floor right close to him. But
after I'd got the divorce, why I sold it, and it
helped a sight about getting here; the minister
there he gave me some money, they've got a
Stranger's Fund in his church to help folks that are
sick and poor and don't belong in the town but
happen there; and what with that and going hungry most of the way, and getting a long lift on a
canal-boat, here we are. I hope to goodness he
won't find us! He was just as mad as could be
when I got the divorce; he was off with her, too,
but he wanted a hold on pa, and he thought I
wouldn't never leave him; he didn't mistrust how
much I knew about his goings on!"

Happy was at a loss to decide what she could do

with and for Adelaide; but she had learned to do to-day's duty, and not to-morrow's, sure that one was the best preparation for the other; and the first thing to be done was to clothe both mother and child properly. Fortunately Miss Lavinia had left a good store of unworn underclothing which had been packed away in the garret for some time of need, and this seemed to be the time, for none of Happy's belongings would suit Adelaide's tall figure; for little Happy there was no such provision, and both needed dresses, but calico was cheap, and cotton and flannel could be cut over, and Adelaide proved herself deft at the business. By the end of the week they were both neatly dressed, and the rags of finery departed in the tinman's bag to be torn and cleansed and bleached into beauty and use in quite other forms. Adelaide expressed herself willing and anxious to work, but the difficulty was to find it; Happy shared with her the sewing she had to do, but that was not abundant; all that could be done was to wait, and she did not do this patiently.

Helen Sands, still a little languid from her long fever, called at once to see Addy, but only a few others of her acquaintance were in Canterbury yet, and they did not offer to help her in any way, or do more than call formally. Adelaide had not made herself friendly or agreeable as a girl, and now it was too late. Doctor Sands found in her appearance a clue to the fulfillment of a project he had long entertained; he had the highest opinion of Happy's qualifications as a nurse, and he knew very well how much an intelligent and experienced woman was needed in that capacity among his own patients; he had hoped to get her to assume this avocation, but the necessary absence from her house during a period of preparation stood in the way. She did not like to shut it up; that had been her objection to going with Julia, and Mary Gray had offered just in time to inhabit it, and care for the garden and the old cat!

Here now was a woman who had nothing better to do than to take care of these things and set Happy free. Doctor Sands, as Delia said, never let the grass grow under his feet; he appealed to Happy in the second week after Addy arrived.

"Now, Happy, I've got something for you to do."

Happy laughed; she thought her hands were full with her new inmates.

"Well, Doctor, I thought I had about enough for the present."

"Maybe you do, but we don't always know our possibilities. Now what I want of you is to take up nursing for a profession. You've got it in you, you only want a little knowledge of some few things, and I want you to go into the hospital at

Newport for this winter, indeed for the next year,
and take charge of a ward there; I can get you a
chance to hear the doctors lecture, and you will
come back just the woman we need in Canterbury,
an intelligent and well informed nurse."

Happy's eyes brightened at the idea, but in a
moment they were sadder than ever.

"I can't do it, Doctor," she said, reluctantly.

"I won't take an answer to-day," he said, taking
up his hat. "Think of it for a week, Happy, you
may change your mind; it is a wonderful chance to
do good."

She knew it was; she liked to help and comfort
the sick; she was in fact a born nurse; but of late
Happy had not been as strong as usual, and the
idea of leaving home had met with instant recoil
from her whole heart; but as Dr. Sands put it to
her she felt that perhaps that recoil had been selfish,
that there might be an opening here for more work
for good than had ever before lain in her way. She
thought much and prayed more about it for the
next few days; she was no longer a young woman,
and the delicacy of constitution that her youth and
growth long held at bay, now that the vital forces
began to decline, made itself felt in many ways,
and threatened more. She began to dread the possibilities that lay before her, and instinctively to
husband what strength she had, and save herself

where she could. If indeed this were the thing she could do safely, there was an end of it; she would stay at home and stand in her lot to the end of her days offering such service as she was able to the Lord; but she shrank from being so soon laid aside from activity and labor; and at last resolved to tell Doctor Sands frankly all her doubts and dread.

He heard her to the end with patience and sympathy; for he saw before she had half finished her confidence that she would never have the needful strength for a life of sick-nursing; there was an inheritance of disease and weakness lurking in her veins that might at any moment declare itself, that did practically declare itself now to the physician's eye. He did not think it best to tell her all he learned, but said,

"Well, Happy, perhaps you wouldn't be strong enough. I think you are right, but you would have been such a help and comfort I hate to give up the idea."

"Doctor, I would if I could. I want to, but I know it is impossible, and I don't believe it is my duty to try to do more than I can."

"That's true. I wish you had some great stout woman's body, Happy, with your soul in it."

"Oh, Doctor! don't wish me any more body than I've got now; it is quite enough for my need; but

wait a minute ; don't you think Addy would make
a good nurse? she is so tender and careful with
little Happy.   I do believe she would make a splendid care-taker in a sick room."

"I don't want to trust any of my patients to her
handling.   Beside, Happy, her right place is with
her parents ; they are old and feeble."

"But, Doctor, they won't speak to her."

"Can't you persuade them ?" said the doctor
with a keen look.

Happy caught at the idea.

"Oh, if I could," she said, unaer her breath, but
the doctor heard.

"Try!" he said, as he shut the outer door behind him ; and "try!" sounded in Happy's ears all
night.   In the morning she was startled by a ring
at the door, which she herself answered, for little
Happy had been feverish with a cold all night, and
both the child and her mother were still sleeping.
As the upper half of the door swung back, — for
the house was an old one, and Miss Vinny, seeing
that this sort of door had its advantages, had never
modernized it, — she saw before her a youngish
man, with a bad face varnished over now by a
plausible smile, and forced expression of bland
inquiry.

"Miss Dodd, I believe?"

Happy assented.

" H'm — I — well I feel ruther overcome by the
necessitous circumstance of — ah — asking a stranger
for such — ah — delicate information I may say;
but my name — ah — is Hubbell, ma'am ; and I have
some reason to expect that Miss Dodd can — will
inform me as to the present residing place of my
wife and child."

Happy's heart stood still; here was the man
Addy dreaded at the very door of her house of
refuge ! What could she, a little weak woman do
to protect her ? what should she say ?

CHAPTER XXXV.

BUT even in little weak women there sometimes
arises a sudden courage, a courage purely moral,
that thrills the timid flesh with strange fire, and
exalts the gentle speech to power and steadiness.
It is given them in that hour what they shall say
and do, literally. Happy looked the man in the
face calmly, though her dark eyes shone with unusual light.

" I have no information to give you," she said.

" Well — ah — really, perhaps I might as well tell
you, mum, that I have you may say tracked them
to this place. In fact — ah — I saw my wife last
night through the window, but I perceived she was
retiring, and — well — I hesitated to disturb her.
I had found where she was residing, hm! I could
wait."

" Your *wife* is not here," said Happy, significantly.

The man's dark face flushed, and an evil look
crept into his eyes.

" I perceive Mrs. Hubbell has told her story. I

— well — I forgive her!" here he tried to put on an air of injured innocence, but failed lamentably — as to the innocence. "I am ready to receive her again. It is quite likely she expects her parents will extend helping hands towards her, but I think they will not; in fact they are both very ill I hear, I presume likely at the point of death; and she will have no home now except with me mum; I am willing to — ah — rub the sponge over the past as you may say."

Happy's eyes flashed, the man had relied too much on her simplicity.

"Adelaide has found friends and a home," she said sharply. "She does not wish to see you again, and it is not needful that she should;" with this she closed the door, and quietly slipped the upper bolt. The man swore at her savagely, the thin garment of smooth words fell off from his accustomed speech and betrayed him. Happy trembled like a leaf, but her heart was stout; all the stouter that she heard a brief terrified whisper from the top of the stairs —

"Oh don't! don't! don't let him in."

"I shan't, Addy," she said, ascending toward the speaker; "don't be afraid of my doing that, dear; and he won't try to get in. There! he has shut the gate now, he will not trouble us at present."

She went into the kitchen to prepare breakfast,

wondering if the man had really spoken the truth, and both Addy's parents were dying. The story seemed improbable enough, but it flashed across Happy's mind that it might be her father was really very ill, and the husband thought if he could be brought to forgive his child, her mother, who had been much the most disposed of the two toward her forgiveness, could not withhold it, and if Addy was his wife again he must needs share her improved fortunes. Happy resolved to ask Dr. Sands what should be done, so after breakfast was over, advising Adelaide to keep the door locked in her absence, she went over to the doctor's office, and fortunately found him at home. He advised her to telegraph at once to the post-master of the place where they lived, and find out the truth of Hubbell's story, then further proceedings could be resolved on. She knew Mr. Palmer's address, so she did not need to go home again, but went directly to the telegraph office which was at the other end of the town in the station of the recently built railway. She found the message could not go immediately, as some official business occupied the line, so she left it and went home, finding Addy, who peeped from the window cautiously before letting her in, pale, tearful, and excited.

"Oh, Miss Happy," she burst out, as soon as the door was made fast again, "he's been here, and I

put my head out of the window thinking it was
you, and he saw me. If he didn't begin to coax!
of all the softly talk you ever heard! I let him
know I was aware of what he was after; he thinks
if he gets me back maybe pa'll come round, but pa
won't. I wrote to him when I was most starving
to death and he didn't answer a word. I wonder
if Philo thinks he'd take me in now! not much! I
told him it wasn't no use, I knew what he was up
to, and then he went and said ma and pa was both
dying, and I wouldn't have nobody to care about
me, and all such talk, but I told him I knew better,
'twas one of his lies; he does lie awfully. Then he
got mad and tore and raved and swore like everything. I really got scared out of my wits, but I
didn't come down. Oh dear! what shall I do! he'll
plague me to death."

Happy quieted her fear as well as she could, and
then told her what she had done, and hardly had
the story ended when the telegram in answer to
her's was brought to the door. It ran thus:—

"Mr. Palmer very sick, not expected to live.
Mrs. Palmer well."

Happy perceived at once on the receipt of this
message that Adelaide ought to go home; and
rather reluctantly that she ought to go with her, and
try to effect a reconciliation. It was an unpleasant duty enough, if duty it were, but it seemed the

thing to be done, and she prepared to face it. A person was found to take charge of the little house for a few days, and the next morning the two women and the child set out for the West.

It was a very tedious journey to Happy; the dust, the jar of the train, the dirty cars, the bad air, all exhausted and sickened her, and the ride was tedious enough before they reached Chicago, and little Happy as fretful as was to be expected. They went to a hotel there, and after a brief rest Happy took the train of a branch road leading to Siloam where Mr. Palmer lived, and then directly to his house.

She found things much as she supposed. Mr. Palmer was sick unto death; two apoplectic shocks had made him helpless, but his mind, though weak, had cleared after the last shock, and he lay waiting for the third and fatal attack with what courage he might. Mrs. Palmer was very glad to see Happy; in her trouble and loneliness she felt bitter need of friends, and was softened and refined by pain and disappointment since Happy had seen her. She cried bitterly at hearing Adelaide's story.

"Fetch her right straight home, Happy," she said. "Jehiel can't die till he's forgive her, I know he can't. That's what kep' him back so long. I know it's on his mind. I've heard him call out 'Addy' more than once in his sleep. I b'lieve

you've brought him his last chance for the future,
as true as you're born. If he'd died without forgiving Addy, I dono as I ever should ha' forgive
myself."

So encouraged, Happy went back on the night
train, and early in the morning all three went out
to Siloam. Mrs. Palmer was right; her husband
had been anxiously waiting for some sign from
Addy to offer her forgiveness, and the burden on
his mind had indeed kept it back from peace and
hope. It was like new life to him to see the little
girl, who at once adopted the delighted grand-
parents; and Addy once more at home and assured
of her future, seemed to grow young every hour.
Happy was the only one who suffered; the journey
had over-tired her, and she lay ill for a long week,
unable to sit up.

It was her first experience of helpless illness, and
every fibre in her body seemed to rebel against this
forced submission and restless inability to do for
herself. It was a sharp lesson but one needful to
learn, and as she lay there trying to be patient,
conscious of a weakness she had never before
known, and an irritability hard to endure or avoid
expressing, she pined for her pleasant little house,
the pure air and living waters of Canterbury, and
resolved nothing should ever bring her away from
home again, less important than this present errand.

Mrs. Palmer and Addy were constantly devoted to
her, and all was done that could be, but it was two
weeks before she recovered strength to reach home,
and when Dr. Sands looked at her he shook his
head.   This brief illness told how little real
strength of constitution Happy had, and she knew
it now ; she feared the years that were to come, as
she looked on to the possibility of her inheriting
the disease that had been fatal to her mother.   She
felt as never before that there might be in wait for
her sore physical trials, and her soul sank within
her, but in this strait as in all others she took
refuge in the one shelter for every mortal anxiety;
and resolved to put away thought for the future,
and forget as well as she could, the possibility before her till it became, if ever it did, a near proba-
bility.   But of one thing she felt sure ; she must
not continue to live alone, for she needed both
society and help at times ; she must look about her
to find a proper inmate.

Soon after reaching home she went over to see
Granny Jakeway, and tell her about Adelaide and
little Happy, in whom the old woman took a keen
interest.

"Well, well, well !   You air a blessed cretur, so
you be ! blessed air tne peacemakers, that's a fact
if Scripter didn't say it ; a real fact.   So they've
got settled to hum, — well — well !   I hope that

feller won't pester her no more; it's awful bad to
hev anybody come a hectorin' round so. I've
knowed what it was in my time," and the placid
old woman shook her head solemnly; tradition
averred that her husband had been fond of chasing
her about the house with a broomstick when he was
not dead drunk in the barn; she had evidently
known trouble.

"I don't think he will trouble her any more; it
makes the all difference to know she has found
him out, and has gone to her friends."

"Yis, yis, them kind of cattle don't like to find
the bars up, now I tell ye; it's a dreadful pity she
didn't find him out a spell back, but that's the way
mostly with folks; they find out what other folks
are when seems as though 'twas entire too late.
Well, the Lord knows an' I don't; an' of the two
I'd ruther 'twas Him than me. But I kinder
wanted of 'em to stay long o' you, Happy; you'd
oughter hev somebody else to your house, you look
kinder peaked lately; what if you'd should be took
sick suddin?"

"I know it, Granny; I came here to-day partly to
talk to you about that. I do want some one there
very much."

"I know it! I know it! well, it's an awful good
chance for some poor gal. I wish't I was a gal.
No I don't now, neither! I'd hev to begin at the

beginnin' ag'in and I'm most through, praise the
Lord! But I wish there was a real good gal want-
in' help, but them kind don't, gener'lly, it's the
wicked ones, and them you don't want; there's that
Polly Lagré, now! Her pa died whilst you was
gone away, and her ma she run off you know
several year back, with another Frenchman, and
Polly's run wild ever sence; that Andry woman's
got the other child, she's a goin' to keep it, but
Polly she's kinder boardin' round."

Happy found out afterward that Pauline had
boarded chiefly with Granny Jakeway, and paid
no bills, but this the good old soul did not mention.
She did wish Poll- could go and live with Miss
Dodd, but she dare go no further than just drop a
seed of suggestion into Happy's mind, for she knew
well it would entail on her a great care and burden
if she did take the girl, and that Happy really
needed help, not hindrance.

The seed dropped into good ground. Happy did
not stop to think of her own needs when she heard
of Pauline's orphaned and forsaken condition; she
knew the girl worked in the mill, but that was only
another disadvantage, for without any home, care,
or restraint, she would be sure to fall into bad company. Her father had been careful of her in a
rough imperative fashion, and her early intimacy
with Jack and Nan Gladding had brought her into

the quietest set among the mill-hands, for these two
were among the most respectable of the crowd;
but now there was every prospect of her headlong
levity and vanity getting the better of her good in-
tentions.   Happy felt that she must take her under
her wing, and accordingly after leaving Mrs. Jakeway, she hunted up Polly, and made her proposal
to her.   She would give the girl her board, but she
must do the washing and ironing in return.   Happy
had learned that the best way to help the poor
without demoralizing them is to give them work;
when man or woman becomes the mere pensioner
of another they lose the last hold on their own self-
respect, and sink into paupers at once; it is the
blessing of the curse, the hidden secret of comfort
even in losing Paradise, that we can eat our bread
with the appetite and flavor of toil.   Polly was a
little shy, a little uncertain, but Happy had so long
been her teacher, and was so looked up to by the
best of her companions, that the honor of the position at last got the better of its inconvenience in
her eyes, and she said she would come.   Happy
hardly knew where to put her in the house, for her
own room being in winter over the sitting-room
which was also the kitchen, and the place for meals,
she had only the best chamber left, but Delia suggested that she should have a small chamber finished
off in the attic, and Mr. Packard, who was out of

work just now, offered to do it cheaply; till this
was ready Polly could stay in the spare room.

"And there's one thing more Happy," said Delia,
as she surveyed the apartment after it was finished,
and an old drugget tacked in the middle of the
floor, a rush-bottomed rocker and tiny light-stand
set beside the cot-bed, and a bright chintz curtain
strung across the window, while Polly had herself
illuminated the walls with some gay fashion-plates,
" You'd ought to have a bell up here, and the bell
pull in your charmber, you're right below; so it
could be fixed easy, and if you was took with a
faint in the night-time you could pull the bell and
fetch Pauliny down." .

Happy accepted the advice, and owned to herself
that she slept better for having this means of communication at hand; a sense of utter solitude had
sometimes made her nights weary enough; it is not
good for anybody to be alone in this world; if man
needed society in his innocence and confidence, how
much more in sinfulness and distrust does he dread
entire isolation.   Solitary confinement is worse pun-
ishment than death, for it violates the order of nature and the designs of God, while death only
hastens their execution.

The mere sense of comfort in having another
person at hand visibly restored Happy's health, and
was her first, for a long time her only reward, for

the unselfishness which had prompted her to choose
Pauline Lagré as her companion, simply because the
girl needed a home.   But unselfishness does not
look for recompense; it is of God and wears His
likeness, who died for us that we might live in Him.

CHAPTER XXXVI.

FOR a long time Polly was a very troublesome
comfort to Happy; her inborn levity, her passion
for fine clothes, her desire for society, made her a
most uncertain and uncomfortable inmate. She
always came home with two or three of the mill-
girls, laughing and screaming, and stopping at the
gate to chat with her; and Happy, who had been
educated to think neat and appropriate dress was
part of a woman's duty, was distressed to see
her put on a light blue cheap woolen dress to do
her work in, set off with plenty of cotton lace
about the neck, and dirty pink or yellow ribbons
fluttering at her throat and in her hair. She had
not an apron in the world but the coarse sacking
garment of that name which she kept at the mill to
save her clothes from the machinery, and the first
thing to be done was to make her a store of these
useful articles.

With the appreciative tact of a nature which
always sought to put itself in the place of another,

and judge for them in that way, rather than from their own plane of thought, Happy selected delicate calico, and the remains of an old white dress of her own to fashion some: and put on ruffles and pockets of the jauntiest sort. Pauline was taken with the bait; she admired the aprons with all her heart, and was glad to keep them delicately neat. It was a little matter to do or to tell of, yet out of it a great deal sprang. These aprons shamed Polly's tawdry dresses and she had the taste to perceive it; Happy was delighted to see that her next purchase for winter was a dark blue merino, coarse, but good in color, and to this she added some white ruffles in the neck which Happy plaited for her every week, and a knot of garnet ribbon; then she began, at Happy's suggestion, to keep her hair in better condition; it only needed a little brushing to be very beautiful; purple-black, shining and wavy, it matched well with her bright dark eyes and clear skin; and Polly received so many compliments on her improved aspect, that her vanity was mightily tickled, and she became as careful and tasteful, — with aid enough from Happy's quick eye to cultivate her taste, — as could be desired.

She took naturally to cooking, and learned the dainty ways of that little kitchen and improved on them also. Nobody could live with Happy and not love her, and poor Polly's heart every day clung more and more closely to this kind and sweet woman who had given her so pleasant a home, and who was so gentle and loving to her in spite of all her faults. Insensibly to herself Pauline grew gentler, quieter in all her ways, more careful in selecting her friends ; she did not perhaps enjoy the Bible reading and prayer with which Happy opened and closed every day, though they were brief and fervent, but she could not help perceiving that they were deeply earnest, and so imbibing a certain respect, deeper than ever, for her first teacher in the way of life.

Three years passed on with little incident to Happy now ; she was no worse apparently, than she had been, but in herself she felt a sort of general failure way-marked by the increasing number of things she could not do. She heard now and then from Adelaide ; Mr. Palmer lingered several months after her return, and on his death the mother kept the house still, and Addy and her child lived with her ; as for Mr. Hubbell he seemed to disappear entirely, so that nothing troubled their family peace, except little Happy's childish ailments.

Adelaide wrote affectionate and sensible letters ; trouble seemed to have sobered her nature and given it depth, but she never alluded to religion in any way, or expressed any interest in the best things. After three years she married a young

Methodist clergyman, and Happy could not but
hope she had entered on the Christian life, though
she was troubled deeply to think she should marry
again, and felt that this very step was one that gave
no encouragement to her hopes for the change of
heart and life Happy so earnestly desired to see in
her. It would have comforted this anxious heart to
know that Addy had refused to marry Mr. Simmons
till she had seen her husband's death in a local
paper sent her from the town where he lived, but
Addy said nothing about this.

Helen Sands was still in Canterbury, the delight
of her father's old age, and the dependence of her
home, for her mother had died not long after Adelaide's return to Siloam. Helen had grown up into
an active, cheerful, charming young woman; her
brothers and sisters loved her heartily, and her
father's heart was bound up in her. Mary Gray
was now at the head of a good school in Philadelphia, earnest in everything that came to her hand,
working with her might. She came every autumn
to spend the vacation with Happy, to enjoy the
peace of that little home, and the pleasure of seeing
the orderly flourishing school and well-filled chapel
of the mission, which was doing incalculable good
among the operatives and working classes in Canterbury. Teachers had always been ready and
willing, and of course scholars responded with will

and readiness. It was always more home to Happy
than her own house, and her soul rested there in
praise for the past and peaceful outlook for the
future. Madam's Holden's sweet old face shone
there every Sunday, and Mrs. Reynolds had gathered a Bible class of grown women; while Happy
still kept her own class of boys now grown into
young men; Nan helped in the infant school, Maria Smith, Mr. Packard's sister, led the singing, and
Jack was yet the librarian.

Of Julia Ireton, Happy rarely heard; she came
home occasionally, but her brood of children made
travelling hard for her; she was perhaps a little less
bright and courageous than before, for her oldest
child had died just as it began to run about and
speak, and the blow was dreadful to Julia; in all
her life she never quite recovered from that loss.

Ruth came back every year to her grandmother's,
for a summer visit, bringing now two lovely delicate
little girls, Alice and Rosamond; she herself was
lovelier than ever, but there was a sad shadow on
her face at times that troubled Happy; she seemed
to have some thorn in her garland that fretted constantly, and shaded her expressive countenance
with pain. She was well; and her children were
evidently as dear to her as can be to such a loving
and devoted nature; her husband scarcely ever
came to Canterbury, except to bring on his family

or to take them away. Happy saw him once or twice, but he did not seem improved; the weak look about his mouth had increased, his eyes were gloomy; she almost thought he was petulant once or twice to Ruth, but reproached herself for the thought, Ruth was so evidently glad to have him come, so tender in her provision for all his likings and fancies, so apparently ignorant of his impatient manner.

Happy thought she herself must be growing old and suspicious; and went on hoping that Ruth was as happy as she wished her to be, till about the fourth year after she took Pauline to live with her, when Mary Gray came for her summer rest, and they were one day talking about Ruth whom Mary frequently visited at her home in Philadelphia.

"How do you like Mr. Thorne, Mary?" said Happy, who had forborne to ask the question before, as she had noticed that Mary never spoke of him, and had respected her reticence, till her own anxiety became imperative.

"I don't like him, Aunt Happy. I never said so much to any one before, but it is a fact. I don't like him at all. Partly because he doesn't like me, I dare say; the Thornes are very aristocratic you know, and I am only a school teacher; he is just civil. But that I don't care about if he was only good to Ruth."

"Mary! you don't mean to tell me he is unkind to her! Of all things!"

"He don't shake her, or swear at her, Aunt Happy; and she seems to have everything she wants, but he is so hateful, so irritable; I couldn't eat my dinner if he snapped at me as he does at her; and she is a real angel. I do think she grows lovelier every day."

"I thought he was very fond of her," said Happy.

"I don't know but he is; I think so sometimes. He will look at her across the room with his heart in his eyes, and turn away his head as if he could not bear it, and growl at something or somebody. I don't go there often, now, he is so snappy and disagreeable. The house is pleasant, the children are perfect little darlings, and Ruth is as sweet as a mortal woman can be, but I do *not* like Mr. Thorne."

Happy sighed; there was surely some trouble in Ruth's life she could not touch or see; she must leave her in the everlasting arms that are a sure refuge, and comfort herself with the fact that the Lord can care for his own as human insight and affection never can. It was a rock-shadow that had rested and calmed her many a time before.

This year Julia Ireton came again to Canterbury, bringing with her a pair of creeping twins, and a little fair baby three months old; she had left her two older boys with their father, and her stay must be brief. She wanted a girl to take home with her who could be trusted with children.

"Oh, Aunt Happy," she said, for she had adopted Mary's way of 'calling cousins,' "don't you know of anybody I can get? We have a smart, capable, rather fierce American woman in the kitchen, who would not stay a moment with Irish help, and that makes it so hard! I did not know but I could get some one from the school, or a mill-girl, maybe."

This last word set Happy thinking; she knew the right person for Julia, but would she go to her?

"I don't know, dear, how to tell you at once," she answered. "Perhaps I can get some one. I will think about it, and let you know to-morrow."

"It would be the greatest blessing, if you could, Aunt Happy; the children are so young, and there are so many of them, that I don't give them care enough. I cannot."

Happy laughed.

"Julia, did you never hear that an old maid's children are always brought up just right? I don't give you advice though, out of my own wisdom, but I used to hear mother say often, that nothing was better for them than 'a little wholesome letting alone.' Perhaps if you should neglect them a bit it would be better for both of you."

"But Aunt Happy, even to keep them clean takes half my time."

"Then let them be dirty ; perpetual washing isn't good for children any more than for plants. I used think just as you do about it, and when Delia had been married to Luman Packard quite a while, I asked her one day if she knew Mira was making mud pies. She looked up at my horrified face and laughed. 'I showed her how,' said she ; 'when I came here she was as peaked as a young rat. I was bound to get her out door ; sun and earth make children grow as well as cabbages, so I showed her how to make dirt pies, and she relishes her vittles now, first-rate. I don't want no water-soaked children round me !' And she was right ; Mira is a stout, rosy, neat girl, instead of a white sickly thing."

"Good doctrine, Aunt Happy," sighed Julia ; "but what would the parish say to see the minister's boys playing in the roadside mud-puddles ? "

"I don't know, Julia, and I don't think it is any matter. You didn't marry the parish, it is your husband you have to suit, not the people in Hillside. And moreover, if you are going to be guided by what folks say about you, there'll be no end of your troubles, dear."

"I know that, already, but oughtn't I to try and please them, Aunt Happy? They are looking at us all the time for example as well as precept, my husband says."

"Then set them a good one, Julia, one of doing what is right and best in spite of the strife of tongues. In real vital things I wouldn't give up an inch; in things that are only for your own pleasure or pride I would give up everything."

"Oh, Aunt Happy, I do wish you lived in Hillside," exclaimed Julia.

"And I wish she lived in Philadelphia," chorussed Mary.

Happy's heart glowed and her cheek colored; she loved to be loved; what woman does not? and these two were as near and as dear to her as any but her own children could be. Ruth, perhaps, came closer to her inmost heart, but all her first Sunday class were especially dear, and to know that they returned her affection was the sweetest thing earth had to offer, now.

When Julia had gone, Happy pondered earnestly upon a plan for helping her which had suddenly entered her head at the suggestion that a mill-girl might be found to serve as child's nurse. Why should not Pauline go to Hillside? work was very slack now at the mills; she did not earn half wages, and she had promised to marry Jack Gladding if ever they could earn enough to buy a little house and "start fair," as Jack said. This unusual pru-

dence was the result of Happy's continuous counsel
to both of them ; they had resolved to lay up all
they could spare, and to wait four years if necessary.

"You hadn't ought to ask us to be patient no
longer than that, Miss Happy," said Jack, when the
bargain was made, and Happy laughingly promised
not to interfere beyond that time. She knew
Pauline would have good wages and good care
with Julia, and be able to lay up most of what she
earned ; Jack had found a place as engineer on a
local railway, whose terminus was at Hillside, so
that it would not be absolute separation of the pair,
the only difficulty was that Polly might take it into
her head that she did not want to be a servant.
But this did not prove a stumbling-block ; the one
we dread and provide for rarely falls in our way;
and Happy's example had done more to render domestic service honorable and desirable among the
mill-girls and mission-scholars in Canterbury, than
a host of sermons or moral tales. Pauline knew
plenty of girls who were willing to ask for and glad
to accept old clothes, half-worn shoes, and patched
flannels, but were indignant at the idea of "living
out."

Thanks to Happy's training, — more thanks to
her doing what she had done — Pauline only de-
spised the beggarly pride that was neither ashamed
to ask alms nor willing to work ; and she had friends

enough in her own class who considered Happy
Dodd had made service respectable. No; her only
reluctance was in regard to leaving Happy, and
Julia only objected to her on the same grounds;
but where a person is truly unselfish there are few
others, however well-intentional, who cannot be
persuaded into accepting their good offices at last,
and Pauline went back to Hillside with Mrs. Ireton,
and became as useful and trustworthy as her teacher
hoped and asked for her. She was really invaluable
to Julia, and learned to love the children heartily,
but Happy was once more all alone.

CHAPTER XXXVII.

THE year wore on into November, and Happy had not yet another inmate : she felt that it would not do for her to pass this winter alone, for the dull ail and creeping weakness had at last given definite warning, the finger of death had touched her now visibly, and she had the future to face close as we face a staring nightmare that looks into our eyes with near unwinking horror, and shortens our breath with its oppressive proximity.

She had gone to Doctor Sands as soon as the ominous spot appeared on her breast.

"I want to know the truth, Doctor," she said, and her face was so calm, her voice rang so true, the doctor hoped he could give her good news, but his face fell as soon as he saw that fatal swelling.

Hours of prayer had given Happy courage to ask the question, yet a mortal sickness stole over her as she received the wordless answer of Dr. Sands' expression.

"Shall I have to have it cut out?" she said, as

soon as she could speak. The doctor heard the tremor in her voice.

" No ! " said he.

" I don't advise it, at all. You may live ten or twenty years, or die of something else if you let it alone, and you are not strong enough to bear an operation, Happy."

He meant to speak hopefully, but what an alternative like this offered did not bring much cheer. It was at best the remedy of another death, and the quickest instinct of life is to shrink from dying. Happy turned very pale and hid her face in her hands ; the doctor brought her a glass of wine, but she would not take it. Presently she raised her head ; the word had come to her.

" I will lift up mine eyes unto the hills, from whence cometh mine help. My help cometh from the Lord which made heaven and earth. He will not suffer thy foot to be moved ; he that keepeth thee will not slumber. Behold he that keepeth Israel shall neither slumber nor sleep."

And another promise chorused that — " Fear not ! for I have redeemed thee, I have called thee by thy name, thou art mine. When thou passest through the waters I will be with thee, and through the rivers they shall not overflow thee : when thou walkest through the fire thou shalt not be burned, neither shall the flame kindle upon thee. For I am

the Lord thy God, the Holy One of Israel, thy
Saviour; I gave Egypt for thy ransom. Ethiopia
and Seba for thee!"

The grand and tender words kindled light in her
face and strength in her heart.

"I have called thee by thy name!"

Oh! this is no impersonal affection, no blind
machinery, no "great creative principle" that speaks
thus; it is the heart of a loving Father, an almighty
Redeemer, a Spirit witnessing with our spirit, that
comforts human fear and weakness with this wonderful assurance of love and help. The very terror
of death fled away before this voice of the Conqueror, and Happy could look up and smile at
Doctor Sands, who was brushing away a sort of
dimness from his usually cool eyes, and looking very
hard the other way.

She went home calm yet silent, as a man is who
has looked into his grave, even though he is neither
ready or resigned to lie down in it. She had left
the matter in God's hands: as she had told Aunt
Lavinia. He would not give her dying grace to live
by, but it could not fail her in time of need. What
remained now was to occupy herself more actively
than ever for the good of those around her, for the
time was short, and the night coming, wherein no
man could work; and work came to her in a very
unexpected way.

After she reached home the still and brooding autumn day gathered into a thick cold mist, and then to falling rain ; outside of her door the sodden dead leaves, the withered flowers, the half-bare trees, showed comfortless enough; she kindled a bright fire on the hearth for cheer and company, and prepared herself a warm supper, an unusual thing for her to do, but Doctor Sands had urged her as a duty and necessity both, to take care of herself, and by every means to keep up her strength and spirits. It took some time to finish her work after her supper was eaten, for though the warm food had refreshed her, she felt weakened by the shock she had endured. She was sitting at last, by the blaze, counting up her mercies, and trying to think who would or could come to her for help and company, when a low knock called her to the front door ; she lit a lamp and went to answer the summons.

Opening the upper half of the door as she always did, a woman with a long water-proof cloak on, the hood drawn over her head, handed her a letter, saying in a low husky voice, "It is from Mrs. Thorne."

Happy opened the door at once, and brought the messenger in to the fire ; the woman sat down in the corner half withdrawn behind the old-fashioned mantelpiece, and watched her as she opened the letter ; a letter that it was plain to see astonished its reader deeply.   It ran thus :

PHILADELPHIA, Nov. 19th, 18—.

"Happy, dear Happy ! this is my husband ! Take care of him, hide him for God's sake and mine. Don't, oh don't let anybody find him.   I know you love me, so I send him to you.   Oh Happy ! he did not, I mean he —   I don't know what to say.   I am half wild.   I love him, love him, love him.   Happy, take care of him, my dear good blessed friend.

RUTH."

The letter was so hurried, so incoherent, so crossed and blotted, that Happy was unable to understand it, even after she had read it through ; she looked up at the stranger, the hood had fallen off and re- vealed the face of Mr. Thorne.

Happy exclaimed involuntarily.

"It is really I," he said, answering her thought.

"Why ! Mr. Thorne ! what is it ? what *is* the matter ; what can I do for you ? "

" Hide me ! " he said, deliberately.

"Hide you ? " echoed Happy ; he went on with a rough and forced distinctness that showed the weak nature was at bay, and had put on an aspect of courage to cover its poor despair.

"Yes.   I have embezzled and gambled away a hundred thousand dollars that did not belong to me,

and escaped, on the brink of discovery. By this
time the police are after me. Ruth sent me here.
I meant to kill myself, but she would not — she
seemed — "

Here the mask fell off; the man hid his face and
cried like a child. Fatigue, exhaustion, and cold
had helped the work of anxiety and fear; he was
utterly worn out in mind and body. Happy knew
very well what was first to be done; the kitchen
fire was still burning and with deft alacrity she
made a cup of coffee and cooked the oysters she had
reserved for her breakfast. The guest ate like a fam-
ished creature while she prepared for him Pauline's
bed in the attic; for the windows of that room did
not face the street, and its dark curtain showed also
less light through than the dimity ones of the spare
chamber. When she went down the supper had
vanished, and Mr. Thorne sat in her rocker before
the parlor fire; it was characteristic of the man that
he had chosen the easiest chair in the room, and the
warmest position, but Happy did not observe it.
She busied herself to remove the supper dishes and
wash them, divining that her guest would prefer to
be alone for the present; and when at length she
asked him if he would like to go to his room, he
assented curtly, and she shewed him up stairs,
where, as the noise soon audibly attested, he fell
asleep at once, and slept heavily, worn out to an

extent that forbade the anguish of the mind to dominate over the need of the body.

But Happy could not sleep: this was a new situation for her, to be sheltering and concealing a felon. Her heart bled for Ruth, who was her first thought, and agonies of prayer went up to God on her darling's behalf all the long night. Here was a sorrow in whose presence her own recent terror shrank away ashamed; this grief was worse to bear than death or pain, for it was a living shame: and she knew the innate pride of Ruth's delicate and honorable nature must shrink from disgrace. But she did not know how a woman's love, if it is real and earnest, springs up to meet and defy whatever sin or sorrow assails her husband. She could not understand the chorus of that piteous letter.

"I love him! love him! love him!" yet it was the deep and divine truth; for a love like Ruth's exults in its overflowing strength to cover and abound above fault or folly in that which it loves, and images in its finite measure, the love of God which forgets our sins and remembers our iniquities no more, but pours itself out with the lavish profuseness of the ocean and the abundant vastness of the air, till our very souls are restored to their forfeited places in heaven, and scarlet stains of guilt and passion are washed away so as no fuller on earth can whiten them! Part of an old hymn

ran in Happy's head as she read and re-read that
letter, —

> "And mercy like a mighty stream
> O'er all their sins divinely flows;"

and while she wondered, she loved Ruth more than
ever, if that were possible, and rose in the morning
resolved to do her best to serve and save Mr.
Thorne; but her way to do this did not prove to be
that which either he or Ruth would have chosen,
had it been left to their own selection.

Two or three days passed away before Happy
said anything to her guest on the subject which
occupied both their minds; very long days to Mr.
Thorne, who was obliged to stay in the house of
course, and who found Happy's small store of books
quite out of his line of reading, but was at last
driven to their perusal in sheer despair of any other
way to endure life.

Of course Ruth could not write him, and Happy,
warned by his superior knowledge of the world's
ways, did not dare to write her; all she could do
was to buy a New York paper daily at the railway
station, so that Mr. Thorne could see for himself
what a sensation his defaulting had produced among
his friends and acquaintance, and how pertinaciously
the officers of the law were seeking to find him.
This was not altogether agreeable reading, but it

seemed necessary to his escape that he should watch
the motions of his enemies ; as yet he had not made
up his mind what to do, he would talk it over with
Happy, he thought, though he had little confidence
in her judgment.   Mrs. Holden and Mrs. Reynolds
had both gone on to Ruth directly, when they heard
of her trouble, and village rumor said she was about
to come back with them to Canterbury.   This would
complicate the situation very much.   Happy knew
well she could not keep him there always.   She felt
that Ruth must and would see him if she was in the
village, and so most probably betray the secret ; but
this was not Mr. Thorne's fear at all, he knew his
wife better ; he fully understood that his safety
would never be endangered by any indulgence of
feeling on Ruth's part, — that her thought would be
first and always for him, and his bitterest self-
reproach was for the pain he had given her ; for
weak and wicked as he was, he yet loved her as far
as he could love anything beyond himself.

It was fortunate in one sense that the north-east
storm which had come at the same time this fugitive
did, as if to screen him, lasted several days, as it
prevented visitors, and offered no temptation to
open the windows, and let any sound of conversation
out for the ears of those who might be passing ; but
the weather was not good for Happy, and but for
the natural anxiety of Mr. Thorne to see the city

papers she would never have exposed herself to its
inclemency during the long daily walk to and from
the station. As it was, she took a severe cold, and
dared not even send for Dr. Sands, when it became
oppressive.

The fourth day after Mr Thorne's appearance he
could bear silence no longer; he began himself to
speak of his outlook as they sat by the fire together
one evening; and gradually, led on by her delicate
tact and sympathy he told Happy all his story, from
the very first temptation to his imminent discovery
and his flight. It was the old tale of weakness, self-
indulgence, temptation and sin. He was a man
with refined tastes, fond of beautiful things about
him, luxuries of food, and dress, and furniture; a
lover of ease and the softnesses and elegance of life;
he had not moral strength enough to do right when
he wanted to do wrong, nor religion enough to supply the firmness his nature lacked, though he was in
name a Christian. He had begun with a small
transgression, used a little money that belonged to
somebody else, expecting to replace it; then a little
more which he lost in speculating, to try and replace
the first, and so the matter went on; till he became
desperate of repairing the fault, and used what he
pleased in order to afford himself whatever he
wanted, trying to drown the upbraiding voice of
conscience in the enjoyment of the present hour.

The natural results followed; he became irritable, wretched, restless; he had been professedly a Christian but so much honesty remained to him that he had for the last two years withdrawn from the special ordinances of the church entirely, and rarely gone to Sunday services where he belonged, making the distance from his own church a pretext for worshipping in one of a different denomination, close at hand.

To Happy this seemed a good sign: it showed at least a resolution not to be a hypocrite if he was a sinner: she could see that he had suffered much, that his wife's love and his children's caresses had been so many more stings to exasperate his wretchedness; he might have used Ruth's money to free himself, but it had been so thoroughly tied up by her father's will that she could only receive the benefit of the income, and though that was large enough to support them handsomely, it was but a drop in the bucket to his indebtedness.

Happy listened to his recital with deep interest and compassion; her face had in it a pure and gentle sympathy that encouraged him to the fullest revelation of what he had done; he spared himself in nothing; he seemed to stand aside from himself and paint his own character and faults as a discerning spectator might have done; there was a ghastly honesty about the detail that while it shocked Happy, gave her hope for him. She did not understand a weakness that revelled in excitement, even when that excitement condemned itself. It is the resource of the feeble to go to extremes, and there was something dramatic in this bald statement of unpleasant facts that seemed to restore in some sort Mr. Thorne's self respect.

"What shall I do next?" was the query which ended his long story.

"I think," said Happy, modestly and reluctantly, "I think you would do the best thing in giving yourself up to the law."

CHAPTER XXXVIII.

" GIVE myself up? " said Mr. Thorne in astonishment, turning pale while he said it.

" I think I should." Happy answered firmly.
" I suppose it does sound dreadful, but it isn't half
as dreadful, it seems to me, as being hunted round
the country and never being able to live among your
own folks any more."

"But think of the disgrace of trial and impris-
onment."

Happy looked straight into the fire a moment,
then she said —

"I shouldn't think the disgrace was in the prison ;
— and would there have to be any trial if you told
them everything? "

Mr. Thorne colored ; hitherto he had rather been
concerned for the consequences of his sin than for
the sin itself, but Happy's simple words restored
the matter to its true light.   Still, however, the idea
of prison haunted him, for he had gone over in his
own mind for months, all its possible horrors ; the
loneliness, the want of comfort, the bare walls, the

harsh rule over his every action, the constraint of narrow space, the utter confinement, the longing that he knew would assail him for liberty, all these things had gone again and again through his brain till it was filled with such images, and his heart failed him utterly. He thought he had repented of his sin, but it had been only a theoretic penitence, a sort of transposition of reality into ideality, not one that brought forth meet fruit, in humility and acceptance of consequences; he had known nothing of that longing to confess the whole truth and stand firm at last before God and man, which haunts the radically honest man who has fallen under stress of temptation, and makes it sometimes the very bitterness of sin that he must carry it within him forever, gnawing and stinging like a serpent in the dark, for the sake of those who are dearer to him than himself. Mr. Thorne considered that he had confessed to God, and therefore he might run away from man; and had so settled himself in this conviction that Happy's words stunned him.

She said no more: it was not for her to urge him, only to sow the living seed of truth even in this shallow soil and trust the growth to God.

He hid his face in his hands, and was silent too, for a few moments; then they heard the garden gate swing, and steps approach. Mr. Thorne instinctively darted up the narrow stair, but before he reached the top the upper half of the door opened and some one called — "Happy! Happilony! where be ye?"

It was Delia Packard. Mr. Thorne dared not stir further, he knew his steps would have to be accounted for to the visitor, so he sat down where he was, and Happy went without a light into the little entry, and opened the lower door.

" For mercy's sakes!" exclaimed Delia, " I didn't know but what you was sick or somethin', a settin' without no light!"

" I don't feel very well, Delia, but that wasn't the reason I staid in the dark," answered Happy.

Delia ignored the latter part of the answer in her anxiety for her friend.

" Why, what does ail ye?" she said, as she threw off her shawl, and sat down by the fire: she had left a crack of the door open as she went in after Happy, having stopped to get rid of her overshoes by the front door.

" Nothing but a cold."

" Well, that's bad enough! you'd oughter be careful, for there's better things to have than a cold, though there's wuss ones. My land! ain't it awful about that feller that married Ruth Holden? She's over to her grandma's as nigh heart-broke as any cretur can be and live."

" Have you seen her?" asked Happy.

" Well, I have; but it was a sort o' happenin'

that I did ; I wanted some skim milk this morning,
and I went over to get it, and Madame she came
into the kitchen where Chloe was givin' of it out,
and she says, ' Mis' Packard,' says she, ' won't you
step into the keepin' room a minute ; ' for there was
two or three there after milk ; so I went in, and she
wanted me to ask you to step over there as soon as
maybe, so's to see Ruth, and jest then Ruth she
came through with one of their children. For
gracious sakes ! she looked like a statoot : whiter'n,
colder, n' stiffer : she didn't take a single mite o'
notice of me, no more'n ef I was a stick, and
Madame she never said nothin', not a word ; but
Ruth did look the dreadfullest ! "

" Poor child," said Happy, with tears in her voice.

" Where *do* you s'pose that feller is ? " went on
Delia. " Some says he's gone abroad, and some says
he's a hidin' round in Philadelphy. I don't b'lieve
but what he is. Well : I think of the text of
Scripter — ' Lord what *is* man : that thou art mind-
ful of him ? ' when I think of that Thorne. Sure
enough ! I should think the Lord would get sick of
tryin' to save sech sort o' folks. It's my belief he's
shot or drownded himself, that kind does, mostly :
it's all they're good for. I remember well John
Crane, son to she that was Jane Holbrook, a askin'
me one day if I thought folks that killed themselves
would be saved, — he had spells of bein' luny ye

know, — and I says, real sharp, ' No I don't ! ' says I, ' they aint worth savin'.' And so I b'lieve. They'd as good kill 'emselves as anything."

" Oh Delia ! the Lord is sorry for them : you know He is. Why should they add another sin to the rest ? "

" Well. I wan't speakin' of speritooal things anyway. I s'pose what you say is so, but I was thinkin' of what sort of lives such folks would live after doin' such things. Why, put the case 'twas you, Happy, if so be you can, and you always was the master hand for puttin' yourself into other folkses feelin's, what would you do ef you'd ben in this Thorne feller's place ? "

Mr. Thorne, sitting on the stairs, and so brought to hidden judgement, winced as she said this ; partly, it must be owned, to hear himself spoken of as " that Thorne feller ! "

Happy answered quickly, " I would give myself up to the law, Delia."

" Confess and be hanged, would ye ? "

" Yes, I feel sure I would ; it is so much better to be honest, and take the consequences, than to live in dread of discovery all your life ; why it wouldn't be half living ; and then you know what the Bible says about confessing and forsaking our sins and then finding mercy."

" Yes it does : that's so ; but human natur' don't

always square itself according to Scripter ; the flesh
is dreadful weak sometimes."

"But God is strong, Delia."

Happy spoke to more than she saw ; the grave
faith and honesty of her speech fell on one listener's
ear like a voice of heavenly counsel. God was
strong, he knew ;. strong enough to support even his
weakness and inspirit his dismayed soul, but how
long it was since he had dared to be conscious of a
God ! to pray to, or even to believe in Him ? Out
of the deep dust where he lay now, went up a little
cry for help ; the first for months : " Lord save or I
perish ! " And in its very utterance a breath of
calm stole over the troubled waves that swayed
about him as once about the feet of another weak,
boasting, denying, but praying disciple.

The further talk between Delia and Happy he did
not hear, his head was bowed, his senses quiet; he
had flown outside of the noises of this lower world
into the outer court of the heavenly temple, and was
listening to the voices of the choir who stand before
God, and praise Him for his mercy and truth.
These were what he needed, and for these he prayed
with the sore agony of a helpless child who cries out
in pain for the mother to help, encourage, and soothe
him ; and as one whom his mother comforteth the
Lord stooped to fortify that seeking soul. When
Happy came to the foot of the stairs with the candle

for him, he rose up and looked her calmly in the face.
" Will you send for Ruth in the morning?" he
said.

" I have made up my mind to take your advice at
last, Miss Happy ; I will be honest now, at any rate."

The tears rose to Happy's eyes ; she could not
say a word, but her look was enough. Mr. Thorne
slept that night as he had not slept for a year ; to
have sounded our own misery is to half conquer it ;
he had faced the worst, and the truth had made
him free.

Early in the morning Happy went over to Madam
Holden's, and received a silent fervent welcome from
Ruth, who drew her away to her own room, and
locking the door, threw herself on her knees and
hid her face in Happy's lap. She had not an idea
that her husband was near her, and she was excited
and agitated to discover it, but she agreed fully in
Happy's opinion of his proper course ; she had so
honorable a nature, so true a heart, that no sophistry
could lead her astray. Women are the severest
moralists, theoretically, that exist ; but it is rare to
find one whose practice vindicates their theory ;
yet Ruth faced the stern conclusion of her premises
with unshrinking courage. She heard Happy's
story through and prepared at once to go home with
her ; the interview with her husband is not for
words to describe, but it confirmed his resolve and

increased his strength. That very night, leaving her children with her grandmother, she and her husband together left for Philadelphia, where he delivered himself to the authorities, plead guilty, and was immediately sent to the State prison. It is not within the limit of our story to follow his after life, it is enough to say that in all its course he never ceased to bless and revere Happy, and Ruth held her in even more sacred remembrance. Remembrance I say advisedly ; for when she returned from her final parting with Mr. Thorne she found Happy so ill that Doctor Sands forbade her to all visitors. Mary Parker's younger sister had volunteered to do the work of the house, and being a capable steady girl was accepted by Delia Packard, who took the superintendence. Soon after Mr. Thorne left with Ruth, Happy's cough had begun to grow worse ; the excitement of the last week was over, and she felt that the strain on her mind had been intense, and during it she had neglected the cold which she had taken in going out in the rain so often. A day or two of weakness, of fever, of oppression, came first ; then chills, sinking, unconsciousness. Happy had made no stir or show in her life, she had done what she had to do in stillness and simplicity ; now she lay down to sleep with the same quiet acceptance of what the Lord sent her. She did not complain, she took everything that was brought to her with a

word of thanks, or when weakness forbade that, a
gentle smile ; her face was placid as an infant's in
its mother's arms.

Delia shook her head at Doctor Sands.

"I'd a heap ruther she'd wrastle and fret; my
mind misgives me when folks takes sickness like
that; 'taint for no good. She don't seem to care for
nothin'. Miry, she reads pieces out o' the Bible out
loud to her every day, and seems as if she heard
'em, she looks a leetle extry pleasant, but that's all."

"She is very sick, Delia," said the doctor gravely.

Whatever else he said outside he certainly gave
the impression in Canterbury that Happy's state was
anything but encouraging, and it was touching to
see the daily procession to her little door; it seemed
as if people could not do enough for her, yet no one
could do anything; humbly, calmly, unobtrusively,
Happy slipped out of her life here into the heavenly
kingdom, without a word of parting or expectation,
with no rapture of song or celestial vision. She fell
asleep in Jesus ; and her works followed her.

"There wa'n't no need for her to say anything,"
said Delia, wiping her eyes as she stood by Mrs.
Payson, looking at the wan face, expressive only of
depths of rest such as death alone can give to a
woman. "She done enough, livin', to go without
talkin' on't. I wish't we could all on us leave such

a record ; we could afford to die as still, and rest as quiet."

The chapel was crowded on the day of Happy's funeral ; not only with the church-goers and respect-abilities of Canterbury, but with the poor, the feeble, the aged, and the children of the mission school. Jack and Nan were there, crying bitterly ; Pauline came from Hillside, Robby and Mandy left their work in the mill, even Granny Jakeway hobbled from her attic with strenuous effort and low groans to look her last on Happy's face.

Ruth left her seclusion, and the tears stood in Madam Holden's kind eyes and moistened Mrs. Reynold's cheek as they mingled with the crowd ; and Delia and Mr. Packard sat close by the coffin with Mira between them.

Mr. Payson preached a funeral sermon and took for his text the motto of the chapel : " She hath done what she could." He recalled Happy's past record, her slender means of usefulness, her feeble health, her want of education, her position in life, and then contrasted them with the powers and priv-ileges of others, even of the poorest there before him. He showed them what they could do by re-capitulating what Happy had done ; but there were hearts in the audience that could have added further testimony and more important than he knew of. Ruth blessed, amid her abundant tears, the faithful

Christian courage that had inspired her husband to
honesty at last and had led her dying mother to the
way of life. Mrs. Holden praised silently the memory of one who had done in her weakness what she
herself had planned so long, but feebly delayed to
accomplish. Mrs. Payson wept over the devoted
helper and beloved friend she had lost, and Mr.
Packard remembered with bereaved heart all that
Happy had done to guide himself, his wife, his
child, into the kingdom of Christ; while Mr. Payson
went on.

"To-day her works praise her in the gate; in her
low estate, with her poor means, her health threatened with dread disease, her heart troubled in its
best earthly affections, she wrought out for herself a
record that praises the strength of God in the weakness of man. There is not a heart here that will
not miss her, an eye that does not weep for her. I
myself owe to her honest direct Christian character,
her Bible living, her candor and simplicity, much of
whatever Christian growth I have been able to accomplish in the last few years. She lived in the
spirit of Christ from day to day: she grew into that
divine likeness steadily from year to year; nobody
ever doubted or sneered at her religion, because it
was so vital that it brought forth fruit after its kind.
Her life preached far louder than any sermons; her
example reached where my words never penetrated;

the history of her Sunday school classes, is a history
of conversions and a high type of Christian character, because she both taught and practised the Scripture rule of thought and life. She was the most
unselfish, pure, tender, devoted woman; the faith-
fullest friend; the most conscientious adviser; all
because she abided fully in Christ. Poor, plain,
lame, sickly, and a servant, there is no one in this
parish who could be more missed, who has been more
loved and honored. My dear friends, gathered here
to take your last look at the worn body she has so
gladly left, let her spirit speak to you as you gaze
once more on the pale garment it wore! Wasted
and wan as it is, let it say to you what she would
say herself. There is no use in words, in profession, in mere intention; the use of religion is in
living to God and man; in denying and forgetting
self; in doing, not in dreaming; and you can all do
something for the Lord who died that you may live.

And let us thank God for her, in that he made
death a messenger of mercy; that he spared our dear
friend long days of pain and nights of anguish, and
put her to sleep with a gentleness surpassing a
mother's care; let us thank him more for her life;
for its results and its lessons, its humble, patient,
untiring vindication of the truths of God. It has
been a very quiet life; devoid of romance, of adven-
ture, of outside interest, of large experience; but it

has this immortal and lofty ending, that the Lord hath received her into his holy habitation, as one with clean hands and a pure heart: and said to her that word of high acceptance and commendation we may all well covet as well as obtain — 'She hath done what she could.'"